Hush in the Storm

Julie B. Cosgrove

Published by Prism Book Group
ISBN-13: 978-1940099743 ISBN-10: 1940099749
Published in the United States of America
Contact info: contact@prismbookgroup.com
http://www.prismbookgroup.com

PRAISE FOR HUSH IN THE STORM

"*Hush in the Storm* by Julie B. Cosgrove is a tough but compelling read about a woman spirited away into the darkness and harsh reality of human trafficking. In addition to her terror and confusion over this split-second turn in her life is the unspeakable horror that perhaps someone very close to her is involved in her nightmare. This is a page-turner that will not only entertain but also inform and educate on a topic relevant to our time and culture." Kathi Macias (www.kathimacias.com) is an award-winning writer of more than 40 books, including *Deliver Me from Evil*.

"Suspense and romance touches the shadowy underworld of human trafficking. A recent widow is kidnapped and her death faked, supposedly for her own good. But if she's really a widow, why does she keep hearing her husband's voice? Julie B. Cosgrove weaves a tale that both shocks and informs. *Hush in the Storm* will keep you reading late into the night." Mary Hamilton, author of the best selling Rustic Knoll Bible Camp Series

"Wow. After reading the first seven pages, all I can say is that. Love your imagery. Fiction is definitely your genre." Gwen McKone, author of *God Up Close and Personal*

"How profound your thoughts are and how amazing your writing is. Julie, I only put in a few WOW expressions. If I stopped to tell you all the places I admired, I would not be finished with your edits for days. You over and over surprise me with your insightful ways of expressing yourself." Sandy Wright, North Texas Christian Writers editor and critique expert

"Julie Cosgrove's new novel *Hush in the Storm* is the compelling story of a woman's journey through tragedy, betrayal, and triumph as the heroine addresses issues of grief, love, and modern day slavery. A must read." Joy Brooks, Prayer for Freedom, Fort Worth, Texas

Dedicated to
All who hear the hushing roar of pain in the storms of life.
There is hope…and peace.

PART ONE

Death and Life

Widowed at thirty-one, Jen clings to her humdrum job as a buoy against the swells of grief until a coworker, Tom, kidnaps her and fakes her death at the request of her late husband…or so Tom says.

CHAPTER ONE

AN EERIE THOUGHT pressed a clammy hand upon my shoulder. *What if all you thought was true never actually was?*

Widowed unexpectedly at thirty-one, I naturally longed for what could never be again. Regrets and what-if mantras swirled daily through my mind. I'd learned to push them aside. But this sudden, unsolicited notion surged an icy-hot chill through my body.

My logical side chided me. *Don't be silly, Jen. Of course it was true.* The diamond band on my left hand glimmered with proof. Robert had cherished me, married me, spent five loving years with me...that one night didn't mean a thing.

I shuddered off the question and leaned in to review the balance sheets my boss had emailed.

But the bizarre suggestion whispered once more in the back of my thoughts just loud enough to keep me from concentrating. The numbers on the page became muddled gibberish. I closed my eyes, sucked in a breath, and tried to focus.

People passed my desk and said the same things they always

did—

"Hi, Jen. Doing okay?"

"Sure, I'm fine."

"Hey, Jen. Keeping busy? Best thing, ya know."

"Yeah." Always with a forced grin. "Thanks."

I fiddled with the little gold cross I always wore around my neck, more out of habit than any indication of piety. I hadn't perched on a pew in years, except for our wedding day and at Robert's funeral. But after the latest in the series of sympathizers walked away, I seethed a semi-prayer under my breath. "Dear Lord. Please. Why can't everyone just leave me alone?"

I had a job to do. The report was due first thing in the morning. I had to concentrate on the now. Besides, I never wanted to hear the eggshells crack as well-meaning colleagues tiptoed around my mourning. I was stronger than that, at least in public.

One by one, the other workspaces emptied. The buzz of office machines and human chatter diminished until the only sound was the soft hum from the fluorescent lights and the tick of the office clock, like a steady heartbeat.

At last, a welcomed solitude settled around me in a thick hush. In fact, it was too quiet. I tapped my pencil, then my foot, to dispel it.

A short, high-pitched ding pierced the silence.

My heart jumped into my throat. The elevator? The bottom right-hand side of my computer screen flashed 6:05 p.m. It was too early for the janitorial staff. None of the executives or customers ever ventured down to this dingy basement department with no windows and stale, recycled air.

I swallowed. "Who's there?"

Tom stepped out of the elevator, then pushed open the glass door with the stenciled white lettering proclaiming the owners of this windowless dungeon—Abernathy & Smith Accounting Firm.

"Hey, Jen. Still at it?"

My heart slid back into place.

Drenched to the skin, Tom jabbed his thumb toward an imaginary window. "Did you know it's storming like crazy out there?"

My jaw set, making a dental impression in my now tasteless chewing gum. Of all people to show up after hours, why Tom? Those piercing blue eyes unnerved me. Many times over the past few weeks, I'd find his gaze on me. And now, he and I were the only ones left in the department.

I wanted him to leave—and for these numbers to make sense so I could do the same. I also wanted my life back, but I wasn't about to discuss that with him, or anyone else for that matter. So I responded with non-interest to his remark. "Really? Raining, huh? Thought maybe you'd walked through the lawn sprinklers."

"Cute." Tom rubbed his dark curls as he peered over my four-foot cubicle divider. Tiny drops of water spattered across my work.

I swiveled my chair to face him full on and slapped on my office grin. "So, why are you still here in the netherworld making a puddle inside my cubicle?"

He snorted a quick chuckle. "I forgot my umbrella."

"Oh." Weird that he'd come back for one now when he's already sopping wet.

"That's for tomorrow afternoon's board meeting, huh?" He nodded toward my corner-angled monitor, flinging a few more droplets in my direction, along with a whiff of citrusy-musk aftershave. The fact that it was my favorite male scent didn't ease the tension.

With an eye roll, I wadded up my calculations and tossed them in the direction of the trash can.

He came around to my side. "You've been working at it too long, Jen."

I ran my fingers through my bangs. "It has to get done now, doesn't it?"

Tom arched an eyebrow.

I sucked in a deep sigh, and then let it out to a silent count of three. "Sorry, Tom. I'm just a bit frazzled right now."

He perched on the edge of my desk. "Which is why you need to leave."

He leaned forward to read my computer screen. I scooted my chair over an inch. The second hand on the black-rimmed wall clock across the room went round and round. Why wasn't *he* leaving?

"Tom, look. I hate to be rude but…" I swung away from him to face the paperwork splayed across my desk and tapped my pencil again. "…I need to get back to this so I can get out of here." I wasn't eager to get back to an empty apartment, but being alone with this guy was starting to freak me out, especially when I felt him edge closer.

"Back away from it for the night, Jen. It's time to go." His voice took on an authoritative tone.

I turned, confused. His face softened.

"Come on. Let's get outta here and grab a bite to eat."

My eyes flew wide. "What?" Oh, no. Was he asking me out? I wasn't ready…not for anything like that.

He punched the off button on my monitor.

A flush of fury warmed my face. How dare he?

"Jen. Did you hear me? It's time to go."

A hint of brogue, no doubt leftover from some forgone ancestor, twirled the last word on his tongue. They called his type the black Irish—dark hair, crystal blue eyes. Right now his windows into the soul darkened to a deep, steel gray. Stern. Inflexible. Like my eighth-grade biology teacher's stare when I hadn't paid attention in class, again. That sort of look always made me buckle.

"Well..." I glanced to the office wall clock. 6:15. My stomach responded with a silent rumble to remind me I hadn't stopped for lunch. I loathed eating alone and didn't feel like whipping up something at home. Even eating with Tom was better than the alternatives. "The janitors will be here in a bit anyway. Can't concentrate with them vacuuming, emptying the trash bins..."

His pursed lips curved into a quick grin. "Then let's go. Bob's Burgers is close."

The longstanding downtown diner served old-fashioned, charcoal-broiled burgers oozing with cheddar cheese. Cholesterol-clogging comfort food did sound good. I grabbed my purse off the back of my chair. "Okay." I raised my finger. "But we'll go Dutch."

"Whatever." He raised himself from my desk. "It's too far to walk in the rain, though. Even with an umbrella." He gave a sheepish shrug.

I sighed and dug into my purse. "Where are my keys?"

Tom dangled them in front of my nose. "Left 'em on your desk. But we should take my car."

I shook my head and opened my palm, fingers cupped. "Uh, no. We shouldn't."

"Your choice." He exhaled through his nostrils, plopped the keys into my hand, and then texted something into his cell phone. I noticed his jaw twitch as he slipped his phone back into his jacket.

Was it me, or had his mood taken a dark turn? Had I ruffled his male feathers by insisting we go in separate cars and pay Dutch? I made an attempt to smooth things over. "Thanks for the offer, though."

"I was just trying to save you..."

I touched his arm. "Tom, I don't need saving."

One side of his mouth stretched into a smirk. "You sure?"

At the elevator, he punched the up button. With a swift ding, the steel doors whished open. Acting the cool gentleman I guess, Tom held back the door with his arm to let me pass first.

I humphed. "Still on this floor. Luck o' the Irish. This dinosaur usually takes forever."

"Probably no one else in the building. Just us two." His mouth formed that swift grin again.

Another shoulder-clamp feeling grabbed me. I didn't really know this guy. He'd only worked in my section for a few months. Could I trust him? *Get a grip, Jen. It's just a cheeseburger.*

Tom's forefinger hit the "G" button. Awakened, the elevator jerked, moaned, and began its ascent. His attention lifted to the numbers above the door. They lit up. B2, ding, B1…

There was a jolt, then a bang. The lights went out. We were stuck.

I sensed his presence move closer to me, invading what little space I had. *Oh, no. Don't make a pass at me. Not here, trapped like this.*

I reached for the gold cross as it flapped against my beating chest. This time, I did pray. *Please, God. Please let there be someone else in the building.* Still, I doubted if He'd listen. The Lord hadn't much in the past. Especially the night Robert died. Where was the Almighty then?

Then, in the semi-darkness, I saw a reddish-white glow illuminating the panic button. I reached to push it, but Tom grabbed my wrist and yanked it down.

"Don't press that."

My eyebrows knit together. Before I could ask why, his other hand slipped underneath his damp jacket. My eyes followed it. The glimmer of shiny metal reflected off the panic button's light.

My heart froze.

CHAPTER TWO

ICY DREAD FLASHED across my cheeks and spread to my neck. Tom turned to face me. I took two steps backwards. One hand felt for the wall, anything sturdy. The other crunched my blouse.

"Here. Hold this." His words, like a sharp bark, echoed in my brain, but my hand refused to register a response.

He cocked his head and gave me a blunt snort. "Today. Or do you want to stay stuck in here?"

I blinked. A pocket LED flashlight waved in front of me. That must have been what I saw. Warmth rushed up my neck and back into my face. I relaxed my shoulders and breathed again. "Oh. Thank God. It's a flashlight."

"Well, duh." He raised an eyebrow.

Wait a minute. "You were prepared for this?"

"Yeah, I'm a regular boy scout." His tone was flat, business like. He shook the cylinder at me again. "Just twist it to the right to click it on."

I took it from his fingers, brushing across them with my own. They were warm, rugged. Not the wimpy, cold fish I expected from a fellow accounting clerk.

He knelt on one knee. "I could see better if you point the light at the buttons."

"What? Oh, sure." I fumbled to aim the beam of light over his shoulder.

Being stuck here alone with Tom unnerved me. I decided to placate him. "I'm glad you know what to do." I let out a nervous, girly chuckle. His face softened into a wink.

"Watch and learn." He took his ballpoint pen from his pocket protector and shoved it into the side of the panel. It popped open to reveal a spaghetti bowl of wire. Pen in teeth, Tom began to twist the wires this way and that as he hummed the MacGyver theme song.

For effect, I hummed along as well.

With a moan, the geriatric elevator opened its doors. Cool air rushed in. I felt like clapping and throwing my arms around Tom's neck. Instead I heaved a relieved sigh. "Thanks."

"Piece of cake." He shoved the pen back in his shirt pocket and took the flashlight from my hand. Halfway up the black concrete wall was the ground floor. "Think you can climb up?"

"Sure. But you go first." I ran my hands down the sides of my pencil skirt. *No free peeks tonight, bud.*

"Okay. Good thinking. Then I can lift you out."

His voice sounded downright cheery. Being Mr. Rescue obviously suited him. Come to think of it, he did appear a bit dashing at the moment. And he had brightened my mood with his humor. Maybe he was a decent guy.

"Better let loose of this." He slipped my shoulder bag from my arm, zipped the opening, and slung it up and over the elevator wall. Next, the briefly forgotten umbrella hurled like an arrow for a bull's eye.

"Ready?" The question was rhetorical. His shoes scuffed until they caught some crack or dent in the concrete. With a grunt, he hauled his body weight up and over the edge. Not bad. Almost cat-like. Who knew?

I heard footsteps. Then silence. Where had he gone? Surely he wouldn't leave me? My heart sank to my ankles.

Seconds later the footsteps returned and his head popped back into view. Black locks dangled into his eyes as they focused on me. He pumped his fingers. "Grab hold."

I took hold of his hand with both of mine. His other one clutched the edge of the elevator wall. "One, two, three." With a steady pull, he raised up. My body followed. My knees scraped the concrete but soon, like a seal sliding out of the tank at Sea World, I slithered up and out onto terra firma.

Tom reached down to help me to my feet. "There you go."

I smoothed my skirt back into place and eyed him. "How did you know to do that?"

"What? The elevator panel? I'm an electrical engineer-tech. Or at least I was before I took this desk job analyzing accounting figures for the construction clients." He snatched his umbrella, then handed me my purse and walked toward the glass front door.

I scrambled to match his longer stride while I crammed my left foot back into my shoe. "Why did you take a job here of all places?"

"It has its perks. Indoors. Warmer in the winter, cooler in the summer."

I scrunched my nose. "For real?"

He punched in the security code, pushed open the glass and motioned for me to pass first.

"There were other reasons."

"Such as?"

His face became expressionless, mouth taut. He tilted his head toward the door. "I might explain someday. Not now." He raised his jacket collar around his neck.

"Right," I whispered and slipped through the opening. I got the message. Don't ask. Maybe something in his past embarrassed him. Best not to know. "Sorry, Tom. I didn't mean to pry."

He shrugged the awkward moment away, slid his access badge into the lock, and opened the glassed main door. The rain cascaded fast off the second floor ledge, enveloping us in an urban waterfall. I pressed my back against the building's picture windows. "It's really coming down."

As if on cue, a bolt of lightning zapped across the sky, chased by a huge rumble. Tom raised the umbrella and pulled me underneath. It barely covered us both, but I admired his chivalrous efforts—at least I hoped that's what they were.

His voice filtered into my ear above the pounding of the rain. "We'd better take Seventh. Roads are really slick. Must be a wreck on Dead Man's Curve again. It's a parking lot out there on I-30."

My mind jumped to another rainy commute last autumn…the night I learned why the curve on the fly-away into downtown Fort Worth had that nickname. For the thousandth time, I saw red and blue lights pulsating at the edge of the sharp turn, mirrored in the sodden asphalt. The sound of sirens and news crews refilled my ears.

Tom's face paled, hand to mouth. He touched my shoulder. "Geez, that was where Robert, uh, your husband…"

"Yeah." I waved the awkward moment away and pushed the tears back into the deep, dark crevice where they belonged. "It's okay."

"That's your car over there, right? The silver Mazda?" He pointed with his head. "By the fence?"

I bit my lip. "Sorry. My attempt to lose a few pounds. Park at the far end and walk. Great idea at the time."

"You look fine to me." His hand dipped to the small of my back.

I didn't want to continue that train of thought, not while we were hunched together under his umbrella. I inched forward. "Let's go."

In sync, we puddle-hopped across the vacant parking lot. I turned to point the clicker at my car. Taillights flashed in response.

Tom stretched his arm over the top of the car. "I'll hold the umbrella for you while you get in."

I slid onto the front seat and shut the door. He dodged the raindrops to his sedan. Once he got there, I started my engine.

"Not a bad guy, really," I said to my windshield wipers as they waved back and forth. "He's been a gentleman. Maybe I've misjudged him."

I clicked my seatbelt and ignored the inner voice warning me to drive straight home. I had to eat, so why not eat with Tom? After all, he was Irish. I was half-Irish on my dad's side of the family. Thus the deep ginger-colored hair and occasional flash of temper.

My cell phone rang.

Tom's voice came over the speaker. "You lead, I'll follow. Just to make sure you get there in one piece."

How did he get my number? I didn't remember giving it to him. Surely I must have. I shook it off. *Oh well, widow's fog strikes again.*

With a wave of my wrist, I acknowledged his request. When his car edged behind mine, the ball of my foot tapped the accelerator. As I flicked on the blinker to indicate we were to turn right, my inner leprechaun whispered, "If ye can't trust part of the clan, me dearie, who can ye trust?"

CHAPTER THREE

TOM CONTINUED HIS chivalrous routine when we got to Bob's Burgers. He parked close enough to me to offer the umbrella again, but I whipped out a compact-sized one from my glove box, opened the car door, and fanned it open. "Always keep one in the car, just in case."

"Just in case, huh? Why not keep it in your desk at work?" He pushed open the door to the diner.

"Then forget it, like you did?" I flapped the umbrella back and forth in the vestibule.

"Sorry," he whispered, then looked down and coughed into his fist.

His wounded puppy-dog expression made me cringe. I huffed into my chin. "Tom. Please. I'm kidding, okay?"

He leaned in with a smirk. "I know." Then he winked — again.

A smile broke across my face. It sent a streak into my heart like a ray of sunlight through storm clouds. I couldn't remember the last time my mouth wasn't curved downward. I'd thought my ability to grin had been buried with Robert's body.

"Ah, I finally got you to smile." Tom motioned me ahead.

Close by, sirens howled their warnings. My smile faded.

In unison we turned to watch a fire engine speed by, followed by an ambulance. I grasped the gold cross on my necklace and whispered a prayer for the loved ones of whomever the EMTs rushed to help, hoping their fate would prove different from mine. Maybe God would be kinder to them.

THAT NIGHT I'D walked out the door with a few girls from the office when the emergency vehicles zipped past. A lump lodged in my throat, telepathically telling me what I'd learn seconds later when my cell phone rang. Black Beemer. Wreck. Robert. Hurry.

I don't remember who drove me to the scene. I stared at a bouquet of muddy, white roses splattered on the drenched asphalt amidst broken glass and twisted metal. The petals were highlighted in EMS' flickers—like the neon marquee I'd pictured flashing over him and whoever else had been tangled in the dingy sheets at that cheap motel the night before.

My neighbor Betty, who had a horrible sense of direction, took a wrong turn into a sleazier part of town just in time to see the two of them enter together. Of course she texted me immediately.

My mind spouted rehearsed questions in furious rapid fire as I listened for the garage door to raise and Robert to stroll in—two hours late. How many other times had there been? Was this why he had to work late or suddenly go out of town on business so often? Was all that money he spent really on power lunches?

Robert's green eyes flashed fire. With a clamped jaw, he insisted my accusations were unfounded. His voice steeled. "If you must know, I was there with a coworker. But only for moral support while she registered. She'd finally walked out on her abusive husband, and she was scared."

"Oh, sure. But you couldn't phone me and tell me what you were doing, huh?" I dug my fingernails into my palms. "Please. I'm not a fool."

"And you think I am?"

For the first time in my life I wanted to slap his face. Maybe it was because I saw in his eyes the ability to lie. I grabbed an antique vase, a wedding present from his beloved great aunt, and smashed it to the floor. It shattered, along with my trust in him.

"I can't believe you'd think I'd be guilty of something like that." He stomped from the room and slammed the door. Our marriage vows shook with the vibration, threatening to explode under the pressure.

All night, I tossed and turned alone. He slept on the couch in the den. We left the next morning in smoldering silence. Our individual prides refused to give way to reason.

Robert must have decided to appease me with the white roses now crushed across the highway. He'd probably zoomed too fast around the curve in an attempt to catch me before I headed to my aerobics class. Four days later, they laid roses on his coffin.

I never had the chance...

TOM LAID A hand on my shoulder. "You okay?"

"Yeah." I inhaled a deep breath. Then another. Better. My legs felt more solid. "Just brings it all back, you know?"

He wiped a strand of damp hair from my face, barely touching, but enough to flame my cheeks.

"Still feel like eating?" His voice softened with emotion. "'Cause if you don't..."

I swallowed the black memory. It hit an empty stomach. "Yes. Definitely. I'm starved."

"Yes, ma'am." He tipped an imaginary Stetson, Texas-gentleman style. His voice mocked me, but his eyes didn't. He held the door open, and beckoned me inside the restaurant.

A waitress approached.

"Hi. Welcome to Bob's Burgers. Table for two?" She clutched menus with covers as plastic as her greeting.

"Yes, please." I returned the same expression.

In silence, we followed single file. The bow on her apron swished over her slender backside as she walked. Tom waited for me to choose my side of the booth. Then, he slid in across from me and took a menu the waitress placed on the table.

Through her smacking gum, she asked, "Can I get you something to drink? Coffee? Iced tea?"

We replied in unison. "Coffee."

She nodded and trotted off. Tom eyed the bouncing bow from the rim of his menu. His eyes shifted to me.

I sighed and motioned to the vestibule. "Sorry." I spread my napkin in my lap. "I get cranky when my sugar level drops."

"That's okay. I get wimpy when I'm wet."

My hoot echoed over a thunder clap. Several heads turned toward our booth. My cheeks had forgotten how to stretch into a laugh. It felt good.

Dinner proceeded with scrumptious, juicy burgers, crisp fries, and light conversation—mostly about work and the weather. Safe topics. I sloshed my last french fry through the ketchup pond on my plate. For a second I stared at the design I'd made. It resembled the kindergarten finger paintings my mother used to hang on the fridge door.

A tingle along my spine told me Tom had locked his gaze on me. I raised my lashes and plopped the now-soggy fry into my mouth. "What?"

"You're quite artistic."

I squirmed and repositioned my purse beside me. "No, I like to play with my food. Always did."

He reached over and grabbed my hand, tight. When I jerked as a reflex, he strengthened his grip. "Jen, there is something you need to know. But not here. Not now." His eyes darted around the diner then landed back on mine. "Come back to my place. I'll explain it there. Trust me, okay?"

I yanked my hand into my lap. "No."

He sighed and slammed his back into the booth. "Look. Truth is, I didn't forget my umbrella. I meant to come back for you. You're not safe. You shouldn't be staying after work alone."

I let out a nervous giggle. "What are you talking about?"

He flipped his table knife from side to side, yet his eyes zeroed in on my face. "I told you. Not here. We need to talk in private."

I returned his stare as my mind tried to fill in the blanks. What *was* he talking about?

After a moment of playing dare-you-to-blink-first, he rolled his eyes and leaned forward. "Please. Come with me for the night. I'll protect you. Nothing will happen."

I grabbed my purse, and then my keys. "You're darn straight." I flopped a ten-dollar bill on the table and began to scoot out of the booth.

Tom clutched my elbow. He clenched his teeth in a hiss. "Look, I've asked nice. Now, I'm demanding. You *are* coming with me." He bolted from the booth and yanked my arm. His Irish temper spread from his icy, blue eyes into his flared nostrils. Then, he flashed a badge of some sort inside a black folder. "I'm with the Feds. My job at the accounting firm is only a cover. I was sent to protect you, okay?"

When he re-pocketed his badge, his jacket opened to reveal a black pistol handle tucked in a holster. That silenced me into submission. I nodded rapidly.

He snatched the money from the table and shoved it into my skirt pocket. "I'm paying. No arguments." His eyes cooled back to blue. "Look, I'll explain it all to you later. For now, just follow my lead and you'll be safe. Got it?"

"Yes." The word came out in a squeak.

"Good." He released me from his intense stare, but his hand still gripped my arm. With a slight yank, he spoke low through a clamped jaw. "Let's go."

We strolled to the cash register. His fingers pressed hard into my flesh like a too-tight blood pressure cuff. It sent a pulsating pain through my arm. At last he released me to dig for his wallet.

I watched as he made small talk with Bouncy Bow, handed her cash, then shoved a toothpick in the side of his mouth. The last french fry flipped over in my stomach. Part of me wanted to scroll "help" in the glass case housing the gum and mints. But this gal would never understand. Besides, her eyelashes fluttered only at Tom.

She wiggled her fingers in a coquettish goodbye.

"Goodnight." He sugar-coated his response. Then the sternness in his voice returned, as did the vise-grip on my arm. "We're taking my car."

He pushed open the restaurant door.

A bit of gumption emerged, which my dad always said I'd inherited from his side of the family. I planted my feet into the rubberized welcome mat. "Why?"

His breath steamed in my ear. "Because they're watching your car, that's why. They don't know mine yet. It's new." He motioned me onto the sidewalk.

I raised my hand and twisted around to release his grip. It caught him off guard. My mind screamed *"Run"* but instead, my

Irish temper rose. I pivoted to meet those icy blues straight on and shoved my hands to my hips. Heat seared behind my eyes. "And who exactly are 'they'?"

Tom looked at the diner's neon sign reflected in the wet windshield in front of us. His Adam's apple bounced as he swallowed. Then he drew a steady breath as his gaze shifted to my face. "Look. I told you, Jen. You need to trust me." His words were metered. "Some rather unsavory men want to harm you. I'm here to protect you. Those are my orders." He spun me around, pushed me off the curb, and opened the passenger door.

I grabbed the door handle. "Wait. What orders? From who?"

He wrenched my hand away. "From Robert."

I wilted against the car. "Who?"

His clutch tightened. "Jen. Get in. Now."

His authoritative tone of voice struck an instinctual chord. It reminded me of my father. Like a scolded child, my tenacity melted. I slipped into the front seat.

Sharp pain jabbed into my right arm. The car door slammed. Everything faded into a dark abyss.

CHAPTER FOUR

MUFFLED NOISES FILLED my ears. Men talking? Colored lights flashed beneath my eyelids.

One voice ebbed into clarity. Wait. Robert's? No. No, my subconscious screamed. He's dead. You buried him. This is a dream—a really nasty dream.

"I think she's coming to. Later."

Two sets of footsteps. One moved away, one came close.

A shadow broke the brightness that filtered through my squinted eyes. The cushion under me sank with added weight. I raised my head and tried to focus. Tom's distorted face was inches from mine.

"Jen."

The sound of my name echoed as if I was in a tunnel. A brilliant light moved in front of my face again.

"Jen, come back."

I cracked open one eye. He waved his flashlight's beam at me.

I groaned and clamped my eyes as I rubbed them.

Tom set the flashlight down with a clunk. My eyes flew open.

The light's beam widened, yet lessened in intensity as it made a round spot on the ceiling. I felt Tom cup the back of my head in his hand and turn it toward him. He held a glass of shiny, clear liquid.

"Here, drink this water."

My tongue stuck to the roof of my mouth. "Water?"

"Yes. Water."

My inner voice told me to shove it in his face and run, but my body wouldn't cooperate. My legs felt bolted to the couch. I shook off some of the fuzzy swirling and leaned on my left arm. He held the glass to my lips.

"Take small sips. There ya go."

The cold liquid cascaded down my burning throat. I flopped back on the couch, spent of effort. "Where am I?" I laid my arm over my eyes to keep the room from swaying. "Did you drug me?"

He placed two fingers on my lips. They smelled of public restroom soap. "Ssshh. Rest. You're perfectly safe."

"Safe?"

"Trust me."

Those two words again. Part of me wanted to believe him. I pushed myself halfway up on to my elbows. Painful pressure pulsated behind my pupils, but I strained to see. No one else was in the room. Hadn't I heard Robert? But no, he was dead. *Think, Jen. Think.* I'd heard Tom, not my dead husband.

The dizziness washed over me again. I tried to make a coherent sentence. "You said Robert...gave you...orders? My Robert?"

Tom shifted his weight and placed his hands on my shoulders. He gently pushed me back into the cushions. My spine slid into the micro-suede.

"Yes, your Robert. Before he died." He pulled a blanket to my chin, then flicked off the flashlight. The pain inside my eyes eased as the room faded back into quasi-darkness. "I'll explain it all later.

Promise. Now rest."

I relaxed. The drug's effects still swam in my brain, robbing me of strength.

"Good girl." Tom repositioned the throw pillow behind my head. As he rose, the couch cushion filled my back. My gaze followed his footsteps toward a dim light coming from a doorway. His body went shadowy and out of focus.

"Goodnight, Jen." He flicked off a light and closed the door. It clicked—locked.

The room darkened. His footsteps faded, but I never heard another door shut. Maybe he was in another room off this one. Somehow, that brought me comfort.

I sighed, and then slipped back into a deep, drugged sleep.

SOMETHING WOKE ME. The pitch-black room smelled pungent and musky as if no fresh air had been allowed inside it this century. I eased my body up and tried to adjust my eyes to see through the dark. Clarity oozed in to replace the floating feeling in my brain.

I raised my hand, but couldn't see it in front of my face. Why weren't my eyes adjusting? No thread of light filtered under the door. No flashes of lightning outlined a windowsill, though I thought I heard rumbles of thunder, so it must still be raining.

I strained my ears, but heard no pattering on a roof above me. In fact, I heard no rain at all. Not against a window, nor on a sidewalk. My heart flinched. Where was I?

"Tom?" No response. I swallowed hard so I could call out louder. "Tom!" Silence. Why wouldn't he answer?

This was why my brain had warned me to not follow him to Bob's Burgers. My reluctance to listen to it earlier slapped me hard in the face.

The room sucked the air from my lungs. Nothing seemed right.

I squeezed my eyes tight and rubbed them with my palms. A rush of dread flowed over me.

Then, just as quick, an old childhood prayer zipped into my mind. "God in Heaven, hear my prayer. Keep me in thy loving care."

Seriously? Had I ever believed that? I couldn't remember the last time I felt His loving care, much less know Him to hear my prayers. Not when Mom and Dad died in the mission field. Definitely not when Robert died.

Instead, Dad's favorite adage blared in my head. *Fear and worry never solved anyone's problems.* I shook off the fright and willed my analytical side to kick in.

My hands pushed against my temples several times. Tom said goodnight. We left the restaurant at night, in the rain. So, I hadn't been out of it very long. Either that or I had been unconscious twenty-four hours. No, no. My common sense told me it wouldn't still be raining. It's dark because it's night and there's no moon shining through the rain clouds. In the morning, there will be light.

Except for the faded rhythmic thunder, dead silence shrouded the room. I heard no city noises, no hums of electronics, no ticks of clocks. Not even the soft buzz of an air conditioner. No whish of air against my skin. Did it mean no air came into the room?

I sat erect and inhaled as deeply as I could. *See, Jen, you have air.* Wait. Musty, damp air. That smell. What did it remind me of? Something horrible, and long ago. A cardiac tom-tom beat in my ears like when my upstairs neighbors turned up the bass on their speakers.

I swung my feet to the floor. A scratchy rug scraped against my toes. Where were my shoes? I patted the cushions, then the floor around me. They weren't there. I probed around some more. Nothing. The smell grew stronger.

"Where's my purse? And my cell phone?" I spoke into the darkness, as if it would answer me. *Duh, Jen. You're alone.*

I leaned against the back of the couch. Of course. Tom wouldn't have left my cell phone so I could call the police. Not if he'd kidnapped me. He had, right? But, why? To protect me?

What about all those times he'd look away quickly when I caught him staring at me across the cubicles? Maybe he brought me here for another reason. I crunched my blouse buttons in my hand. No, I didn't want to think about that.

My brain whispered, "No one will know you're here."

I threw off the thought. They will know. I'll tell them. I'll get out and run for the nearest store or house. There has to be a way out of here. There has to be.

I gritted my teeth to keep the anxious feelings inside, determined to get a grip. Somewhere nearby, a tinkle of glass responded to the thunder's vibration. The water tumbler. I stretched my fingers through the blackness to find the end table with the glass of water Tom had left behind. My mouth begged for more of the cool liquid. I downed a big swallow then halted. Was it drugged? *Who cares? My mouth is parched.* I took another gulp.

I stood and got my bearings. My feet scooted along the rug, reaching to feel furniture legs. No coffee table. I inched further and stumbled at the edge of hard, rough concrete. My toes shuffled across the floor five more paces. My hands waved the air in front of me. *Why can't I see?*

Thunk. My fingers jammed into a wall as stone-cold as the floor. Concrete, too? I followed it around to the left, its icy dampness penetrating my fingertips There was a crack, then—ooh, yuk!—a sticky something which kept wrapping around my fingers. A spider web. Like in attics.

I shook my hands and stomped my feet. "Oh, God. Get it off. I hate spiders."

In an instant, hundreds of wiggly legs scurried across my body. I slapped my clothes back and forth. My dad's voice sounded in my head again. *Steady, Jen. Your imagination is running rampant.*

Then Robert's voice sounded, just as stern. "Calm down, Jen. Don't be a baby. That spider probably died years ago." His words sounded so real, as if through a loud speaker. I pressed my temples again. *Calm down.*

With a shiver, I continued to probe around the walls. No windows. Surely there had to be one. Then I could open it, get fresh air, breathe, and maybe have light to see. The awful odor would finally go away.

Within a few sidesteps I reached the corner. My heart leapt. How small was this space? I bumped into the end table. The now-empty glass crashed to the floor with an echoing shatter.

The noise made me jump back to the sofa like a guilt-ridden child. Crouched, with my chin buried in my knees, I strained to hear Tom's angry footsteps. He'd told me to rest. What would he do to me? Should I risk getting cut in an effort to clean it up?

No one came. The initial rush of relief gave way to a niggling question. Why hadn't he responded?

Was Tom gone? Was I all alone?

Would he ever come back?

Would I die here?

A dizzy dread flooded my brain.

The dead air was stifling. The stench made me cringe. Why?

Memory flooded in. The awful smell was like my grandmother's trunk. The one I'd been locked inside when I was little.

CHAPTER FIVE

I WAS FIVE. I'd discovered the trunk in my grandmother's attic and hidden there during a game of hide-and-seek with my cousins while the adults milled around downstairs at my great-uncle Dave's wake. The latch accidently fell into place when I pulled the lid over me.

The clothes stank of old-woman body odor and damp mold. Raised in the city with all the street lamps and neon, I'd never been in real, pitch-black darkness before. No light came through the trunk. I couldn't see my hand in front of my face. I banged on the lid. No response. I shoved it with both hands as hard as I could. It wouldn't budge.

Was this what it felt like to be in a coffin, like the one they'd just buried Uncle Dave in? My first funeral. I remembered staring at the shiny humped box. It frightened me. Had he died in there?

Dad told me Uncle Dave wasn't in the coffin. He was in Heaven. Just a shell which was once his body lay inside. I wasn't so sure. It seemed a horrible place to end up. No wonder he'd died. Probably of fright. Was that to be my fate too?

I banged and banged on grandmother's trunk. Tears flooded my face. No one knew I was there. Would I die in there and be left like Uncle Dave?

I prayed like they taught us to in Sunday school. But Jesus didn't open the trunk. So I screamed over and over. Finally, Dad found me. He lifted me out and carried me back down the stairs. I clung to him as I cried my heart out. My mother cried as well.

I had nightmares for weeks. I'd wake up in the dark and shriek again. Dad refused to give me a nightlight. "That's for babies," he said in his stern, fatherly voice. "Stop blubbering. You're a big girl. You don't need anyone but God in Heaven. Now go to sleep." He closed the door.

I whimpered into the dark as I hugged my teddy bear. "But I do need someone. Here. Now. Not way up in Heaven."

THAT LITTLE GIRL fear returned now, just as vivid, as I stood in the darkened room. It edged into my throat and stung the back of my tongue. The darkness pressed hard against me. My mouth tasted the horrible musty odor. I shook my head. "No, no, no. Panic go away. Breathe. I have to breathe. This is not my grandmother's trunk."

I heard Robert's voice again. "No, it's not. That was a long time ago. You're a grown, intelligent woman, Jen. Act like it."

My dead husband was talking to me. Was I going mad? My palms became clammy. I wiped beads of perspiration from the corners of my forehead with my shirttail. Yet the trunk-like smell stuck in my nose. I had to find fresh air.

Desperation forced my body to push through the crushing pain in my chest. Inhale. Exhale. Each breath fought to get out, yet couldn't. They became more and more shallow. Was I suffocating? Was I running out of oxygen?

I raised my eyes and almost began to pray. Then my brain clicked. Of course. The ceiling. Small people could crawl through duct work. I'd seen it in the movies. I was petite enough. It would mean an even tighter space, but only for a while. It would lead somewhere, so I wouldn't be stuck. And there would be air. I had to try.

I leaned my head back on the sofa and willed my breaths to deepen, to suck in as much oxygen as my lungs could muster, no matter how foul. The riotous heartbeat lessened in my ears. The wooziness faded little by little.

Okay, Jen. One, two, three. Both hands grabbed for the upholstered backrest. I wobbled onto the cushions. On my tiptoes like a novice acrobat, my stretched-out fingertips scraped across what had to be ceiling. But why so low? It felt solid and cold, just like the concrete walls and floor. No acoustic tiles to pop out. No escape.

My fingers shook. I couldn't catch my breath again. Fright pushed hard against my upper body. My stomach burned. I slid back on to the sofa and rocked back and forth, forcing gulps of air in and out through the vise grip around my torso. Sobs stuck in my windpipe.

I pressed my eyes against the palms of my hands and willed the logical part of my brain to surface. *Think, Jen, think. Tom got out, so can you.*

An icy cold splashed my face and spread to my arms. Wait. He'd said goodnight and turned off a light. A light.

I slapped my forehead. Idiot. *Why are you feeling around in the dark getting yourself all scared as if you were back in that trunk?* I raised my voice to the ceiling. "Dad, Robert, you're right. Fear and worry doesn't do any good."

Adrenaline rushed in with renewed hope. I leapt off the sofa toward where Tom's voice, and the door, had been.

A sharp sting pierced my heel. Ouch. Glass.

I hobbled on one foot, pulled out the shard, and tossed it aside. I felt the warmth, then the coolness of my blood as it oozed from the slash. No time to worry about that. I wiped it on the itchy rug strands and ignored the stabs of pain.

Mime-like, I shuffled across the floor, felt for the doorjamb, then the light switch. Nothing. My hands scooted across the smooth surface to the opposite jamb and wall. Nada. The switch must be located on the other side of the door outside the room. But why? So I couldn't turn it on? What purpose did it serve?

I bit my lip and willed my fingers back across the door. No knob? I traced my palms in larger circles. No knob.

How in the world did this thing open? The door *had* opened. It had to have hinges, right? Maybe I could ease off the bolts? But with what? My mind pumped questions as fast as my rapidly beating heart.

I felt for the curled metal of hinges. None. What kind of door was this? This was no ordinary basement room. The door was metal, like an elevator. Except there was no seam where the panels opened. Like a mausoleum vault door.

Trepidation grabbed my chest. A concrete encased tomb. This room was designed to keep me in. My childhood voice echoed in my brain—*a horrible place to end up.*

And I'd thought my cubicle at work was coffin-like. Now I really felt buried—like my Robert. At his funeral, a grave no longer seemed like a horrid place. Remaining alone above ground did. How often, in my grief, had I wished I could dig down to Robert's coffin and crawl in there with him?

I cried out to the darkness. "I didn't mean it, God. I didn't mean it. Help, me, okay? I'll start going to church again if You do."

The hardheaded, Irish attitude my father tried to instill in me oozed onto the musty floor. I flattened my back against the cold, hard steel to keep my composure from melting into a puddle of helplessness. The room swirled.

Who was this man named Tom? Why had he brought me here, then, left me alone?

An image loomed in front of me of a panting tiger, tail drooped, as it paced back and forth on concrete in front of bars. My first trip to the zoo when I was seven. I hated it. Something inside me wanted to release all the animals and yell, "Run."

Now, I was that pathetic creature. Tom was my zookeeper.

In a burst of panicked survival mode, I turned and pulled with all my might at the crevice between the door and the jamb. Again, and again. My knuckles cramped. Three of my nails broke off.

I suckled my fingers as my shoulder slammed into the rigid door. It didn't do any good. I stomped my foot in frustration. Ouch. Pain shot into my gashed heel. I slid to the floor and rubbed it, as I sniffled in short, raspy gasps. Now my shoulder throbbed as well.

Oh, why had I gone to dinner with him? And why had he brought me here? Where was I? Hushed silence crowded the darkness to smother my moans.

No one knows you're here. Just like when you were playing hide and seek.

Nobody would worry if I didn't come home. My grief-instilled solitude had pushed away what few well-meaning friends we'd had. Life had taught me to rely only on myself. So, I'd constructed a fortress of self-sufficiency to encase my sorrow, like a precious jewel in a locked, velvet-lined box. Not even I remembered the combination code.

WE'D ONLY LIVED in Fort Worth for three months when Robert died. He'd been transferred from San Antonio to the main headquarters of his advertising firm. I loved San Antonio, and after graduating from college there, I'd been ecstatic when I landed a teaching position. But love and wifely duty called. Besides, the private middle school where I taught math was closing due to lack of funds, so it made sense.

For some reason, Robert didn't want me to teach in Fort Worth public schools. None of the private schools had openings. His boss's wife found me the accounting job. We'd also found a comfy, second-level apartment close by. *Oh, how I want to be there right now.*

Through the pitch dark, my mind's eye saw two iridescent green eyes mournfully gazing up at me. They belonged to the only heartbeat who might notice I wasn't around—a stray cat I'd been trying so hard not to adopt. Who'd feed the poor, helpless kitty?

A sudden dread swallowed me. Who'd feed poor helpless me? This was Friday. Nobody would phone over the weekend to see if I was okay. The only neighbor I'd befriended, Betty, was out of town visiting her grandkids. I'd stopped going to church years ago, so I had no church family and no acquaintances outside of work. No one would have an inkling I was missing until mid-morning Monday, at the earliest, when some coworker noticed my empty cubicle.

Oh, no. Tom and I worked together. He'd thought of that, too, hadn't he? This was all planned out. When he showed up at work on Monday, he could give them some lame excuse for my absence— like the flu, or my back gave out—something to explain my not being at work for several more days.

A shiver darted through me. Tom could keep me locked in here for a week and no one would be the wiser. Could I last that long, here in the dark with no piped-in air, no water or food? Surely he'd come back. Surely he'd open the door. He'd been nice so far, hadn't he? He said he was assigned to protect me. To hide me from "them," whoever they were.

The seclusion crushed down on me. I wanted someone to find me, carry me out, hold me. I wanted my dad. I wanted Robert. But both lay helplessly in coffins under the earth in the dark. Sort of like me. A whimper stuck in my throat. "I don't want to be alone anymore, Lord."

Tears stung my eyes as I gulped back the bitterness in my mouth. I squeaked a prayer through the boulder in my throat. "God, please, please help me. I'm sorry I haven't been to church. I'm sorry I haven't talked with You. I was just so mad when You took Mom and Daddy to be with You. I needed them here. I was only in junior high school. And then, You took Robert away." I twisted my shirt tail through my fingers. "Don't punish me. I want to live...I do."

The dam burst open and my sniveling turned into a wail. I buried my face in my hands. Sobs shook my body.

Finally, the desperate screams came. They pushed into my throat and out of my mouth, over and over again. "Help! Somebody. Help me."

CHAPTER SIX

THE METAL DOOR behind me disappeared.

I fell back into air and landed onto Tom's shoes. Every muscle in my body wanted to fling myself at his feet, beg for mercy, and blubber like a child. I willed myself to resist such a pathetic display of cowardice, but not before a few sobs gurgled through my lips.

"Whoa, there. Calm down. You okay?"

Above me was the bottom of a metal tray clutched in Tom's hands. My nose twitched in response to the smell of butter, scrambled eggs, and toast. And coffee! Freshly brewed coffee.

My captor stepped back and brushed past me. I fell flat on my back, staring at a dimly lit hall ceiling. The air smelled fresher. I closed my eyes and drank it in. *Thank you, Lord.*

I sat up, my legs tucked behind me.

"Don't bother running. The hall is a dead end. You can't get out, Jen." He placed the tray onto the end table. "Trust me, right now you don't want to."

That word again. How could I trust him?

Tom stopped, his eyes fixated on the mess now highlighted by the wedge of light from the door. Shattered glass, smeared blood. "Jen?" He turned around and glared at me. "What happened?" His voice echoed across the concrete walls. Loud. Stern.

"Don't be mad," I whimpered. "Please. I didn't mean to."

He rushed at me. I cowered.

"Where are you cut? Show me."

His tone sounded sharper than the pain in my heel. I uncurled my foot and held it out. He lifted my leg, flopping me back to the floor again. His thumb pressed into the sore.

"Ouch!" I jerked, and pulled myself upright, but he held my ankle tight, turning it toward the light. I squeezed my thighs together, remembering my knee-length pencil skirt. He concentrated on my heel and didn't appear to notice.

"Okay. Could be worse." He laid my foot down in a slow, tender motion. "It's not a deep slash. You'll be fine. No stitches needed, thank goodness." He perched on his haunches. "I don't have a first-aid kit here."

"You're not mad at me?"

Tom humphed. "Don't be stupid, Jen."

Stupid? His words might as well have been a slap to my cheek. My Irish temper began to rise. "You locked me in a pitch dark room with no light."

"I know. It was night."

"For hours. Hours." My voice quivered. The knot in my throat twisted tighter.

"You were supposed to be sleeping."

"Oh." I wiped the residual tears from my cheeks.

Tom nodded toward the tray. "I'm sorry. I thought it'd take you a long time to sleep it off. I didn't mean to freak you out." He rose and extended his hand to me. "Come on and eat."

The beckoning aroma made my stomach growl. Still, I planted

my rear end to the cold concrete. I glanced away to the darkened corner of the room where the spider web had snagged me. "There are spider webs in here." My hands ran up and down my arms. I looked at him, my eyes hot with fresh tears.

He pulled back his hand. With his feet slightly parted, he folded his arms like Mr. Clean. His Adam's apple moved. "Sorry. I'm not that great at housekeeping. Do you have a phobia to spiders? It wasn't in your portfolio…"

"I cried out. You didn't answer." I swallowed the urge to melt into sobs again.

His cheeks reddened. He waved at the tray. "I didn't hear you. I went to get breakfast."

My hands dropped to my lap. "Oh. Right."

He took two steps toward me. I scooted back two on my rump.

"I'm not mad, Jen. Honest. It's all right." His voice became calm, comforting. "I'll clean up the glass and the spider webs in a minute, okay?"

I nodded, afraid if I opened my mouth again it would open the tear ducts as well.

His voice softened. "Please, while it's hot? I'll sit here with you while you eat. Then if you need to use the, uh, john…well—"

His words reminded my bladder it had been ages since it was emptied. But hunger won out. I got to my feet and hobbled toward the couch. Then I remembered the glass, the water, and the drugs. A chilly splash burst across the crown of my head and cascaded down my spine. "Is it safe?"

"Probably not. It's take-out." He remained stone-still, staring at me. Then his lips curved into a smirk.

I stared back, trying to decide whether to trust him.

He blinked. "Oh, for goodness sake." He reached down to the end table, grabbed a point of toast, and jerked off a piece with his teeth. In between chomps he said, "There. See?" He tossed the half eaten slice back onto the tray, then mocked a gag, and grabbed for his throat.

"Very funny." My temper gauge inched higher. He'd scared me out of my wits, and now he made fun of me? I glanced at the shards of glass on the floor. Part of me wanted to slash him with them and dash out of there. A bigger part wanted the rest of the toast.

Tom's eyes must have followed mine. I turned to see his face harden. His foot swept the glass across the concrete to the spider-webbed corner with several swift kicks.

I shuddered off my anger and pulled the tray onto my lap. My eyes scanned my cage, less ominous in the pale light which emitted from the hallway. No more than eight feet by another eight or nine, and solid concrete. *See Jen, it isn't a trunk or a mausoleum. Just a room.* Or was it?

Through the dim illumination, I could make out the furniture in the room—couch, end table, and a straight back wooden chair to the far left of the door. Normal enough. But no light fixtures hung from the ceiling. No lamps. No electrical outlets interrupted wall space. No light switches either. And, as I suspected, no windows. I looked to my right. The sliding steel door was retracted into the wall. An incandescent light bulb encased in wire above the door was the only light source for the room, but it wasn't on. The walls were institutional greenish-gray. Institutional?

I wiped my palms, which had begun to sweat again, and swallowed the creeping angst with a sip of coffee. "Where are we?"

Tom shot me a sympathetic smile. "A safe room."

"Where?"

"Somewhere in Fort Worth." His tone indicated that was all the information I was going to get.

His weight sunk next to me. Our hips touched. I bit my lip. His arm swooshed over and behind me. He rested it on the sofa back, a little too close to my neck. With his other hand, he wiped the hair from my eyes. I flinched at his touch.

What was he going to try now? Was this when the rape part began? I curled my arms around my waist. My fists clenched, pumping attitude back into my soul where fear had invaded. I got ready for a fight. What could I use as a weapon? Hot coffee. I could throw the hot coffee in his face.

He must have sensed my thoughts because he reached across my lap for the Styrofoam cup on the tray. "Don't even think about it. Trust me."

"How can I? You kidnap me, drug me, trap me in the dark, and don't come back for hours."

I expected him to lash out, but instead he placed the cup back into my hand, rose to his feet, and walked a few paces. His voice became gravelly. "I'm not here to hurt you, Jen. Really." He stretched out his arms. "This is all for your safety. We have to keep you out of sight right now."

"We?"

Tom huffed into his collar. "Never mind." He scooted the wooden chair toward me. Straddling it backwards, he shielded himself with the spindles. Yet, his body language oozed confidence. He draped his elbows over the curved top rail. With a nonchalant, limp-wristed gesture he motioned toward the tray. "Go on. Eat."

If I could have grabbed one thought off the merry-go-round in my brain, I'm not sure what it would have been. Fear? Anger? Hunger? Gladness…to see him? Another slurp of hot caffeine slid past my vocal chords and became liquid courage. I straightened my shoulder blades and met his eyes. "If you're not going to tell me where I am, at least tell me why I'm here."

He stretched back in the chair, like a cat studying his wounded prey. "I could. But the less you know, well… it's for your own good, Jen. And as far as where you are, it's an old bomb shelter in a basement of a building. Probably built during the Cold War days in the 1950s. That's all I can say." He motioned to the tray. "Now eat, or I'll take it away."

Ticking him off wasn't the way to win him over to my side. I dropped my eyes to my plate. To make him think he'd won this skirmish, I shoveled eggs into my mouth. I pointed with the flimsy, plastic fork. "I have to admit these taste great. I was famished. Thanks."

He released himself from the chair and walked to the door.

"Wait. Leaving already? Didn't you promise to stay while I ate?" Another forkful of room temperature eggs slid into my mouth.

He stopped at the threshold, but remained facing out into the hall. "Don't play coy with me, Jen." He tapped the door jamb but stared straight ahead. "I am on your side in this."

Was he a mind reader? A shiver touched my neck.

"You're here because I'm supposed to protect you. The best way right now is to keep you out of sight. I wish you'd believe me. It'd make this all a lot easier."

I poked at the remaining nibbles of my breakfast. "Convince me."

With a sigh he pivoted to face me. "That's what I've been trying to do."

I looked to see if his eyes held any truth.

His face became less crimson and, after he inhaled deeply through his nose, his tone flattened. "Look, you obviously need some more time to sort this out."

My eyes widened. *Oh, no. Don't leave.*

"I'll let you eat in peace." In the shadow of the hall light, he rubbed the back of his neck. "I'll be back in a little while to take you to, you know, the toilet."

"Wait! Turn on the light." The door swished shut, cutting off my reply.

Too late. One click of the locking mechanism and the blackness returned. So did fresh tears. Fear gripped at my chest once more. I was alone...in the dark, again.

I blinked back the urge to cry out and swallowed more coffee—creamed, sweet with a hint of aspartame bitterness. A tightness clinched my throat. Tom knew how I took my coffee. He really had been watching me closely at work. The cup shook in my hand. I slammed it onto the tray, except I missed. Hot coffee splashed onto my wrist. Ouch. Dang it. I sucked my hand to ease the singe of pain.

"Oh, for Heaven's sake. Why? What is this about?" I screamed to the low ceiling, which didn't bother to enlighten me with a response.

Neither did a booming voice from Heaven. Not that I expected a miracle. I was hardly like one of the saints in the Bible. Still, a part of me wanted to be, so I'd be close to God. Especially now. Who else could I turn to? Everyone I loved was dead.

A sob shot into my throat again. I shoved the tray off my lap, got up, and paced in front of the couch, ignoring the sharp twinge in my heel. I ran my hand over my head in an effort to calm down.

I closed my eyes, breathed, then opened them again, recalling what the room looked like. Seeing its shadowed corners made it less scary. I calculated the dimensions. Perhaps this was a bomb shelter left over from the Cold War era when everyone was afraid the Russians would invade. Yes, of course. That would explain the metal door. But how had he found it, and why put me here?

Tom's words echoed. "To protect you." From what? From whom?

My brain ached from thinking, and my bladder cramped.

Where was he? I felt my way toward the door to pound on it, then my big toe stubbed into hard wood. He'd left the chair in the middle of the room.

First my heel, then my shoulder, my wrist and now my toe. "I hate this dark. I hate you." Hot tears filled my eyes.

I shoved the chair out of the way with every ounce of frustration in my body. It screeched across the floor and slammed into the wall. The echo bounced into my ears.

Nature called—hard. The sharp pressure only magnified my helplessness. My fortitude waned. I willed my body to wait. "He said he'd be back."

He needed to, soon. I scrunched in my stomach and tapped my teeth together. Hurry. Hurry.

After an eternity, the door swooshed open and Tom's form filled the threshold. I squinted my eyes in the sudden light.

"Ready?"

"Two hours ago." I grumbled and brushed passed him into the hall. Grayish-green, like my room. Cold and void of any adornment. One bare light shone from the ceiling. The place reminded me of Alcatraz.

"Sorry. I was, uh, delayed." His tone sounded almost genuine.

"Where?" I jiggled my legs.

"Straight ahead."

I quickened my pace.

"Wait." He grabbed my left hand and pinned it to the small of my back. "I need to escort you. Sorry. Protocol."

"Uh, how am I supposed to...?"

"We'll work it out."

Right. Anger bubbled inside me, shoving down the fear. How is humiliating me going to protect me?

Tom pushed me forward. I stutter-stepped, then found my

stride.

"Keep going." His voice was flat and all business again. Had I made him angry? Had he heard me toss the chair or scream my hate for him? Was it the cause of his sudden streak of meanness?

I stopped. "Tom? I'm sorry. Thank you for coming back."

He nudged me forward again. "Sure. Turn left at the end of the hall. First door on the right."

He held the door open for me and leaned against it. The room held only a toilet. No sink, no shower, no window. Grayish-green painted cinderblock lined three walls. It reminded me of road-stop restrooms, without the privacy of a stall. At least it smelled better.

The commode was industrial steel. No tank. Prison like. No porcelain lid with which to whack him up the side of the head. He'd thought of everything.

A package of baby wipes lay on the chipped, green linoleum floor. He picked it up and wiggled it at me. "Can you, you know, with me here?"

I clamped my teeth hard together in fury. "*I'll* work it out."

He laughed. "Okay, Missy Hardhead. *I'll* avert my eyes."

Thank goodness, he actually did. He opened the package, pulled out two baby wipes, and waved them in my general direction while staring at the ceiling. I strained my arms to grab them.

Then I tried. But my modesty—or was it pride?—overruled my bladder. "Tom, I can't do this." I don't know what I despised more, the sheepishness in my voice or him for putting me in this predicament.

Eyes still averted, he stepped two paces outside. "Okay, I'll be right out here. Holler if you need help." His voice was droll, echoing in the bare hallway. "Tough girl for trying, though. Robert said you would be, once I hit your Irish-temper button."

I stomped my foot. "You're lying. You never knew him."

"Oh, contraire. I knew him long before you did. He worked undercover for the Feds, too. But you probably didn't know that."

Right. My bladder finally loosened. I responded loudly to cover up the sound. "Convince me. Tell me a story about you two."

"Very well." I heard his feet shuffle. "When he confessed he'd fallen for you after the NIOSA dance, I told him he was nuts and to break it off immediately. Spies aren't supposed to fall in love."

I covered my mouth with my hand. He knew about how we'd met.

THAT DANCE.

Fiesta Week is the yearly San Antonio version of Mardi Gras, except it commemorates Sam Houston's rag-tag troop's defeat of Santa Ana's forces on April 21, 1836. Night in Old San Antonio, NIOSA to the natives, lasts all week. Always a crowd-hater, I'd gone on a Thursday evening only after three days of persistent pestering by two fellow teachers. The lively beat of Greek music in the pavilion, and fabulous Gyro smells, drew me to the door.

Robert swished by, grabbed my hand, and propelled me into the communal kicking, shuffling, and twirling to the beat of lyras, mandolins, and zilia. His musty-green eyes sparkled behind lush, dark lashes against olive-colored skin and a Mediterranean nose. His touch oozed warmth. Perspiration magnified his cologne and mystified my endorphins.

We danced for what seemed like hours. I'd never had a better time in my life. I clung to him for tutelage in the moves, a habit which continued through our courtship in multiple ways.

TOM'S VOICE BROUGHT me back to the present.

"I tried to talk him out of it. Told him to never call you. I even destroyed that piece of the program you'd scrawled your phone number on. But alas, he'd committed it to memory. Your hooks were already imbedded in his heart."

A tear dripped over my cheekbone. Oh, my gosh. How did he know Robert had memorized it? For the first time in my life, at the ripe old age of twenty-six, I'd given a strange man my phone number. On our second date, he'd rattled it off to prove his interest. That impressed me more than any sweet nothings he could have said. Six weeks later, we posted the wedding bans at St. Sophia's Church per Greek Orthodox protocol.

Oh, how I missed Robert. My legs felt as limp as Ramen noodles as I pulled myself back together. I shut the lid, plopped onto the john and sat there, fully dressed. A new sob bounced in my throat. I sucked in a few deep breaths to shove the memories back into the deep hiding place between my heart and my mind. *You have to concentrate on the present, Jen.*

"You okay, Jen?"

"Yeah." I wasn't, but I'd never admit it to him. I flushed the toilet to signal I was done.

Tom led me back to my captivity without any argument from me. I padded along, numbed with renewed grief. We reached my cell. "Here we are. Home sweet home." His tone was a touch sarcastic.

I stood in the middle of the darkened room. A sudden wave of loneliness rolled over me. Unable to face him, I whispered, "Please, don't go."

Tom's grasp loosened. He brushed the hair off my neck, sending icicle prickles down my spine. His fingers fell softly on my nape. He leaned into my ear, his breath hot on my skin.

"Sorry, hon. Have to. But I'll be back in two or three hours. Try to hang in there, okay? " His lips softly pecked my forehead.

I felt his warmth drift away and heard the door close and lock.

The darkness returned. A growing storm of emotion, past and present, swirled like a tornado threatening to form. I fell to the floor and sniveled in the blackness. Why was he playing this game?

CHAPTER SEVEN

I ROCKED BACK and forth. Then an idea popped into my head. The glass shards. I might nick my hands picking a large enough piece, but I could have some sort of weapon to defend myself. Just in case his mood turned foul. In micro-moves, I felt with the palms of my hands. Nothing. I scooted to the right. No glass.

I made it all the way to the corner, then crammed my tailbone against it. When did he clean it up? He was with me the whole time I was in the john, or so I thought. Then I vaguely remembered two voices when I first came to. Was there an accomplice? Robert? Was it really his voice I kept hearing? *Could it possibly be? No, Jen. You buried him.* But then again, the funeral home director had adamantly refused to let me see the charred body…

I bopped my forehead with my palm. *Don't be ridiculous.*

In the dark silence all I could hear was my own out-of-breath puffing. The storm inside me brewed again. I closed my eyes to the room and willed the emotions to go away. Buck it up. Fear never did anyone any good. You're a grown woman. The two male influences in my life, though both dead, hounded my thoughts.

I don't know why it surfaced in my thoughts, but it did. I remembered the story about Jesus calming a storm. Probably from church camp. Maybe He'd hush this storm inside me now. Worth a try? I said the Lord's Prayer for the first time since leaving Agape Academy for Girls. My breath became less shaky. Okay.

I tried to recall as much of the 23rd Psalm parroted each day in the chapel for the five years of my stay, except on holidays and summer breaks of course, when I was temporarily released on good behavior to my grandparent's ranch. I'd thought parochial school had been a prison. It was minimum security compared to this room.

I racked my distant memory to recall the familiar voice of the headmistress as she'd say the first few word of the passage before we'd join in. How we loathed her rhinestone-studded glasses dangling from bright red silk cords, like a breastplate of honor. Now, I'd love to hear her voice, and see her stand in front of me. The verses always brought serenity to her face. I secretly envied her faith, though I'd never have admitted that to my school chums.

Girl's school hadn't been all bad. I'd made fast bonds with the other nerds and endured the slashes of sharp-tongued gossip mongers. I learned to ignore the constant eye rolls of the perfectly figured, bronzed goddesses dripping in diamond tennis bracelets and pearls. Their daddies owned half of the Texas counties by the same last name, and their debuts later made front page headlines statewide. Not my crowd. I was pale with reddish-brown hair which had an annoying wave in it—not curly, not straight. My blue eyes had too much hazel in them to be stunning. Both my parents had worked for a living. Plus, they were part-time missionaries, which really alienated me from the "in-girls."

Agape Academy was where I learned to drag a cigarette, shave my legs, and develop a passion for Bach and Monet. The last two lessons I still considered useful.

I also developed a deep-seated desire to remain virginal until my wedding day, until Robert persuaded me otherwise on our third date. Some of that lofty goal was born out of religious brainwashing, but mostly it was defiance to prove I had something the society girls didn't—control. I had a lot of first dates in college, and a few second ones. Never were they hot and heavy enough to melt the Ice Princess.

And then came that one night of Greek dancing. I would have followed Robert into the bushes behind the Arneson River Theater, and I think he knew it. He acted the gentleman and just brushed his lips on my hand when he said goodnight. His restraint stoked the smoldering flames in my heart. Oh, how I missed his touch.

My mind returned to the present. Still no Tom. How long had it been?

Don't panic, Jen. He'll be back. Yeah, and then what? *Don't think about it. He hasn't attempted that yet. He has been nice, actually.*

I closed my eyes and repeated the Lord's Prayer. I'd often recite it and Psalm 51:1-15 while on my knees under the headmistress' glare. Not that I ever did anything major. Mostly it was punishment for something public high schools would consider normal teenage defiance. My knees had ached for days after kneeling on those parochial school hardwood floors.

Now, I knelt on the equally unforgiving concrete floor. Did the words contain some magic power to summon Divine help, or were they empty phrases?

The door swooshed open. Grayish-yellow light splayed before me. Perhaps they weren't empty phrases after all.

"On your knees? I didn't know you prayed. Wait, you were in the dark?"

Was he kidding? I clenched my teeth, willing my tears to defy gravity and return to my eyes. I sat back on my heels. His footsteps sounded behind me, and then stopped. I heard a light switch flick. A soft glow began to ease into the corners of the room. Tom came around to face me.

"Ah, geez. I meant to turn on the light over the door. But then you pushed my buttons and I guess I just left." He bent down to my level. "I'm sorry, Jen, really. I'd kept it dark before to help you sleep. But when I brought you breakfast…I mean we could see okay with the door open, right?"

I looked away.

Tom swallowed hard. "I forgot when it closes…Why didn't you call out?"

"I did." Tears formed as I bit my lip. Part of me was angry, part still scared. I felt the veins in my neck bulge.

"I didn't hear you. Honest, or I'd come running." He gently squeezed my shoulders. "Wow. You're all in knots."

I sniffled. "Wouldn't you be?"

Tom plopped to the floor, scooted behind me, and proceeded to massage my neck, upper back, and shoulder blades. "I really am sorry, Jen. Here, this will ease the tension I've caused you."

My body became like jiggled gelatin. Images of riverside bushes loomed in my mind. I shoved them away. Twenty-four hours ago I didn't even like this guy.

He patted my waist. "Better?"

"No." I'm not sure how convincing I sounded.

"I'm trying to be nice, Jen." His hands rubbed down to my hips.

The old familiar alarm went off in my head, the one only Robert had been able to silence. I jumped to my feet. "Look. If you're going to do it just get it over with, okay?"

"If I was going to do it, I would've kept you drugged. I was only…" He stood and brushed himself off. "Never mind. Come on, let's sit down, and talk about it."

My eyes narrowed onto him as my breath continued in quick, short spurts.

He waited, hands folded as if in penitent prayer.

After a moment the heat from my face dissipated. I mumbled, "Okay. Sure." I flopped on the couch and stretched my legs out hoping he'd get the hint and take the chair.

But he meandered over to me, hands in pockets. Before he sat, he pushed my legs aside. "That's not what this is about, Jen."

I tucked my legs under me and stared at him as he eased down onto the cushion where my feet had been. "What *is* this about, Tom?"

He averted his eyes again, this time I think to organize his thoughts. I waited. Finally his chest heaved as he returned his gaze to me.

"Robert was more than a good friend. We were in the military together. Worked together. I'd have given my life for him. You." His eyes targeted my face. "You, Jen, were the most precious thing in his world. I promised to protect you against all odds, at all costs. That's what this is about."

"I don't understand."

"You're dead, Jen. According to the article on page 16D of today's newspaper." He shut his eyes to quote from it. "Tragic car accident, uncannily on the same curve as where her husband met his fate. Explosion so massive, they are scraping the ashes for dental work. Suicide is suspected."

"No." My heart flipped upside down in my chest. Thunderous beating filled my ears.

"Afraid so. The best way to get the bad guys off your trail. Of course, we had that scenario ready to go before you came with me into hiding. It was part of the plan. But I can't read you in on any more. I am not running point on this."

Read me in? Point? Sounded like what they'd say on a CIA drama. Did real agents talk like that? Maybe the federal badge he'd flashed at me in the diner was fake. I never got a good look at it. Was he some sort of psychopath? That seemed too fanciful. Something else was going on. Someone else was behind this. "I don't believe you, Tom."

He cocked his head as a sneer edged across it. "It's believable. You've been even more withdrawn and moody than normal for months now." He reached in his shirt and pulled out the newspaper clipping. "Here. It's hard to read in this dim light." He flicked on the flashlight and aimed its beam at the headlines with today's date on the top.

I widened my eyes.

"See?" He clicked off the penlight and waved the clipping in front of my face. "Local woman killed on same road as late husband."

"How dare you?" I grabbed his shirt and slapped his face as hard as I could. Then I beat on his chest over and over.

He took it without flinching and let me play it out. When my anger subsided, he gathered me into his arms. I drew into a fetal position and whimpered. "Everything's gone. Robert, my life, everything."

He stroked my hair. "I know, hon. I know. It's for the best, really."

I was drained of any desire to fight him. I limp-ragged into his embrace and sobbed. He rocked me gently back and forth until the crying softened to sniffles.

When sensibility returned, his statements sunk into the cognitive portion of my brain. "Tom, you mean the wreck was part of it? The sirens, before we went into Bob's Burgers? That was my car?"

I felt his chin nod against my temple. "Uh-huh." His answer vibrated off his shirt into my ear.

I raised my head off his chest. "How? I'd just driven it. My car was in the parking lot."

He released his grasp and rubbed his forehead. "When we planned this op, I was to convince you to take my car to go eat. Then they were to wreck your car, which of course they did. They had to burn yours so the VIN would be traced."

"But I took my car."

He shifted and turned to face me. "Yeah, that was a bit tough to work out. I told them I doubted you'd go with me in my car, so we came up with a Plan B. They switched yours for a stolen Mazda of the same make and color. No one ever really looks at their license plates at night so we figured in the pouring rain you wouldn't notice."

"But my keyless entry?"

"Easy enough to switch out while you were smoking your nimble fingers over the calculator keypad. You always leave your purse dangling on the back of your chair." He wiggled his forefinger back and forth in front of my nose and clicked his teeth. "Bad habit."

I sighed and scooted back, pressing my lower spine against the armrest of the couch opposite him. I drew the throw pillow to my chest. "Go on."

Tom picked at a piece of lint on his pant leg, and then looked straight at me. "I'd texted them Plan B was in place. I slipped your real keys in the trash can by the elevator so they could do the switch while we were detained in there."

He saw my mouth form a question. "Yes, the elevator malfunction was planned. That's when the exchange was made.

They filled the stolen car with your personal effects—umbrella, your morning coffee thermos, cell phone cord, CDs—so you wouldn't suspect anything."

"How did the police know it was me in the wreck?"

"They…"

That word again. Who were "they"?

"…took your stuff and scattered it all around the wreck as they pretended to be bystanders. I'd given them your purse and cell phone before we drove away from the diner—after you were, well, knocked out. Those, by the way, were found later over the rail at the scene. The police figured opportunists had pilfered through them for info, and then tossed them."

"Where is the car now?"

"The stolen car? After we left the restaurant, they swept it clean and got rid of it. It'll probably turn up in Nuevo Laredo today."

I sat up straight. "You keep saying 'they.' You're part of a group?"

"Yes…and no."

Right. Obviously he wasn't going to tell me. But someone had planned all this. I didn't want to really know but I had to ask. "What—I mean who, did they use for my body?"

He looked at his hands. "I dunno. Some O.D.'d prostitute probably. They're experts at this sort of stuff, Jen. They know how to make an anonymous body be whomever they want it to be."

I threw the pillow on the floor and paced the room. In the edge of my vision, I saw his head move back and forth with me, like a spectator in a tennis match. Mine felt horrible, pressed with emotion, lack of sleep, and worry. "I need some aspirin. My temples are splitting."

"Here." He reached in his pocket and pulled out a small, plastic pill bottle. He tossed it to me. "Catch."

I reached and missed. It rolled across the floor.

"Oops, sorry." His smirk reappeared.

I shrugged. *Don't let him raise your blood pressure.* I slapped a quick grin across my lips and cocked my head. "My fault. My eye-hand coordination always sucked."

Tom reached to retrieve the bottle. "I know. Robert said he gave up trying to teach you tennis. He loved that sport."

Now he'd pushed my buttons. My red-headed personality tingled. I slammed my good foot onto the concrete. My fists jammed into my thighs. "Stop it."

"What?" He scrunched his shoulders.

"Stop talking about Robert." I gulped back tearless anger. Either my tear ducts were tired of producing them, or maybe I was dehydrated.

He bowed his head, and the little boy act resurfaced. "If you say so. But it's kinda hard to explain this without mentioning his name. This was all his idea. He sensed he'd put you in danger." He handed me the aspirin.

"Really?" I raised one hand to my eyes and pushed the hurt away once again. Control, Jen. Don't appear so vulnerable. It's what he wants. He's egging you on.

I shook the pillbox. "Do I get water for these?"

He snapped his fingers. "Right. Back in a few."

I waggled my neck and felt the tension pop. Better. Then, my eyes widened once again as I watched Tom press his hand to the door. It magically opened, as in a Sci-Fi or spy movie.

Tom turned his head back to me. "Don't go anywhere now." Then, he winked again.

My blood simmered.

To prove my aim was better than he thought, I threw the pillow at him. But by the time my projectile reached the door, it had already sealed shut again. Rats.

Through the dim wire-caged light above me, I watched the throw cushion slap against the steel and slide listlessly to the floor. At least he'd left the light on this time.

CHAPTER EIGHT

HE NEVER CAME back. A shake of the bottle told me he'd only given me two. Guess he didn't want me to O.D. and end up being a body "they" could disguise for someone else. Whatever.

I downed the pills with what little saliva I could muster. I sat on the floor, my back against the couch and stared at the soft, grayish light emitting from the bare bulb over the door. At least I could see the walls caving in on me. Thank God for small favors.

Over the next few hours I sang every hymn I knew, then Beatles songs. I'd regressed to "Row, Row, Row Your Boat," by the time the door slid open. I squinted into the dingy yellow beam of light that brightened the room and tapped my arm where my watch once was. Where was it anyway? Probably it'd been strewn across the road with my other stuff. More proof.

"Sorry. Something came up I had to take care of." He walked toward me. "Having fun, yet?"

"Oh, all kicks and giggles." I wiggled to sit straight and threw my shoulders back in defiance. Chin up, show him strength.

Tom seemed unimpressed. He slid down onto the floor next to

me. "I've gotten permission to fill you in on a bit more of what's going down."

He'd changed into khaki pants with a black T-shirt stretched across his chest, dangling loose at the waist. His upper chest muscles rippled underneath the cotton. He handed me a waxed paper cup with a domed lid. A bright yellow and white striped straw stuck out of the top. "Here, better than water. It's a low-cal almond milk, banana and strawberry smoothie, no whipped cream."

"From the Yogurt Tree?"

"Yep. That's what you usually order from them, right?" He dangled it carrot-like in front of me.

"How—?" I reached for it.

He winked with satisfaction and slowly lowered the cup. I snatched it and sucked down the cold liquid, savoring the sensation as it slid down my throat and coated my stomach. Pure heaven.

He then rattled a sack. "And, ta-dah. Smoked turkey with Munster on rye, extra romaine, no onions, with low-fat mayo." He peeked inside the paper bag. "Oh, and sea salt pita chips."

How did he know? A chill equal to the second swallow of smoothie raced down the back of my head. *He had been studying me that closely. Oh, my God.*

"Yes, I have been. Part of the assignment. A rather nice part, I might add." He gave me a quick grin.

I felt my eyes grow bigger. Had he read my thoughts again?

Tom wadded up the sack. "Never play poker, Jen. Your face reveals your thoughts before you open your mouth." He scooted away to give me a bit more elbow space. "Besides, if I were you, that's what I'd be thinking." His voice changed to a higher pitch. "Oh, no. He's been learning all about me."

I shook off the embarrassment, chomped down on the

sandwich, and tried my level best not to roll my eyes into the back of my head with delight. It tasted so wonderful.

He wiped a dollop of mayonnaise off the corner of my mouth. Then with a slight grunt, he hoisted himself, sauntered over to the chair, and straddled it again.

Did he do it to give himself a dominating appearance, or was he confident I'd not try to escape? Did he ever do anything spontaneously, or was every move calculated? Did I even know this guy who forty-eight hours ago set my teeth on edge? The wimpy-nerd routine had obviously been his mild-mannered Clark Kent act. Not that I'd go so far as to say this was Superman in front of me. No, he was more like Lex Luthor, the calculating, crazed nemesis of the caped superhero. Yet, in a way, he was so benevolent toward me, as if he sympathized with my situation.

I stared at the sandwich. "If you ordered this, then..."

"We must be close to work?" He leaned back and flexed his arm muscles. The T-shirt strained a bit more. "Good try. But no, not really. However, I did have to make an appearance today for a few hours. Everyone is teary-eyed over your demise, by the way. You were really liked..."

I stomped both feet hard onto the concrete floor and ignored the pain as it shot into one heel. "Stop it. Stop it, now." I threw the sandwich onto the wrapper.

It's all a lie. I'm alive. I had to get out of there and tell the world none of it was true. As if from nowhere, an idea slammed into my mind. If I let him see me as vulnerable, then maybe he'd drop his guard. I buried my head between my knees, my hands grasping the back of my head, and whimpered out loud. Maybe being a blubbering female would pluck at his heart strings and bring him closer like it had before.

It did. He sighed. "Aw, geez, Jen."

My faked weeping increased. I heard the chair legs scrape the floor, then his body slid next to me. He laid a gentle arm across my back and drew me to him. "Ssshh. There, there. I know this is tough, but..." He kissed the crown of my head.

Something inside me snapped. *Now*, my psyche screamed. *Do it now.*

I shoved my elbow deep into his diaphragm. He groaned. In a split second I was on my feet. I jabbed my knee into his groin. He let out a pained roar, then rolled to the side in a fetal position. I dashed for the door and down the hall.

At the "T," I turned right. The toilet and a dead end had been to the left. My bare feet slipped along the tiled floor, trying to get traction as I rounded the corner. I reached another wall. No door. I could hear his grumbles and groans as he edged closer. Frantic, I felt the walls for a panel, something. He'd gotten in. There had to be an exit.

"I told you there's no way out."

I swiveled to see him leaning against the wall, half-bent, his face grimaced with residual pain. He raised one hand. "Please." He drew a shallow breath and shook his head rapidly several times. "Truce, okay?"

I stared at my incapacitated captor. Part of me wanted to rush to his side and look after him. The other wanted to snap his neck. His eyes beckoned me to choose the first.

"For the last time...I am not...here to hurt you." The sentence came in short spurts as he eased his torso upright.

"Oh?" My voice bounced off the narrow walls. I hoped it hit him in the face.

Tom swallowed hard and waved his arm back down the hall. "Look. Go back. Eat your food. We'll talk, all right? I won't touch you again."

I let out a humph and proceeded defiantly past him back to my cage with one couch, one chair, and a wooden end table. I don't know why. Maybe my favorite deli delight drew me back there. Or, maybe deep down I knew my only way out was with Tom.

He knew it, too. I could see it on his face. Probably another calculation on his part. He'd planned this well. Whatever this was, it felt more and more like a late-night movie.

I sat on the couch, he in the wooden chair, this time flipped to the normal position, facing me. He slouched, arms on his knees, but remained alert. As I slurped the smoothie and reveled in my food, he kept his voice even-toned, matter-of-fact.

"Look, I know you have no cause to trust me. I've lied to you, kidnapped you, drugged you. I'm not who you thought I was, and I'm telling you your husband wasn't either. That's a lot to take in."

"No. You think?" I garbled between bites.

My sudden burst of sarcasm amused him. His eyes twinkled. "Robert warned me you'd have a feisty side. But still..." He shook his head and wiped the laughter from his eyes.

A wave of deep melancholy washed over me. If this guy was being truthful, and it seemed he might be, then Robert had been the liar. He had a secret life. Our whole marriage, supposedly built on trust, had been a farce. "Did he ever even love me?" The words squeaked from my heart into my throat.

Tom looked me square in the eye, jaw set. "Deeply." He blinked and focused on an invisible spot hovering over my left shoulder. "That was the problem. Still is. He tried his best to keep you cushioned from it all, but..." He shrugged.

Still is? What did that mean? I sat in silence, waiting for him to formulate his thoughts. He heaved a deep breath, nodded to himself, then returned his gaze back to my face.

"Yes?" I flipped my hand back and forth at him. "Go on."

"Jen, Robert was investigating some pretty sleazy guys. They've discovered who you are. You can still be used as leverage to get my organization to back off." He sighed. "I don't know how much I should tell you. The more you know the more"—he glanced back into space then found the word he wanted. His eyes fixated on me once more and continued—"vulnerable you will become, and more likely, if caught, to actuate the headlines about your sudden and premature end." He stood, hands jammed into his pockets again.

Fear rose to conquer me again. I forced it back with the last swallow of the smoothie. "You mean, they'll kill me." There was no need to make it a question.

"Probably. After they use you to get to me. You see, they're now aware I know too much. And that Robert and I were, well, let's say colleagues."

"Who are you?"

He snorted. "Just the same ol' Tom you always knew."

"Oh, sure." I slammed my back into the cushions, crossed my arms over my chest. "If you want me to perhaps, one day, begin to trust you an itsy bit..." I raised my thumb and forefinger to barely touch, emphasizing the minute amount. "Then drop the dramatic cloak-and-dagger act, okay?"

He stopped mid-stride and hung his head like a schoolboy in front of ruler-whacking headmistress. Then I saw the glint in his pupils. I threw the now-empty smoothie cup at him.

Tom ducked in mock fear and laughed, shattering the silent echoes in the bare-walled bomb cellar. It made him so attractive with those glistening blue eyes, dark locks, toned muscles, and wry smile. Hollywood would have snatched him up for a contract in a blink.

Oh, how I wanted to hate him. I loathed myself for not being able to, no matter how hard I tried. Why did I ever agree to go with him to Bob's Burgers in the first place? He'd known I would. He'd played me.

"Exactly how long had you been planning this?"

Tom wiped his eyes with the back of his hand. "Robert and me? Months. At least two before, well, you know. The night he died."

I blinked back fresh tears. "If you knew he was in danger, why didn't you do something? Why didn't he?"

He stepped toward me, then rocked back, obviously thinking of the last time he let my womanly weakness sway him. A touch of pain still showed in his jaw line. "Jen. It couldn't be helped. It was inevitable. The odds were too much stacked against him. Robert knew it too." He waved his hand around my prison walls. "That's why we prepared this. First for him, then for you, or so was the original idea. Fake your deaths. Have you both hide out for a while then re-emerge with new lives, new IDs, in another part of the world."

This cage would have been a second honeymoon seclusion. The two of us, Robert and I, tangled in the darkness. If only I hadn't overreacted about him and that woman in the seedy hotel and…no, I refused to go in the deep hole of regret again. I had been there too many times already.

I opened the pita chips and plucked through the bag for the right piece. I needed time to collect my emotions again. Tom politely waited.

I crunched, then swallowed. "Want one?"

That took him back. His face brightened. "No, thanks. Already ate. I guess I have answered your questions to your satisfaction then?"

"Hardly. I'm just tired." I looked away.

"It's a lot to absorb, Jen. I understand." He glanced at his watch. "Look, I need to do something. I'll be back in a few hours. But first, do you want to, uh, you know?" He nodded toward the opening in the wall and the hallway.

"Yes. Please."

He bobbed his head twice. "Let's go." Then he stopped and shrugged. "Sorry. Bad pun."

I laughed, in spite of myself. "Yes, it was."

We walked down the hall. I stopped in front of the door to the restroom. With one eyebrow raised, I smirked, "Are you coming in again?"

"Screw protocol. If you promise not to dismember me, I'll give you your privacy." He leaned in. "Besides, as I said. There is no way out."

"You did, twice now."

He motioned me toward the lone steel toilet and shut the door.

I did my thing, then opened the bathroom door. He was in the hallway, leaning against the wall, texting a message on his phone. The gun's butt peeked out over his belt. I sighed. Either could be my passage to freedom, but it would do no good for me to try and grab one of them. He was way too strong, and I knew deep down he'd never let me catch him off guard again.

I walked past him and back to my vault in submission. His footsteps followed. We didn't speak. Back in the room, I refused to look at him.

"Jen. I am sorry I have to keep leaving." His shoes shuffled across the concrete and then stopped at the door. "There is a lot I need to do to make this work."

"Oh, sure." My voice dripped of insincerity.

"Look," he huffed. "Let me do my job, then maybe we can both leave this place, okay?"

A few minutes later I was alone again, locked in my cage with one lousy light bulb over the door illuminating the room with its mighty forty watts. Pita chips don't taste as good in semi-dark, not by yourself.

I wanted Robert. Then, I wanted Tom.

CHAPTER NINE

TRUE TO HIS word, Tom came back. This time he had a discount store's sack. "If you promise to be a good girl and not whack me over the head—or kick me somewhere else..." He cringed. "I'll give you a present."

I almost expected him to jiggle like a bowl full of jelly and say "Ho, ho, ho" as he dug into the bag. But then again, he had neither a white beard nor a big belly. In fact, his physique was rather...I stopped myself in mid-thought and looked at the wall. A wave of guilt splashed over me. Even though widowed, I still felt married.

He pulled out a small camping lamp. He ripped open a package of D batteries and slipped them in the base, then twirled it upright again with a dramatic flair. With a wiggle of his eyebrows, he flicked it on.

"Here ya go." He set it on the end table.

The stark whiteness of the bulb pierced my pupils. Little colored spots flashed in front of me. "Why now?"

"I thought you might like some more light. It's getting dark outside."

I blinked several times then shaded my eyes with my hand. "Very funny." The pressure behind my retinas began to ease as my eyes became accustomed to the beam.

His mouth jerked slightly to one side as he dropped on the couch next to me. "Give it a minute. Your eyes will adjust. Look what else I brought you." He patted my knee, but it didn't feel like a seductive pass this time. More like a schoolboy giddiness. He pulled out a paperback. Of course it was by my favorite mystery author. Why was I not surprised?

"Entertainment? Guess that means I am not going anywhere soon, huh?"

"No, 'fraid not, dear. I was hoping we'd be able to clear out tomorrow, but it's not looking favorable. Some of them need more convincing that you're really out of the way."

"Some of who?"

He gave me a you-know-better look. "And last, but not least, as they say." He handed me a small, battery-operated video game. "Can't allow you to have the Internet. Sorry." Another shrug. He pointed at the screen. "But it does play sixteen different solitaire games."

"Is this a hint you won't be staying?"

"Do you really want me to?"

I couldn't choose an answer.

"Yeah, I thought so." He got to his feet. He raised his face to the ceiling and pointed. "By the way, see that little dark dome in the far corner? Camera. I'm right above you, so wave when you feel lonely."

I shot him a look.

He blushed hard. "It's not what I meant, Jen. Honest."

"Freudian slip?"

He leaned over. I inhaled his cologne— citrus, slightly musky.

The one Robert refused to wear even though it was my favorite. Did he know that, too?

He brushed his fingers across my cheek. "Perhaps it was."

Then he was gone.

New questions spun like a merry-go-round in my head. Had he been watching me all this time? Surely I'd have noticed the hump when I felt around the ceiling. No, not in that corner—the spider-web corner. Maybe he installed it while I was in the restroom? Would he have had time? Concrete would be hard to drill through, wouldn't it?

No, the camera had to have been there all along. Not your typical bomb shelter then. I felt like a rat in an experiment, or a pawn in a game of chess.

Speaking of games, maybe they would keep my mind off all these questions he'd never answer. I grabbed the video device. After five hands of Klondike and three of Golf, I decide to test his statement after all. I stood on my tiptoes, stuck my tongue out at the black dome, then wiggled my fingers behind my ears. A distant thud, thud, thud came in response from the general vicinity of the ceiling.

That freaked me a bit. Was he telling the truth about the reason I was here or was he toying with me to get me to rely on him in some twisted, sadistic way? I'd read about stuff like this—the ways captors try to psych out their victims. Was this all a fabrication, a means to get me to depend solely on him? I had to admit it was working.

I flopped onto the couch, buried my face in the back cushion, and bit my lip. Maybe he was a sociopath, and I his latest prey. He and Robert were never "Feds." It was all part of his delusion. It made more sense than hiding me from "them," whoever they were—the same "they" who'd also killed my husband even though the police were convinced it was an accident.

Yet there was an underlying "Tom-ness" which always remained—steady, deep-flowing like a river's current. Caring and seemingly honest. Could I trust that part of him?

"I have to believe him," I scolded my psyche in a whisper. "But dare I?"

Suddenly his voice, though tunneled, pierced the room. "Please try to believe me, Jen."

A chilled splash hit my face again. So he could hear me as well. Which meant he'd heard my sobs, my Bible verse chants, even my singing. Dear Lord, what has he thought of me? Had he enjoyed watching me fall apart? The thought sent anger and embarrassment simultaneously seething through my veins.

His voice sounded again. "For the umpteenth time, I am doing this for your own good. Really."

I raised mine in response. "Then let me out of here."

"No can do."

"Why not?" I slid my legs to the floor, sat primly, and stared at the dome. "If you are hiding out as well, why aren't you down here?"

"Is that where you want me?"

The question was loaded. I didn't dare respond.

"Make up your mind, Jen. Time to decide if you believe me or not."

I stared at my lap.

He cleared his throat. "Jen, listen. I'm giving you space, okay? I know you're lonely, vulnerable. Robert was my dearest friend. I swore to him I'd protect you. I'd never, ever betray—"

"Shut up!" I threw the paperback at the black humped intruder on the ceiling.

Silence.

Heat flooded my face, so I flung myself onto the couch, my back to him. I shoved my fist in my mouth to stop the sobs from erupting. I felt violated, exposed.

I prayed the Lord's Prayer once more through squinted eyes. It was the only way I knew to get through to the Almighty. I'd been away from Him for so long, I didn't know how to pray on my own. Is that why He killed Robert and put me here? To punish me for turning my back on Him, as I now did to my captor?

Or was it to get my attention?

"God, You have it. I'm sorry I got so angry with You. I'm sorry I blamed You for Robert's death. I'm sorry I've kept You out of my life. Help me, please."

I wrapped the blanket around my shoulders. The dam of self-reliance, which I'd prided myself for maintaining, crumbled. Mourning for Dad, for Robert, and my once mundane life crashed over me in waves. My soft sobs lasted until disjointed dreams took over.

THE NEXT TIME I awoke, a small paperback Bible lay on my chest. A take-out egg, cheese and sausage muffin, apple slices, and foamy vanilla latte sat on the floor next to the couch on a tray, along with a long-stemmed peppermint carnation and a scribbled note. "I wish I didn't have to do this to you. I'm just following orders. I prayed for you. Tom."

The syrupy words almost dripped from the ink and rolled down the sides of the note. "Please." I growled to the black sphere. I wadded the paper and tossed it at the dome, of course missing the mark. Peppermint carnations and white roses had been my wedding flowers...but Tom probably knew all of that. I crushed the bud in my hand and chucked it as well. I hoped he was watching.

I'd swallowed the last of the latte when the wall slid open. But no one was there. A voice came from overhead. "Go ahead. You know where it is. By the way, there isn't a camera in there. Just in the halls."

I nodded to the black ceiling bump and walked to the doorway, half expecting it to close on me in a cruel joke. The now familiar hall stretched ahead. I noticed another black bump on the ceiling by the bare bulb. "This is like the Twilight Zone. I swear I've seen this episode," I mumbled under my breath.

As I turned left, another one glared back at me. But where was the exit? Tom hadn't materialized out of thin air. Then I saw it. A thin dark outline in the ceiling—rectangular, ten feet above my head. A hatch. Smart. I tapped my forefinger to my forehead and pointed to it as I nodded to the dome.

"Thank you. I knew you'd figure it out." Tom's voice cascaded down. "It's all electronically controlled by my body temperature. Works best because yours, of course, is sub-normal. 97.2 as I recall?"

So that was how he got in and out.

"Why all this monitoring? Was that part of the original plan?" If Robert and I were to have shared this mausoleum-like place, would Tom have been watching? The thought made my stomach squeeze tight.

"Not originally. But now, since I have to keep you...well, let's say safely out of the public eye..." He paused. "As attractive as you are, you're still my best friend's wife. It seemed better if we have separate quarters. So I rigged this system."

"You mean best friend's widow."

"Semantics. Jen. You still feel married, don't you? That's why you tense up whenever I'm close?"

His intuitiveness made my skin crawl. I changed the subject. "Are you in a windowless area, too?"

A long pause. Finally the response came. "No, Jen. I have a

lookout point. But we're not anywhere you'd recognize. We made sure of that."

We again. I was sick of him talking as if he and Robert were still cohorts in this whole bloody thing. Robert was dead. "I'd like a few minutes of privacy now."

"You got it. Turning off audio for ten. Take your time. I am still monitoring the hall, though, so I'll know when you're finished."

I nodded, ducked into the cinderblock closet, and closed the door. Baby wipes *and* toilet paper had been carefully placed in reach. So was the morning paper. I stifled a laugh. Maybe he was trying to make me comfortable after all.

I NOW HAD the run of the place, so to speak. Room, hallway, two dead ends, john. Cozy. I tried not to dwell on the fact Tom was watching me like a lab experiment. Truth be told, I didn't know. He could be there, or gone. He could come back, or not. He could appear suddenly with food, or another syringe. Rape still remained a possibility. But surely by now...?

My mind couldn't make sense of it. The man was a blank slate I couldn't figure out. On second thought, he was more like a chameleon. Kind and sympathetic one minute, all business-like and calculating the next, then back to soft and caring. Originally wimpy and dull. Next, seductive and manly.

Almost as if he behaved one way when he was sure we were alone and another when he thought someone was watching and listening through that little dome. But who? His agency? Like on the old TV game show *To Tell the Truth*, I wanted to call out, "Would the real Tom please stand up?"

Either way, he spelled danger with a capital D. From now on, I'd have to be on my toes. I simply couldn't play into anything. I couldn't reveal my emotions. Nope, I couldn't give him a clue. The best way to get the upper hand was to keep him guessing. I'd be totally stoic. I'd show him who had a poker face.

A SLIGHT WHIRR came from the hallway, then his soft-shoed stride into the room. I'd been doing sit-ups, trying to keep the blood circulating.

"Hate to interrupt your workout." He sugar-coated a grin and sat down in the chair. I swung my torso around and folded my legs to the side.

"Yes?"

His face brightened. "Good news. Your confinement may be close to an end. I think I have it all arranged. Things are settling down. Your funeral..." He cleared his throat. "Uh, memorial service was this morning." He handed me the obit section, in case I hadn't seen it in the loo where he'd left the newspaper each morning. Which, I hadn't. Maybe my subconscious had kept me from that part of the paper. I blinked and looked away.

"I know you were an only child, but I think you still have two or three cousins living? Guess they had to wait for them to arrive. Anyway, management gave everyone in our department a half day off today, so some of your coworkers attended. I, by the way, have the stomach flu, so I didn't go." He felt his own forehead for effect. "I'll be off work at least two or three more days as well."

So that's where he's been. At work. As if all was normal. I gave him a fake pout. "Ah, too bad."

Tom cleared his throat. "We know they were watching the church." He smiled. "They must have been convinced it wasn't faked. It seems they have slithered away for now. So now we can make our move."

I glanced back at the paper. The reality of the words in print grabbed me. To the world I really was dead. I bit my lip as tears pooled in my eyes. So much for my stoic facade.

"Well, that display of nonchalance lasted a long time, Jen." His tone sounded mocking. He reached over and patted my shoulder. "Good try at it though."

"Go to hell."

"Probably would, except I confess my sins, regularly. Keeps me on the straight and narrow."

"I'm sure." I scrunched my mouth in disbelieving disgust.

He exhaled deep and long. "Jen, please. I was trying to lighten things up here. I didn't mean to tease you."

I snorted. "Right."

He looked peeved, then a bit wounded. "Look, lady. Have I hurt you? Have I mistreated you? Have I molested you?" His words came zipping at me like automatic weapon fire.

"No. Not yet."

"Okay, then." His anger fizzled.

But I wasn't through. I was tired, irritated, and trapped. My tongue-lashing began in earnest. "Oh, you've been the perfect host." I stood with my palms jabbed into my hips. "You kidnap me, drug me, leave me here alone in an, an"—I waved my hand around the room—"oversized coffin in the pitch black."

"Coffin? Coffin, you say?" He pointed at the door, and yelled. "Don't you get it? You are in this sealed-off room *so they can't find you.*"

I stared into him.

His eyes narrowed. "Darn it, woman. I brought you your favorite foods, let you go to the restroom when you want, gave you a pillow, blanket, water, a lamp, a book, a—"

"Bible? Nice touch." I waggled my finger under his nose. "And don't judge me, Mr. Holier than Thou."

His jaw steeled. His Irish eyes blazed. Every muscle in his

upper arm rippled. I'm sure the words he mumbled under his breath would've burned my ears.

I jumped back as he pivoted to my face, his fists clenched. They hung in mid-air, and then one dropped to his side. He raised a finger at me, shook it at my nose as his face reddened even more. Then, with a wipe of his hand across his head, he turned to pace the floor. I'm sure I saw steam rising from his head.

Minutes passed. My feet were cemented to the concrete, afraid to flinch until I noticed his arm muscles slowly ease, a sign his scorched mood was melting. I'd seen a new facet to this dark jewel. It wasn't pretty.

"Sit down." The command was even, voice low.

I did as I was told. He turned and stood in front of me, legs planted apart and stiff. He peered down at me as I perched on the edge of the couch. "Let's start over, okay?"

I nodded. His blue eyes softened. I watched his chest swell and slowly deflate to normal.

"Jen." He took another cleansing breath, and then proceeded. "Robert and I've been colleagues a long time. We are, well, like freelance errand boys for the agency. The government tells us what they need done, and we do it. I'm called an asset, you see."

My heart jumped. "Are? Do?"

"What?"

I jolted to grab his shirt. "You said we *are*. You and Robert are, not were."

CHAPTER TEN

HE WAVED THE thought away. "I meant me. I am, he was. Sorry."
He took my hands and lowered them.

I grasped at the straw, refusing to let go of the thought. "He's
alive, isn't he? You said it was the original plan. You faked his
death, too. Just like mine." My eyes darted back and forth, my mind
racing. "I heard his voice when I was just coming to. I've heard it
since."

Tom's eyes widened, just briefly, but long enough for me to see
what I'd said surprised him. I peered into his face, searching for a
chink in the armor, a crack in this veneer of a story.

He stepped forward and squared my shoulders. "No, Jen.
Sorry. No."

I gulped back a sob. "No?"

The blue in his eyes floated with emotion. "No." He stroked my
hair. "He's gone, honey. The Robert you knew is no more. Really."

I looked at his face, blurred through my tears. It seemed
transparent with sincerity.

Tom swallowed hard. "I wish it wasn't the case. I honestly

loved the guy."

"So did I," I squeaked, then folded myself onto the couch. He'd thrust a needle into my balloon of hope. It deflated into the pit of my stomach.

"I know that, Jen." His voice was velvet and low. "So did Robert."

I closed my eyes and laid my head in my hands.

He gently touched my arm. Then he cleared his throat. "I'm sorry, Jen. Your imagination has been getting the better of you. It's my fault for leaving you alone down here. But those were my orders, hon."

I nodded, and buried my head further into my palms.

He was silent for a few moments. Then in a low tone, he said, "Get yourself together. I'll be back in an hour or so. I need to check in."

Tom's footsteps faded, then the whirr came and went. I was alone once more. But this time, I was glad. I needed to weep in solitude, despite the black spy-dome on the ceiling.

I SAT ON the couch with my arms laced behind my head and stared at the ceiling. My brain was numb. Tired of thinking, tired of crying, tired of being. My eyelids hurt from the salty tears. I no longer cared what happened to me—well, almost.

So the world thought I was dead. Next week, the missionary relief fund that had sponsored my parents' excursions would get my life insurance check. My distant cousins would divvy up my annuity for their kids' college funds. The stray cat would slither off to find another softhearted victim. Someone else would balance the quarterly figures at work. The earth would keep revolving.

What would happen to my grandmother's buffet or my mother's wedding china? I shrugged. Who knew? Funny, I'd never thought of all that before. Why would I have at the age of thirty-one?

I crunched my knees to my chest and wrapped my hands over them. What was going to happen to me? Would Tom go ahead with this act, play with my emotions, then eventually do me in? Or would he fly me to some distant land and pretend we were husband and wife? People were abducted every day. I remembered a young girl who finally escaped after years of captivity. But no one had declared her dead. Just missing. Her family never gave up hope.

It wasn't the case with me. I'd have to prove I still existed. Until then, like that girl, I must play along and wait to make my move. Whether it was today or three years from now, I'd have to be secretly on my guard.

I looked at the dome and narrowed my eyes. I could participate in this game. I had no other choice. Tom had made that very clear.

"You win," I whispered to the ceiling. No thump came in response.

TOM CAME BACK, now dressed in jeans and a collared Polo shirt. His cologne was freshly applied, his face clean shaven. I stared at him, wondering what roles we were going to play now.

He knitted his brows, then softened them. "Look, if you promise to cooperate..." He placed two fingers on the butt of the gun jutting out of his jeans. "I'll let you come upstairs and shower, okay? I have a change of clothes waiting for you."

I turned back to stare at the ceiling. "Do you plan to watch?"

"More than that." His tone iced over. "I plan to be in there with you and ravish you over and over, all sudsy and wet."

I whipped my head around, my mouth open.

He grinned from ear to ear. "Gotcha."

I rolled my eyes, then lifted myself from the sofa and headed for the door, conscious of his eyes on me, most likely as they had been on Bouncy Bow at Bob's Burgers.

He stopped at the dark rectangle in the ceiling, then raised his hand. On silent command, a stairway lowered. He motioned upward. "Go ahead."

"You first." I dropped my hands to my skirt.

His cheeks turned a darker shade of pink. "Okay, but when you get to the top, turn right. I'll be waiting. Just keep to the hall and away from any rooms with windows. We have a visitor staked out across the street I'd rather you not meet."

"Why, because he's a cop?"

"Hardly."

"Then why risk this? Why not give me more baby wipes and leave me in the coffin?"

He inhaled. "I wish you'd quit referring to it like that."

"It seems appropriate," I said as we ascended the stairs. "I am, after all, dead."

He made no comment, just the next directive. "Let's go."

I climbed up after him, trying not to notice the tight muscles in his backside, and then followed him through another unadorned and grayish-green concrete hallway about ten paces to a partially opened door. Two other doors on the other side of the hall were closed. His quarters?

"Well, go on in."

Obediently, I peeked inside. A shower, a toilet, and a wall-hung sink. The place smelled of bleach cleanser and the porcelain sparkled. Bad at housekeeping, huh?

An opaque skylight perched out of reach by at least six feet, but no window. Daylight streamed through from above, accenting the sterile feel of the room. Bug carcasses lay in the edges of the glass. I knew how they felt.

The door closed softly behind me. I waited for a lock to click. None did. No lock on the knob on my side, either. Probably protocol. Whatever.

I turned to see a T-shirt and jeans hanging on the back of the door. A pair of hiking tennis shoes lay in the corner with a pair of underwear and socks draped on top. No need to look at the tags. They'd be my size and brands.

I jumped at the tap on the door. "Is it all you need? Did I forget anything?"

I scanned the rest of the room. A toothbrush and toothpaste nestled above the spigots on the sink. A towel and a washcloth lay neatly folded on the commode lid. On top of them lay a woman's disposable razor, deodorant and a hair brush. I pulled back the shower curtain to see shampoo and soap perched on a bench. What? No hairdryer so I could electrocute him?

"It's fine, thanks." But he already knew it, didn't he?

"Okay. I'm walking away, now. I'll be just down the hall. The audio is on. Sorry."

I looked to see a familiar black dome bearing down at me. "Geez. Just audio, Tom? No video? Sure that's protocol?"

In a pig's eye. Okay, let him get his jollies then. I undressed, stepped into the shower, and swished the curtain closed. I made sure I took my sweet time under the scorching stream of water. His turn to wait for a change.

TOM WASN'T THERE when I opened the bathroom door.

"Run," my brain yelled, but as soon as my muscles registered the command he appeared in the hall, outlined by another skylight behind him at the far end.

"All done?"

I nodded, running the towel through my hair. He meandered toward me. Then he stopped, hands in his pockets, and leaned against the opposite wall.

"Hate to see the hot water bill after that long shower you took. Glad we'll be bailing from this place."

"We are?" I stopped, not sure if this was a good thing or not.

He looked perplexed, maybe a little peeved. "Yes, I told you so."

I pivoted and hung the towel on a hook inside the bathroom door. "Now?"

He reached down to pick up a small backpack. It was the same grayish-green as the walls. Definitely old Army surplus. "Yes. Right now."

He brushed past me into the bathroom, gathered the toiletries, and shoved them in the bag. "Here," he pushed it toward me. "Take it. It has a change of underwear and another T-shirt. We're traveling light."

I grabbed the bag. It was light. Obviously it didn't hold any of his things. Guy's clothes were heavy, at least Robert's had always seemed so. "What about you?"

He pointed. "Mine's down there." A similar backpack lay under the skylight's beam—worn, well-used, generic.

He pulled a trash bag from his pants pocket, shook it open, and stuffed my dirty clothes into it. I watched him at his task. "What are you doing?"

"Preparing to destroy evidence."

I lunged for the bag. Tom pulled it away.

"That's my favorite blouse and skirt you're trashing."

He didn't bother to look up. "I know. So do they. Which is why I'm getting rid of them."

They again. I was sick and tired of this proverbial they. Maybe

[78]

this guy was psychotic…and paranoid. I shoved the thought deep into my gray cells.

Another voice inside me, somewhat resembling my father's stern tone, surfaced…yet, it was still mine as well. *Let's not venture there, Jen. Not yet. You need some evidence he's lying to you. Remember, you must be patient and observant. Play it cool and pacify him for now.* Had God just spoken to me?

Tom bore a hole through me with his stare. "Uh, as in now?" It was a semi-command.

I blinked. "Oh. Right."

He pulled me gently by the elbow down the hall, grabbed his backpack without slowing his stride, and led us around the corner to another steel door. I glanced to see the butt of his gun tucked in his belt again.

"Are we—I mean, am I really in that much danger?"

He pulled his jacket closed. "Yes. The men who killed your husband will kill us both if they find out I faked your death. That's why we only have a small window of opportunity here and you wasted half of it in the shower."

"I'm sorry, Tom. It just felt so good to get clean."

His expression eased. "Yeah, I know. But we have to go. Okay?"

Sincerity, etched with a touch of dread, seemed to swim in his blue eyes. I nodded.

He stopped and squared my shoulders again. "Jen. I need you to do two things for the next twenty-four hours. One…" He held up a stiffened finger. "Trust me." He waited for my nod. "Two, don't question what I tell you, just do it."

I nodded again as I bit my lower lip.

He studied my face for a moment. "Good. When I open this door we will go through a corridor into the next building and ascend another flight of steps as quietly as possible."

His words sank into my head. The fact I had been underground, just as I was each day at work, sent a brief shudder through me. Was that why my work station had been moved to the lower levels about the same time Tom arrived? Was it part of a master plan to keep me out of view from "them?"

How ironic my pitch-black coffin-cage of the last few days had been underground as well. Appropriate somehow. Since Robert's death, my whole world had seemed buried. I often thought they might as well have dumped the dirt over me five months ago. One thing this captivity with Tom had taught me. I now knew, even after all those months of grief, I still wanted to live. I was stronger than I thought.

"Jen, listen to me, okay?" Tom shook me slightly.

"Okay." I refocused on his words.

"You will hear restaurant noises. Ignore them. Just go to the end of the hall to the back door. An Oriental girl will be there. She'll be wearing jeans like yours. She's with me. Trust her and do as she says. Go with her quickly. Don't look back or acknowledge me. We don't know each other. Just follow her and get on the first bus that comes. Got it?" He shoved a day pass into my hand.

"Yeah. Tom?"

"Yes."

"Is it okay to be scared?"

He squeezed my arm. "Sure, hon. Just don't show it."

He prodded me forward. I walked ahead, feeling my prison tether lengthening, thinning. Each step took me further from both his shackles and his safety. Half of me wanted to run as fast as I could and not look back. The other half wanted to run back to him. Odd to have my captor also be my savior.

My senses spun in ten different directions as I passed the

clamor and clatter of the kitchen. I smelled soy sauce and ginger, heard high-pitched foreign voices. Chinese? Vietnamese? I couldn't tell if they were male or female.

A smudged and paint-scraped backdoor lay ahead. It was a sharp contrast to the spotlessly clean hallway I'd left behind with its shiny green and white checkered linoleum floor. I stopped briefly, three paces from the jamb. For just a moment, I thought I saw a shadow off to my left. A too familiar whiff of aftershave filtered through the cooking odors. I heard an American male's soft voice. My heart surged.

"Robert?" I turned, but no one was there. I blinked, but only the empty hall lay in my vision. Tom was gone.

Should I run? Something told me he'd anticipated any move I might think of making and was, like a master chess player, already at least six plays ahead of me, the novice in this spy game. The floor even looked like a chessboard. I caught the symbolism. I had to play along like a good little pawn.

I proceeded with Tom's instructions. The upper part of the door had a window, covered by a grime-encrusted, frosted windowpane. Sunlight etched through in a diffused, pale yellow. Street sounds—car engines, honking horns, shuffling shoes and chatter—could be heard through the exit. In the dingy reflection of the glass I could barely make out the hall I'd just traversed.

Sucking in my breath, I reached for the doorknob. It smelled of peanut oil and aged brass. I twisted it and stepped back into the din of the real world—alone and free, yet still very much a captive.

CHAPTER ELEVEN

NO ORIENTAL GIRL waited by the stoop. I heard air brakes and saw the city bus pull to a stop at the corner a few doors away. Its doubled-glass accordion doors opened with a hiss, beckoning me to come ahead.

"Get on the first bus," he'd said. I felt the day pass in my hand, took a deep breath of fresh air, and walked up the chipped concrete steps to the sidewalk. I pushed through a few people toward the public transit vehicle. Then, I saw Tom get on the bus. I hastened my step, but an arm grabbed me. "Not this one, the next. You can't be seen together."

I turned to look into two dark eyes, lashes lined above and below with bright blue, coming to a point past each pink-shadowed lid. They were soft, knowing, and kind, set in porcelain skin with pinkish-bronzed blush. She looked younger, yet in some ways older than me. Streetwise, not cubicle naive. I'd gone from a girl's school study cubicle, to study stalls faintly reeking of cigarettes and beer in a college dorm, to teaching in a square room, to my subterranean accounting cubicle. How much of the world did I know? Her eyes answered back *not much.*

She carried a large shopping bag, and shoved my backpack into a bright pink one, stuffed with tissue paper. "Here ya go." She smiled and hooked my elbow through hers.

I smiled back at her and matched her stride. Two friends out on a shopping spree. How grand. I followed her lead as she chatted non-stop. I couldn't understand much of it over the clamor of city street noise, but the tone was friendly, trickled with giggles.

A half block down and across the street we came to another bus stop. A clear-acrylic, three-sided wedge plastered with ads from professionally printed to hand-scratched messages encased a metal bench. A black man bopping to tunes on his iPod noticed the two of us and scooted over to make room. I mouthed a thank you. He broke the rhythm briefly with a nod. We sat down. My companion began chatting again as I looked up and down the street. We were facing the opposite direction from the bus Tom had boarded.

I interrupted her in mid-sentence. "Isn't this the wrong direction?"

She giggled and slapped my arm. "No silly. We're going to my Auntie's for supper. Remember? She lives off of Bluebonnet Circle."

Four more people appeared—a man with a briefcase, an older woman with plastic grocery bags cascading from her wrists, and a young mother holding her child by the elbow. His stubby fingers were laden with Kleenex strands and milk chocolate. The same color dribbled down his Donald Duck T-shirt. His mother fussed with his face, clucking. "Why did I let you have that ice cream cone? And why didn't I bring those wipes? Never mind, here's our bus."

None of them looked like international terrorists, or spies, or bad guys—whoever "they" were supposed to be.

The bus screeched to a stop, five tire rolls past the bench, of course. A mini panic of humans jostling for seats pursued mostly with apologetic smiles and grunts. I waved my day pass under the indicator, which illuminated green. The driver nodded. I broke a quick grin in response, then felt a push in my right kidney.

"Let's sit back there."

My companion swiped her pass, and then shuffled me ahead to two seats, facing the rear exit. I grabbed the pole, set my shopping bag down and sat on the hard, curved-plastic seat. The back of my knees felt something sticky. I scooched over a tad.

"Here's your purse, silly." She handed me an off-white, scuffed, vinyl shoulder bag.

"Thanks. I'll leave my head behind someday, I think." I giggled, getting into the role.

My cohort winked in approval. Then, both eyes pointed to the purse.

I looked inside to find a red wallet with two twenties, a ten, four fives and a few ones. There was a pre-paid Visa card and a driver's license. The picture looked like me, but something was wrong. Debra Ann Fuller? DOB 8/19/86? I glanced at my new BFF and knitted my brows.

She bobbed her head in an affirmative gesture. "I'm Mae Lin. You're Debbie."

I read the rest of what was printed on the license. 5656 Bryant Irvin #1225, Fort Worth, Texas. *Okay, lots of complexes along that street.* Eyes: Blue. *Thank you.* Hair: Red. *Please, I prefer auburn.* My fingers thumbed through the rest of the wallet's contents. A major medical card and three coupons. When I saw the dog-eared photo of me and Tom leaning against a tree, I coughed. Modern photographic technology at work. We were smiling and holding hands. How cute.

A small, pink cell phone rang. I glanced at Mae Lin, who flashed me a smile and turned her head to watch the road. I clicked it on. "Hello?"

"Hey, hon." Tom's familiar voice sounded through the airwaves. "Debbie, I can't make it to Mae Lin's aunt's house for dinner. Gotta work late again. But I'll meet you at ten at the McDonald's on Berry for a hot fudge sundae, okay?"

"Okay. But you are not off the hook yet, darling. This is the third time this month."

"I know. Your Travis is a bad boy. It's my new manager, you know. I'll make it up to you. Promise. Just meet me at Mickey D's."

So he's Travis now and I'm Debbie? Right. I was beginning to get the hang of this cloak- and-dagger stuff. "All right then, Travis." I tried not to emphasize the name too much. "I guess. But you better bring me something good."

"Love, I'll bring me. I'm always good. Bye."

Gross. "Ha, ha. Bye, sweetheart." I saccharined it for effect. Mae Lin widened her eyes in mock disgust.

I sat and watched the streets zip by us. Marquees, canopies over stores, and blurs of people walking by reflected in the sun-shaded green glass of the bus window. Mae Lin slid an emery board over her long lacquered nails. "I don't like the shades of polish she gave me."

"I think it's cool."

"Really?" She fanned her hand in front of her and cocked her head. White and purple streaked nails with tiny rhinestones gleamed back. "Oh, well. Auntie will have a fit. She thinks nails should be short and one color only, preferably pale pink."

"And no eyeliner or large earrings, right?" I rolled my eyes. "Totally old school."

"Prehistoric."

We giggled in unison.

"Got any gum?"

"No. Wanna mint?" She dug in her flowered purse and brought out a small shaker. I stretched out my palm and hoped the candy wasn't drugged.

Two miles later, after we'd sucked on our mints, she leaned in. "This is it." She pulled the cord above our heads and the bus whooshed to a stop. After it rocked back, I stood, grabbed my shopping bag and my purse, and followed Mae Lin off the bus.

"This way. Not even a block."

I gazed behind me to see if anyone else disembarked. We were alone on the sidewalk, except for a woman sweeping her stoop a few doors down and two teenage boys leaning against a mustang, chatting through bluish-gray cigarette smoke. "Are we really going to your aunt's?"

Mae Lin looked straight ahead and smirked. "Yes." She pointed to me and back to herself. "You and I work together at Pauline's."

"The department store downtown?" For thirty years or more it had been an exclusive small boutique until tourists and the glam gals in Dallas discovered it. Suddenly, it blossomed into three store-lengths of chic merchandise, absorbing the children's shop and costume jewelry store next to it.

"Uh-huh. You work in accounting, of course, Debbie." She put a forced emphasis on my name, as if to remind me. "Travis thought it might be more comfortable for you in conversation to have a similar job like you, well, did."

"Who else will be there?"

Mae Lin shrugged. "Who knows? Auntie's door is always open."

She clicked her heels a few paces faster and nodded to a Craftsman cottage with urns of tousled pink and white vinca flanking the steps. A tabby cat lay in a horseshoe shape, its tail dangling from the railing. Wind chimes tinkled when a long red card with Oriental characters printed in bold black strokes twisted in the breeze and collided with the silvery tubes.

I sucked in my breath, plastered on a smile, and prepared to be Debbie, whoever she was.

Mae Lin rapped twice on the knocker, then opened the door and called out in what I guessed was Chinese. She motioned me inside. Immediately my nostrils were assaulted by pungent sweet and spicy aromas, which set my salivating glands into overtime. Auntie returned the call from deeper inside the cottage, most likely the kitchen.

We set down our packages and purses. A small, thin woman with graying hair tied tightly into a bun shuffled across the floor, hands wiping on her apron. Her narrow eyes sprang into black diamonds at the sight of her niece, then widened across her wrinkled face. She looked as old as time and eternally beautiful all at once. "Mae Lin."

The two embraced, and held the hug for a moment or two in genuine joy of seeing each other. Then the black diamonds focused on me. "Ah, you are Debbie?"

I stepped forward and extended my hand. "Yes."

The woman bowed slightly. I folded my hands and did the same. She smiled. "Then come, come."

Mae Lin winked as we followed the old woman's shuffle past a tidy living room mixed with Victorian furniture and Oriental art. Strangely, the china floral teacups, crocheted doilies, and jade dragons seemed to work well together. A happy, round-bellied Buddha welcomed all to the hearth and her home. So did the sapphire-glazed pottery filled with salmon geraniums angled to catch the afternoon sun.

We walked down a narrow hall past a dining room with more Oriental screens and a low, red lacquered table. Scooted under it were individual benches, each decorated in unique, yet well matched, patterns of brightly colorful fabrics. Ferns flanked the windows with rolled bamboo screens. They were edged with Victorian mahogany molding, probably original to the cottage. White spider mums, delicately arranged in a cobalt blue vase, sat in the center of the table. The aromas became stronger as I entered a bright white and blue kitchen. Auntie's place was very Zen, yet somewhat old-fashioned and cozy at the same time, perhaps due to the simmering pots on the stove and the little woman who now joyfully hovered over them.

"Sit." She motioned to a Formica table and chrome chairs reminiscent of the 1950s. Three round woven mats topped the table. Teacups in blue and white Oriental patterns were in the center, and a teapot of like design with a wrapped bamboo handle perched off to the side on a trivet. The woman poured steaming water into the teapot, inhaled and nodded, then clunked the lid back over the opening. A slight fragrance of oranges and roses steamed through a small hole in top.

"No one else tonight, Auntie?"

"No, just us. Good quality time." She patted her niece's hand, but frowned. Snatching it, she held it to the fluorescent light and clucked her teeth. "Purple and white. Mae Lin." Her tone was like a master scolding a puppy who'd piddled on the ancestral rug.

Mae Lin jerked her hand back. Playfully she said, "Want to see my toes?"

All this time I was casing the joint, in gumshoe lingo. No doubt, this pink cell phone I'd been given was being monitored. Surely Auntie had a phone. I could slip off to use the bathroom, and instead seek it out. But who would I call? The police?

Hi, 911. I know you think I'm dead, but here's the deal... They'd probably think I was a nut case.

Maybe I could call my boss, or Janet, the girl who worked in the next cubicle. But I didn't know her number. I'd had it in *my* cell phone, but of course, that was probably at the bottom of the Trinity River by now. Betty, my neighbor, wouldn't be back until, when? What day was this? Not Sunday. Maybe Monday or Tuesday?

I felt a sharp jab to my shin. Two pair of blue-lined dark eyes bore holes into me. "Auntie asked you how you liked working at Pauline's."

"I'm sorry. I'm feeling a bit, uh...do you have a restroom?"

Mae Lin shot me a don't-dare-try-it look. I smiled and followed her aunt out into the hall. She pointed to a door wedged under the stairs with a tile that read W. C. hanging on it. Right next to another door—the back door. What a stroke of luck. I had money, and ID. I could make a dash for it, then wander into the police department. If they saw me face-to-face, maybe I could convince them.

I thanked my hostess. She bowed and shuffled back toward the kitchen. I ducked inside the tiny washroom.

Before I closed the door, I heard Mae Lin's voice. "Auntie, since it's just us girls, I'm setting the alarm. It's getting dark outside. You can't be too careful these days."

Drat.

CHAPTER TWELVE

THE HOT TEA settled my nerves. The evening went well. Mae Lin's aunt, Mrs. Chang, was intelligent and her stories of growing up in Mao's regime were fascinating, frightening, and unfathomable. Born into a family of five boys and two girls, she and her younger sister, Mae Lin's mother, had been smuggled into Hong Kong, then to Seattle. Girls were not valued in Mao's China and her parents feared for their lives. The family had decided she was old enough to take care of her sibling on the long journey.

When they left hand in hand, Mrs. Chang was thirteen and her sister four. She never saw her parents or brothers again. They were raised by relatives who had been living in America for two generations. Her sister married a chef and later moved to Fort Worth so they could open their own restaurant.

Graduating from the University of Washington, Mrs. Chang became a teacher. She met her husband, a Navy pilot, who later shuttled private jets. He went to his ancestors after forty-two years of marriage. They had three sons—now living in Houston, Toronto, and Fort Worth. When her husband died, her eldest son and Mae-

Lin's mother insisted she move to Fort Worth to help in the family restaurant.

A tingle shot up my neck. It must have been where Tom, uh, Travis had held me captive. How did he know these people? Had Robert?

My thoughts began to swirl. Perhaps our move to Fort Worth had been a set-up? A cover for Robert and Tom's covert activities. Was Robert's boss in on this? Was that why his boss found me the accounting job, using what Robert called his "connections"? And why Robert begged me to take it instead of teach? The pieces of this puzzle began to fit together, but I didn't like the picture it formed. Tom was right. My life with Robert had all been a sham.

I heard a faint ringing coming from the front hall. "I think that's your cell." Mae Lin motioned with her eyes. "Mine plays Beethoven's Fifth. I'm into Beethoven."

I excused myself and dashed for the white purse. On the fourth ring I punched the button. "Hello?"

Nobody was there. I looked at the screen and saw the voicemail symbol. I tapped it and it asked me for a password code. What? I paused, then figured he'd make it easy for me. I plugged in the one I used at work to log onto my computer. Bingo. A mechanical female voice replied, "You have one message. First Message."

A strange woman's voice came on. "Hi Debbie. It's Mom. Hope you're having fun at Mae Lin's aunt's house. Call me before you head home."

Who in the heck was this and just how many people were involved in this thing? I came back to the table and placed the pink cell phone beside me. "It's Mom. She wants me to call her before I head home."

Mae Lin nodded. "Well, then you should. Besides, it's nine-twenty. Auntie, it's past your bedtime. Maybe we'd better say goodnight." She hugged the narrow-shouldered woman and kissed her forehead. Then she grabbed a dish scrubber and soap. "We'll wash these dishes for you first."

Half an hour later, we were all hugs, goodbyes, come back again soon, then out the door.

I stopped a few paces past the front stoop, cell phone in hand. "Exactly who is my mother?"

Mae Lin laughed. "This is where we part ways, my friend. Take the Number 7 bus to Berry. McDonald's is right there. Be smart. Call your mother." She looked both ways and dashed across the street. I watched as she disappeared around the corner.

I walked to the bus stop and sat down. What was I thinking? All I had known to be true I now questioned after a day or two of listening to the tales of a possibly delusional coworker? So what if Tom knew Robert? It didn't mean anything else was true. But then, who was Mae Lin and this mother I was supposed to keep calling? It made no sense. I shook my head and held it in my hands.

Now away from my coffin captivity my mind became more astute. No, I couldn't believe Robert had lied to me. He was in advertising, and had been good at it. That's why he'd traveled a bunch. Lots of businessmen do every day. And maybe he had been helping that secretary make a life-changing decision. She'd tried to tell me so at the wake, but I wouldn't listen.

My Robert had been an honest, loving, and good man. That's what I had to believe. Not this. Tom was just jealous. When I didn't respond to his innuendos and stares at work, he'd made this whole thing up to nab me in an effort to get me to fall for him. Maybe he saw the family restaurant when he rented the basement. Then he met Mae Lin and hired her to act the part. It was plausible, right?

I firmed my jaw. I was not playing this game anymore, and I definitely wasn't calling "Mother." I had a day pass. I could go anywhere. I decided to get on the next bus, no matter what its number.

I took the cash out of the wallet, ripped up the picture of me and Tom—or Travis, or whoever he claimed to be—and shoved my so-called driver's license deep into the sewer opening under my feet. I stuffed the purse into the bus stop's mesh wastebasket and covered it with newspapers and an open box of leftover Kentucky Fried Chicken, complete with a half-eaten drumstick. That woke up the flies. They buzzed my arm in protest. I shook them off with a shudder, then sat back down.

The Number 7 bus was the first to arrive at the stop. I got on it and rode to Berry, but I didn't get off. The map indicated this bus route went downtown. A plan solidified in my thoughts. I'd walk a few short blocks to the Greyhound station, and then buy a ticket for San Antonio.

When I got to the San Antonio bus station, I'd use a pay phone to call one of my old friends to come get me. I'd explain I'd been kidnapped. Maybe they hadn't yet heard of my so-called accident. I could start over again. Who'd stop me? I closed my eyes and let the rumble of the tires jostle my anxiety away.

The bus pulled to a stop. The doors swooshed opened and I heard footsteps coming toward me. Two strong hands wrapped around my arms. A familiar citrusy-musk cologne hit my nostrils.

"You missed your stop, dear. Something told me I'd better come get you."

I turned to see sapphire-blue eyes narrow into mine. He waved to the bus driver and shot him a pearly smile. "Never mind. She gets confused when she's, well, you know." He raised a cupped hand, thumb toward his mouth indicating I'd been drinking. "I'm giving her a ride home. I got her."

Yes, he did. Again. He coaxed me down the stairs. The bus

lumbered away, along with my passage to freedom.

Tom's expression became harsh as he shook his forefinger inches from my face. "You should have called your mother."

I slapped away his hand. "My mother's dead." I started to walk off, where I didn't know. Just away from him.

He matched my steps, then laced his arm through mine as he jerked me to a stop. "Didn't you see the old Chinese saying Mrs. Chang had on the plaque in her kitchen?" His breath was hot against my face.

I stared at him. So he did know her. Was she part of all this? Not that sweet woman. Mae Lin said her door was always open. Maybe she was an innocent puppet. Then again, her husband had been in the Navy. So had Robert. And Tom.

He turned me around and began to walk us in the opposite direction. His thumb dug into my forearm as he pulled me closer. "It says, 'The obedient dog knows the freedom of his fence, but the disobedient dog is chained.'"

His tone of voice rattled me, but I was determined not to let him see that fact. I plastered on a blank expression and held my tongue.

He leaned in, with a death grip near my elbow. "I thought you understood, Jen. I told you to follow my instructions, and you said you would."

I looked away.

He tugged my arm to get me to look into his face gain. His eyes glistened like fiery ice under knitted brows. "This is serious business, hon. What part of 'they will kill you' did you not understand?"

There was a Celtic lilt at the end of his words. I'd managed to flare his Irish temper once again. "Tom, I—"

He waved away my thought. "Too late. You tried to jump the

fence. I'm afraid it's time you were chained again."

Mae Lin appeared as if from nowhere. She gave him a look, which he returned. I saw his Adam's apple wobble.

I looked down. In her hand was a syringe. I felt the jab before I could protest.

CHAPTER THIRTEEN

I WOKE UP and stared at metal scaffolding above my head. The floor was hard and cold. Concrete again. But I wasn't back in the basement. I was in a garage or something. Motor oil and gasoline fumes burned my nose. Bright fluorescent lights dangled from the ceiling. One of them hummed loudly at me. Tom sat on a rusted blue oil drum, talking on a cell phone.

"Yeah. I know. She almost ruined the whole set-up. Wait." He looked in my direction. "She's coming to. Right, I will."

I groaned and tried to focus as much as possible without the room spinning. My hands were wrenched behind my back. I felt a hard plastic band rub against my skin. Cuffed. My legs were crossed and tied as well. My cheeks were stretched. I could only open my mouth a crack. My tongue probed through my teeth to touch tight metallic material. Duct tape.

I tried to scream, but only a "Rrmmmm" came out.

He knelt beside me. "You made us do this, Jen. We have to protect you, even if it is from yourself. You have no idea who you are dealing with."

My eyes zeroed in on his face. I tried to speak again, then flopped my head back down. Why try?

He brushed a strand of hair off my forehead. His touch nauseated me. I flinched.

"Are you going to be a good girl or not?" His tone was flat.

I nodded affirmatively.

He yanked the duct tape. "Ouch!" I'm sure half of my lower lip went with the adhesive. I tucked part of my lip into my teeth and sucked the blood from it.

"Do you have any idea how much trouble you've caused?" His shoulders were rock solid, his demeanor as harsh and cold as his icy stare. "For the love of Pete, Jen. I'm risking my life trying to keep you from danger. You know?"

I scooted to a semi-sitting position. "Okay. I get it. I'm sorry."

"Are you? Why, because I caught you?"

He looked away, not expecting a response. He was mistaken. My anger boiled. My voice shook with emotion. "My head feels like lead, my mouth is killing me, and my ankles are cramping. Besides, this grungy place stinks like old sweat and gasoline fumes."

His jaw twitched as his fist balled.

I sucked in a deep breath to slow my mood. "So, my dear *Travis*." My voice dripped with sarcasm. "To answer your question—yes. I *am* very sorry you caught me."

He spun on his heel and flipped out a knife. His nostrils flared, like a defiant bull ready to charge the red flag. Through clenched teeth he mouthed, "Look. I have tried everything I can to persuade you that I'm doing this to protect you." He leaned in, the blade inches from my neck, then snarled. "I'm tired of trying to convince you."

I leaned back and squinted my eyes. But the blade didn't slash my throat.

Instead, he slipped it between my ankles and snapped the plastic. "There. Maybe it will prove I'm on your side in this. But until your attitude improves the wrists stay tied."

I continued to glare at him. "I suppose you want me to thank you, now?"

His knife hovered over me. His muscles crinkled, the blue veins intensified. He lowered it to his side and stomped off. I heard him seethe. "One potato, two potato..."

"Lord's Prayer works." I flung the words at him, hoping they'd pierce deep. His back tensed, and he cracked his neck, but waited before he turned around. When he did, I watched his face as it eased from red back to his normal shade. The man transformed from a raging bull into a human being as he walked toward me. But I imagined steam still snorted from his nostrils.

"You know, I always prided myself on staying cool under any duress. Ice in the veins. But you, woman. Somehow..."

"The feeling's mutual."

He edged toward me. His eyes still flickered with icy blue heat. "I don't know what Robert ever saw in you."

I smirked. "As I said, the feeling's mutual."

"Geez." He kicked the drum. From the look that flashed across his face, I think he regretted it.

"Feel good?" Something told me to stop stoking this fire, but I couldn't help myself. I wanted to hurt him, and at the moment, words were my only weapon.

He set his jaw, took two steps toward me, then turned and walked out of the garage bay into the moonlight.

Seeing my chance, I crawled across the floor toward the back door. My knees ached as they pressed against the hard pavement. Then I heard his shoes thump left, right, left. I scooted back as fast as I could to my original place.

He scanned me over, and smirked at my grungy knees. I expected chastisement. Instead he turned and dropped some coins into a vending machine. A soda can clunked down the chute. I heard the tab pop and the carbonated whoosh. He meandered over to where I crouched, his frame loomed above me. "Diet. Right?"

I nodded. He squatted and held it to my lips. The fizz tickled my nose. He pulled it back, waited for me to swallow, then pressed the can to my lips again, tilting it a touch more. I guzzled quickly. Then he set it down on the floor and walked back to the machine, jingling coins from his pocket.

I couldn't help it. Carbonation bubbles stuck deep in my esophagus. They exploded out of my mouth in a very un-ladylike bullfrog sound.

Tom's shoulders moved up and down as he stifled a laugh. He plunked a few coins in the machine and punched his choice.

My cheeks flushed. "Excuse me."

He popped the top, sipped, and then pointed the can at me. "Your stomach's empty. I shouldn't have made you guzzle it. My fault."

My gaze shot to the floor. Had he done it to humiliate me, to put me in my place? It worked. After a deep sigh, I looked back at him.

He raised an eyebrow. "Are we going to be decent to each other now?" He set his soda down on the oil drum and came over to me.

I sucked in my breath as he approached, unable to read his stone-set face underneath a thick five o'clock shadow. I gave him a brief nod and looked back at the concrete.

"Okay." He elevated my head, locking my view to see only him as those blue eyes glared into my soul. He flipped the knife back and forth in front of my face. "Let's try this one last time."

I bobbed my head in submission and licked my lower lip. He

brushed it with his finger, his face just inches away from me. "Sorry I pulled so hard."

His warm breath smelled a lot better than the rest of the garage. So did the remnants of his citrus-musk scent blended with day old, manly sweat. He leaned around me, our torsos touching. I heard a snap, then felt my wrists being released from their plastic bonds. Or was it a heartstring he'd just plucked?

With a sideways grin, he rocked back. "Better?"

The blood rushed into my arms as I pulled them forward and rubbed them.

I almost hugged him in thanksgiving, but stopped in mid-thought.

Outlined by the moonlight, his countenance loomed in front of me as his eyes watched for my reaction. I could see the muscles in his arms, the solidness of his chest. Part of me wanted to cling to him for safety, another kiss him, and yet another slap the living fool out of him. I tried to choose one, but couldn't. I remembered my inner voice's advice from the day before. Keep cool. Yet one look at him and I felt my knees weaken.

My savior, my captor—with black locks, sapphire eyes, six-pack abs and a cologne that stirred my senses. I was drawn to him like a hummingbird to a trumpet flower. As his stare fixed on my face, I could sense him thinking the same about me.

One of us was obviously mad as a hatter for thinking what we were thinking. But which one?

CHAPTER FOURTEEN

I SIGHED, RUBBED my arms, and tried to keep any emotion from registering on my face. "Tom, to be honest, I'm too tired to argue anymore."

"Tired of?"

I flashed him an incredulous look. I waved my hands around me. "All of this."

He cocked his head. "You don't care for the choice of accommodations?"

I crossed my legs and tucked my feet under me. I picked up a pretend daisy and began to pluck its petals. "You drug me, you're nice to me, you drug me, you're nice to me. Geez, Tom. I want off this roller coaster."

He scratched his head with the blunt edge of the knife, then folded it closed. He stared at the crack in the concrete between us as if all the answers were going to magically appear out of it. I waited for his response.

"My neck's on the line here as well, Jen. I have my orders. I told you, I'm not the one running point in this."

I cocked my head. "It can't be Mae Lin. My supposedly dead husband, then?"

He raised his eyes, their blue washed into a dull color of faded blue jeans. "Let go of that string. No matter how hard you tug, it won't unravel to reveal anything you want to know."

I rolled my shoulders to reduce the stiffness. "I just want to go home. Go back to the office, back to my mourning. Back to my empty life and feed the stray cat that keeps hovering around my patio."

Tom's face softened. He reached for my hand and held it in a soft caress. "I know. I'm sorry. But it's impossible now."

My eyes clouded. Through damp lashes I firmed my nerve. "Okay, so now what?"

He pushed his eyebrows together. The wrinkle lines on his forehead became cavernous. I guess my shift in subject startled him. But I wasn't going to reveal a chink in my armor into which he could slide his hand and twist my heart again. I repositioned my legs, drew them to my chest, and wrapped my arms around them for protection.

He wiped his hand over his face and it became all business—focused, stern, determined.

"We wait here until three a.m. Then we take the clunker behind this station and head south. It's already filled with gas."

"Why not now? Or is it another protocol to stealthily sneak off in the wee hours?"

He huffed. "Because I am dead tired too, okay? I need to sleep for a few hours. I'm trusting you not to thump me over the head with a torque wrench and leave." He reached in his pant pocket and pulled out six spark plugs. "But just in case I'm wrong, I took the liberty to remove these. Robert said you were mechanically challenged. I'm betting you can't change out plugs."

"No." I picked at a loose string on my jeans.

He leaned into my face. "Cars without spark plugs don't go very far. And we are in the middle of nowhere in an abandoned gas station. I wouldn't try it on foot."

"Thanks for the info." I stood and stretched, then turned back to him. "I am allowed to move around a bit, right?"

"As long as you keep your paws off the tools, ropes or anything else you'd want to use to maim me." He stood as well, but instead of walking toward me, he pivoted, walked to the oil drum, and grabbed his soda can. Leaning against the barrel, he studied me. "Be smart, Jen. I'm your best bet right now. You really have no inkling what's..."

I interlocked my arms. "Enlighten me."

His face hardened again. "You know I can't. We've had this conversation." He walked to the far end of the garage, into the shadows. "By the way, they insisted on tying you up. They'll probably have my neck for letting you loose. But I couldn't stand to see you pinned there like a calf in a rodeo."

"Thank you, Tom." I meant it

He raised his finger. "Uh-uh. It's Travis now. There is a restroom through that door, and a small office with a fridge. You'll find sandwiches in there, and bottles of water. Sorry, no Yogurt Tree today."

There was a moan of stretching canvas. I heard him grunt, then sigh. In the shadows I made out his horizontal form on an army cot. He laced his hands behind his head and looked at the ceiling. "We've got about six hours. Eat if you want. There's another cot here if you get tired. But I warn you, I might snore." With that, he flipped over on his side, his back to me. The cot made an echoing creak as it stretched under his weight.

I wandered over, found the other cot, and sat on it. "Why did you untie me, really?"

He rolled back to face me. "Against all protocol, I've become involved. Just like Robert did. At first I hated you for that, by the way. But now..." He swallowed. "I can deal with the fact I honestly care about you."

I leaned forward and rubbed one hand over the other. Was he telling me the truth? Did I dare respond back what my heart was beginning to feel? I wasn't about to let my guard down—not just yet. "Then why did you gag me and tie me up to begin with?"

He inhaled, held it a few seconds, then released his breath. He repositioned his head on his arm. "I told you. I didn't. They did."

"You mean Mae Lin?"

He waggled his head.

"Okay, but you let her drug me."

"That was your choice. You tried to run. I had to do what they said…for your own sake. I really don't want anything to happen to you, Jen. So, be good for a change, okay?" He yawned, then closed his eyes. His breathing deepened and slowed.

I sat in the shadows of a grungy, smelly garage in the middle of God knew where. As I listened to his soft snores, I couldn't deny the fact that Tom's, uh, Travis's presence comforted me. I didn't want to be alone again. Still, maybe I should have reminded him to call me Debbie.

I'M NOT SURE how long I sat there watching him as he sawed the zzzz's in a fetal position. His face was peaceful, almost childlike, except for the day-old beard. His charmingly disheveled hair cascaded into his eyes like a sunshield. I resisted the urge to push it away, or to stick his thumb in his mouth to complete the look. Part of me wanted to slither next to him, to spoon together tightly, feel that closeness of a man and woman again. But he was not Robert.

Then again, maybe now I wasn't the same Jen, that is, Debbie. Sheesh. Would I ever get used to the name change? How long would we have to be someone else than who we were? Or had he been pretending all along?

I sighed, slapped my knees, and rose to my feet. He stirred, mumbled incoherent syllables, then fell back into a deep rhythm, his chest softly rising and lowering. I tiptoed into the office, and wrinkled my nose at its old, musty smell.

Oh, no. Not going there again. I shoved the memory of the trunk in the attic as far back in my mind as I could, hopefully never to surface again. I refused to let the ghosts of my past haunt me anymore. Besides, this was no mausoleum. The ceilings were tall, though rust-tinned.

The walls were a dingy, faded mustard. Near the ceiling, a small, single-paned rectangle of a window huddled beneath layers of the same colored dust. Cobwebs dangled undisturbed from the rusty lever and elbow shaped hinges, evidence the window hadn't been cracked open in a dog's age. A desk and narrow metal table had been shoved against the wall opposite the window. Yellowed car manuals and an old phonebook cluttered the table, along with a cardboard holder for pamphlets. In the tabletop dust, an arrow pointing down and the word FRIDGE had been scrawled. Sure enough, a brown square with a chrome handle was tucked underneath. Splashes of rust spotted the hinges.

"Thanks, Tom. Or Travis, or whoever you claim to be. Got it."

Above the table hung a faded calendar depicting a well-endowed girl in a red-checkered halter top and tight cut-offs that barely covered her buttocks as she leaned over the hood of a Mustang. She wore cowboy boots and a smile, not leaving much else to the imagination. The remaining calendar page read AUGUST 1986. The ninth day was circled in red.

That was the year, day and month I was born, according to the fake Debbie ID. I backed against the edge of the dusty Formica-topped metal desk. Both knees buckled. A ripple of fear spread throughout my body as I slid to the floor, my spine bumping against drawer handles.

This was too uncanny. If this was somebody's elaborate idea of a joke, I wasn't laughing. Were they purposely messing with my head, trying to break me? Who were these people?

This all felt like a chapter in *Alice in Wonderland*. Nothing seemed real. Except maybe the Mad Hatter in the next room. Was Mae Lin the Queen of Hearts screaming, "Off with her head?"

Who was I supposed to believe? Tom? Mae Lin? Robert? When did people in my life stop telling me the truth? I waved my hands back and forth in front of me to erase that thought. I didn't want to play this game anymore. I wanted to go home.

The room wobbled back and forth like a number two on the earthquake Richter scale. Pain sliced through my head as anxious vertigo ensued. I buried my hands in my face, pressing my palms against my eyelids. The room smelled like my grandmother's trunk. Was it the frightful memory which freaked me out? Or maybe, because there was a lull in this storm, I now allowed all my fears to surface. Maybe it was the drugs or the fact I had not eaten in...what time was it, anyway? Heck, what day was it?

My throat tightened and I regurgitated the boulder-sized sob which had been inching its way up. The pressure released a geyser of emotions as I wailed, "God, please get me out of here."

This time, He didn't oblige. What would I have to do to make Him hear me?

CHAPTER FIFTEEN

I BAWLED UNCONTROLLABLY for a few minutes until the sobs lessened to shallow sniffles. Totally spent of emotion, I wiped my nose and eyes with my T-shirt.

I shook my head. Why did I just lose it? "Jen, get a grip," I hissed to myself. "I know you've been drugged, but please."

I looked around the room.

The date on the calendar had to be a coincidence. Or maybe "they" had found this place and seen the calendar. Sure, it had been planted in someone's subconscious so they used it on my fake ID. I had to stop letting my imagination run away with me. This was not a mystery novel. This was my life.

Still, throughout this temper tantrum, no Tom/Travis had rushed to my side. My knight in dull, dented armor still snoozed soundly in the garage bay. Disappointment and relief surfaced. I chose relief.

My throat chose water. I stretched to grab the fridge handle and peered inside. The bulb was burned out, naturally. Still, in the moonlit room, I made out two plastic wedges holding convenience store sandwiches, two oranges and three bottles of water. My guess was there had been four and Tom had already guzzled one. There were also two mega-sized Snickers candy bars.

"That's more like it." My wrenched female hormones craved chocolate-covered serotonin over anything nutritious. I ripped open the packaging and chomped down on the nougat, peanuts, caramel and ah, milk chocolate, as it melted on my tongue. Nirvana. With each chomp of my guilty pleasure and swig of cold water, my muscles eased, my stomach unknotted, the band around my cranium loosened.

I closed my eyes as a velvety darkness enveloped me, rocking me into slumber. Like Alice down the rabbit hole, I slid into a netherworld. In my dream, Tom was my knight in shining armor. He had slain the Queen of Hearts—who had pink eye shadow and purple nails— then stabbed Robert, the evil dark king, through the chest. He drew me into his arms. Our lips touched…

Something moved in front of my eyelids. My brain registered it, filtering through the cloudiness of deep sleep.

"Jen?"

I groaned. My eyelids were still heavy, my mind begging to tumble back down into the dream's scene. I felt pressure on my arm, like a blood pressure cuff. Then my neck and torso shook. The words came stronger, clearer. "Jen."

"What?" I floated back into grogginess and yawned.

"Get up. I overslept. It's past time."

I opened my eyes to see Tom crouched in front of me. He rocked back on his heels and waved the telltale candy wrapper in my face. "I see you already ate?"

I stretched, air hitting my waist as the T-shirt unstuck from my back. "Yeah." I grinned with a guilty shrug. "Sort of. And shouldn't you be calling me Debbie?"

"Right. I should be."

"I can't seem to call you anything else but Tom."

"I know." A hand pumped in my face. "Come on, sleepyhead."

I yawned like a cat in a sun-drenched windowsill, and stretched some more. He cleared his throat and outstretched his hand further. I grabbed it, and felt my body effortlessly float upright. "Upsy-daisy."

I laughed. "Who says that anymore?"

Tom scrunched his shoulders. "My mom did. Every morning to get me up for school."

"Nauseating. Did you want to throw your backpack at her?"

"Every morning."

We both chuckled, then I realized he had me drawn to him, arm around my waist. My hand was in his, pressed against his chest. My other clasped his love handle, not that he had much of one. I expected the waltz music to begin.

"Tom, let go."

He whispered in my ear. "You first."

I gazed into his eyes, almost navy in the darkened room highlighted by a breath of moonlight filtering through the dusty window above us. My hand moved slightly in his, but he tightened his grip.

"Tell me, Jen." His voice graveled. "Once and for all. Do you want me to keep being the gentleman, or are we both going to cave to what we know we want?"

I heard the *Jeopardy* tune, and then realized he was humming it through his smile. My fingers pressed against his lips to stop it. He kissed them.

"Jen. I really do care for you. Now I see what Robert saw in you."

"Tom—" I stopped. I didn't know what else to say.

The kiss came. It deepened, swirling my emotions down an abyss too long not traveled. He enveloped me in his arms, lifted me to his level, and arched our bodies over the metal desk…

A bright light flashed on us. "Agent Walker. Get a hold of yourself."

There stood Mae Lin, dressed in tight-fitting black, holding a flashlight. Two humongous thugs stood behind her stifling laughs with their fists. "So that's why you didn't make the rendezvous. I should have known." She jerked her finger toward the garage bay. "Conference. Now."

Tom cursed, released me with a thud on the desk, and pushed through the little crowd out of the office. Mae Lin snorted, motioned to one of the men to follow her, and pointed for the other to stay with me. The door shut with a wham, rattling the glass window above me. A mist of dirt drifted down the moonbeam.

The gorilla-sized man moved to block the door, legs spread in an at-ease military stance. He held a gun. Naturally he pointed it at me. His stone face cracked a lusty sneer. Was he trying to decide whether to pick up where his colleague had left off?

I inched my way around the other side of the desk, putting it between us. His gaze locked onto me like a laser beam to a target. He didn't flinch.

Behind us loud shouts rat-a-tatted like bullets flying, fast and furious. Something clanked to the floor, followed by a groan and several loud thuds. Then silence.

I bit my lip, afraid to move, lest Godzilla-man leap for me. In a minute the door opened and he inched aside, his glare still glued to my chest, as his tongue ran along the side of his mouth. Mae Lin whispered something to him. He became stone-faced again, nodded, and passed through the doorway.

Purple and white dagger-like fingernails lashed out and

slapped me across the face, hard. "Slut."

"Ow." I rubbed my stinging cheek. She'd drawn blood. "Wait. It's not my fault. He's been drugging me. I was tired. I didn't have the strength to, to…"

"Shut up." She wrenched my arm behind me and pushed me through the opening out of the office. Godzilla grabbed my other arm. They slid me across the garage through the back door, scraping my hip on the side door's jamb.

A non-descript white minivan waited, engine revving. "Get in, witch, and stay quiet."

With a hefty shove, I stumbled and belly-flopped into the cargo section of the van, the metallic floor grid pushing into my face.

The side door closed with a vibrating slam nanoseconds after I tucked in my feet. There sat Tom, his right eye already swelling, blood trickling down his slashed cheek. "Guess we should have chosen the gentleman route."

Across from us crouched Godzilla No 2—the one who had guarded me. The barrel of his pistol pointed intermittently at our heads.

"Meet, uh, Joe. That's the .45 mag's name. The guy holding it is Chuck." Tom leaned in and his breath brushed my neck. "He has very little sense of humor."

A pylon-sized hairy forearm shoved us apart. "Enough. Stay quiet."

"So much for dinner and the other Snickers bar, dear." Tom scooted off to the left.

We sat in silence, bodies tousled back and forth to the movement of the wheels under us as the van navigated over rough country roads. Every once in a while Tom glanced at me, then I at him. I was sure we were thinking the same thing. If Mae Lin hadn't busted in, would we have? And would we ever have the chance to find out? Or, would we both be joining Robert in the hereafter...if he was really dead? I mouthed that childhood prayer of protection just in case.

The cargo area of the van was separated from the cab by a metal wall. There was no window or peep hole. Through the wall we heard a muffled sound of country music from a crackly radio.

Tom inched over to Chuck's side of the van. "Come on, Chuck. She's still half out of it. You can't blame me, caged up with her for days. She is a looker. A guy can only take so much, ya know?"

I stared at him. What?

"Look." He motioned his head to the metal divider. "They can't hear us. Gag her, cuff her. I'll go first. You watch. Then you can have her."

Chuck's eyes widened. He licked his lips.

"No," I squeaked.

Tom raised his leg and slammed his heel against my chest, pinning me to the side of the van. "Didn't we tell you to shut up?"

The goon's smirk spread. "I don't know."

"Come on. She's hot lookin'. Cushy thighs. Firm breasts." Tom wiggled his eyebrows.

"Hmmm." Chuck grabbed me by my T-shirt, and then slammed me face first to the floor, his full weight on top, knocking the breath out of me. He locked his knees into my hips.

I felt plastic clamp around my wrists, then wedge into the skin of my ankles once more. Like a fish on the jetty, I was flipped over. Chuck's beady eyes were right above mine as gray duct tape came down across my mouth before I could scream. His vice grip clamped down on my knees and spread them wide.

Tom shoved him away. "Oh, no. I get her first."

Chuck's eyes became one thin line buried in bushy eyebrows. His fists pumped. "Why?"

"Because I had dibs," Tom's voice was forceful. "I'd been all through if you'd all been a few minutes later. Let me finish what I started, man."

Tears dripped down the sides of my face into my ears. So he didn't care? It was a ploy to get me to...I gulped. Days earlier I'd wondered when this part was coming. Dear God, was I now to be a victim of two men?

Tom leaned into my face as his hands flattened on my hips. His voice was barely audible over the whirr of the tires. "Quiet. Lay still. Nothing's going to happen. Promise."

My eyes stretched wide. I mumbled through the tape. "Says who?" It came out more like *shumz zzoo*.

I could sense Chuck's massive torso hovering above us. More guttural growls emitted from between his teeth. I closed my eyes. One of Tom's hands left my hip and slid to the small of my back.

My wrists snapped free. The pressure lifted from my chest. I opened my eyes to see Tom fling around and whack Chuck square in the jaw with his knee. The gorilla buckled against the side of the van. Tom kicked him again, and punched him with both fists laced together. The massive man went limp.

I scooted to a sitting position.

Eyes still on his prey, Tom reached behind his back toward me, his hand outstretched. "Duct tape?"

I inch-wormed for the rest of the roll which had ended upright in the back corner of the van, then nudged it toward his feet.

He winked. "Thanks. Be with you in a minute."

I was not confident that was a good thing, considering my predicament. I rubbed my wrists and then pulled the duct tape in micro-steps from both sides to the middle of my mouth. My lips were still recovering from the last tug.

Tom glanced in my direction. "Sorry, hon. I had to catch him off-guard. It was the only way…"

He ripped a piece from the roll and plastered it over Chuck's mouth. He wrapped the man's hands, then grabbed for more plastic cuff strips and secured Chuck's wrists and ankles, rendering him helpless, if he ever regained consciousness. The whole thing must have taken no more than four heartbeats. He finished his thought. "But you must have known I'd never…"

I looked down and suckled my lower lip as I blinked back the tears. A shudder traveled up my spine.

"Ah, hon." Tom crawled over to me and cut the restraints from my ankles. His hands cupped my face as he peered into my eyes. "You okay?" One hand moved to smooth my hair back from my forehead in tender, caring strokes.

My lips quivered, half in pain, half in relief. I buried my face into the chest of the man who moments ago I'd thought was going to gang rape me.

CHAPTER SIXTEEN

AFTER A FEW moments my breathing slowed. Tom pushed me away from his warmth and gently planted my back against the sides of the van. "Take a deep breath. Another. Good, girl. Stay put, okay?"

I bobbed my head, the shock of what had just happened easing. In its place my temper began to bubble. Had he really just put me in danger like that? I was so tired of his games.

Tom slipped his folded knife into his jeans back pocket, then he bent to frisk Chuck, found the pistol named Joe, and stuffed it into his own waistband. "This was the last time I let someone gag and tie you up, I promise." His voice was still low, tender.

"Really? Versus what? Drugging me?" I snorted and looked away to a rusty seam inside the van. How dare he?

He turned my chin back to him. "Jen, it was an act to fool him. I've told you. I'd never harm you. I promised Robert..."

"Yeah, I know. Yadda, yadda." I pushed my face away from his grasp.

"You're angry."

I titled my head, daggers shooting from my pupils into his. "Ya think?" He moved toward me, but I raised my hand. "Don't. Don't."

Tom recoiled, the hurt puppy dog inching into his expression.

I wanted to slap it off him. I'd never hit a guy in my life before I met Tom, and now I'd wanted to hit him for the second time in a few days. My hand raised, shook, then returned to my lap.

"Go ahead." He swallowed hard. "I deserve a slap in the face."

"I still want to." I thrust my finger at his nose. My cheeks flamed. "Don't you dare say, 'let's start over.' Don't you dare. I hate you. I will get as far away from you as possible. First chance I get."

His teeth clenched together, the vein on his forehead turned red. "Woman, I was trying to save you."

I glared back. "You could have tried a different way."

We hit a huge bump, knocking both our heads on the inside top of the van. Chuck groaned, then his body went limp again.

"Fine," Tom hissed. "Run away. Be on your own where I can no longer protect you." He blinked and lessened his jaw. "By the way, we're in the middle of New Mexico, in the desert, in the dark. Good luck, lady." He did a chivalrous bow and swooshed with his hand to the back door of the van. "*Vaya con Dios*. Go with God."

"New Mexico?" I scooted back and shook my head. My brain tried to absorb his words. How? I had been drugged. I had no concept of time. I could have gotten to the gas station by car, helicopter, even in a small jet.

He clutched my arms and peered into my face. "Look, let me get you and me away from this mess first, okay?"

I lowered my head and nodded.

His grip eased. "Stick with me for another twenty-four hours. I'll get you to some place safe. Then, we can have this conversation."

I buckled. "That makes sense."

He edged to the door of the van, then turned back to me. "I won't ask you to trust me anymore, Jen. I'm telling you to. Sunrise is about two hours away. We'll have to move fast."

Freedom rattled outside this van, blocked by the presence of another Godzilla and a feisty, ticked-off Oriental girl in the front seat. I ran my hand across my cheek, remembering the force of her fingernails. He'd said they'd been the ones to tether and gag me. Were these people the "they" Tom kept referring to? If so, then why had he instructed me to go with her in the first place back in Fort Worth?

We were jostled again, shaking my thoughts back to his voice. He explained we must jump and roll. "Tuck your head and knees in, jump at an angle so you land on your side, then roll, roll, roll until you stop. I'll be right behind you."

My mind flipped back to a lecture in girl's school. Tuck and roll. How to get out of a car you didn't want to be in because your date was drunk, or trying to do something against your will. The other girls in the dorm jeered at the female cop and muffled their giggles. For some reason I absorbed it, word for word, the officer's gestures imprinting in my mind. Was it because somehow God knew I'd need that info now?

I bobbed my head at Tom, my jaw set tight. "I know how to do this. Let's go."

He shook off a brief disbelief. "Okay."

He slid open the van's side door. The dark air blasted against my cheek. Below, lined shadows zipped by in rhythm to the thunk of the tires. He spoke into my ear. "One, two, three." He shoved me in the small of my back and my body left the van.

My hip hit first, then my head. I bounced then landed on my other shoulder. Pain seared through me as my face scraped the asphalt. I rolled again, into the shoulder of the highway and prickly plants. Gravel wedged into my cheeks.

Two hands propelled me upright. "Can't stop. Go." Half-stumbling, grabbing for tufts of grass, I scrambled with him across the humped landscape. I felt his fingers laced through my jeans belt loops, tugging me forward.

I slammed my feet to the ground, forcing us to stop. "I need to catch my breath."

He brushed residual gravel from my cheeks. "Later. Keep going." He locked his arm through my elbow and jerked me forward.

We took off in a fast trot through the desert brush. We ran, and ran. My lungs burned as I tried to inhale, my tongue stuck out like a panting dog. The calves of my legs cramped. My hips felt like gelatin, but on we trekked.

Finally he released me and hunched over, hands on his thighs. His chest heaving. I fell onto my back, then curled my legs to my torso.

He sputtered. "One minute. No more."

"Are...are they..." I gasped for air.

He turned and looked back. "Not sure." He wiped his hand across his forehead. "The sun'll be up soon. We're sitting ducks. Must find cover." His sentences were chopped, forced. He nodded. "Go."

I scrambled to my feet. Tom grabbed my arm and set the pace. For the next hour or so we said nothing. Off to our side the predawn desert colors emerged. Purples faded to oranges and pinks, gray shadows evaporated to reveal sage-colored grass and caliche dirt. Already the sun's temperature warmed my back. Ahead lay sheep ranchland, dotted with cacti and squatty-treed hills underneath amethyst mountains. I stopped. "Which way are we headed?

South?"

He tugged at me to keep moving. "Very good."

I pulled my arm away. "Wait. Mexico?"

He slowed his pace, but continued to pull me along in his wake. "No. Not that far south. Just Loving."

"What?"

Tom swallowed. "Loving, New Mexico. Not far from the Texas border. An hour or so by car to Pecos on Highway 285. I know of a place we can rest for a while. At least I think I can get you there. All these hills look alike." He stooped to catch his breath. He swallowed then continued. "Then we'll hitch a ride on to Odessa, maybe San Angelo."

"So we need to find the highway?"

Tom shook his head. "No, Jen. We can't take that way. Too populated. But I figure we can hitch a ride along the county roads in a produce truck or something." He shaded his eyes from the rising sun and surveyed our surroundings. "Here, roll around in the dirt a bit more."

"Excuse me?"

He got down and squiggled back and forth like a horse scratching its back. Then he flipped over and rubbed his stomach. He leaned on one side and looked at me. "Blending in. Camouflage? In case they search by chopper."

I plopped down next to him, rubbing caliche on my skin and shirt.

"That's right." He rubbed his legs. "Dirt bath. Of course, this is useless if they have thermal scopes, which they probably do..."

"Pessimist."

"Realist." He stood and dusted his backside. Again, he flexed his hand in front of me. "Well, at least your hair matches the caliche. Come on, lady. We've got to keep going."

I sucked some saliva in my mouth and swallowed. "You keep saying so."

He smiled. "Yeah. And I probably will keep doing so until we reach a safe house. Ever been on the lam?"

"No. I suppose you have, tons of times."

He didn't answer. He kept his gaze ahead as he walked, and I stumbled, over the veined terrain of gullies, brush, and rocks. The slash on my heel from the broken glass in the coffin-room reminded me how deep it had penetrated.

He wrapped my arm around his waist. "Here, I'll lead. Hold onto my belt."

"Thanks." I melted into his strength.

He waved the thought away. "No problem. I know your heel must hurt like the dickens. You're doing fine." Then he returned to my question. "I've had survival training. Been in a few tough scrapes." He stopped and pointed. "See those mesquite trees?"

I cupped my hand over my eyes. "Sure."

"They're clumped together. That means water of some sort."

I felt a surge of vigor. "Well, come on, then. We gotta keep moving, right?"

He roared back and let loose a laugh, though a dry, thirsty one.

A few minutes later we were crouched over a small, half-dried stock pond shooing away two buzzards. "Not today, my friends," Tom heckled.

Ahead was a semi-paved road. "Do you think there's a ranch? A phone?"

"Maybe. Don't want to take the chance." Tom flipped out a cell phone.

"Where did you get that?"

"Chuck gave it to me." He winked, then waved it for a signal. "He was also kind enough to give me this." He dug in his pocket and pulled out a money clip bulging with folded money. "Tonight may be rustic, but tomorrow night perhaps we'll find a hot bath and bed."

It didn't sound like an innuendo, more like a dangling carrot to keep me going. My eyes returned to the cell phone.

"Won't they be able to track it?"

He nodded, studying the screen. "Probably. Which is why we are leaving it here. Just needed to get my bearings." He punched up a map. "About a half mile that way should be the Black River. We can follow it to the safe place. Hmm, I'd say it's about three or four hours away."

He tossed the phone into the pond with a kerplunk. One buzzard did a quick two-step backwards, then waddled away. Small ripples vibrated outward to slither into the muddied edges. With one more slap of water on his face, he stood. "Ready?"

I stood up from my haunches. "Tom?"

"Yeah."

I wiped my mouth. "Isn't this a bit too easy?"

"Mae Lin probably hasn't realized Chuck isn't still guarding us. But she will as soon as they stop for gas."

"But we'll be at your safe place by then?"

He shrugged. "Assuming I actually find it. The instructions were a bit on the vague side."

I grabbed his arm. "You sounded so confident. Are you sure we can?"

He grinned. "Prayer will help. 'Show me your ways, O Lord. Teach me your paths. My hope is in you all the day long.' Psalm 25."

The man continued to amaze.

Tom winked. "And the name's now Travis. Remember that. Let's go." He headed up the mound back to the vast grasslands which surrounded us for miles on end.

I had to admit, I was impressed. Perhaps one of his personas was a Bible-thumpin' preacher. Why not? I still had no clue who this chameleon really was. Maybe I should just quit trying to guess.

CHAPTER SEVENTEEN

WE WALKED MOST of the morning, but at a slower pace. Tom had us follow a riverbed, which was low at the moment. He told me because it was September, the end of an Indian summer, so the snow-melts that swelled creeks in the spring had long evaporated. The water still was deep enough to cover our ankles...and our tracks. Its coolness eased the burning in my heel, gouged by the broken glass in the cement room. I'd lost track of the days. How long ago had it been? Evidently not very long, since my foot still hurt.

In the near distance cars zipped along County Road 720, but Tom insisted we stay off the road for now. The river bank hid us partially from view.

"Why are we heading to Loving? Was that our destination?"

He shook his head and grabbed at a low lying mesquite limb to pull it away from our path. "Actually, our contact is the other way, in Carlsbad."

"So, that's where they will think we're headed?" I dodged the branch as it swished back.

He sucked a thorn from his finger. "I hope so. And we are stopping short of Loving. In the hills. Where I am taking you, I don't think Mae Lin would ever figure I would."

"Then she knows this place? Isn't that risky?"

"Maybe, but it's the best card I can play—and, it's my last."

I knew better than to ask for more of an explanation. In time, when he thought it was right, he'd tell me. I had to trust in that, and maybe trust more in him.

He stopped and reached down for a clump of small, yellow berries. "Here, wild Mahonia. The natives call it *Agritos*." He dropped some in my hand, and plopped the rest in his mouth.

They had a different taste. Not bitter. Not sweet. Like something you'd put in a fruit cake for someone you didn't like very much.

He chomped, and then spit out a stem. "You may have seen their purple-clustered cousins in gardens in Texas. Also called barberry. You know, Oregon grapes? But those berry in the spring, not the fall like these."

I shook my head. "Not exactly grapes."

"Anyway, they are edible." He reached down and plucked some more. I followed suit.

"Wheat farmers hate them," he said between munches. "They're nasty weeds."

I shuffled to keep up. "How do you know this?"

He saluted. "Courtesy of the U.S. Navy survival training, ma'am."

I smiled. He'd definitely flipped back to savior-mode, for now.

THE SUN WAS high in the sky. We'd stopped to munch on other edibles Tom discovered in the desert tundra and to sip river water. "If we're lucky," he said between slurps, "we won't get dysentery."

"Very funny, Tom, er, Travis." I hoped he was joking. "I still can't get used to your new name."

His eyes warmed. "I know, *Debbie*. I came to care about you as Jen."

My cheeks flushed with heat.

Suddenly he grabbed my hand. "Ssshh. Wait here."

I heard male voices. He motioned me to stay low, then scrambled up the riverbank. He greeted them in Spanish. "*Hola. Como está?*"

My Tex-Mex was rusty and the wind was blowing the other way, but the gist of the conversation was this—Tom said something about *marido*, which means husband. Was he telling them I was a widow? They said they were migrant workers. I imagined more like illegal immigrants. They chatted some more then I heard him say, "*Gracias. Buena suerte.*" That much I knew. Thanks and best of luck.

A few minutes later he returned with some beef jerky, two tortillas, two bottles of water, and a somewhat bruised and blackish banana. A lighter band of skin, not crusted in dirt, showed where his Rolex watch had been on his now bare wrist.

He smiled and doled out the traded goods. "The safe house is about six miles to the southeast, so I have us on the right track after all. We can stay there and rest. But I warn you, hang close. Most likely we will not be alone, but we may be the only *gringos*. We'll have to win their trust."

"You mean a hole-up for illegal immigrants?"

"Right, and maybe a few petty drug dealers."

"Oh, great. And this is the safe house you spoke of?"

"You got a better plan?" He peeled the banana and handed me half.

"No." I snatched the bruised fruit and devoured it, slimy black and all.

"Here." He released the dollar bills from the clip, took a few ones, and then handed me the rest. "Put it where the sun don't shine."

I took the cash and went to stuff it in my bra.

"That's the first place they'll look. Much lower." He pocketed the ones and turned away. I unzipped my jeans and slid the rest of the wad between my legs.

He waded into the river, took the money clip, and shoved it under the water. Tan mush swirled around him in an ethereal dance before the water slowly turned back to green. He tramped back out again and sat next to me. "They won't find it until the spring rains."

I tapped his naked wrist where his watch once sat. "You seem to be losing things."

He pecked my cheek. "Never you, my dear. A promise is a promise."

"Something tells me that watch had sentimental value."

"It did. Your husband gave it to me when we were in the military. I needed a waterproof one."

Tom raised up, ripped off a piece of jerky with his teeth, and strode downstream. It fit. Robert was always generous with his money, which meant it was hard for us to ever save any. I could tell by the tone in Tom's voice they really had been good friends. Maybe that is why I felt this attraction...I shoved back my pheromones and followed, as I chomped on a stale tortilla and swigged the water.

"I guess the hot bath and fresh sheets are out of the question tonight, though, huh?"

He raised his hands in the air. "We'll see. If your sore heel gets to be too much, I can carry you."

"I'm fine."

He shaded his eyes from the sun to judge my expression. "Yes, you are."

I felt my cheeks warm again, not from the sun's rays.

THROUGHOUT THE DAY Tom tried to match my stride instead of vice versa, giving me a concerned look every now and then. I'd smile. I vowed to myself there would be no more complaining.

Twice, we rested for about a half hour. The sun, which had been beating onto our heads, began to edge to the west beyond the mountains. Barely visible, through a clump of trees past the river, stood two shacks. The fellow travelers had given us good directions. By the time we reached the dirt path, my legs ached so badly I could barely lift them. My heel throbbed. The blisters on my ankles and big toes had popped about two hours previously.

Two quasi-military types emerged from the brush, their automatic rifles cocked and aimed at us. Tom grabbed my arm and pulled me to his side. "Let me do the talking. You understand Spanish?"

"*Mas de que hablar, pero sí.*" (More than I can speak, but yes.)

He looked impressed. "*Ta bueno, chica mía.*" (Very good, my girl.) He winked, then added, "Same story. Lovers running from your pathologically jealous husband."

I shoved my hand to my hip. "So that's what you told the others. Why?"

"So"—his voice edged with irritation—"we can stick together. Remember in the Bible about Abram and Sarai? He lied to the Bedouins or Egyptians or whoever and said she was his sister? Same thing." He stopped. "Well, sort of."

"Tell me that story."

"Later." He gave me an incredulous glance. "You really went to parochial school?" He clicked his tongue. "Sheesh. Didn't they read the Bible there? No wonder you didn't like the one I left with your

[127]

breakfast. I thought it would comfort you."

"We did, well, some. I usually didn't pay attention."

Tom shaded his eyes from the sun. "Ah, I see."

I suddenly felt inept. Add Bible study to the growing list of things to do if I ever got out of this mess. "Anything else I need to know?"

"Hush." Tom raised his hand and waved. *"Hola. Estamos amigos. Necesitamos ayuda."* (We're friends. We need help.)

Tom went through the whole story, and from his gestures, I guessed he told them about meeting the men on the road. The two remained expressionless, casing us with their eyes and the tip of their rifles.

One grunted to the other. He dropped his weapon and began to pat me down. He stopped when he reached between my legs. Two gold teeth gleamed at me as he rubbed. I sucked in my breath, then swallowed. "Period. I'm in my, uh—*¿Que dice? Tiempo a mes a la mujer. ¿Comprende?* Woman's time of the month."

Tom rushed him. "Hey, stop that. *Alto."* The other man shoved his weapon across Tom's chest.

Tom continued. *"Está es la mujer. ¿Comprende?"* (She's a married lady. Understand?)

I scrunched my eyebrows. Why did he say that? My wedding band told them so. But for some reason, it made a difference. The man lowered his weapon and hissed something in Spanish to his partner, who still held my crotch. My searcher pulled his hand away, stepped back and nodded.

Tom rushed to my side, the concerned lover. He buried my head in his shoulder. "Good thinking," he whispered. I squeezed his side.

The first man pulled me away by the elbow. "No. You two stop. Later, when she's clean, *si?* Then *Jefe* have her. Maybe we

[128]

watch." He laughed and shoved me, then motioned to start walking.

Jefe? Their chief. I turned to Tom, who winked and whispered, "It's okay. I know him. You'll be safe." He nodded for me to go ahead, but not before I saw his jaw set. What was he not saying? He dropped back to walk behind me, followed by the second gunman.

I was taken to the first dilapidated wooden shack. The elements had stripped away most of the paint, the exposed wood dusty gray with flecks of white and green. Outside I stood like a statue as I was stripped of my opal ring, wedding band, and gold-stud earrings. Then, the gold toothed, tobacco-stained smile of my frisker widened.

A grubby, tan hand reached down the neck of my T-shirt and pulled out the small gold cross dangling from a slender filigree chain. My mother had given it to me for my thirteenth birthday. She and Dad had been killed in a private jet crash a year later on the way to the Yucatan for a week-long missionary trip. That day I stopped talking to God. But I never took it off. It kept her close to me.

"No." I grabbed it back before he could jerk it off my neck. My eyes swam. *"Por favor. Este de mi madre. Está muerta."* (Please. It's from my mother. She's dead.)

His look softened for a second, then he grunted. The man whipped me around and shoved me in the back with the gun toward the door of the shack. *"Allí. Va."* (In there. Go.)

Then, I was shoved inside. I glanced at Tom and saw his brows knit into one line across his face. The door slammed shut and I heard a piece of wood slide across it to lock it. The room was dark, dank, and somewhat cooler. A dirt floor was littered with four woven hay pallets. Faded Indian blankets lay crumpled on top. Two other women crouched in a corner. The only light was what eked through the loose-planked walls.

I inched over in the dim lit room, they backed away. *"¿Hola?"*

No response. As I drew closer I saw they weren't women, but girls. Neither looked over fourteen. My heart sank, wondering if they were the children of the gunmen, or their playthings. *"¿Su mama o su padre está aqui?"* I asked them if their parents were here.

One sniffed and shook her head. The other looked down at her lap. No parents around here. I'd guessed right. They were playthings. *"Yo soy Jen."* I patted my chest.

One volunteered their names as she handed me a half bottle of warm water from behind her mat. *"Soy Monica."* She nodded to her roommate. *"Y, está es Marisol."*

I took the water, and gave them both a piece of jerky from my jeans pocket. In broken Spanish, a hint of English, and a bit of sign language, we talked in hushed voices. They'd come to America to be maids or nannies. They'd traveled for six days in trucks and on foot. Both had been prostituted repeatedly, first to raise money for their passage, then by a white man they called *Jefe* when they got here. He'd have one of them with him each night to teach them how *gringos* liked it and how to speak English. Marisol was sure she was now pregnant. She'd been throwing up for a week.

An old pang hit my heart. I remember seeing the plus sign on the wand. Giddy because I had wanted kids, I showed it to him. But Robert said he wasn't ready to be a father. He hadn't yet asked me to marry him. After several tearful arguments, I gave up trying to persuade him and agreed to take the medicine which would end my pregnancy. Maybe if he'd let me have that child my loneliness would have ached less. I'd still have a bit of him, of our love. Now, I had only emptiness and regret. Another reason I quit praying to God—out of shame.

Maybe it was what drew me to Marisol. This poor girl, way too young, had nothing but trouble ahead of her with an unwanted child in her belly. In a way, her shame was forced on her, just like mine was on me. Life was cruel and unfair.

The door opened and an old woman entered, then three tin plates of food were set in front of us. I thanked her, then took the bottle of water she handed me. The seal had been broken, the water a bit muddied. It had obviously been refilled from the Black River or a nearby stock pond. She nodded and tossed me a tampon, wrapper torn, from her skirt pocket. I guess my story had worked.

I took it and nodded. *"Gracias."*

She began to back out the door. I stopped and grabbed her skirt. *"Un minuto. ¿Donde está mi amigo?"* (Wait a moment. Where is my friend?)

The woman smirked and left.

Monica said Tom probably was all right for now. They might rough him up a bit to show him who's boss then hold him for ransom, or use him in a drug trade as a shield.

I prayed for my savior-captor, hoping he'd have the wherewithal to come out unscathed, then whispered, "Amen." The other two made a sign of the cross on their chests. One kissed a rosary she took from her pocket. In silence, we ate our beans and rice with our fingers.

The sun set and the air cooled rapidly. We wrapped the dusty blankets around our shoulders, talked a bit more, then crawled onto our pallets. Weariness overcame me and I fell into a deep chasm of dreamless sleep.

DURING THE NIGHT, in my sleep I heard hushed, angry voices. One was Tom's. The other…but it couldn't be Robert. The loneliness, the memories all this had conjured up, even my growing feelings for Tom all were playing tricks with my mind. Again, I shoved the idea to the back of my brain and told it to go away. Two pairs sets of footsteps shuffled further away from the shack, the slam of a wooden door echoed through the night. In minutes, the crickets began to sing again. I let myself drift back to sleep.

Later, the door opened and Monica was escorted out by a man with a flashlight. She crossed herself and went silently without struggle, already knowing her fate. I heard Marisol's soft weeping and the clink of prayer beads.

The wooden door whammed shut and the shuffle of feet distanced. I bit my lip to thwart my own tears and held tightly onto the cross around my neck.

For the second time in one night, I prayed for someone else besides myself.

CHAPTER EIGHTEEN

IN THE MORNING, Monica returned with tortillas and watery oatmeal, definitely the instant variety. We were each given a bottle of water about the same color as the oatmeal. I spent the day teaching them Tic-Tac-Toe in the dirt and Rock-Paper-Scissors with our hands. Occasionally we'd hear men's voices outside the hut. None of them sounded familiar and all spoke Spanish. Marisol would cringe, Monica stiffen her back. I craned my neck, ear poised to detect Tom's voice. But I never heard it again. Nor did I hear the voice that haunted my dreams.

In the early evening, when the sky was splashed in a purple haze behind soft hues of peach, we were led from the hutch into a closed-in camper truck. Three men already waited in the bed. One had blue eyes. I rushed and sank next to him, clinging to his chest as one of the captors hopped in and closed the latch.

"Keeping up the act, hon?"

I didn't answer.

He wrapped his arm around me and whispered, "You okay? They didn't do anything to you?"

I shook my head. He stroked my hair. I heard his chest heave in relief. "Whew. That story of your period was brilliant. When I told the *Jefe*, he laughed..."

I arched my eyebrow.

"Um, never mind. I'm glad you're okay." His voice cracked as he squeezed my waist.

I raised my head to study his face. His slashed cheek was crusted over and the eye swelling had gone down. His day old beard, now two, was less prickly to the touch. "You're unscathed, too, I see."

He leaned in. "For now. We aren't out of the woods yet. We know a lot."

"*Silenció.*" One of the gunmen poked us with his automatic rifle. I scooted to sit opposite of Tom, my spine flattened against the backside of the truck. I placed my feet against his, in an attempt to hold on to him. He smiled.

The seven of us were stacked in like a cord of wood. The air was stifling, mixed with bad breath and body odor. But then, I doubted I smelled like a rose.

We rode in silence through the night, catching tidbits of sleep in between bumps. Once, we were let out to find a bush, then given sips of stale water. Monica and Marisol appeared relieved to be given the night off. Tom eyed them cautiously as we stepped back into the camper shell. "They're only children," he hissed. "I had no idea they took them so young."

I looked at him. "They're being held against their will. Told they'd be nannies or maids. Now they're...you know."

He lowered his eyes. "I know."

I kept my voice as low as possible. "Tom, we have to help them."

"Sshh." His voice vibrated in my ear as he lifted me into the bed of the truck. "We have to help us first."

We scooted to the back and propped against the cab, knees scrunched so everyone could sardine back inside. His feet found mine again as we sat opposite each other. The truck's engine choked and sputtered, then decided to turn over and run once more. We jostled back to the unpaved road. Small clouds of dust penetrated the camper into our nostrils.

Tom shifted his weight and exhaled a slight cough. A few minutes later his breathing deepened and slowed. Why is it men can fall asleep at the drop of a hat? I tried to do the same.

CHAPTER NINETEEN

OUR GUARD SHOVED his gun into my ribs. I squinted.

"*Gringos. Arriba. Vámonos.*" (Get up. Let's go.)

Tom shook off the mental cobwebs, then looked at me. The camper door was open, the truck stopped. Edges of dawn were lightening the shadows of the brushy land. The other men, Monica, and Marisol were already outside. We scooched our way out as our guard backed up, his barrel aimed in the vicinity of our chests. Tom exited first, then turned to help me down the back bumper.

Another Hispanic man with a gold chain around his neck came around, gun also pointed at us. "Because you did good for us *mi amigo Travis, Jefe diga*, er, say, we let you go."

Tom nodded and shook his hand. "*Gracias.*" The two men exchanged looks.

I scanned our surroundings. Where were we? Dry prairie brush stretched out endlessly from all sides—no trees, no hills, flat. The road was paved. A sign with a black silhouette of Texas on it and white letters identified the road as FM 1062. We'd crossed the border.

A bottle of dirty water was shoved into Tom's hands. His partner's grungy ones slid down my hair to my breasts. *"Jefe tiene buen gusto en las mujeres. Pero ahora él elige los más jóvenes."* Both men laughed.

I picked up on the Spanish words for good, women, and now, but could not decipher the rest. What had he said? Whatever it was, it must not have been nice. Tom's face turned pale then hardened. He pulled me to him.

"Cálmate. She goes with you." The gold chained man laughed. *"Jefe* says he already has those two."

Whoever this *Jefe* was, he was in the shadows or giving orders over the phone. He obviously did not want us to see him. I figured it was for our own good so we could not identify him to authorities. What I couldn't figure out was why they were letting us just walk away. "Will they shoot us in the back?"

Tom's eyes softened into a smile. "They wouldn't chance it. Don't worry."

"What did that one say?"

Tom gulped. "That their chief used to like beautiful women like you. Now he likes young girls." He looked away, to something over my shoulder. I saw his eyes take him someplace. I didn't have a clue where, but it seemed painful.

The gunmen pushed the others into their designated positions as the truck revved up dust. As the camper door closed, I caught Monica and Marisol's gazes. Their pleading eyes stung my heart. I nodded farewell. They returned the gesture. In a silent bond I swore to them, God and the world, I'd find them again. I'd find them and set them free. My eyes bore the promise into theirs as they rode away.

In my peripheral vision, I saw Tom eye me, then watch the truck leave. We waited until it was a speck enclosed in a dust mite on the horizon, then simultaneously turned to each other.

"I know you want to help those girls, hon. But..."

I blinked back a tear. "I know. We have to help ourselves first."

He wrapped an arm around my waist and patted it. "Yes, we do."

I turned toward the sunrise, which had yet to fully form, and peered into his face. "What did they mean, you were good?"

Tom looked around, anywhere but at me. "I ran an errand for them. Cocaine, I guess."

My hands grabbed his shirt. "What?"

He pushed them down. "I was the only one seen. I made sure of that."

"By?" I shielded my eyes to the rising orange-yellow disc over his shoulder. The rays haloed his head.

"The authorities. See, now I am wanted criminal." He flashed me a brief smile. "So, I'm not going to run to the police and tattle."

I looked at him, trying to read his expression. "I guess you have slithered on the edge of illegal before."

Tom grabbed my elbow and motioned to walk east toward the dawning sun. "Yes, and crossed that line a bit as well. I think we are somewhere outside of Amarillo." He took the bottle of water, swigged it, and swished the liquid around in his mouth. Nodding, he swallowed. "Don't think it's drugged. Take only a swig. We'll need to use it sparingly."

My voice quivered. "I was sure they were going to kill us."

He winked. "I had a long talk with *Jefe*. He told them, 'No.'" He strode a few more steps then turned and winked back at me. "You can thank me later."

WE WALKED IN silence for a good while. No cars traveled the road which stretched out in a shimmery ribbon ahead. The sun inched its warmth up my back. My T-shirt stuck to my skin. Beads of sweat slid down my cleavage and the back of my neck. Oh, how I wished I had a scrunchie to put my hair in a ponytail. I stopped, then yanked a piece of Johnson grass stalk growing near a barbed-wire fence post. Winding my hair into a figure eight, I slid it through, bent it, and weaved it back again. I grabbed another and did the same higher up.

Tom's eyes widened, his smirk returned with a smug curve which seemed to wane between fascination and approval. I cocked my head and said "What? I'm hot." Then walked ahead.

"Yes, you are." It was no more than a whisper, one I chose to ignore as we passed a green highway sign which read "Canyon 16 miles." I hoped it was a town, not a landmark. I wanted a hot bath, a cold Diet Coke, and a juicy cheeseburger.

To steady our pace, we talked, about nothing and everything. He kept jamming his hands into his jean pockets, then taking them out to wipe his brow on his T-shirt. It was as if he didn't know what to do with them. Was he nervous for some reason?

Thinking it was better if I didn't ask, I told him tidbits about my childhood when prodded by his seemingly innocent questions. He revealed almost nothing about himself other than that he was raised in Chicago by an elderly Irish-Catholic aunt. His dad had left his mother early on, then she left when Tom was seven. "Went out on one of her dates and never came back."

He shrugged off my concerned look before I had a chance to comment and kicked a small rock in the road with the side of his foot. Then, he continued. "I joined the Navy right out of high school and went into Special Forces training in Virginia. That is where I met Robert."

His story fit. Robert had been in the Navy Seals—the 6th. An ounce of trust rose in my heart again.

From behind us I heard a mechanical chug. We turned to see a blue Chevy pickup heading in our direction. Tom pulled me to his side and held out his thumb. The truck slowed, brakes objecting. The windows were down and the radio blasted a Patsy Kline oldie. A man in a dingy Texas Rangers baseball cap leaned over the cab seats and peered through the passenger side at us. "You lost?"

"We picked up a hitchhiker. He did this." Tom pointed to his cheek. "Then stole our car, our money, everything."

I looked away, hoping the driver didn't see my reaction to Tom's lie. I hated lies, no matter how legitimate they seem at the time.

The man sized us over. He pointed to the bed of the truck with his head. "Okay. Hop in. I'll take you as far as Canyon up the road. You can see the chief of police there about it."

Ah, so Canyon was a town. Good.

Tom reached out and, in what I guessed was a manly fashion from the set of his jaw, shook the man's weathered hand. "Bless you. This is Debbie. I'm Travis."

I wondered why he used our Mae Lin given names, but added, "We're mighty grateful."

We climbed into the back of the truck, empty except for the pungent odor of manure and hay. A silver tool kit splayed across the back between us and the cab. Our rescuer had the sliding window open. Patsy continued to serenade our journey.

Tom latched his arm around my waist to steady me over the bumps, I supposed, as we edged back onto the highway. Not that I minded. His hip bone pressed against mine. I handed him the water bottle, with maybe two remaining swigs. He motioned me to drink first.

The breeze coming off the truck bed felt marvelous, cooling my sweaty skin, though after a mile, the Johnson grass clips gave up the ghost. My hair whipped my face and Tom's. I grabbed most of it, twisted it, and held it with my hand.

He slipped his arm away, then he scooted to the right and looked off across the prairie. A slight sense of abandonment etched the corners of my emotions. I blinked it away and turned to look out my side of the bed. I refused to fall for this guy. I still loved Robert. I stared at the white circle around my left ring finger. I wouldn't betray his memory, even if my wedding band was gone.

Ten minutes later, we entered Canyon, population a little over twelve thousand according to the census sign that zipped by. We pulled off onto 11th street, then turned onto 3rd. In front of City Hall, our benefactor found a parking space. He tapped on the cab window. "Here ya go. Betty at the information desk right inside there will tell you who to talk to."

I looked at Tom. He gave me a hush signal with his finger to his lips then motioned for us to get out. We walked around to the driver's side. Again, firm Texas handshakes were exchanged.

We waved as the rancher pulled away. Two secretaries returning from lunch gave us the twice over before proceeding up the concrete steps.

"What do we do?" I hissed. "We can't go to the police, can we?"

Tom looked around. "No. Let's head for a diner. I'm starved. You still have the wad well hidden, right?"

I'd almost forgotten. "Yes, but we must smell and look a sight."

At the corner a block up and over was a convenience store and gas station. "Let's go there." He swallowed and pointed. "You know. Use the restroom. Wash up."

As we crossed the street and approached the gas station, he stopped. "If you can slip me the money, I'll buy us new T-shirts. I see some hanging on a display in there."

Luckily the unisex restroom was on the side, and unlocked. I slipped in, retrieved the cash, opened the door a crack, and handed it him. A moment later there was a knock. "Psst, Jen. Here."

A pink Tony Romo jersey appeared along with a brush and hair clip. God bless the Dallas Cowboys...and Tom. I hissed back. "Don't you mean Debbie?"

"Ha-ha."

I slipped on the jersey, brushed my hair, and emerged feeling revived and a bit more civilized, even if I did smell of truck stop soap.

He held up a T-shirt with Palo Duro Canyon on it, wiggled his eyebrows, and exchanged places with me. I'd just stepped away when the restroom door cracked open again. A twenty waved at me. "Oh, here. Buy us lunch."

I went inside to browse our choices, nodding to the clerk who leaned on his arms as he smoked a cigarette behind the counter. He barely acknowledged my presence, then went back to stare at the newspaper in front of him. Moments later, the bell on the glass door tinkled and Tom appeared, clean shaven, wet hair slicked back, sporting his touristy tee.

I walked toward him, my arms laden with two ice cold bottles of water, two plastic wedges of egg salad sandwiches, two oranges, and two Snickers bars. His laugh disturbed our host behind the counter. He glared at us with a how-dare-you-interrupt-my-day expression. We slapped it all down on the glass that displayed cheap jewelry and lottery cards.

He rang up our food and bottled waters, then held out a mammoth hand for our legal tender. "Ten seventy-five," he grumbled. The toothpick in the corner of his mouth wiggled in a semi-circle as he crunched it between his molars.

I handed him the twenty. The clerk huffed. "No exact change, huh?" He punched open the till, took his sweet time counting back the change, then returned to the sports section splayed out in front of him.

"Have a nice day," I responded with a sugar-dripping lilt I knew would set his toothpick on edge. Tom chuckled under his breath.

We scooted into a once red Formica booth and chomped on our feast. I had no idea how famished I was until my taste buds felt the soft mayo and egg delight. Every ounce of inner strength was required to not cram the whole sandwich wedge in my mouth. My mother's voice to eat slow and chew like a lady echoed in the back of my mind. *Yes, ma'am.*

Tom pointed his sandwich at me. "Eat slow. Your stomach isn't ready for a full meal, yet."

"I know. My mother was just telling me so."

He leaned in. "What?"

I shook my head and swallowed another bite. "Never mind. Lame joke."

"Uh-huh." He peered out the window between the taped advertisements. "It's clouding up. Let's see, exactly how much cash do we have?"

He reached in his pocket, slipped the wad into his lap, and began to mouth the numbers.

"Why?"

He glanced at me then back to his counting. "We need shelter. And real baths. Possibly more clothes? And ointment and bandages for your feet."

I'm sure my expression revealed my shock that he knew more than I'd let on.

His blue eyes smiled back at me. "I noticed you not trying to hobble. There just was nothing I could do about it. We wouldn't have gotten far if I carried you."

I raised my chin. "I wouldn't have let you."

He grinned. "Yeah, I know" He reached in his pocket for the change from buying our T-shirts and asked for mine. "One ninety-two, fifty-four. We need to make it last. We'll have to share a room."

"I figured that would be the case." I refused to blink or look astonished. We'd shared just about everything else up until now, except...I wondered if he thought the same. We'd waltzed around it so often we could win first place in a dance competition.

"Good." His shoulders eased. "Thanks for not putting up a fuss."

I leaned in. "It's the only thing I'll put up with tonight, mister, okay?"

His eyes twinkled back at me as he handed me the wad of money. "I figured that would be the case."

CHAPTER TWENTY

OUR CHOICES WERE limited since we were on foot, and mine were killing me. The first motel we saw was the Buffalo Inn near the campus of West Texas A&M. The room rate was cheap, and it came with a microwave, mini-fridge, and "Cable TV." The motel sign on the glass door stated they provided a free all-you-can-eat continental breakfast.

"We'll take them up on that." Tom grinned as he held it open for me. His attention turned to a middle-aged man behind the counter who was busy eyeing us from head to foot. Tom told the man our story to explain why we were without any wallets, car, or IDs. "We do have cash, though. My, uh, assistant hid it...in her shoe."

Well, it was the place I'd stashed the money when we left the gas station. The extra padding felt good against my swollen heel. I took off my shoe and produced the folds of bills.

"How much is it for one room?"

He eyed us again. "Forty-five for a single. Fifty-five for two beds. Did you tell the sheriff?"

Tom shook his head. "Not sure it will do any good. They're long gone." He scratched his head. "Insurance will want a report though, right? We will in the morning."

The manager continued to eyeball us. "We're not supposed to check you in without proper ID, per Homeland Security."

Tom gave him the most sincere smile I'd seen yet. "Right now, my colleague and I are just dead on our feet. We both need baths and a good night's sleep."

The manager shifted his weight to his other foot. "Well, I guess I can make an exception."

"We'll take the double."

"Okay. Your choice." His gaze moved rapidly between us as a sneer curled the side of his mouth. "But you two don't need to pretend. If you want the single...well, I don't ask questions."

I started to protest his innuendo, but Tom held me back. "It's okay. The man can think what he wants." He narrowed his eyes to the manager, then tipped his imaginary Stetson in a thank you.

Down the road a few blocks was a Walmart, so we decided it would be cheaper to shop and fix dinner in the room. We walked to get groceries, underwear, jeans, and two new T-shirts. We also purchased socks, bandages, Neosporin, toothbrushes, and paste. The hotel provided soap and shampoo. All total, after paying for those and the room, we had $52.13 left.

"You're quite a bargain hunter."

"Robert used to tell me Lincoln squealed every time I held a penny. I'm that tight-gripped with my money."

"Robert. Right."

I scrunched my brows. The fond tone whenever he'd mentioned Robert's name had disappeared. I wondered if Tom would tell me why if I asked. Probably not.

Tom shifted his load—he'd volunteered to carry back the

majority of the packages to our lodging since I was hobbling. Beads of new sweat formed on his temples and dampened his curls. I swung the two smallest ones on an arm, enjoying this latest expression of chivalry.

He cast his eyes away to the navy tinted skyline. Rumbles cascaded, then a fork of white blitzed across the horizon. A veil of lighter navy filtered to the ground like a bed skirt under the clouds. The wind lifted the distant smell of damp prairie grass into the air, swirling bits of roadside debris in a miniature waltzing dust devil. "We'd better pick up the pace."

"Race ya." I laughed and took off, unburdened by heavy groceries and forgetting my feet hurt like crazy.

"Hey, no fair." His voice faded behind me, then his footsteps quickened to catch up.

The first nickel-sized drops splattered on the driveway as we entered the motel parking lot. Sheltered from the shaking of thunder and the rush of water as it gushed off the eaves of the breezeway, Tom unloaded our newly-acquired wealth into drawers, the fridge, and countertop as I massaged my feet.

He glanced over at me as he slid the remaining bills into the Gideon Bible, and then snickered. "Serves you right."

I stuck out my tongue as he tossed me the bandages and ointment.

We took turns showering, ignoring the old wives tale about lightning traveling down the pipes to electrocute you if you bathe during a storm. As I towel-dried my hair, he spread the hotel curtain back with one hand. "Wow, look at it coming down out there." He turned and smiled. "Like the night we—"

"But now you aren't dripping all over my computer."

He displayed his fake hurt little boy face. "Did I do that?"

My apple core missed his left ear by a smidgen. He chucked it back at me, then flopped onto his designated double bed.

I plopped onto the other one and studied the bedspread pattern with my fingernail. I took a breath through my nostrils and decided now was the time for the answers he'd promised. "Tom. Why did you kidnap me? Really?"

He fluffed the pillows piled behind his head and started at the ceiling. "Robert didn't have an accident, Jen. He was killed."

"So you implied. But they did an autopsy. The insurance company went over the car, what was left of it, with a fine-toothed comb. Nothing"—I emphasized the last word with my finger pointed at him—"ever showed anything else than an accident." I shook my head. "Nothing."

Tom waggled his head. "Yeah, yeah. He'd just been going too fast and lost control. I know." He glanced in my direction then back at the ceiling. "Less questions that way."

"Was it all faked, Tom? I mean his death. The way you planned mine. Is that why they wouldn't let me see the body?"

I'd tossed the question out. Tom caught it. His jaw twitched, but he continued to stare at an old water stain etched on the acoustical tile, sort of resembling an amoeba. For a moment, silence stagnated between us.

Then, after a quick sigh, he volleyed it back to me. "Jen, don't ask questions like that. You'd never believe the answers anyway."

"Why? I'm tired of all these clouded secrets."

"It's how these people work. They're professionals who can make almost anything happen. The less you know, the safer you'll be."

I slammed both hands on the bed and yelled, "For Pete's sake. Who are 'they'?"

"I honestly can't tell you." His voice remained controlled.

"Arggh." I leapt up and paced in front of the black TV screen.

The storm had wiped out the satellite signal. I stopped in front of his bed. "You mean you won't."

He sat straight, hands on his crossed knees. "No, I mean I'm really not sure who they are. Robert ruffled a lot of illegal feathers in his job."

"As an advertising exec?"

He shot me a get-real glance. "It's above my intel level. I do have an idea who 'they' might be, though."

I tried another avenue. "Who is Mae Lin? I gather she really isn't a teenager."

"True. Asians can pull that off. They have an ageless look of youth until late in life." He glimpsed in my direction and shifted his weight. "She's another asset, er, freelancer, with the same government agency that hired Robert and me. Well, sort of." In response to my rolled eyes he offered another tidbit. "We'd crossed paths before. She's kinda my boss in this. Or was, until I escaped with you. As I said, I didn't run point."

"In my kidnapping and alleged death, you mean." I didn't say it as a question. I sat on my bed and looked as deeply as I could into the layers of this man. Reading tea leaves through an onion would have been easier.

"Yes, and my getting the job at your company so I could keep my eye out for you."

I saw the bait and yanked the line. "Wait. You said Robert made you promise to look after me. But you came a good two months after his accident."

He huffed. It seemed he was searching for patience with me. "Yes," he replied slowly. "He knew his life was...let's just say, precarious, after the last job he did for the good ol' U.S of A. He contacted me and made me promise if anything happened...well, you know."

"And when it did—*if*, like you say, it did—that convinced you it wasn't an accident?"

"I notified our contacts and told them I thought it wasn't. I conveyed what he'd made me promise. Then I was read in as much as they'd let me know. Basically, all I was given was the instructions on how to proceed."

I scooched back onto my elbows. "Go on."

"I was just supposed to keep a watch on you. Stay low profile. I had your house tapped, by the way." He held up his forefinger. "Audio only."

"Gee, thanks."

He made a slight bow with his head. "It's not like I stayed up all night listening. It'd pick up if the phone rang, or if certain words were said. Then it would kick in and record. I'd check it every morning before I left for work."

"You're kidding."

He gave me a superior, know-it-all look. "No. It's true. The government uses the technology to monitor cell phone use across the borders all the time. It's how they monitor drug lords. Certain words trigger a beep. Like an alarm."

I shrugged. "Okay? What words?"

"Whatever it is programmed to." He leaned back again on his pillow, hands laced behind his head. "Oh, you know, like help, don't hurt me, gun, knife, etc."

I rose to pace again. "I don't believe you."

Tom's gaze traced my footsteps back and forth. After a moment, his voice softened with a sigh. "Try, Jen. Please."

I stopped, turned back toward him, but stayed on my half of the room.

He motioned to my bed. "Will you sit? You need to stay off your feet."

[150]

I obliged.

Tom turned over on to his side to face me. "Look. I didn't know things were going to turn nasty. But they did. They tried to get to you twice. That massive short in your computer keyboard before you moved to the basement? The break-in of your apartment?"

I waved my hand at him. "Uh-uh. The police said it was a random burglary. There had been several in the area."

Tom gave me an incredulous look. "And you believed them, huh?"

I sat back against the headboard. "Why me? Because I was Robert's wife?"

"Yes. They have no idea he kept you in the dark. They think you are an asset as well."

I pounded the bed. "Then tell 'them,'" I cupped my fingers, "I'm not."

He sat up to face me, mirroring my posture. "You think they'd believe me? I'm a pawn, too, Jen. Honest. I am way down here." He lowered his hand a foot off the floor.

I grabbed a pillow and held it close to me. "You said you two had planned this kidnapping thing months before."

Tom came to sit on the edge of my bed. "Look, Jen, we did. We were to fake both of your deaths. Robert knew that'd involve kidnapping you. Your Irish head is too hard to come peacefully."

I gave him a daggered look. Outside, a rumble of thunder responded as well.

He glanced through the curtains at the lightning flash that followed, then turned his face back to me. "When I heard he'd died, I asked for permission to carry it out, for your sake. At first the agency said no. Then things began to happen to you. I got permission to go undercover at your work."

"And..." I hugged the pillow closer.

"And, let's say some pretty shady guys were observed tailing you. I reported it and got the go-ahead."

"To kidnap me?"

He shrugged. "I had a job to do. I was told to keep you safe until the coast was clear, so to speak. Get you to trust me, then escort you out of town to a safe house. Sort of a prelude to the witness protection program."

I threw the pillow aside and shoved my arms into a pretzel in front of me. "Trust you? Was pretending to care for me part of the master plan? Play on the widow's vulnerability?"

His face registered pain. "No. That wasn't part of the plan. It just happened, Jen. And I do care for you. Really."

I threw him a mental dagger. "Oh, so that explains why you're the one who drugged me at Bob's Burgers, huh? And why you let Mae Lin shove the needle in me at the bus stop. Oh, and how many times was I gagged and shackled?" I jerked back my shoulders. "Because you *care* for me."

"Are we going over that again?" He sat erect, his hands palms up in front of him. "Look. I asked you to cooperate first both times. The syringe was plan B like I told you before."

It was my turn to waggle my head. "But since I tried to run, you had to take drastic measures. That's your justification?"

"I didn't approve of the hand tying and gagging. I never meant you to be hurt in any way." He stood and shoved his hands under his arm pits. "They figured I'd messed it up. Not gained your trust. So, Mae Lin and company got involved when you put up a fuss."

"And what is her angle in all of this?"

He sucked in air through his nose. "I told you, she is sort of my boss. She's higher up. I report to her."

"Was Robert?"

"Higher up? Yes, I guess. There are layers, hierarchies. He was recruited before he left the military, then later he recruited me."

It still didn't make sense. Especially my husband leading a secret life which required him to fake his death. "So you were really just following orders, is that it?"

He rubbed the back of his neck and nodded. "Yes. That's it."

"To kidnap me and drug me. Then fake my death. What a way to protect a gal." I slid off the bed to stand opposite him. "Next question. When did you two install the cameras in the ceiling, and why?"

His foot twitched. "I told you. So I could keep an eye on you and keep my distance. Because, Jen, like you said, you're a vulnerable widow."

I threw out the bait. "Or, because Robert didn't trust you with me. He was there at the coffin. Admit it. You knew he wasn't dead. He'd faked it himself just as you two planned."

He rubbed his hands over his face. "Jen. Give it up, okay?"

"But I keep hearing Robert. I thought I heard his voice in the coffin room. Then, when I left to meet Mae Lin, I sensed him there. Then, at the shack, I thought I heard his voice." I bore into Tom's eyes searching for truth.

His jaw twitched...again. His eyes dashed to the bedspread.

I slapped my hands to my hips. "That's why they let us go, isn't it? Robert told them to. That's why you took us there."

Tom shook his head. "No, Jen."

"I did hear him. Tell me, Tom. Tell me. Robert knows the white *Jefe*, right? He's trying to bring him down. He just couldn't acknowledge me because he's undercover." My pursed lips pleaded for it to be true.

Tom's face screwed into an even more painful look. His eyes reddened. "Please believe me, Jen. Your Robert is gone. Don't keep trying to think he isn't. It'll drive you nuts."

I pivoted and slammed my hands onto the cheap lowboy dresser that half served as a mini kitchen with microwave and dormitory-sized fridge. I stared at Tom's reflection in the dusty mirror. I willed the tears not to edge into my eyes with what little backbone I had left. It all seemed so unreal, yet way too real. Besides, I was dead tired, traumatized, and my feet stung like mad.

"I'm so sorry, Jen. About all of this. Taking you there was a mistake. Just let it go, okay?" He swallowed hard and looked to the window.

"And admit he's dead."

Tom's head bobbed quickly several times. He swung his feet to the floor and stared out the curtains.

The air thickened between us.

He was right. It was time I let it go whether I believed it or not. Which also meant, if Tom was being truthful about 'all of this,' my marriage had been a lie. The Robert I thought I'd known really was dead because he never existed.

If that was the case, I had to move on, gathering whatever pieces of my life this Greek man had torn apart. I might never have the whole picture, but the bits Tom offered were my tools to process this whole thing. Maybe it was best I didn't know more. This much hurt enough.

I willed the quest for the whole truth back into the pit of my stomach and prayed for it to never again be refluxed. Some things should stay under the rock where they had slithered.

RAIN PELTED AT the window as thunder rumbled through the canyon. I watched a flash of lightning through the half-drawn curtains and then turned my attention back to Tom. "So, what now?"

He came to me and placed his hands on my shoulders. "I

frankly don't know. I disobeyed orders. I escaped from Mae Lin with you. That kinda complicates things."

"So, now we're running from two organizations."

Tom scrunched his shoulders. "Well, if you count our Hispanic drug and human trafficking friends who are making sure we don't go to the police, then three."

"Great." I kerplopped onto the edge of the bed, simultaneously with a shuddering clap of thunder.

We both jolted at the sound.

The curtains moved back and forth to reveal a small spider-webbed hole in the glass. A chunk appeared in the opposite wall past the beds in a puff of drywall dust.

"Duck!" Tom grabbed my hands and pulled me to the floor between the beds.

We crouched on our knees, facing each other.

"Okay," Tom whispered. "That wasn't thunder."

CHAPTER TWENTY-ONE

HE CRAWLED OVER me and grabbed the motel phone's cord. The phone clunked to the ground. A faint high pitched hum hit my ear. Then three short tones in rapid succession.

I scooted aside. "What are you doing?"

Tom cupped the phone from his mouth. "Dialing 911."

"The police?"

He gave me a frustrated look. "That's usually what people do when they've been shot at." Then he released his hand. "Yes, my name is Travis Walters. We're at the Buffalo Inn. Room 115. Someone just shot at us through the window."

I watched as he nodded, repeated yeses, and gave terse bits of information into the receiver. I noticed he'd used the name on his fake ID. Or was it fake?

He hung up. "The cops are on their way."

"Shouldn't we have done something else? I mean the drug guys said not to..."

"Something else? I am unarmed. We have no IDs. I am not Jason Bourne, okay? This isn't the movies." He scooted around to lie sideways facing me. "Just stay down, shut up, and wait."

"You gave them the name of Travis."

His face was expressionless. "It's my real name, hon."

"Really?"

"Well, for all intents and purposes, that is."

I groaned, then buried my head in the musty carpet.

WITHIN MINUTES WE heard the siren, then the screech of tires. Tom, er, Travis, poked his head above the bed when the knock sounded at the door. I straightened from the floor. He waved for me to stay put, then eased past the end of the bed and rushed, bent low to the door. He rose, peered through the security peephole, then nodded back to me as he opened the door.

"Officer, please come in."

A man resembling an actor out of an old TV Western entered. He must have been six-six easily, and almost as broad as the door. He tipped his Stetson to me and flashed his badge. Actually, that was a protocol courtesy. His uniform and the .45 caliber pistol holstered to his hip were enough credentials for me.

"You two report shots?"

Travis—maybe if I said the name enough times I'd get used to it— pointed to the wall. "Yeah, it hit over there."

The officer narrowed his eyes and swaggered over to examine the white indentation in the sienna-painted wall. He picked at it, then nodded. "Ah, there it is."

Travis edged over, but the officer put out his hand.

"Stay back. Don't touch anything. I'll be right back with an evidence kit."

We watched Officer Juarez, or so his badge stated, exit the hotel room, turning slightly sideways to get his frame and the police paraphernalia on his belt through the opening.

I asked in hushed tones, "If you're Travis, who am I? Jen, or Debbie?"

My partner in crime gave me a quick smirk. "Who do you want to be? Both are traceable."

"I prefer my own name."

He frowned a bit then nodded. "Okay. Do so, then. Probably less chance to get facts wrong." He thrust his finger at my nose. "But remember, you've been reported as dead."

"Yeah. I remember."

Officer Juarez returned with a baggie, gloves, and tweezers. He was talking on his cell phone. "Yeah, definitely looks like a rifle. Maybe a .22. Want me to question them here or bring them in?" He craned his head to look back and forth at the two of us. "No. I doubt it. Okay."

He pocketed his phone then scratched his head. "Folks. I think it would be wise if we went to headquarters and let you tell your stories there, okay?"

"Sure," I volunteered.

Travis shot me a look, then sighed. "We'll have to ride with you." He screwed his mouth to one side. "No car. It was stolen."

I looked away. Lies.

Officer Juarez gave us a blank stare. "That's usually how it works, son. We take you. But first, let me get your names." He reached in his pocket, pulled out a notebook and pen.

The man who once was Tom didn't even flinch. He spoke with the sincerity of a saint. "Travis. Travis Walters. I told them that on the phone when I called."

The policeman shifted his gaze to me. "And you?"

I took a step forward, an old habit from being called on by the teacher. "Jennifer Westlaw. Mrs."

He raised an eyebrow at my emphasis on my married status.

He moved his pen back and forth between our chests. "Not, uh, related?"

"No. Coworkers." Travis smiled. "And friends. I mean, I was with her husband."

"Was?"

"He's deceased. Car accident."

Each time I'd heard someone say it, it seemed false. *He's not dead, just gone,* I'd tell myself. Now maybe it really was false. Especially since I kept hearing his voice. Didn't matter. He was still gone. Tom was right, let it go.

I slumped onto the bed with my arms laced around my waist. Officer Juarez cleared his throat. "Sorry, ma'am. Recent?"

"Last April." I croaked out the response. *Or so I've been told.*

"Sorry for your loss."

I set my jaw and bit down hard on my tongue to keep from voicing how I felt about that saying. So many people spouted the hollow, politically-correct sympathy phrase in the first few weeks after the funeral, I swore I'd puke if I heard it one more time.

The officer cleared his throat. "IDs?"

I gave Travis a "now what?" look.

He caught my eyes, then released them and looked straight into the policeman's. "Stolen. Along with the car. By drug dealers. In New Mexico. They held us for one, no…two days in a shack, then shoved us in a camper truck…"

"With other illegals," I added.

Travis' eyes widened as he locked onto my face. Evidently, I'd said too much.

The officer's narrowed. "Other illegals?"

"I…I mean we guessed they were." The cat was out of the bag. Well, I was glad to at least tell the officer something I knew was true. Besides, maybe the law could help find Monica and Marisol.

"There were two Hispanic teens." I rushed to the officer then stopped just short of his personal space. "Marisol and Monica. They were being held against their will, and well…" I cast my eyes to the rug. "You know. Trafficked." I looked up again. "One was barely pregnant. Still had morning sickness. I doubt if either was over fourteen or fifteen."

He held up his hand. "Whoa. Let's go down to the station and figure out who you are first. Then we'll talk about drug lords, teenage illegals, human traffickers, and who the heck might be shooting at you."

I stepped back into place. "Yes, sir."

Travis gathered the motel key and loose change from the dresser top and shoved them in his pocket. "Okay. Let's go, then." He shot me a sharp look.

Led by Officer Juarez, we formed a mini-parade for the few spectators who'd gathered on the sidewalk or dangled overhead from the second floor breezeway that ran the length of the motel rooms. Obviously, we were the most excitement in Canyon in quite some time. I felt one pair of eyes dig into my back, and turned to see the manager standing stiff with his arms crossed. He didn't seem pleased. I wondered where I'd be laying my head tonight.

I'D ONLY BEEN to the headmistress' office once in my entire parochial career. Not that I was a goody-two-shoes. Okay, I was. Detention hall for smoking or saying a curse word was the extent of my crimes. My father had been a city councilman, so it'd been engraved in my conscience that every move I made was being observed. My grandparents hammered the point into me—if I did anything to tarnish his reputation or our standing in the community, even after his and Mom's death, untold Irish ancestors would swoop down on me in my sleep. So, riding in a squad car to police headquarters sent my sweat glands into overdrive and my heart palpitating. Tom must have seen the havoc this played with my psyche. He squeezed my hand.

"Just tell them the truth, Jen. All of it. It's the best way. Don't worry about me." His voice was low, but I could still hear him over the hum of the squad car's engine and AC.

"But If I tell them everything..."

He shifted to face me, his hip pressing into mine. He squeezed my knee. "Don't leave anything out. They'll know if you do, Miss No-Poker-Face." He tapped a finger across my nose and winked.

Tears welled in my eyes again. Why did I want to protect him? He'd yanked me out of my mundane mourning, then set me on a fast-moving roller coaster ride of drugs, guns, and lies. Part of me admitted it had been great. I had longed for the unexpected to yank me from the grip of grief. What we'd been through in the past few days held a certain dangerous, and almost romantic, thrill. I almost hated to see it end. I hated to see us end before we began. "Will I ever see you again?"

He leaned over and pressed his lips against my cheek. "Can't say, my dear. I wouldn't think I'd be assigned to you anymore. If I get out of this." He nodded toward the front of the police car.

I didn't like the finality in his voice. It sounded as if he'd never be assigned to anyone again—ever. I had an image of his body being dumped in some remote river, weighed down by cinderblocks. They would naturally be the gray-green color of the ones in the bathroom down the hall from the room where he'd first held me in as captive—uh, protected. A sort of poetic justice.

"Tom?"

"It's Travis, remember?" His lips curved into a soft smile.

"Whoever you are—stay alive." I leaned in and pressed my mouth on to his, tasted its sweetness, then scooted away to stare out the car window. I blinked back tears, not wanting to see his reaction or for him to see mine.

I heard him breathe in and then whisper in an exhale. "Ah, geez, Jen. Why now?"

AT THE STATION, we were escorted into a room typical of most police stations. I couldn't spot a two-way mirror like I'd seen on TV crime shows, but the interrogation area was just as bleakly sparse with four walls, a door and an undecorated window with burglar bars. The only furnishings were a chipped wooden table in an oak stain, and four institutional-styled oak chairs, as uncomfortable as they looked. On the wall was a calendar from a local bail bondsman and a poster from TxDOT with a slogan to remind everyone to not text and drive.

Officer Juarez brought in a stenographer with a laptop and introduced her as Grace. Another officer named Mercedes brought Travis a cup of coffee and a cup of water for me. I almost laughed at the pun of the two girls' names, but no one would have understood. But truly, to have both Mercy—which is what Mercedes means in Spanish—and Grace around me right now made me think perhaps there was a God who cared.

We hit a snag when they asked me for my name, date of birth, and social security number. Grace entered them into their database, knitted her brow, and scooted the laptop to Officer Juarez's viewpoint.

Travis slunk into the chair and sighed. "Here we go."

Grace and Officer Juarez looked at us, then each other.

Travis splayed both his hands on the table. "She's not dead. Obviously. I helped set it all up to protect her from the mob." He looked at me then back to the policeman. "She had no idea I'd done it."

[162]

Officer Juarez leaned in, eyes glued to Travis' face. "Wanna explain that?"

I opened my mouth to speak, but he held out his hand, still staring at Travis. "I want to hear his explanation first." He then turned to Mercedes. "Why don't you take Mrs. Westlaw, or whoever she is, to the break room? You two can have a nice long chat in there."

She nodded and grabbed my arm.

Officer Juarez added, "Oh, and take really good notes."

As I was escorted out, I turned to lock eyes with Travis. His expression told me volumes without him opening his mouth. "Goodbye. Don't worry. I love you."

I blinked back the tears and walked with Mercedes down the hall as Grace closed the door. That was the last time I ever expected to see Travis, or Tom, or whatever my savior-captor's name really was, alive and free.

CHAPTER TWENTY-TWO

I JERKED MY elbow from Mercedes' grasp. "Where are you taking me?"

She looked me in the eye. "We have a lot more questions. Officer Juarez feels you'd be more likely to answer them truthfully if you are not in the same room as that—" She pressed her lips in disgust. "Man."

"That man," I hissed, "has been protecting me from drug lords, from thugs, from the desert heat, from people shooting at me."

She gently shoved me forward. "Yeah, right. Come on."

"Am I going to get to go back to the motel?" I thought of the rest of Chuck's wad Tom had stashed inside the Gideon Bible while he unpacked our haul from Walmart.

Her regulation shoes clunked along the linoleum floor in purposeful long strides. I shuffled to keep up. Her vise grip on my elbows began to sting.

"Going back to the motel is out of the question. Your things will be delivered here to the police station." Mercedes motioned to a nondescript door. "In here."

Inside was a typical break room. A worn Formica table and khaki-brown folding chairs with worn, avocado-colored vinyl cushions, obviously from the 1970s, reflected the sterile coldness. The room smelled of burnt coffee and leftovers scrunched into the trash can from someone's garlic-laced lunch.

Grace came in. "You wanna a Diet Coke?" She yanked on the handle of the harvest gold fridge. It opened, bottles and jars tinkling in response. She held up a can, popped the tab, and handed it to me before I could answer. I took a chug. The cold fizz felt good in my throat. I nodded a thanks.

She returned the nod, and then grabbed two—one for herself and one for Mercedes who now straddled one of the chairs.

I spent the next hour talking to the two of them, telling them all I could remember. My brain hurt, my body was exhausted, and my temper simmered just below the surface. Finally, after six pages of notes, Mercedes stood. "We've got what we need." She nodded toward Grace and left.

Grace said, "We're supposed to wait here. It won't be long."

I nodded. Right.

THE CLOCK'S LONG hand on the wall moved a half hour more. Grace chatted about safe topics—the weather, the sports teams, all about Palo Duro Canyon. Officer Juarez entered, his frame filling the doorway. "Is she ready to sign?"

I stared at each of them. "Sign what?"

He slapped three forms in front of me. "Charges against Travis Walters."

"Why? For what?" My tonsils clamped against my throat. I swallowed the last of the soda and ran my fingers over the rings on the Formica from the condensation on the can to avoid his face. I didn't like where this was heading.

[165]

Officer Juarez leaned his large frame across the table. "Look at me." I jumped. He stared me down. "He kidnapped you. That's illegal. He drugged you against your will. That's illegal. He committed fraud by faking your death. He stole a vehicle." His stubby fingers stood erect emphasizing each point. When he got to his thumb, he added, "And, according to you, he admitted participating in a cocaine delivery."

I firmed my chin. "You'll have to ask him. I didn't witness it. I was locked under guard in a shack."

He slammed his hand on the table, jolting my emerging stubborn resolve back down my throat. "Yeah, yeah, we know."

It was nearing 11:00 p.m. Mercedes stretched. "Look, let's stop for the night. We'll make calls to Fort Worth in the morning."

Officer Juarez rounded his shoulders, casting a shadow over me. "Fine. We'll start back up in the morning."

I rubbed my eyes and nodded. He'd frazzled me. Relief flooded when he turned and walked out. Then he slammed the door. All three of us jumped. Even the soda cans on the table rattled in his wake.

I turned to the two women. "Where's Tom? Uh ...Travis?"

The two shot each other a glance. "Don't you worry. You're safe," Grace said in an assuring tone.

"We'll get you a cot and you can sleep in here," Mercedes replied.

"Am I being held against my will?" I tried to keep my voice steady.

"We can hold you pending further investigation, yes. But I doubt you want to spend the night in the drunk tank."

Grace reached for my hand. "It's really for your own good, dear. Stay here and get some rest. You've been through the wringer."

I shook my head and shoved the forms across the table. "I want to see him. I won't sign any papers until I do."

The two exchanged looks again. Grace squeezed my fingers. "We'll see what we can do. Tomorrow."

Another officer brought me a cot, and Grace brought me a blanket and a bare pillow. "Sorry, we don't have sheets around here."

"I understand." My personal items from the motel were delivered. Not Tom's though, or the motel Bible. Some praying soul in the future would have a pleasant shock. Well, they say God works in mysterious ways.

Grace showed me to a restroom down the hall and stood guard as I freshened up. Then she led me back to the break room. "Good night, Jen." Her voice was soft. "Try and get some sleep, okay? There will be an officer up front if you need anything."

She turned off the light and closed the door.

In other words, stay put and don't try something stupid like running or hunting for Tom. Big brother is watching. With a deep sigh, I laid down on the lumpy cot, and chose not to think about the many drunk and disorderdly bodies who had used it before me.

I lay awake for some time trying to send telepathic messages to Tom. Whether it had any effect, I wasn't sure. It didn't feel that way. I tried a prayer, but it seemed to bounce off the ceiling back into my head. The room at last turned fuzzy as I slipped into a now-too-familiar chasm of dreamless sleep.

I WOKE TO the sound of the station's coffee pot groaning over doing its duty. The smell of coffee grounds filled my nostrils.

"Good morning." Mercedes shook a bag of sweetener, and then grabbed the pot as remaining droplets hissed on the hot plate.

I watched her stir her coffee, rubbed my eyes, and yawned.

"What time is it?"

She glanced at the wall clock. "Eight oh-five. You must have been tired. You were dead to the world." Her smile was as saccharin as what she sprinkled into her coffee. She was obviously playing the role of nice cop today, hoping I'd rely on her. I wasn't buying it. It fit her as well as a secondhand-store sweater, stretched in all the wrong places.

"Can I see Tom now?"

"You keep calling him that, but he claims his name is Travis." She sat down and sipped her coffee. "Want some?"

I rubbed my hands across the back of my shoulders and my neck. "I told you. That's the name I knew him by. Do we have to go over it all again?"

Her sweet look faded. "Not now. Let's get you cleaned up a bit, and then some coffee and food in your belly. Maybe then your mood will change."

She grabbed the bag of a few clothes I'd purchased at Walmart and led me to the locker room showers. She sat on one of the benches and held vigil while I bathed. As the hot water untwisted my aching muscles, I thought of the shower in the bomb shelter. And Tom. Where was he? Had he spent the night in a jail cell? I hoped he was okay and they hadn't roughed him up. Then, I heard his voice in my head. *Don't worry about me.* He had been on the edge of the law before and crossed over a few times. Yeah, Tom would be okay. But would I?

Grace was in the break room when Mercedes and I returned. She pulled breakfast tacos out of a bag. The savory aroma permeated my nose. My stomach responded with a huge growl.

I devoured two, hardly chewing them, as Grace set up her laptop. She shot me a sugary smile. "Well, shall we begin, again?"

I sighed and leaned back in the chair, my arms and legs

[168]

crossed. "If we must." I waved my hand and took a deep drink of coffee. "Fire away."

In flat tones, I re-answered all their questions. Mercedes stood, her face twisted in a scowl. "Okay, Grace. Let's start making phone calls." She pointed at my nose. "You wait here. The morning paper's over there."

I sat in the break room and read through the local paper. I did the jumble puzzle and the crossword of the day. Policemen filtered in, nodded, grabbed coffee and left again. I knew better than to ask any of them about Tom. But I strained my ears for his voice. I felt alone and on edge. I needed his strength. Mine was waning rapidly.

I stretched my fingers in front of me then tapped them on the table. It was way too quiet. Maybe they were all busy and had forgotten I was in here. A thought flashed across my brain.

Should I make a dash for it? Find a back exit? No. They'd stop me. Then, I would be arrested for real.

I drummed my fingers some more and stared at the second hand on the wall clock. Stay strong, I told my psyche. Don't let them wear you down. No matter what.

Mercedes came in at 11:15 to escort me back to the examining room.

"Well, we are getting somewhere now." She pulled over a chair. "Luckily, since it's been only a week since you were declared 'probably deceased, pending further investigation'"—she held up her fingers as quotation marks—"there's no probate court documents or inheritance papers to reverse. No death certificate yet to nullify as false."

I leaned in on my elbows. "That's good, right?"

"Yep." She sipped from her can of Coca-Cola. "Here's even better news. Your credit cards have not been deactivated nor your bank accounts closed, though they were in suspension and being monitored for activity."

I leaned forward. "Were?"

"We have convinced them you are now alive and found. Your bank has agreed to wire you one hundred dollars for bus fare and a meal. Our department doesn't have the funds for two tickets."

"Two?" My chest tightened. Was Tom coming?

"One for me. Protocol."

The word popped my bubble. I hated that word.

"You must be accompanied then turned over to the authorities in Fort Worth."

My eyes popped open, as did my mouth. Oh, no. That meant more questions. "Will they detain me as well?"

She cocked her head. "Look. The good news is by the time you get there, you should be able to have access to your money. New cards will be reissued to you within a few days."

"It doesn't answer—"

"I haven't finished." Mercedes shifted in her seat. She went on to explain that since forensics had determined the crash as "suspicious," a hearing to determine whether my demise, if proven, had been a suicide or an accident had been set for the next Thursday.

I half-listened, still thinking about what lay ahead in Fort Worth. I twisted the foil that held my breakfast taco. They weren't telling me the whole truth. Why?

Mercedes continued, flipping through her handwritten notes. "Your life insurance has not yet processed a claim, their actions pending that verdict, and according to your agent, underwriting was still trying to discover who could be claimed as your beneficiary." She peered at me like a school vice principal.

I gave her a sheepish shrug. "I hadn't updated my will or policy since my husband, Robert's, death." *Or supposed death.*

She remained silent and shuffled through her notes again.

I looked down at the white mark on my ring-less left hand. What had I been doing? I had been thinking only of Tom. I was still for all intents and purposes a new widow. I should still be mourning, not yearning for another man's arms. I felt adulterous. A wave of dizziness swooshed over me. My cheeks became icy, my palms clammy.

Mercedes' chair screeched as she scooted it to get up. "I'll be back in a few."

She closed the door softly, but the click blared in my ears. I buried my head in my arms. God, I wanted to go back in time. If I'd never gone to Bob's Burgers for that stupid cheeseburger...

CHAPTER TWENTY-THREE

GRACE ENTERED, JUGGLING her trusty laptop, a glass of water, and a writing tablet. "I'm going to sit with you while I make some calls. This way you can listen in and answer any questions that arise. Let's start with your apartment complex."

I straightened in my chair and nodded. "Yes, good. Please." If I'd had ruby slippers I'd have clicked them together and chanted, "There is no place like home." I envisioned my sofa, my own bed, my books, even the stray cat. I hoped he was still hanging around.

With her cell phone in her ear, her eyes darted over the screen, one hand swishing the computer mouse in small, sharp moves.

I bit my lip as she spoke with the management of my building. "Oh, that's good news." She nodded at me. "You say her personal effects are still part of a police investigation since, as of yet, her body has not been found?" She gave me a thumbs up. "Well, guess what? It's turned up in Canyon, Texas, with a pulse, no less." She laughed into the receiver.

If it had been anyone else, I may have laughed as well.

Grace's fingers clicked across her laptop's keyboard.

Occasionally she asked me a question, showed me her screen, then pulled up more information. It freaked me out how much of my life was accessible on the Internet.

"We have special clearances. But a lot of it is public record. You have to be careful these days."

Tom had been right. I was glad I'd given them my real name and told the truth. The more Grace's research confirmed what'd I said, the nicer she became.

She called my office and spoke directly with a very surprised Mr. Abernathy. Tsk, tsk. Poor man. He had lost two employees back to back. Being the meticulous OCD accountant, he never could tolerate chaos. I sat back, contented to listen to her end of the conversation. I wasn't ready to speak with him, or anyone else in that dungeon yet.

Just when my stomach was feeling empty, Mercedes brought us lunch and iced tea. She presented a stack of papers transcribed as my testimony.

I again pushed the papers away. "I said I wouldn't sign unless..."

Mercedes' eyes narrowed, their blackness deepened. She shoved them closer and wiggled the pen. "If you don't, you will be under arrest for aiding and abetting."

I gulped. "But he kidnapped me."

A sneer crossed her lips. "And you refuse to press charges or give us information about him."

I locked my elbows on the table. "Because I don't know who he is."

Mercedes leaned across and squared her eyes to mine. "Then why do you insist on protecting him?"

I slumped to the chair, my fingers crossed over my eyes. I silently counted to three, then lowered them.

Grace pulled a chair next to mine. She took one of my hands. With the other, I wiped a tear before it dripped down my cheek.

"Honey, what you are going through is understandable. Really."

I looked at her, seeking out sincerity in her eyes. I saw a glimpse of it.

"It's called Stockholm Syndrome. Out of pure self-defense, you begin to identify with your kidnapper. You develop a loyalty to them. They get you thinking they're protecting you, not detaining you for some foul purpose yet to come. It's a mind-game they play." She peered into my face. "You know, to keep you in their control, so you let down your guard."

I unclenched my teeth. "Really? This happens a lot?"

Grace patted my hand. "It happens a lot. The ol' cat and mouse."

The warmth of Tom's breath and the stone-strength of his arms filled in my mind, then guilt over betraying Robert surfaced. "I was falling for him," I said to the table in front of me.

Mercedes sat down and gazed at me. "Yeah, we know. Sly dog. And good looking to boot."

I raised my eyes to her, pleading for the truth. "He said he cared. He said he loved me."

They both nodded. Grace replied, "They usually do. That way you'll do what they want."

Mercedes tapped the pen across the signature line. I grabbed it and held it in my hands. Then I set it down again. "No. No. It was more than that. He, Travis, helped me escape the Chinese thugs, and then the drug lords. He took care of me in the desert. He—"

"—was a conniving, manipulative weasel," Mercedes finished. "Trust us, we see it all the time." She handed me the pen. "Now, sign."

I bit my lip as the teardrops slipped down my cheeks onto the paper. I hovered the pen above the signature line. A large portion of my heart and my mind wouldn't accept that Tom, even if he was now Travis, had manipulated me. I'd thought so in the beginning, but too much had passed between us. Yet I knew there was something he still wasn't telling me. "This still is not stating that I am pressing charges, right?"

Grace and Mercedes exchanged glances. Grace spoke first. "Right. It's just your acknowledgement that this is your testimony about what happened."

Mercedes finished the thought. "However, we still have enough to hold him until further investigations are completed, and to possibly book him."

I sighed and sent the lump back down my throat. "I understand. But I don't want him to ever think it was because of me. And, I won't testify against him in court. Ever."

Graced touched my shoulder. "When the dust clears and you're able to separate yourself from the emotion of what's happened, call them." She handed me a State Attorney General's pamphlet on victim's rights. A phone number was scrawled on it. "That's my cell. I'm here, too, in case you just want to talk."

"Okay. Thanks." I meant it. I looked first at one then the other. "Please, can't I just tell him goodbye?"

Mercedes sighed and rose from the chair. She shoved it so hard it rattled against the table. "Geez," she scowled. She left the room, shaking her head.

I turned to Grace, my eyes still holding the question.

She patted my hand. "No, sweetie. It's not allowed. Sorry."

I bit my lip so much it bled. "Why?" I gulped.

"It just isn't."

I grabbed her sleeve. "He is okay, right?"

Grace shoved a tissue box toward me, clucked her teeth, and left the room as well.

The door clicked, echoing against the bare walls.

Once again I was alone, in a confined place, and nothing was in my control. The story of my life. When would this madness ever end?

CHAPTER TWENTY-FOUR

THE DOOR OPENED with a clamor. Mercedes stood there in full uniform, her police cap half shading her face.

"We've coordinated with the Fort Worth police to get you safely home. I'm to escort you by squad car to Amarillo, then by bus to Fort Worth. A female officer will intercept you at the other end and take you to headquarters for more questioning."

I plastered on a smile. "Great. I can hardly wait to be grilled for another few hours." I got up and walked over to her, my hands folded around my waist. In unison our steps clicked down the narrow hall. In the main squad room, Officer Juarez flipped through a clipboard. When he saw me approach, he tipped his fingers to his head. "Good luck, Mrs. Westlaw."

I shot him a sarcastic grin.

In the squad car, I asked Mercedes, "I have one question. If I was supposedly in so much danger I had to have my death faked, isn't that going to put me in even more jeopardy now to suddenly return alive?"

She shook her head. "We're still trying to sort out his story. No one's convinced you ever *were* in any danger."

I twisted to face her, my eyes so wide they stretched my forehead. "What do you mean?"

Mercedes looked straight ahead. "We think this guy may be, uh, delusional." She leaned her head toward me and looked at me out of the corner of her eye. "You may have been one lucky lady to get away from him when you did."

I shook my head. "No, no. I don't believe that. He was smart enough to fake my death. He set it up, switched the cars. Arranged the room in a basement. Wired the cameras and sensors."

She turned toward me. "So?"

"That all took planning and intelligence. Not exactly delusional behavior, is it?"

"I'm not a psychologist. Are you?" By the look on her face, it was a rhetorical question.

I shook my finger at her. "Mae Lin and her goons were real enough. The gas station in New Mexico? Trust me. That was real."

Mercedes shrugged, the edges of her lips curled down a bit. "Maybe so. Sometimes these nutcases suck other low-lives into their vortex of deceit. You have to admit his story is a bit, well, fanciful."

"But someone did shoot at us. A bullet was wedged in the motel room wall."

"Maybe it was the drug lords giving you two a warning."

"So you all believe that part. About the shack in New Mexico. And Travis protecting me in the desert to get me to safety."

She shifted in the seat and looked out the car window. "All I know is I'm to get you on a bus. Perhaps, by the time you arrive in Fort Worth, the Metroplex investigators will have some answers."

She obviously didn't want to continue this conversation. It would be a long ride back to Fort Worth if I pursued it further. Maybe the authorities in the Metroplex would be more open to believe what Tom had said and done. I had to admit his methods may have been unorthodox, but I couldn't doubt his motives. Forget the Stockholm Syndrome garbage. He had cared for me, and I for him. I already missed him horribly. *Sorry. Robert, but you were the one who lied to me. Not Tom.*

I switched subjects. "Promise me you'll will try to find Marisol and Monica."

She glanced at me, her head wobbling to the rhythm of the car's tires over the road. "I wish I could. Needle in a haystack. Maybe, if the one you say is Marisol delivers a baby..." She shrugged, leaving her thought to dangle.

"But that could be seven months or so from now. She could be anywhere by then."

She gave me an uh-huh look.

I blinked back tears and stared out the squad car window.

After that, our conversation was sporadic and sparse. Mercedes had not lived up to her name in my book. But I silently swore to the Almighty and creation, as soon as I got my life straightened out, I'd do everything I could to find Monica and Marisol. Then I'd track down Tom.

ALL THE WAY back on the bus, my thoughts solidified into one goal. I'd spread the word, however I could, to whoever would listen, about the plight of these young immigrant women. I knew it happened every day. That didn't matter. In fact, it made me even more determined to stop the other Monicas and Marisols out there from getting into the same mess. Maybe Robert, if he was alive at all, was somehow involved in it all. Maybe he was undercover, trying to stop it, too.

In the din of the bus' engine as it traveled toward Fort Worth, I made a vow to God. I whispered, "You put me through this for a reason, right? This human trafficking has to stop. Show me how, Lord. I'll be a better believer. I'll go to church and read the Bible. Just show me how."

A strange peace washed over me. It was more than an aftermath calm, now that I'd been released from the whirlwind storm and was headed back home. No, this was something deeper, more permanent. I wished I had the Bible Tom had given me in the concrete room. I wondered where it was now, and the rest of the things in those backpacks. I prayed God would let some needy soul find them.

I closed my eyes and pushed my head against the back of the scratchy Greyhound seat. For the first time in a long while, a sense of purpose coursed through my veins. At last, I'd found a hush in the storm, a ray of hope piercing through the thick, ominous clouds of grief which had encompassed me for so many months.

I'd discovered the ability to love once more, and to begin to forgive—Tom for manhandling me in the beginning, Robert for lying about who he was. Now, I had to forgive myself for the intense feelings I had for them both. Perhaps they were cut of the same cloth. Maybe I had been suckered in twice. But there it was. It didn't matter.

What mattered was I could now reach out beyond my little hunched up world and possibly make a difference. And I had only one person to thank for that. This mystery man named Tom, or Travis, or whoever he was, who'd jumpstarted my dead heart. He'd heard my silent screams.

I felt like a chick bursting out of an egg. I now had something to live for—a goal, a reason to propel myself beyond my next breath and reach beyond my personal sorrow to help someone else on this planet. The dirt had been cleared off of me. I no longer crouched two stories underneath the world. My life had begun, again.

I prayed with all my might Tom's wouldn't end anytime soon. I owed him that much, and more.

PART TWO

Life After Death

Jen begins a journey to find the trafficked girls. But in the process she finds something else — a secret which further endangers the girls' lives, Tom's, and hers.

As Tom once told her, she must first save herself.

CHAPTER ONE

AN IGOR-LIKE voice whispered in my head, "We have ways to make you talk."

I stood on the threshold of a sterile room, deep in the bowels of the Fort Worth Police Department downtown. The space contained only a small sink, metal cabinet, stool, and examining table. My mind leapt to forensic examiners, surgical instruments, and syringes.

On the table was folded the way too familiar blue and white dotted robe, one-size-fits-none. My story had already been examined inside and out through two hours of questioning. Now they were going to examine my body?

The female police officer, her badge said Washington, cleared her throat. "Take your clothes off and put on the robe."

"All of them? Now? With you here?"

She wedged herself between me and the door, legs straddled and arms crossed. "Uh-huh. Protocol, part of the job." Her face softened into a semi-smile. "Don't worry, honey. I've seen it a thousand times before."

I've never undressed and robed so fast in my life.

I shut my eyes and tried to find my breath, dreading what was going to happen next. Frisk me? Probe me? Truth serum? I squirmed onto the table and wrapped the robe further around my knees. My feet felt like ice cubes. A shiver ran from them all the way to my shoulders.

Officer Washington turned my clothes inside out and shook them, felt the hems, and then hung them on a hook. She shot me a grin but didn't move another muscle until there was a tap on the door. Then she opened it and moved aside.

A doctor entered. Thank goodness she was a woman, too. "The police have assigned me to examine you."

"Why?"

She took the stethoscope from around her neck and put the ends in her ears as she gave me a curious glare. "To make sure you're okay, of course." She nodded to the officer, who then slipped out the door.

She was too thin. Her hair appeared a bit unruly, as if she permanently lived in between chaos and sleep deprivation. But her eyes were warm. I wish I could have said the same for her medical instruments.

She was silent as she tapped and prodded, other than stating matter of fact commands such as, "Breathe deep. Again. Cough. Does that hurt?"

I returned the favor with my own one word responses.

She touched my feet, eyed me with curiosity again, and tenderly treated them with Betadine antiseptic, antibiotic ointment, and fresh bandages. Then she brought over a syringe and a vial of liquid. I scooted back and drew my legs in.

"It's a tetanus shot, just in case." She winked at me as she filled the syringe tube. "It won't hurt much." She edged over to my left side and raised the robe's sleeve to my shoulder.

Right. I turned my face to the wall as she dabbed my arm with alcohol and plunged the needle into my flesh.

At last she stopped punching and probing, scribbled a few notes, and then peered at me through her reading glasses. Her face etched into an empathetic expression. "You can expect to feel out of sorts. You've been through some rather harrowing experiences."

I shook off her comments and squared my eyes to hers. "I feel fine. Really. In fact, I actually feel better than I have in..."

She held up her hand. "Nevertheless, you need to take it easy for a while. Let the dust settle."

I gave her a "whatever" look.

She leaned toward me. "You're pumped up on survival adrenaline. You have not eaten right. You haven't slept well. You're still showing signs of dehydration." She extended a bony finger for each point she made. "I recommend your primary doctor do a complete lab work-up on you. Check for parasites, bacteria. Not to mention fungus and vitamin deficiency."

Her words slapped like ice water on to my face. I swallowed hard and nodded. My thoughts returned to the oatmeal-colored water I drank in New Mexico during my brief encounter with the drug lords.

Then, Marisol's and Monica's faces materialized in my mind. I saw them disappearing in the back of that truck, pleading for me to take them with me. What medical care would they ever get? I squinted my eyes and looked at the ceiling to control my emotions.

She patted my knee. "Promise me you will make an appointment in the next few days."

I took a deep breath and nodded rapidly. "I will. Promise."

"Good. You can get dressed now." She turned to leave the room, stopped, and then added, "You will probably have nightmares. That's normal. Your mind has a lot to process."

I blinked and stared at the floor. "I know. It's all still a whirr." My voice squeaked as I gulped back tears.

The doctor pulled her hand from the doorknob and walked back to the examining bench. She grabbed a pad. "I'm going to give you a prescription for fifteen anti-anxiety tablets. Just in case. I suggest you fill it and have it handy. These things have a tendency to surface suddenly. If you get dizzy, feel your chest tighten, or become short of breath, take one. If you get no relief within fifteen minutes, call your doctor or 911. Don't take two."

I nodded. Her voice softened. "Look, don't let them push you, okay?" She motioned with her head at the door. "If they want to talk to you any more, tell them I said not for a week or so."

I raised my eyebrow. "And they'll agree to that?"

She shrugged, whipped off a sheet of paper from her prescription pad, and wrote on the back. "Here, take this."

I took it and saw it was a phone number. I knitted my brows. "What's this?"

"It's my cell. Call me anytime." She squeezed my shoulder. "I mean that, okay? Any time." She emphasized the word "any" with another squeeze.

I tapped the piece of paper across my palm. "Thank you. I think I'm okay, but if anything begins to bubble up..."

She winked. "Good. Take care."

She slipped out of the room. I dangled my bare legs off the examination table and stared at the speckled linoleum, then the bare walls, and dark brown rubber baseboard. Part of my mind agreed with what she'd said would happen and I needed to prepare for it. But the rest of me refused to believe it. Tom had given me the gift of feeling alive again. Marisol and Monica had provided me the gift of purpose. God? Well, I figured He was in it all as well, calming the storm just as He had done in the Bible.

I whispered under my breath as I stared at the sterile room. "Where are you, Tom? When will I see you again?" I swallowed hard. I needed him, but so did those girls. I prayed, "Lord, help me find Tom, so he can help me find them."

There was a knock on the door, then it cracked open. "Mrs. Westlaw?"

I grabbed the examining robe close to me. "Yes?"

Officer Washington entered. "I'm afraid I will need to escort you out of the building."

"Why?"

She leaned against the door and heaved her chest. Her badge flickered in the fluorescent light. She snorted. "Because the reporters have descended like vultures."

I slid off the table. "What reporters?"

She crossed her dark muscular arms. "Honey, you're front page news. Dead yesterday, now alive." She waggled a long finger at me. "That doesn't happen every day."

"Guess not."

She stared at me, one eyebrow cocked. A few uneasy moments of silence passed. Finally, I uttered the obvious. "I need to get dressed."

Her lips raised to one side. "Uh-huh. That would be a good idea." She shifted her weight and planted her feet to the floor, her body blocking the exit.

"And you are supposed to stay in here with me again?"

She tapped her temple. "Smart lady."

I turned my back to her. My hand shook as I tried to clasp my bra. I pulled on my panties, jeans, and T-shirt in three seconds flat.

Officer Washington escorted me by my elbow down the hall to the police garage. Another officer waited by a squad car. He looked very young and his nervous mannerisms screamed rookie. I scoffed. "I hope he has his driver's license."

Officer Washington's lips curled to one side. "Yeah. Got it last week from what I heard."

My shoulders relaxed a bit as I shot her a grin. She had a lot more wit and spunk than Mercedes. Things might be looking up.

To my left I could see the reporters huddled like racehorses waiting for the starting gates to open. Bulbs flashed, lights flicked on and a hundred voices all began at once.

The policewoman pulled me to her and yelled in my ear. "Ignore them. Don't make eye contact. Just get in the vehicle." She opened the door, placed her hand on the top of my head, and pushed me down into the back seat.

I sat, my hands laced in my lap between my knees as the din of voices continued, hardly lessened by the steel walls of the squad car. Officer Washington slipped in beside me and tapped on the black, webbed metal cage separating us from our rookie driver. "Go."

The reporters stormed the car as soon as the engine started, a sea of microphones and eyes pressed against the glass. I turned my face away and closed my eyes.

"Go!" Officer Washington said again, her tone more terse. With a screech of tires, we were off.

As the car left the garage, I looked back. Several of the news media dashed after us. One still had his hand on the door handle. Eventually, they all dropped away. I slammed my back against the upholstered leather and breathed.

I heard a chuckle. "Get used to it, girl. They aren't going away for long."

She was right. When we pulled into the gated community where I lived, even more of the press lay in wait. I saw news vans from all three local stations. Their twisted antennas stretched high into the air. Several men had cameras hunched over their shoulders.

"What's the gate code?" the male officer's voice bellowed from the front seat. Those were the first words he'd spoken.

"Huh?" I thought for a moment, racking my brain beyond the past few days. It seemed at least a year had passed. "It was 9333 star. I guess it still is."

His window lowered. Immediately, crews and reporters rushed forward, their questions battering me. The officer waved back microphones with his hands. He cursed at them to move away. A few did.

Officer Washington jerked off her jacket and covered my head. She pulled me down on to the seat, my head in her lap. "Lay low."

The car jerked ahead. Then I heard the bump of the tires over the gate track. The jacket's liner stuck to my mouth and my nostrils. It smelled of musky perfume.

"Whew. That was insane," the driver's voice called back to us. The jacket came off my head. I combed my fingers through my hair and peered over the front seat. "Turn right, then go to the third building. Mine's in the first entry, second floor."

We pulled into the section where my unit was located. Everything looked normal. A girl walking her dog stopped, jerked the leash, and turned abruptly in the opposite direction. Two guys leaning over the bed of a truck stopped their conversation to stare at the cop car.

Officer Washington opened the door for me and the two of them escorted me upstairs. They tapped on my door and another uniformed female opened it. She was petite with a plastic grin.

"I'm Federal Agent Bonita Hernandez. Welcome home." She motioned me inside.

I entered and looked around. Everything was in order, yet it wasn't. It looked almost too neat and tidy. Then it hit me. I swung around to Agent Hernandez. "You've searched the place?"

She closed the door and stood straddle-legged in the foyer of my tiny living room. "The FBI did. Dusted for fingerprints, too. But I've cleaned most of it up." From her proud smile I knew it was considered above and beyond the call of duty.

I gave her a weak grin and rubbed the back of my neck. "Thanks."

"You rest. We'll get what's left of it tomorrow."

"Tomorrow? Are you coming back?"

Officer Washington coughed into her hand, and then handed the agent a clipboard. She nodded, flipped through the papers and signed off on the police forms. "That should do it, then."

The black policewoman retrieved her paperwork, turned back to me, and winked. "Well, I'm outta of here. Good luck, honey."

With that, my first protector disappeared out the door. I felt a quiver wiggle up from my toes, like when my mother left me at daycare for the first time. Wait—how silly. This was my apartment. My refuge I thought I'd never see again. I turned to the Fed. "Well?"

Agent Hernandez flipped the deadbolts to the locked position and planted her feet into my carpet. "I'm staying. No arguments." Her tone meant business, and she had a gun.

"Fine, stay a while. I am too tired to argue."

"Oh, I'm staying for more than just a while." She motioned to my tan couch. "Have a seat. By the way, your answering machine has been going nuts."

I turned to look on the side table. The red light flashed twenty-six. My box was full of messages.

"Go ahead. We've already heard them all."

"We?"

"Your government, who has assigned me to be your bodyguard

[191]

until everything calms down." She shoved a thumb at the front door.

I snatched the pad and pen I always kept by the phone, inhaled a deep breath, and pushed the button. My heart wanted there to be a message from Tom, but my brain knew better.

Some were well-wishers I barely knew. Six calls were from the office. More from local news anchors. Five were requests for my appearance on talk shows. "Already?"

My guardian smirked. "Oh, trust me. It has only just begun."

The last message was a Canyon police sergeant stating Travis Walters had escaped custody while being transported to Fort Worth for indictment. He was yet to be found. If he tried to contact me, would I please let them know?

A brief smirk crossed my face.

She tapped the machine with her fingernail. "That is another reason why you're stuck with me for a while." She laced her thumbs through her belt. "I am your constant companion, *mija*. At least for the next few days. Just in case your friend decides to get in touch with you."

I stretched out on the couch. "You might as well leave, then. He won't. He told me so."

She shifted her feet. One eyebrow arched high, touching the wrinkles in her forehead. "Really? And when was that?"

I refused to look at her. "Before we were taken in. In Canyon, at the motel."

"Doesn't matter. You're not allowed out that door"—she shoved her finger at my vestibule— "without me glued to your side. Unless you *want* to get locked up. Got it?"

"Yes'm." I rolled my eyes and rubbed my forehead.

Déjà vu. Captured again. I wondered if she'd bring me Yogurt Tree smoothies. Doubtful. Maybe she'd at least leave the lights on tonight.

I sat up to face her. "Is this considered house arrest? What are my charges?"

She stood her ground. "Mrs. Westlaw. Someone kidnapped you, drugged you, took you across state lines, shot at you. You need protection right now and I am it."

I laid my head back and nodded at her badge. "Why the Feds?"

"If even a smidgen of your testimony is accurate, this is beyond local involvement."

I crossed my legs and dangled my foot. "So, y'all think what Tom said about my husband's, let's say, covert activities, is true, then?"

"I can't tell you anything at this point." She pressed her lips together and crossed her arms over her chest in response.

I dropped my hands in my lap. "Right."

So, here was yet another person who couldn't give me details. I was getting quite tired of being kept in the dark, pun intended. I massaged my temples. "My head is killing me. Can I have some water and Advil? A bottle's in the kitchen cabinet near the glasses."

Agent Hernandez released me from her stare with a nod of satisfaction, turned and went into my kitchen. I heard a cabinet door open, the clink of glass, and then the rumble of ice cubes in the freezer bin. She called out through the pass-through. "I am assigned to you for your own protection, so get used to it." She nodded at my kitchen window. "Besides, you'll need me to help keep those reporters away. A few have already filtered through the gates."

I craned my neck to peer out the vertical slats in my sliding door's blinds. There were cameras and about twenty people across the apartment parking lot. I got up and pulled the cord, collapsing a few of the blinds for a better view. A female reporter in a navy business suit was interviewing my neighbor, Becky. Two others were talking to their cameramen. Several were seated on the curb, legs stretched out, pounding on their laptops with cell phones cocked on their shoulders. Several apartment dwellers milled around the perimeters.

One man looked up. His shout rang out. "There she is." Heads turned and the small crowd rushed across the pavement. Others came out of nowhere and ran toward my unit. I heard thundering footsteps on the stairs.

Hands grabbed me and pulled me out of view. "Are you nuts?"

Quick bangs sounded on my front door. Voices yelled out my name. Then more pounding. The agent had her backside to my door as if to barricade me from the mob of reporters in case they broke the door down.

It was more than I could bear. All the events of the past few days crashed on top of me. I covered my ears with my hands, ran to the bathroom, and slammed the door shut behind me. I paced back and forth a few times, and then folded onto the toilet seat. I rocked back and forth, my arms wrapped around me. Would I ever live a normal life again?

"Dear God. How am I going to survive this? I want my solitude. I want my quiet, mournful life back." I couldn't believe I'd just admitted it. Impossible. I'd seen too much to go back. The vow I'd made on the bus echoed in my thoughts.

I changed my prayer in midstream. I hoped, under circumstances of duress, it would be allowed. "God? Help me think this through. How can I find Marisol and Monica with those reporters hounding me and a federal agent watching my every move? Tom would know. But he will never come for me now. They might even evict me from my apartment if this doesn't cease. Oh, God, then what? Please hear my prayer. Amen."

An idea—no, a command clear as day—came to me. It entered

my brain from some outside source stronger than my own thoughts. "Use them. Use the reporters."

My back muscles tensed with a surge of purpose. I wiped my cheeks, blotted my lower eyelids, dabbed on some makeup, and combed my hair. I grabbed a fresh blouse and slacks from my closet, and spritzed some lavender body spray into my armpits. With one more look in the bathroom mirror, I whispered, "Okay, you can do this," and opened the bathroom door.

With locked shoulders, I strutted down the hall to the living room, my eyes zeroed in on the front door.

Agent Hernandez held up her hand. "Wait. You can't."

"Watch me." I shoved her arm aside and took the deepest breath I could muster. Then, I grabbed the doorknob.

CHAPTER TWO

I HAVE SEEN the rush of paparazzi on the news when a celebrity hits town or does something outlandishly bad. I never fathomed I'd be their victim. The onslaught was mind-boggling and threw all my senses into overload.

The crowd of reporters had multiplied in just a few minutes like dividing cells in time-lapsed biology films. A cacophony of voices yelled at me simultaneously, crashing against my ears. Cameras flashed and clicked. The shove of humanity bumped against me, jostling me against the door. My shoulder blades ached from the pressure and I couldn't raise my arms. At last, I took as deep a breath as I could muster while being pinned in against the crowd of bodies and screamed at the top of my lungs, "Stop!" In a nanosecond, silence reigned.

"I have a brief announcement." I swallowed the bile which had bolted into my throat, burning my tonsils and tongue. "I was kidnapped, yes. By a man from work."

Questions began again, the mob pushed forward. I raised my hands before they pinned me again. "But wait. While I was in his custody, I witnessed something heinous."

A din of voices and microphones were shoved in my face. I pushed them away. "Please, I'll explain. Just, back up, okay?"

Agent Hernandez appeared at my side, our shoulders touching. Her arm splayed across my chest in a gesture to protect me. "Back off, people." Her authoritative bellow made it easy for everyone to hear her. "Now."

A few precious inches of space emerged between me and the first row of wide-eyed reporters, camera lenses, and mics. I smiled at her and nodded a thank you. "I guess I do need you here."

Her tensed jaw twitched. "Make it short. Don't say much."

I inhaled a pocket of fresh air. "That's better. Thank you. Now, as I was saying—"

Immediately the questions began again as more voices pursued their own train of thoughts. "Tell us what it felt like?" "Did you know him well?" "Are you lovers?" "Are you going to return to your job?" "Did he hurt you?" "How did the police find you?"

I stared at them, my mouth clamped shut. I remembered one of my elementary school teachers using silence to command the room. I hoped it would work. To my surprise, it did. The butting, shoving for position, and yelling stopped. Then, it was my turn again.

"I said I have a brief statement. If you won't let me speak without interruption, then I'm going back inside." I pushed my hand behind me and rattled the doorknob. Again, the mob backed up in unison to give me space. Better.

One female reporter with big brown eyes and shiny long hair smiled. "Forgive us, Mrs. Westlaw. Please, what did you want to say?" Her microphone had FOX NEWS on it.

I stared at her, wide-eyed. "FOX News? I've made national news?"

Her expression warmed. "Yes."

My eyes caught the CNN logo on another mic, and then MSNBC on another, as well as several of the local TV stations' insignia. I recognized others from places like San Antonio and Houston, even Austin, the state capital.

The faces faded into a blur. All I saw were the news logos looming at me from long, black wands and round knobs inches from my face. Everything inside me shook. My mouth went dry. I closed my eyes. My knees buckled and I slid against the door as strong arms encircled my waist.

"Mrs. Westlaw?" Agent Hernandez's voice echoed.

"Give me a minute." I croaked out the words. "This is rather daunting."

There was a shuffle of feet. I realized the door to my apartment had opened when my back support vanished. My assigned bodyguard linked her arm into the crook of my elbow and pulled me inside. She slammed against the door and commanded, "Breathe."

I inhaled three times. Each effort let more air into my lungs. Clarity oozed back into my head.

"I repeat. Are you nuts?"

"Agent Hernandez, I want to tell them something about those girls."

"Why?" She craned her neck forward, invading my space.

My eyes locked with hers. "So maybe someone can find them. Please."

She knitted her brows as if the wheels were spinning in her brain. After a few seconds, she pushed me behind her and cracked open the door. "Give her five minutes, folks, to catch her breath. Then she'll make her statement."

"B...but?" I stammered.

She slammed the door and flipped both deadbolts again. She

pinned me against the wall of my tiny vestibule. "Hear me. Those illegal immigrant girls? Do not mention their names." Her finger thrust in my face. "Do not."

"Why?" I locked my chin.

"Do you want them to die?" She released her grasp on my elbow and jerked her head toward the door. "Give these reporters their names and it will be plastered all over the news across the nation. The coyotes will kill them rather than face exposure. Is that what you want?"

I stood there, hand to mouth. My eyes welled. I shook my head as one tear escaped and slid down my cheek. "No, no."

She backed off and stood, hands on her hips, displaying her FBI badge hooked onto her belt. It flickered in the overhead light of my miniscule foyer. "Next, they'll come after you to shut you up. Oh, you can be sure of it."

"Okay," I said. "What do I say?"

"Keep it vague. Say you don't recall a lot of what happened. Just say you want people to be aware of human trafficking, especially of illegal teens. You want to urge people to call their congressmen and report anything suspicious to their authorities."

I nodded.

Agent Hernandez pressed her hand on my shoulder. "Look. What you're doing is admirable. Really." A momentary softness eked through her face. "Just stay calm, state your facts, and then nudge me. I'll yank you back inside before they maul you."

I laughed. "Got it."

Straight-faced, she jerked her head quickly for me to move aside. She grabbed the doorknob, turned to me, and whispered, "One, two, three."

Immediately, the din level rose from murmurs to ear-piercing. Again, I was slammed against my own door as human bodies and recording devices inched in. Then, a loud shrilling whistle came from the direction of the stairs.

Everyone stopped and turned.

"Let the lady speak, for Pete's sake," a way too familiar masculine voice boomed.

I craned my neck, rising on tiptoes, but all I could see was a crown of curly black locks and an extended arm as it waved. The disc from a gold Rolex reflected the afternoon sun. Then he disappeared down the stairs.

So, Tom had not only escaped, he'd replaced his watch.

I felt my cheeks flush. My bodyguard looked at me and grinned. She knew it'd been Tom. *Shoot. Miss No-Poker-Face strikes again.*

"Arrogant idiot," Agent Hernandez scoffed, and then barked commands into her com. "Suspect spotted in stairwell. Team One, guard the complex exit. Team Two..."

Good luck. He'll slip away from y'all every time. Why had I worried?

In spite of the roar of the cameras and voices, the storm within me suddenly calmed.

CHAPTER THREE

TOM'S BRIEF PRESENCE steeled my nerve. He was alive and well, and he had found me. He'd find me again when all of this chaos of public scrutiny settled down. When the time came, my heart knew I'd leave with him without any argument. Wherever he was, that was where I wanted to be. Until then, I had a job to do, and it didn't involve an accounting cubicle in a basement office. My attention turned back to the reporters.

I yelled to the heads hovering around me. "I will make a statement and entertain no questions until I am through. That's the deal." Their attention returned to me, forgetting the brief escapade on the stairs. Good.

A few minutes seemed more than enough to tell the reporters about Marisol and Monica. Yet, on the other hand, days wouldn't have done their plight justice. I spoke slow and purposely, describing the shack and the conditions, but not divulging the number of women, their names, or their physical descriptions. I told them how we were let go after my coworker, Tom, had been allegedly forced to transport drugs, then how he had kept me safe and secure until we could hitch a ride into town. I also stated that he, in no way ever harmed me or mistreated me.

A male reporter, in his early thirties from what I gathered, asked me, "Why did he kidnap you in the first place?"

I smiled. "He said he was protecting me from shady characters whom, he was convinced, were responsible for my husband's fatal wreck last spring."

"Oh boy," Agent Hernandez said under her breath. She shifted her stance.

I gave her a quizzical look, then immediately knew I'd just handed over the utensil to open the proverbial can of worms. The shouting hoard of questions erupted again. Black, meshed microphones shoved toward me as the pelting of new questions began.

"He was delusional, then—is that what you are saying?"

"Uh, no." I shook my head and opened my mouth to explain. I was cut off by the next question which came from a woman to my left.

"Brenda, KTXB. Were you afraid for your life?"

"Where did he hide you?" Another reporter bellowed above the other voices.

One reporter shoved his microphone closer to me, arm stretched to where the cuffs of his shirt looked tauter than a rubber band. I expected the cuff button to pop off any second and shoot into the FOX newswoman's eye. "So are you saying your husband was murdered?"

"No. I have no evidence..."

A blonde in a tweed suit and fuchsia blouse shoved her mike in my face. "Did he sexually assault you?"

"NO!" I screamed above the din.

"That's all." Agent Hernandez stepped between the crowd and

me. She shoved me into my apartment as what seemed thousands of voices hurled at us in unison. She backed in, slammed the door, and flicked both bolts. "That," she pointed back with her thumb, "was stupid, girl. Stupid."

I curled up onto the couch, wasted of effort. "I know. Now. But at least I let some of the nation know what's happening to illegal teens."

She straddled her stance over me. "As I said. It's admirable, just not too wise. Wanna drink?"

With grateful eyes I pleaded a yes. "Sherry, in the kitchen pantry."

The agent smirked. "Coming right up."

I sipped my sherry, letting the liquid warmth trickle down my gullet as my bodyguard watched the local news. Not surprisingly, a good portion of it was about me. In a surreal way, it was like watching a movie of myself. My numbed brain wasn't really registering any of this stuff yet.

But my heart was anything but numb. All I could see was those curly black locks disappearing down the stairs. I could almost smell his citrus-musk cologne.

Why had he risked showing up with all of those reporters around?

Had he telepathically heard my prayer?

How had he escaped?

My mind flooded with questions and my heart with resolve. I knew I had no way of reaching Tom. But at least I knew he was alive and free. He'd find some way to get hold of me later. Of that I was certain. I just had to bide my time. He certainly wasn't going to risk another contact as long as this hunk of a female federal authority was attached to my hip, or reporters were camped out on the apartment's common areas day and night. No, his brief appearance had just been a signal.

He would wait it out. So could I.

ON TUESDAY, LIKE Rip Van Winkle after a hundred-year snooze, I woke to life again. A week had passed since I last saw Tom or heard his voice, other than in my dreams. Reporters no longer staked out my home, thanks to my apartment manager's repeated complaints. The phone had stopped ringing every fifteen minutes. My assigned bodyguards were less of a constant presence. But I knew I was still under constant surveillance by both them and the news media.

The stray cat slithered back onto my porch wanting food and attention. I received notice in the mail that my life insurance policy had been reinstated. So had my credit cards, though new numbers had been issued. I even had a driver's license now, as well as a settlement for my toasted Mazda for $17,582.47, which an agent deposited for me into my checking account. To the world of cyberspace and commerce, I existed once more. Dang, I supposed that meant I'd have to file my taxes.

I never thought I'd get tired of take-out, but after seven days of it, my whole system was out of whack. Delivery was prohibited, so I had to call it in and have a federal agent retrieve it. Over breakfast tacos I pleaded, "Please, let me go to the grocery store. All this eating out is playing havoc with my digestion."

My latest protector/delivery person, named Shelly, nodded and patted her stomach. "I've enough sodium the last two days to last me six months. You write up your list. I'll call and see if I can get permission."

Two hours later, I answered the door to find a familiar Hispanic woman on my stoop. I leaned against the door jamb, one eyebrow arched. "Well, Agent Hernandez. Long time no see—face-to-face—that is. What has it been? Three days?"

She humphed and gestured with a wave. "Car's waiting. You get to go yourself—with me."

The idea of having the freedom to see other than my four walls exhilarated me. With money to burn, I was the kid let loose at the carnival. I wandered aisles, drove my companion bonkers, and spent $326.92 on groceries, cosmetics, and "see-buys." I was only pestered by the press twice in the store and once in the parking lot as we loaded the bags of groceries. A definite improvement.

Afterward, I decided it was time to return the six messages the office had left on my answering machine. The operator put me straight through to my boss without any hesitation.

I refused my old job, which of course they had already filled. My boss stumbled over his words in relief.

"Legally, we had to offer it to you. I mean it wasn't your fault you didn't report in per policy. And you did have a history of exemplary work."

"I need time off to recover, both physically and mentally," I confessed. "I'm just not sure how long. It wouldn't be fair to take an undetermined amount of leave of absence. Just tell HR to pay me for my sick leave, vacation, and overtime."

His chair squeaked. "That is very generous of you, Mrs. Westlaw."

His sudden formality in addressing me made my stomach flip. I wondered if "Legal" was listening in.

"Of course, I probably won't sue you either." I let that statement dangle.

He cleared his throat. "For?"

I humphed. "For hiring a psychopath who likes to kidnap coworkers, and for not screening him properly, of course."

The chair squeaked again. I heard muffled whispers. I stifled my giggle. This was fun.

[205]

"Uh, let me check with the partners, but I am sure we can throw in the bonus we were going to offer you when your next anniversary came up in November. As I said, your work was—"

"Yes, I know. Exemplary." I swallowed down a burst of laughter. The firm never gave out bonuses. They were too bottom-line conscious. "But, just a bonus for all the harassment and horror I've been through?"

Silence. I counted to ten.

Another throat clearing sound came through the phone. "Would say..." His voice briefly faded then came back. "...Uh, $45,000 be fair?"

I decided to release the fish from the hook. In spite of my animosity for the job itself, I held very little for him. "That seems fair to me. Of course, I'll need it in writing. And I assume the figure is after taxes. Plus, I'd like you to pay my COBRA benefits and still contribute to my 401K for the next twelve months."

"Yes. Of course. It seems like a reasonable severance package. Good day, Mrs. Westfall. We will have Legal draw it all up along with your termination papers. You can expect that and the cashier's check by Fed Ex tomorrow."

"Good day, Mr. Abernathy."

I hung up and squeezed Tom Cat. "That, my friend, just bought me some breathing room and you more cat food."

MY DILEMMA WAS how to find the girls without endangering them. I'd received two calls from publicity agents asking if I wanted to write a book about my ordeal. The idea intrigued me. Maybe that would be one way to get my message out. Write my memoirs. I wasn't sure I was quite ready. However...maybe in a few months or so.

I replayed the messages from the reporters who wanted me to

interview for talk shows. That would be another way. I recalled Agent Hernandez's warnings. But I could keep it vague, and concentrate on social awareness. At least I might get people to call and want to help out. Maybe, since I had witnessed the horrors firsthand, it would be my foot in the door to agencies who dealt with this issue of human trafficking.

I wrote down the phone numbers to call each one. In a matter of hours, I was booked on a complimentary flight to New York, complete with private escort to a swanky hotel room. I was to appear on FOX Sunday, and do a taped interview with one of their well-known interviewers. Then on Monday, I was to appear live on the Today Show. The producers of a nighttime talk show in L.A. would make arrangements in another week or so, then get back to me.

I decided to try the local news first as a trial run. Channel 11 agreed to interview me in my apartment. At five minutes to ten the next morning there was a slight tap on my door. A middle-aged woman in business attire and a camera man stood on my stoop. "I'm Veronica Wells. This is Joe."

A man in jeans and a baseball cap lugging a black case gave me a wave. Behind him, Agent Shelly bounded up the stairs.

"Wait a minute. What's this about?" She flashed her badge at the reporter.

"They're here to interview me." I kept my voice nonchalant and steady.

Agent Shelly raised an eyebrow. "Uh, no they aren't."

I ushered the two inside. "Yes, they are." This time I was the one to close the door and flick the bolts. It didn't matter. I figured the Feds would hear the whole thing anyway. I was fairly certain my apartment was bugged. I asked the reporter to be seated, and then I poured glasses of ice water for them and one for myself.

"I have never done anything like this in my life," I admitted after a few gulps of fortifying H2O.

"Few people have. Their horrific stories make the news. You can't prepare for that."

She walked me through it all, and knew what questions to ask, when to stop the camera, and when to resume.

I thanked her profusely at the end. She smiled genuinely. "You did well. I hope they find those two girls, and the man who terrorized you."

"But he didn't. Really. I didn't give that impression, did I? He protected me."

The reporter turned to her cameraman. "Joe, I'll meet you in the van in a minute, all right?"

Joe nodded, packed up his gear, and shook my hand. "You did fine. Pleasure to meet you. Glad you're safe."

Veronica turned to me after he'd softly closed the door. "Jen. May I call you Jen?"

"Sure."

"Jen, I see trauma victims all the time in this business. Do you have someone who can talk you through this? If not, I know some names."

I waved her comment away. "Yes, I do. I know all about Stockholm Syndrome. It doesn't apply to me." I wanted to scream, *Tom is not crazy and neither am I.*

She patted my shoulder. "Good. It'll take time to sort through all that has happened to you. Don't rush it."

With a smile, she rose, smoothed her skirt, shook my hand, and left.

Agent Shelly, who had camped on the stairs leading into my unit, scowled at me as I motioned she could enter my apartment. The rest of the afternoon, she kept giving me the "look." I was obviously in detention. I felt like strapping on a penitent face and getting down on my knees to recite the 51st Psalm, just as I had in girl's school—well, sort of.

At last she divulged what had obviously been relayed through her earpiece. "Your little stunt cost you more quality time with me, lady. Congratulations."

"It's my apartment. I can invite whomever..."

"Not if you know what's good for you." She shook her finger at my nose. "Our job is to keep you safe. The other taxpayers are paying for this, you know. So why not give us all a break and cooperate, okay?"

I gave her a silent nod. But I was still going to New York.

The days dragged on while I waited to hear from the stations in New York. I decided to log a diary into my laptop while all the recent events were fresh in my head. It passed the time. But the more I wrote, the more anxiety crept back into my day. I couldn't sleep for more than two hours at a time. Normal apartment living noises, like my lead-footed neighbor upstairs, made me jumpy.

I fumbled through my desk to find the prescriptions the police doctor had given me. I sent Agent Shelly to get the real one filled, while I called the number scribbled on the back of the other. She answered in three rings, which surprised me.

"Doctor Jacobs? It's Jen. Jen Westlaw."

"Mrs. Westlaw. I am so glad you called. How are you?"

"It's starting to sink in." My hand quivered, as did my voice.

"Did you fill that prescription?" Her tone sounded maternal.

"Yes, I did. Just now. Do I take them any time?"

"No more than one of them four times a day, but yes. Just be careful, and do not drive or make any legal decisions."

"When will it stop?" My voice pleaded for her to say soon.

"Would you like the name of a counselor? I know a very good

one who specializes in trauma. It might help you, Jen, to sort through your experience."

I thought for a moment. "Would everything I say be kept confidential?"

"Yes, of course. It's the law."

"I agreed to go on talk shows."

She sighed deeply into the receiver. "Are you sure you're ready for that?"

"I thought I was. Now, I'm not sure. I did one interview for Channel 11. It was like opening Pandora's box. All the emotions just poured out."

"Jen, I'd advise against it from now on. Don't be the latest thing on the news. You don't need it."

I closed my eyes and felt strength surge back into my heart. "I know. But two other girls do."

"I'm not sure I follow..."

I sighed. "Doc. Thanks. I appreciate you letting me call. Really. If I need the counselor, I'll call back for the name and number."

I clicked off before she could respond. Rude of me, I know, but I was still a novice at how to act more assertively, and yet remain cool, calm, and in control. Anyway, I figured with these interviews, Tom would keep track of me. Maybe I could send him a cryptic message over the airwaves. But how? It would have to be an innocent remark that had no meaning to anyone else. Something he'd said or I'd said which related back to our experience. Something the Feds would not pick up on. Maybe about Snickers or Agritos.

I'd think about that... and how to convince these Feds to back off so I could travel.

CHAPTER FOUR

AGENT HERNANDEZ STOOD in my foyer. After ten minutes of bantering, she and Agent Shelly finally admitted no one could stop me from going to New York, or L.A. or anywhere else. I was not under arrest, but both of the Feds advised against it.

"You think, if I begin my public speaking career, I might be in danger?"

Agent Hernandez nodded. "There are lots of advocates against human trafficking, Jen. Non-profits, lobbyists. You don't have to fight this battle."

"I witnessed it. I have to tell what I saw."

She placed her strong hands on my shoulders. "We can't protect you. Unless you agree to come into WITSEC."

"Witness protection?" I took two steps backwards. "New name, new life? Like on the TV shows?"

"Yes." Agent Shelly chimed in. "Tell us everything you've held back. We'll relocate you and protect you. Then, when these coyotes are arrested, you can help us shove them into a deep, dark hole by testifying."

A thought gripped my heart. How would Tom ever find me then? "If I did, would it guarantee Tom, well, Travis to you, immunity?"

Agent Hernandez clucked and released her grip. "How do you know he's not knee-deep in it?"

I shook my head. "What?"

She stepped back and leaned against the wall. "Look. You said he told you he ran drugs for them that night."

"So?"

"So, they just let you two go in return?" The agent huffed. "Trust me. It doesn't work that way. They would've shot him in the head and let the buzzards find him, then they'd have trafficked you."

I wrapped my arms around my waist and stared outside my sliding glass door, not really seeing anything. "He wouldn't be involved in that."

Agent Shelly stepped into my line of vision. "How can you be so sure?"

I pointed to my chest. "My heart tells me so."

Agent Hernandez sighed. "Jen, hearts lie."

"Look, you two can gang up on me all you want. I *am* flying to New York. Now I'd like to take a nap." I walked down the hall to my bedroom and, once inside, slammed it shut.

I ARRIVED AT JFK International at 2:26 p.m., with new clothes in my bag thanks to a mega shopping spree with Becky. I wasn't sure why my bodyguards let us go alone, but I'd relished in the freedom. I bought two pair of shoes, seven outfits complete with jewelry, and had my hair styled in a more chic, New York-ish style. Surprisingly, only three reporters recognized me during our outing and I wasn't about to be interviewed via Smartphone tape-recording apps. We told them to shove off and they did. Having power over them felt good. My inner confidence dial increased a few notches.

Standing in front of the mirror in my plush room at the Waldorf Astoria, I had to admit the new tailored business suit and slightly feminine blouse also gave me a boost of self-assurance. So did the bling of the earrings dangling beneath the edges of my new cropped hairdo. Tomorrow I'd look put together and professional, even if I did say so myself.

A young woman called my room. She asked if I'd found the schedule which had been faxed to me. I located it on the desk in a sealed envelope with my name, next to a bouquet of yellow roses. "Did the studio send these?"

"Yes. And dinner in your room is on us. Order what you wish. The T-bone is succulent, by the way."

Yellow roses and T-bones? Was it because I came from Texas? How cliché. "Thank you. What am I to do now?"

"Rest. Tomorrow will be a full day."

She proceeded to go over the itinerary. The studio would pick me up at 5:45 a.m. What followed would be a blur of directions, makeup, advice, and rehearsed answers to questions before the Sunday morning five-minute segment, which was scheduled for 7:35 a.m., right after the news cap. Then, I would be given a tour of the studio and introduced to several other people. I was to wait in the green room with a catered brunch until around 10:00 a.m. before the taping of the other show.

The studio rep was professional, yet warm and caring. Together we walked through what would happen and how I should respond. After a half hour, I had exhausted every possible question my brain could muster, so we hung up. I sniffed the roses once more, poured myself a glass of Diet Coke from the mini fridge, and walked around my expansive, four-room dwelling, feeling like mini-celebrity.

I'd just slipped into the cushy white hotel robe and was preparing for a steamy bubble bath soak when the phone rang. A lady's voice was at the other end.

"Mrs. Westlaw? My name is Juanita and I am with the NHTRC."

"The what?"

"The National Human Trafficking Resource Center. How long are you going to be in New York?"

"Another day, I guess. I have an interview on FOX News, then a taping, and then another for the Today Show."

"Good. I'd like to drive up from D.C. and meet you tonight, if that is okay? Do you have dinner plans?"

"No. I was going to eat in my room." A thought hit me. "Do you want to join me here?"

There was silence. "Sure. Why not. That way we can speak in total privacy. I'll see you around eight o'clock. Okay?"

I hung up, and then realized I didn't know this woman from Eve. How naive of me. Did the National Human Trafficking Resource Center really exist? How had she gotten my number at the hotel? A brief chill surged through me.

Was this a plot by one of the operatives Tom worked for, or perhaps Mae Lin's group? Had my "Mother" just called me? My mind raced.

I opened my laptop and Googled NHTRC, which did indeed exist. But a nagging thought tugged at me. How did I know the woman coming to my room was from there?

I called the concierge and asked for the number that had just called my room. I dialed it and Juanita answered. My heart sank back into my chest.

"I'm sorry to bother you. I—I just wanted to make sure..."

"Mrs. Westlaw. I apologize. I should have explained. FOX News contacted me for a comment about your interview and gave me your information. They interviewed me about three months ago. They didn't tell you I'd call?"

"No." I sank into my hotel bed with relief. She sounded legit. I rubbed the perspiration from my left temple. "No matter. I'll see you at eight. You have my room number, right?"

AT FIVE AFTER eight, I answered a rap on my door. A young woman in a tailored business coat with ponytailed, black hair and beautifully chiseled cheekbones stood on the threshold. She extended her hand, then immediately two men busted in as well. One grabbed me and gagged my mouth with his fist before I could scream. The other flicked out a blade, then shoved it under my chin.

"Don't say a thing. Listen to us."

I nodded more with my eyes than my head, since the blade already pressed against my skin.

The woman smirked. She brushed my cheek with her manicured nails. "Good. Then listen well. You are calling off all of these interviews. You suddenly became very ill. Got it?"

I blinked what I hope she'd interpret as a yes.

She nodded to the goons and they shoved me to the couch. One stood behind me, blade still at my throat. The other towered over me. He had to have been a fullback in college football. His muscles rippled as he punched one hand into the other. He was dressed in a uniform with a NYFD insignia. Why? In my peripheral vision I saw the arm of the other man was covered in the same uniform color. What was this?

The woman took off her long raincoat. She was in surgical

[215]

scrubs. She sat on the couch beside me. "By the way, I am not from the NHTRC, you idiot."

"So I gathered."

She grabbed my arm, her nails digging in. "You never met those girls. You were just making it up to get attention."

I jumped to face her, but was shoved back into the couch. The knife blade pressed against my throat again. The male voice behind me growled with a Hispanic accent. "Sit still or I'll cut you good."

The girl looked at him. She seethed through her teeth at him in Spanish. It was slang, and I couldn't catch it all. She turned her face back to mine. "Let's get her out of here."

"No!" I screamed, but a pungent smelling cloth over my nostrils and mouth prevented any more from leaving my throat. I was being drugged...again. I tried to jerk free, but the room faded into a floating darkness.

I AWOKE ON a plane. The girl sat across from me, as did my two newly assigned bodyguards. One of them growled in Spanish, "*Está despierto.*" (She's awake.)

"Welcome back." The woman moved to face me.

I rubbed the back of my neck to clear the fog. This was getting old. Can you get brain damage from being repeatedly drugged? I tried to focus on her face. "Where are we?"

"Probably over Kentucky."

The small plane's engine labored like an angry swarm of bees. An air pocket bumped our seats and rattled me from my toes to my still-queasy head. "Can I have some water?"

A bottle was shoved on my lap.

"Thanks." I struggled to focus enough to release the cap seal. The bottle was jerked away.

"Here." One of the goons twisted the cap and thrust the bottle toward my mouth. I guzzled a few gulps, spilling half down my front. He snorted a grunt, which I gathered from his gold-toothed grin, was his laugh.

"*Jose, alto.*" (Stop.) The woman spoke to him in hissed tones. The goon pouted and handed me the half-empty bottle, then backed off and sat down.

"You are headed back to Fort Worth. You suddenly got very ill—stomach flu. High fever. Probably combined with emotional exhaustion. That is what the networks were told."

I squinted at her. "How did you get me out of the hotel?"

"The hotel thinks FOX called us in to care for you, but we had to call an ambulance. We helped you into the ambulance, which took you to the airport. These ENTs and I were hired to transport you home."

"I see."

The girl leaned in. "Forget all about this crusade, Mrs. Westlaw. Go back to your mundane world and live a long life."

"I can't do that."

"We'll help you change your mind." She nodded to the first goon with the gleaming tooth.

A humongous fist smacked across my cheek. My jaw snapped. Then another smack hit my chin and jerked my head up like a rag doll. The inside of the airplane blurred into a stinging pain, then all went dark, again.

WHEN I CAME to, the plane's humming again filled my ears. The woman was reading a magazine. One goon was cleaning his nails with the edge of a knife. Both had changed into T-shirts and jeans. Goon Number Two had as well. He was loudly sawing logs, his gold tooth shining like a stalagmite in his cavernous opened mouth.

"We will land outside the city at a small private field in a few minutes. You should be able to get home from there."

"What?" I rose. My jaw ached. Pain shot into my right ear and temple. My cut lip had swollen, making it feel as big as a rolled-up washcloth.

The woman set her magazine on her lap and leaned in. "You tell no one about this. You make it home. You are to stay in your apartment and recover from the flu for the rest of the week. Do not answer the phone or the door."

"Why?"

"Because you value your life and are smart." She bore into me with dark daggers in her eyes. *"¿Entiende?"*

"Yes, I understand." I glared at her. She stared back in a dare, whoever blinked first, lost. I chose to blink first.

She smirked. "Good."

"But what do I tell the Feds?" I slurred the question through my fat lip.

"They're gone. When you left for New York, you sent a clear message you no longer wanted their protection. They were reassigned."

Now that really made me feel stupid. Oh, if I could rewind the clock a few days. Maybe I'd learn to control my Irish hardheadedness.

The drone of the engine changed, and the wings dipped. The plane dove for terra firma and landed with two jerky hops, rushing wind, and a screech of tires.

"Get up." Goon Number One ordered me as Goon Number Two opened the door and let down the stairs.

I was pulled from my seat and half-dragged to the doorway. Then, someone's hand thrust against my back and shoved me. I stumbled down the steps, then splayed across the tarmac, scraping my knees and the palms of my hands.

The plane's propeller began to whirr and the engine rev. A goon tossed my suitcase in my general vicinity. The woman called from the doorway. "Have a good, long life, Mrs. Westlaw. We will be watching."

With that, the door closed and the small plane rushed down the runway and reached for some light bluish-gray clouds in the black of the night sky.

There were no lights on anywhere, except on what appeared to be a small red and white painted hangar a good football field's length away. I sat on my tush, wondering where in the world I'd landed, and what time it was.

CHAPTER FIVE

I GOT UP and brushed myself off. My head and jaw throbbed and my knees stung. I wobbled over to my suitcase and grabbed the handle. The bar raised to hip height as I tilted it on its wheels. Slowly, blinking back panic and tears, I breathed three deep breaths and began to walk toward the light.

On the horizon I saw hotel signs and the familiar golden arches of McDonald's. Praise God. Civilization. I made it to the fast-food restaurant on pure gumption and inner strength—from where I do not know. Perhaps it was Divine Guidance.

I entered the brightly lit dining room and spotted a short hall to the right with a restroom sign. The place smelled of coffee, fries, and hamburgers, all of which sounded marvelous. I hadn't eaten since I had lunch on the plane to New York. But first things first.

I lugged my suitcase into the restroom and fumbled through it to find my purse. My wallet still had money, credit cards, and my newly acquired replacement IDs. I leaned back against the tiled wall in relief.

The woman's words echoed in my brain. "We will be

watching."

"Join the club. So are the Feds, I'm sure, plus a few of the more tenacious reporters, and maybe the cartel. God in Heaven, help me." I shivered it off and raised myself to the sink. My left jaw was already a nice shade of greenish-purple. My mind felt mushy. I think I stared at the running water for at least two minutes before dipping my hands in it to splash my face.

But within minutes, I was Humpty-Dumpty back together again and ordering food. I asked the man who served my meal as politely as I could, "Where can I get a cab this time of night?"

He eyed my suitcase. "Ma'am, this ain't New York City. You're in Burleson. It's after one in the morning. Ain't no cabs running for hours."

Burleson? "Oh, okay." I smiled and grabbed my tray.

"Why don't you go back to your hotel room and get some more sleep. They can call you one later."

I gave him a nod, then cringed from the sharp pain it sent to my jaw. I slammed the tray to the counter and held my hand to my face.

"Ma'am?" He touched my arm, head tilted, and eyes landing on my cheek. "You okay? Should I call anyone else for you?"

"No. I'm fine." I brushed my jaw. "Car accident on the highway. Jaw hit the airbag. They released me and got me the hotel room. I just needed food. Thanks." Had I just lied to his face? What was happening to me?

I sat quietly and ate my meal, barely tasting the hamburger and fries I could only chew in small bites with one side of my mouth. A young couple with eyes for no one else huddled in a corner booth, their hands intertwined. My heart ached, wishing it was me and Tom. It seemed like ages since we were tossing an apple core back and forth in a hotel room in Canyon, Texas.

I dragged my body and suitcase across the road to the La

Quinta. Now I remembered why the town of Burleson sounded familiar. Robert once brought me here to a Mexican restaurant when we were both craving real San Antonio style Tex-Mex, not the trendy stuff with sour cream and chipotle. So, I was only thirty minutes or less from my apartment in south Fort Worth. Good.

A man of Arab descent gave me a room without much conversation other than asking for my credit card and ID in a heavy accent. His breath reeked of curry. He gave me my key and a map of the motel's layout, then returned to his foreign newspaper. The letters all looked like up and down squiggles.

"Thank you." I shot him a quick grin, which shot another sharp sting into my jaw, and then lumbered down two halls to Room 127. I swiped the card and the little green light appeared as the door lock clicked. I opened it and entered through a blast of stale AC into a clean room decorated in mustards and burnt orange. A queen-sized bed beckoned to me.

Quite honestly, that was all I remembered.

AT 10:45 A.M., according to the illuminated dial on the motel clock, I groaned and rolled over. I'd never even turned down the bed. For a moment I thought I was in New York, until my scraped-up knees brushed the quilted spread. Right. Not New York.

I crawled to the restroom and examined my face. The bedspread's pattern had left an impression into the now spreading green and purple cheek. Just gorgeous.

After a marathon hot shower, almost matching the one I'd had in the coffin-room, I applied as much makeup as I could to cover the bruises, changed clothes, and called for a cab. When I got back to my apartment in Fort Worth, the tom cat rubbed my legs repeatedly in a figure eight dance. I picked him up and snuggled his fur. His wriggling told me he was more interested in the can of chicken and liver cat food in the cupboard. I laughed. "Typical male."

Perhaps it was my imagination, but I couldn't shake the feeling that eyes were watching me. I checked the lamps and my phone for listening devices. I didn't find anything. Out the sliding door I noticed Becky taking trash to the dumpster. Her eyes turned to my balcony. I closed the vertical blinds. I didn't want anyone to see my face right now. It would only lead to questions whose answers would be too fanciful or put me in danger.

When she tapped on my door, I answered through the crack, hiding my left jaw.

"I thought you were in New York?"

"I got violently ill. They sent me home in a private jet."

"Can I bring you some homemade chicken and rice soup?"

That sounded wonderful. "No, I'm fine. Thanks, though. I'm going to lie down now."

I closed the door. Another falsehood had rolled off my tongue. I hated lying more than getting a root canal.

I slept some, downed a pint of Rocky Road, and vegged out on a good Hallmark movie. Tom Cat, the no-longer-stray kitty since I decided to officially name him, curled in my lap and purred softly.

BECKY CALLED ON the phone the next day. "You're better?"

"Yeah."

"I knew something was wrong when I taped the midday show and it wasn't you, but..."

"I got sick. Stomach flu, maybe food poisoning. Maybe nerves. I don't know. I am just dead tired from it all. I'll call you in a day or so."

I placed the phone back into its holder and closed my eyes. I couldn't do this on my own. I needed help finding Marisol and Monica, but obviously the best way to do that was not through mass media. There had to be another way. But how?

Agent Hernandez had said if I told them everything, they'd protect me. But if I was in witness protection, how would that help me find the girls? And how could I then write my memoirs, which I had decided to do. The contract from a well-known publisher lay on my desk and a ghost writer had already been assigned. Still the residual pain in my jaw cautioned me to proceed with caution, if at all. I wasn't sure what to do.

I was rusty at this sort of thing, but I tried to pray again. Not a short "I need You" prayer, but the concentrated "be with me" kind. I got down on my knees by my couch and folded my hands. After reciting the Lord's Prayer, I winged it.

"Dear Lord. I know I need to lay low. Protect Marisol and Monica. Protect Tom. Teach me the patience and wherewithal to handle this passion You have placed on my heart. Show me my next steps. Guide my decisions and moves. Oh, and please, protect me, too. In Jesus' name. Amen."

I rocked back on my heels. I didn't feel Divine intervention, but I did feel less antsy. At least that was something.

Realizing I'd eventually need some income if I put off the book deal, I searched the want-ads and online for a new job—preferably one with the Texas Department of Human Services or with one of the immigrant welfare organizations. Maybe I could legitimately get my hand on resources. Perhaps I could even work at home doing data entry.

I bought a used Mazda and signed up for spring classes at the Tarrant County Community College in Spanish 202 to boost my prospects of an interview, and on a whim, Bible 101 starting in June. I figured Tom would approve.

I even went to worship, twice. I figured God would approve.

The pastor at the church closest to my apartment was younger than I expected, but had a kind, round face. His sermons were actually rather good. He only stepped lightly on a couple of my toes each time.

On my second visit, when I stopped to shake his hand at the back of the church after services, he held on to mine firmly. He bent forward to my ear. "I know who you are. If you need to talk..."

A spiritual zap coursed from his hand, up my arm and into my heart. For the first time in weeks tears flooded my eyes. I nodded, tongue-tied, released my hand quickly, and bolted down the church steps. I felt dozens of eyes on my back as I wound my way through the parking lot to my car.

I turned the key, and then turned it off again. The dam of calm I'd created cracked, then burst. Streams flowed from my eyes onto my steering wheel, flushing out every ounce of angst I had refused to admit still existed. I felt drenched from inside out, like an inward baptism of sweet release.

The parking lot emptied. I looked up to see him close the front doors to the church. I dashed from my car and ran to stop him. "Wait. Pastor Jake."

He froze in his task, and shaded his eyes from the noonday sun.

Out of breath, I reached the church steps. As I gripped the wrought iron railing, I panted my response with what I am sure were runny-mascara, raccoon eyes. "Yes. I do. I want to talk."

"Now?"

I bit my lip as he studied my face, as if he could peer into my soul.

After a moment he nodded. "Come inside. The women's luncheon yesterday left a ton of food in the fridge." His deep brown eyes twinkled with care. "Want to help me make a dent in it?"

I grinned and bolted up the stairs. "Sure. Thanks."

He held the wooden door open and beckoned me inside. I

slipped back into the cool hominess of the sanctuary.

A flashing shudder zipped along my spine as I heard the lock click. Déjà vu? I turned, wide-eyed, to stare at him.

The minister must have sensed my reaction. "I'm sorry. I don't want you to feel uncomfortable. It's just that the elders are always getting on my back for not locking up." He scratched his head. "We had a robbery a few years back."

"Oh." I bobbed mine in response, feeling my cheeks flush with nervousness. I glanced at the service schedule posted on the message board.

"Would you rather sit outside in the reflection garden?"

I shook my head. If I couldn't trust a minister…

His face softened into a cloud of tenderness. "You have every right to be antsy after what you have been through. Come, tell me about it. It's all confidential, as you know. I promise I won't write a book and make a million dollars, okay?" He cocked his head. "Though it is tempting…"

What a great sense of humor and keen sense of understanding. I liked him. "Yeah, the press would love you for that."

He waved his hand to brush my comment away. "So would the IRS—and the Church Council."

I smiled back. Yes, I liked him very much indeed.

CHAPTER SIX

WE SAT IN the church kitchen and munched on chicken salad croissant sandwiches, ambrosia, deviled eggs, and gooey chocolate brownies, then washed it all down with sweetened peach tea. Rarely had I been so ravenous. In fact, I had been eating bird-like for weeks. That cleansing cry must have helped.

He listened, I talked. I told him everything, blow by blow. He didn't judge even when I got to the part about what happened in the office at the garage in the middle of nowhere. He only stopped to occasionally comment in trained therapeutic sympathy. "I see. Please, continue."

He kept his eyes fixed on me, until I told him about the faked rape in the van. At that, his poker face of impartial counsel cracked—just a bit. He took a sip of tea, twisted his neck muscles, and said, "Go on. What happened next?"

Finally, I finished my tale, ending with my midnight ride in the private plane. The clock on the back of the oven read 2:35. Pastor Jake leaned back in his chair, hands laced behind his head.

I drank more peach tea and picked at the last brownie.

His gaze went to the ceiling then, after a moment, came back to zero in on my face. He leaned forward, hands folded across the table. "Do you believe God is in control?"

I stared, wide-eyed. What?

He peered into my face and patiently waited for my response. I had none to give.

Pastor rubbed his hands together and spoke in a low, evil, mad-scientist tone. "I won't unlock the door until you answer me."

I snorted a nervous laugh, then looked down at the faint white stripe around my left ring finger.

The minister leaned in. "What are you thinking about?"

I tugged at my lip with my teeth. "Why I haven't replaced my wedding ring. The drug lords stole it."

"Perhaps because you don't know if you should. Do you really believe your husband's dead?"

"I don't know." I shoved both lips into my mouth and clamped them shut.

Pastor Jake got up to refill his glass with ice from the machine in the back of the tidy kitchen. He said, his back to me, "Now you have two questions to answer."

"To you, or to myself?"

He turned and lifted his glass upwards. "To Him. But you can tell me. That's my job."

I sputtered a snicker. "Do we need to move to the pews, then?"

He walked over, his shoes barely making a noise. His eyes narrowed as his smile faded. "If that would make you feel better."

I traced around the plastic fork with my finger. "Can I get back with you?"

His grin returned. "Deal. Come back to see me on Tuesday morning. Ten. Don't be late."

He reached in his pocket for a ring of at least twenty keys. I followed him down the hall as he jingled them to locate the right one. I suddenly realized he'd never removed his suit jacket and tie. Perhaps that had been purposeful so he'd appear more official. How thoughtful. I knew then I'd be back.

He got to the door and unlocked it. "Go in peace."

Under my breath I replied with the common end of worship response. "Thanks be to God."

I heard his hearty laugh as the door clicked shut.

ALL THE WAY home I pondered his second question. Did I believe Robert was actually dead? Up until a month ago, I'd never doubted it. What if he was still alive? Was my love for him still alive—that was what Pastor Jake had meant. Was Tom's uncertain whereabouts the reason I'd not replaced my wedding ring? And, did I have any right to feel the way I did about him?

I shook it all off. Maybe I wasn't ready to answer question number two. I returned to Pastor Jake's first question, the God-in-control one. In a strange way, it seemed a lot less threatening.

I had no answer for it either, though. I figured I was supposed to have replied, "Why, yes. Of course I do." The trouble was—I wasn't sure I did. What evidence did I have that the Lord had any control over my life? A few eerie suggestions whispered into my brain? A feeling I wished was there more often? It's not control. But then was it because I wouldn't let Him take the reins?

Once in my apartment, I Googled the first question Jake had asked me. Did I believe that God was in control?

It seemed a core question many people would ask a man of the cloth. He'd probably learned that fact in seminary the first year. Start with that basic question when you were faced with a person who had lapsed into a semi-believer. See if they still knew the answer.

The computer screen responded with the following choices—

Is God in control?
Is God in control of everything?
Is God in control of our lives?
Is God in control of my life?

I sat back. Wow. The words illuminated in front of me had an eerie progression from everything in the universe down to me. Option number one referenced a passage from the first chapter of Ephesians.

"God 'worketh all things after the counsel of His own will: That we should be to the praise of his glory.'"

What did it mean?

I scrolled further down through a succession of blogs asking how He can allow bad things, or if He didn't, would we be just puppets, yadda, yadda. Nah. Too deep. So I scrolled back up.

I'm not sure how long I stared at the computer monitor and that verse. My thoughts whirled like autumn leaves in a wind gust. Both questions Pastor Jake had asked spun around me. What did one have to do with the other?

I tapped my fingers on the desk. "God worketh all things." Had God orchestrated all of this so-called adventure to zap me out of my zombie-like mourning blackness? Could it be Tom, or Travis, or whoever this shadowy figure was whom I'd brushed against for one week, had come into my life for just that reason? If so, I would be eternally grateful. But Tom had done more than help me find a new purpose in life. He'd given me back my life.

Suddenly a desperate yearning to find him surfaced. I flicked off the computer screen and circled my bedroom. After an hour of brain-racking exercises of how I could get a message to him, I gave up. I tried to shove him out of my thoughts by watching a movie I'd taped ages ago but never got a chance to see. My mind kept blanking out. Over and over, I had to rewind to catch what I'd missed. At last I surrendered, downed an anti-anxiety pill with a glass of water, and undressed for bed.

It didn't work. I tossed and turned all night trying to remember how Robert's touch felt, or how his lips pressed on mine. But what seemed etched into my skin was Tom's touch. The yearning to be with him made my whole soul ache.

About three in the morning, I threw the covers aside and once again paced. Tom Cat sat on his haunches. In the moonlight, his iridescent eyes peered into me. I turned to him, hands on my hips.

"I can't think about him, Tom Cat. I can't. I have no right to." I waved my hands frantically in the air. "I don't even know who he is. Where he is. If he's still—" I couldn't say it. He had to be alive. He had found me once. He'd find a way to contact me again.

Tom Cat stretched out a paw and tagged my nightgown. I knelt by the bed, stroking his back. "Oh, Tom. Oh, Tom."

Once again the tears flowed.

Tom Cat purred as I drenched his fur with my sobs. And they said cats hated water.

CHAPTER SEVEN

MONDAY DAWNED WITH me in a self-enforced fog, doing everything I could to not think, emote, or remember. I started with my laundry, scrubbed the grout in my bathtub enclosure, wiped baseboards, and yes, washed my windows as best as I could, living in a second-story apartment. I played Scrabble on the computer, then Gin Rummy, then Find a Word until my brain went limp. About dusk, I hopped in my car, drove through a Mexican fast-food to get chicken enchiladas, and then through the Dairy Queen for a hot fudge sundae. I figured either I'd sleep like a baby or be up all night with physical ailments—a blessed relief from the emotional or spiritual anguish which had been doing the same thing.

On Tuesday morning I fed Tom Cat, did my stint in the apartment weight room and mini-gym, ate breakfast, then caught up on emails and the Facebook news of all six of my contacts. I still questioned the attraction of this social media thing. Maybe if I tried harder, I'd make more friends. But honestly, I didn't care to share recipes or see everyone's pet pictures.

Then I bathed, did the makeup routine, and dressed in business clothes. I chose a long skirt with a lace collared blouse and linen jacket. I honestly couldn't recall what the other ladies had worn on Sunday.

At twenty until ten I was out the door and headed to meet Pastor Jake. Three times, I talked myself out of turning around and heading home. I parked and sat, staring at the front door of the church for a good six minutes, until a rap on the driver's side window jolted me.

"Not backing out on me, are you?" Pastor Jake's muffled voice and shining gaze seeped through the car glass.

I pushed the window button. "No, I just—" I stopped. "Yes. I was thinking about it."

He wiggled the door handle. I unlocked it. He nodded and opened it for me, extending his other hand to help me out of the driver's seat.

"Thanks." I slid out and watched as he closed the car door.

As we walked to his office, he chatted easily. "Let's see if you still say that in an hour. I have been known to beat confessions out of people. I didn't show you the dungeons beneath the church." He slinked along, dragging one foot with the opposite shoulder slightly humped like Igor in the novel *The Hunchback of Notre Dame*.

I laughed. It felt good.

Pastor Jake straightened his back. "The office is over there off to the left side."

He was dressed casually, in not the normal suit, white shirt, and black tie.

"Why the incognito?" I shuffled to catch up to his longer stride.

"My white shirts are in the wash."

I chuckled. "You know something? In one minute you've gotten me to laugh twice."

He puffed out his chest and winked. "I sensed my astute wit

wouldn't fall on deaf ears."

His smile was contagiously warm. Did they learn how to do that in seminary or was this a gift? I knew he was trying to ease the tension for me. With each grin, another twisted tangle in my stomach loosened a bit.

Pastor Jake led me through the door and down a short hall. He opened a glass door with "Church Office" painted on it. Inside, an elderly lady, with blue-white hair neatly gathered into a bun at the nape of her neck, pecked away at a keyboard. Her nose scrunched as she peered over half-moon glasses.

"Mrs. Edwards. This is Jen. She's my ten o'clock counseling session."

The woman twisted to gaze at me, nodded, and returned to her computer screen. Pastor Jake scooted around the desk to place his hand on her shoulder. "That new program still giving you fits?" He turned to me. "It's the latest member database on the market. A gift from one of our more influential members."

Mrs. Edwards' thin, slightly bent shoulders heaved in confusion.

Pastor Jake leaned into her ear. "Call tech support and speak to Angelo. He'll be happy to walk you through it again." With a pat on her back, he motioned me to the next room.

His office was what I expected. Old, but well-made furniture in mahogany and green leather were sparsely placed on an oriental rug. Floor to ceiling bookshelves filled the wall behind him. Several crosses and mementos were scattered amongst the various books, some paperback and some not. A photo of a young woman who shared Pastor Jake's smile propped center stage on the middle shelf. I gravitated toward it.

He followed, hands in both pockets. "My little sister. She's getting her masters at UT in Physics. She got all the brainy genes."

He sat in his chair and motioned me to choose one of the green leather straight back ones in front of his desk. He shuffled a few folders and papers, then leaned in to face me. "Okay, so what are we discussing today? Question one, or would it be question two?"

I wiggled my bottom in the chair while my eyes bore a hole into my interlocked thumbs. I sucked in half the air in the room, let it out, and spurted my desire. "I want to find those two girls I told you about. You know? Monica and Marisol."

A smirk emerged. "Avoidance so soon? We've barely gotten out of the starting gate."

I bit my lip. "I mean it. I can't stop thinking about them, about what is happening to them. Over and over, and…" I blinked away tears.

He reached across the desk and motioned with his hands for me to take them. I did. Then he bowed his head and closed his eyes. "Let us pray," he whispered.

We did. Rather, he did and I listened, sniffling every now and then. Bowing my head made my nose run. After he said "amen," he reached over and yanked a tissue from the box on the edge of his desk and handed it to me.

I blew my nose.

"I found something you might want." He flipped through the papers in a stack. "Ah. Here it is." He handed me a tri-fold brochure. A Hispanic young girl's face stared at me from beneath the words "Coalition Against Human Trafficking."

"I got this at a conference a while back. It's a start."

I flipped it over and read a contact phone number on the back. "Area code 202?"

Pastor Jake leaned back in his chair again. "Washington D.C., I think."

I scrunched my face together, like Mrs. Edwards.

He raised his hands in surrender. "I know. This is Texas. But they may have contacts here. Believe it or not, the DFW area is supposed to be a major hub for this sort of thing. I can also check with the neighborhood ministers' coalition and see if anyone knows of someone you can speak with."

Gratitude washed over me. "So, they may be filtered through here?"

He raised a finger. "It's not much to go on. Don't get your hopes up too soon. You really need to get the police to help."

I rolled my eyes. "I tried that. In Canyon."

"Ah." He nodded. "Needle in a haystack was their answer, right?"

I stuffed the brochure into my purse. "Something like that, yes."

"Jen." His face took on a parental sternness which aged him by ten years. "May I call you that?"

I nodded.

"Good. Then just call me Jake. Most of the members here do." He tented his fingers. "I know these young girls' situation is horrid. I can't blame you for wanting to find them and help them. I just want you to also help yourself."

I gave him a blank look. Tom had said the same thing.

Jake extended his arm across the desk and waggled his forefinger at my nose. "Don't play dumb. You know what I mean. Don't use this cause as an excuse to not process your own harrowing experience. You are going to have to be strong, mentally and emotionally, to pursue this. That means working through your own trauma first."

My eyes dashed to the corner of the room.

He came around and perched on the edge of his desk. "Remember your flight to New York?"

I wiggled a smidgen in the chair. "Yes. So?"

"Those poor flight attendants. No one listens to their spiel before takeoff. I know how they feel...every Sunday morning in the pulpit."

I laughed again.

His eyes sparkled back into mine. "Seriously, do you know what they tell parents?"

I knitted my eyebrows and shook my head.

He sat up straight. "To put the oxygen mask on themselves first, then their kids."

Comprehension jabbed me.

A little smile told me he'd seen it. He went back around to his chair. "You have to save yourself before you can save others."

I cocked my head. "Isn't that Christ's job?"

He reared back and laughed. "Touché." He bent over his desk. "I'm free on Thursday at two. See you then."

He rose and motioned me to the door.

Mrs. Edwards was still at it, all scrunched up. At least she was on the phone. "Yes. Did that. Okay. Then what do I do?"

I envied her. If only there was an Angelo to guide me through my steps. Angelo means angel in Spanish. Who was mine?

MY FINGERS FROZE over the keyboard. The cursor blinked, suspended at the email address. What was I going to say? "Dear Anti-Trafficking Organization, I was kidnapped, then hid for safety with two Hispanic teenagers trapped in a prostitution ring." Would they think me a nut case?

Maybe I could call, pretend to be a reporter writing an article for the church newsletter. No, too formal—and another lie.

I clicked off the screen and stared at the brochure. The beckoning eyes of the girl on the front bore into my soul. Her gaze was straightforward, blank of emotion as if, even at that early age, hope had been squeezed out of her, drop by drop, forever. I'd seen that same look in Monica's eyes the night they came and got her from the hut. I blinked to break the force of the stare.

My hands grabbed my wireless phone. I punched the toll-free number and sucked in a deep breath of fortitude. Ring. One. Ring. Two. A man's voice answered.

"Oh. Yes, hello." I don't know why I expected to hear a woman's voice. I swallowed. "I would like some more information on human trafficking."

"I see. Exactly how can I help?"

"I had a brief encounter with two young girls being held against their will in a hut in New Mexico." I stopped and breathed. "One was already pregnant. She was fourteen, maybe fifteen."

The man gave a small clearing cough. "Okay?"

"I want to find them. Get them out of that situation. I don't know where to begin."

A short pause, and then he responded. "How did you get my number?"

"From my pastor." Well, I guess he was now officially my pastor. "He had a brochure from the conference. It has a young girl in green on the front."

"That's from 2009. Five years ago."

I flipped the pamphlet over. "Oh, yes, I see that now." My resolve deflated.

Another pause. "You said you were in New Mexico?"

"Yes. Er, no. I live in Texas. Fort Worth." I took a deep breath. "I was kidnapped in New Mexico."

"Kidnapped?" For the first time his voice showed animation.

"They let me go, but these two girls, they'd been, well, with them awhile." I stopped. How much info did he need? I switched the subject to Monica and Marisol. "They said they were promised jobs as nannies. They had to pay for their transport into the U.S."

"So they had money?"

"No." I paused. "They had to pay, well, you know, with their bodies."

He cleared his throat again. "Right."

I waited, not sure how much else to tell him.

I heard him inhale. "Look, Ms., Mrs.?"

"Mrs. Westfall."

"I see. Mrs. Westfall." He sighed through the receiver. "My name's Ed. First things first. Did you tell the police?"

I shifted in my chair and let patience rule. There was no need to get my Irish up. "Yes, Ed. They said it would be impossible to trace them."

"Yes, it would."

"But surely there is a pattern. A route these traffickers take to get the girls to wherever they take them. If I could—"

He cut me off. "Mrs. Westfall. Your efforts are noble. But you escaped these animals once. Don't put yourself in danger again."

I planted my feet to the floor. "Your brochure says you provide a safe haven for trafficked adolescents. And," I emphasized, "direct services to victims in the United States."

"Yes, we do. But we don't have the resources to go looking for individual girls."

Ed's words slapped my face. I gathered my thoughts for a moment. "I have to do something."

"I understand." His voice became more soothing. "Do you have a pen?"

"Yes." I craned across the computer desk to grab one, and flipped over the brochure. "I'm ready."

"Call this number. It is a hotline for reporting human

trafficking. It may be hard, since you don't know where they are now, but..."

My voice raised in excitement. "Thank you. What is it?"

"1-888-373-7888. It's a division of the U.S. Department of Human Services. It was set up as a response to the TVPA, well, now the TVPA-R."

My pen paused. "The what?"

"TVPA." He enunciated each letter. "It means the Trafficking Victims Protection Act that passed in 2000. It has since been revised."

I flopped back in my desk chair. "I had no idea."

I heard his chair creak as he shifted his body weight. "Mrs. Westfall. You are not alone. That's why we need people like you to spread the word. You may never be able to help those two girls, but you can help others. God bless you for your fervency."

With that, he ended the call.

Now I was even more confused.

No more than a minute later my landline phone rang. "Hello?"

A mechanical, graveled voice replied. "Stop shaking the bushes, Mrs. Westlaw, or we'll shake you." Click.

I let the humming tone ring in my ear as my mind tried to grasp what just happened. Had someone bugged my home phone? When? As if it was on fire, I tossed the wireless receiver onto the bed. Then I dashed to the windows, closed the blinds, and double-bolted my doors.

Tom Cat mewed. I picked him up, grabbed my purse, and locked us both in the bathroom. Then, I dug for my cell phone and dialed Agent Hernandez. Maybe a companion right now wouldn't be such a bad idea. Then again... I hung up before it rang twice.

I refused to be threatened. If I was rattling cages it meant I was doing some good. I apologized to my furry friend, unlocked the bathroom door, and re-opened my blinds.

If she called me back, I'd let the Feds in to do a sweep for listening devices, and agree to have them monitor the comings and goings in my complex for a while. But nothing more than that. No roommates. I deserved my privacy as much as possible.

THURSDAY AT TWO in the afternoon, I opened the glass door to the church office. Mrs. Edwards was not at her station. I tapped on the desk. "Hello?"

I heard footsteps. Jake came out, this time in full minister-mode—vested suit, white shirt, black tie.

"You cleaned your shirts, I see."

He ran his hand down his front and knitted his forehead. Then the light went on. "Ah. Yes. I guess I did. Come in."

I stopped midway. "Where is Mrs. Edwards?"

"Dentist." He cocked his head and propped against the door jamb. "Are you uncomfortable being alone with me? We were alone in the kitchen the first time."

I readjusted my purse on my shoulder and walked toward him. "No, of course not."

I'd just lied to a man of the cloth.

He sat down. So did I.

"Okay, have you done your homework? Asked the questions?"

I inched forward in my chair. "I called the number on the pamphlet and talked with..."

He leaned back and held up his hands. "Whoa. Stop."

"What?" I scooted back into the chair, my hands in my lap.

"Jen, stop avoiding the main issue. You are torn between mourning your husband who isn't the man you thought you married, and missing another man—the one you can't decide who or what he is. Ask yourself, why did he, this Tom, have such an effect on you?"

I gulped down the emotions rising in my throat. "I have."

"You don't look as if you have an answer."

I bowed my head. "I don't."

"Keep asking, then. Until you know that, you can't move forward."

I turned to stare out the window. "I know. It's just too jumbled. It's like putting together a jigsaw puzzle with the pieces all on the gray side."

He pushed the tissue box toward me, and then clasped his hands over his desk. "Jen. Turn them over, one at a time and look at each piece. Ask God to help you find the next, then the next. Let Him guide your path."

I smirked. "Ah. Back to question number one?"

He winked. "Always."

I turned my head and stared at the tree in the reflective garden outside. The limbs jiggled slightly in the breeze, but the tree was sturdy, well-rooted. I wanted to be that tree. For me, for Monica, for Marisol, and yes, for Tom.

"I love him."

"Your husband or Tom?"

"Yes." It came out in a whispered squeak. I blinked, glanced at Jake then back to the tree.

He said nothing. I knew he was waiting for me to speak again. My eyes filled, blurring my view of outside. I wrapped a tissue around my fingers, then unwrapped it and dabbed my eyes. "The trouble is, I don't know either of them, do I?" I shot him a look.

"How can you love someone you don't know?"

I nodded as I took a breath. "Exactly."

"Are you angry with them?"

The answer spurted out of me. "Yes."

"Are you angry with yourself for being duped?"

The answer was the same, but less emphatic. I glanced down at the tissue, wrapped around two fingers this time.

He leaned in for the zinger. "Are you angry at God?"

I bolted from the chair and went to the window. "Don't go there."

"It's my job to go there. You know that, Jen. Are you angry at God?"

I spun around with venom in my eyes. "Yes." I screamed.

Jake rocked back with his hands laced behind his neck, just as he had in the kitchen before. He propped one foot on the opposite knee. "Good."

I splayed my hands in confusion. "Good?"

"Uh-huh." His eyes glistened brighter yet. "Which means two things." Jake held up a finger. "One, you still believe in Him, and two…"Another finger joined the first one. "You have answered the first question. You believe He is in control. Otherwise, why would you care enough to be angry with Him?"

Flies could have buzzed in and out of my mouth and I not felt them.

He winked, flipped open his calendar and tapped a page. "Next Friday. Same time?"

I plopped in the chair, arms wrapped around myself. Wow, this man was good.

FOR TWO HOURS I paced and processed my session with Jake. I felt as weak as a horse that had just been ridden hard. I chose to hang up the emotional saddle and return to my mission. I flipped the pamphlet over in my hand. How was I to find these girls? If I raised awareness, it might not be a warning over the phone this time. Those goons from New York might raise their ugly heads and snatch me again.

Then, an idea gleamed inside my brain. I sat, cross-legged, half yoga style on the bed and slapped my own forehead. I had to get the attention off me and on to finding the girls. Duh! TV interviews wouldn't do that. Maybe I could eventually write the memoir, just not now. This couldn't be about me.

It was about Monica and Marisol, and hundreds like them. I'd go on an incognito, underground trek, with the help of Jake, and maybe Grace from Canyon. That way, even without Tom, I'd find out more about the world of trafficking. Make contacts. Seek them out. Needles can be found in haystacks—I just had to risk getting pricked when I least expected it. Maybe I already had.

I uncrossed my legs. Or, I could go the other route. I could make it all about me and stay in the limelight. I clapped my hands. Tom Cat jerked.

"Sorry, guy." I leaned over to stroke his fur under his collar. "Mommy just had a brainstorm."

What a better way to point to the problem? Not through sensationalistic media, but through legal means. Get involved with the big guns like the nonprofits and lobbyists, and then glean info from them. Be their local spokesperson and become a public figure. Let other people help me with the legwork. Rally the troops. Then it would attract way too much attention for anyone to try and mess with me.

I hugged Tom Cat, then set him down. Yes, that was the best route to take.

I rose from my bed and spun around the room as two feline eyes tracked my movements. I picked up my adopted stray and buried my cheek in his fur. "I have a new direction to go, Tom Cat."

But first, I had to get over my fear of public speaking. That interview with Channel 11 had unnerved me to no end. I Googled the topic and Toastmasters International popped up. A local club met at a restaurant two blocks from my house on Tuesday evenings. Cool. My plan emerged like a butterfly from a cocoon.

The phone rang. My heart flew out of my chest and then back in. I bent over the bed. The caller ID said "Name Unknown." I took a deep breath, and then clicked the talk button. "Yes?"

"Tom says to drive to Arlington. Now. Meet him in the cough syrup aisle at the Walgreens on West Park Row near the University." Click.

I knew that voice. It wasn't mechanical. It was Chinese, and female. Mae Lin.

CHAPTER EIGHT

TINGLING SPREAD OVER my head and down my arms. Was this a trap? I remembered her slap across my face. She was not my friend. Perhaps she wanted to lure me somewhere I wasn't familiar with so she could...what? It made no sense.

I dug through my wallet and stared at the card from Grace in Canyon. If I heard anything, call. I reached for the phone, tapped it twice with my fingernail, and then got up to make a cup of tea.

As the mug of water circled round and round in the microwave, it gave me time to think this through. Was the "him" I was supposed to meet really Tom? He and Mae Lin hadn't parted on good terms. Why would she be his mouthpiece now?

The microwave dinged. I held the steaming cup to my face and breathed in the vapors. Just smelling the Earl Grey steeping eased my brain muscles. I sat down and sipped—slow, methodically. No, I was not dashing off to some drugstore in another city. No way.

But what could I tell the police? A strange voice which might have been the Chinese girl who was involved in kidnapping me left a cryptic message on my phone? Uh-huh. They'd rush over on that tip. Sure.

Tom Cat jumped onto my lap. I stroked his fur. "You are the only male I can trust, now. Well, you and Jake."

The light bulb went on. He knew the whole story. He was astute. "Yes." I hugged the animal again, set him down and punched in the number to the church. Mrs. Edwards answered. "I'm sorry. Pastor Jake is in premarital counseling with a couple. Can I give him a message?"

"Yes. Please." I thought for a moment. "Tell him Mae Lin called me."

I had to spell the name for her twice.

Three computer Scrabble games later my cell phone rang. Sure it was Jake, I didn't check the caller ID. "Hi. What shirt do you have on now?"

"A blue one. I'm here at Walgreens. Where are you, Jen?"

The hint of Irish brogue in his voice sent a rush of ice through my arm, then heat. Tom. I wanted to yell at him, hug him, but also hang up on him.

"At home," I replied coolly. I slurped my tea for effect.

A few seconds of silence followed. Then the phone clicked off.

Clarity slapped me in the chest. Had that been Tom, or someone pretending to be him?

"Jen, you're stupid, stupid." I hit my forehead with my palm. Now, whoever wanted me to come to Arlington knew where I was.

I grabbed my keys, hopped in my car and drove the opposite way, west toward Weatherford. Then I took Loop 820 around, down I-35 and back to my apartment complex via three side streets. I sat in the parking lot and watched the cars come and go. Each one knew the gate code or had a clicker. Tom didn't have either. Neither did Mae Lin. It was a gated community, but of course it was possible to sneak in after another car before it closed. I couldn't stake out my own apartment complex all day.

"The Feds could," I said out loud to my steering wheel. But that would mean telling them Tom, or someone pretending to be him, had contacted me. Then would begin the surveillance and companions 24/7. I didn't want on that merry-go-round again.

I slammed the steering wheel with the heel of my hand. This was ridiculous. I couldn't cower in my car all day waiting for someone to show up with a gun tucked under a jacket.

I felt idiotic. This wasn't TV. No spies or cops and robbers lurked inside those apartment gates. This was real life. I started the car, pointed my clicker at the gate, and went home.

As I walked in the door, Jake called back. I told him about my phone calls to the Anti-Trafficking Coalition, the one from the Chinese woman, and the man who sounded like Tom.

"You were wise not to go."

"Jake, may I ask you something. And tell me honestly."

He laughed. "Yes, I believe God is in control, too."

I scoffed at him in jest. "Please. I'm serious. Do you think Tom is, uh, was a psycho?"

I heard him blow his breath out over the receiver. I waited.

"I never met him, so I can't answer that. In abnormal psych courses in college I learned true psychopaths can be geniuses. They can be cunning, devious and lure other people into their games. They seek out vulnerable, unhappy people and suck them into their delusion. Look at Hitler."

I chuckled. "Hardly the same."

"True, but still..."

For a moment we both were silent. Then he said quietly, "Jen. If he calls again, call the police and tell them. He isn't worth your time, or your love. That will fade. It was all part of the excitement and chaos. Your feelings for him are trying to fill a void, so you keep things stirred up instead of facing life."

His words pressed hard against my heart. He was right. I nodded into the phone. "Okay. Got it."

"Jen, listen. Adrenaline rushes can be addictive. They make us feel alive. But they are dangerous. You need to pray yourself through them."

After we hung up I paced for a few minutes. His words floated around me, not quite sticking.

I tore up the agent's card and stuffed it into the bottom of the sack lining my trash can, then scooped Tom Cat's dirty litter into it, tied it together, and walked it to the dumpster. Grace's card, the officer from Canyon, I kept. She might be able to help me find Marisol and Monica and get in touch with statewide anti-trafficking groups. Besides, I liked her.

My cell phone buzzed with a text message. I picked it up and swiped my finger on the app. The words blared off the screen. *I'm still here. Please come. Have Snickers.*

My heart jumped into my throat. Only Tom knew the significance of a Snickers bar to the two of us. Maybe he'd be all the protection I needed. I texted back: *Okay. Coming now. Got Agritos?*

I dashed to my car, got in, and plugged the partial address into my phone's navigation search. Walgreens. West Park Row. Arlington. Thank God the GPS lady was smarter than most humans. She understood exactly where I needed to be. Within a half hour, her soothingly calm voice had guided me to my "destination straight ahead in 400 feet."

WALGREENS WASN'T CROWDED. I noticed three employees, a hunched-over wisp of an old man adjusting his glasses to read the labels in the laxative aisle, and a young woman with purple streaks spiking out of her hair browsing the hair products. No one was in the cold and flu remedy section.

I'd never been to Arlington, though Six Flags, the Rangers' ballpark, and the Cowboys' stadium close by, made it a tourist's mecca. T-shirts for each of them crowded for display space near the candy aisle. I chose a blue and red Ranger's shirt, size medium.

"Want me to buy you that one?"

I squeezed my eyes shut and took a breath to keep from squealing and flinging myself into his arms. I put the T-shirt back and brushed through the hangers, which made the shirts wave back and forth almost in a hello. I cleared my throat. "Long time no see."

"Miss me?" His arm, sporting the new gold Rolex, reached out to take a Ranger's shirt off the display rack. I smelled my favorite brand of cologne. His breath was warm, and smelled freshly minted. Was it for my benefit to snare me in his webs of deceit again? Or did he really care? I turned my back to him so he couldn't read my emotions. "Was I supposed to?"

He scoffed. "Well, perhaps not since you've moved on to greener pastures. I mean, the way you've been hanging around that young minister." He made a disapproving click with his tongue. "Alone, behind closed doors no less."

I swung toward him, my Irish temper bubbling to the surface.

He cocked his head. "Ah, I see. Is it because he's safe? Or do you like the challenge?"

The temperature in my cheeks increased by at least ten degrees. "Because of you, I am seeking counseling from that pastor."

His grin widened. "And signed up for Bible courses, too. Glad to be a good influence on your life."

"How…How did you know?" I sputtered.

"I have made it my job to know, lady." He leaned in and brushed his lips over my right cheekbone then moved them to my ear. "I have been watching you, hon, even in your travels. I wasn't the only one. Others in New York watched to make sure you did the right thing and came home."

I gasped. "If you knew about those goons on the plane, why didn't you intervene?"

"I couldn't, Jen. It would have brought me out into the open. I am still wanted, you know."

I flipped around. "Stay away from me. Crawl back into your delusional underworld. I want no more to do with you." Another lie.

The manager came over. "Is anything wrong here?"

Tom scratched his head. "She doesn't want me going to the game with the guys instead of her." He rolled his eyes for effect.

I thrust my hands onto my hips. "Oh, sure. So, I guess Miss Buxom, always-wearing-a-too-tight-T-shirt Sheila is one of the guys, huh? She gets to go with you."

The manager spun on one heel and backed away from the line of fire.

Tom's eyes twinkled. "See, we make such a good pair."

"Not anymore."

He rubbed the small of my back. "I've missed you. I just had to wait until things cooled down a bit."

My eyes became hot. I jerked away from his touch. "I mean it, Tom. Go away."

He held up a Snickers candy bar. "Then, why did you come?"

I looked away.

"Your finger is still bare. Never replaced the wedding ring, huh?"

I clenched my jaw and stormed out of the pharmacy. I half-wanted him to follow me and half-wanted to put as much distance between us as possible. I walked to my car and stood there trying to collect my thoughts. Hadn't he just admitted to knowing about my being shanghaied in New York? Then why hadn't he stopped it? Surely, if he was truly the big underworld man he claimed to be, it would have been a piece of cake.

Then, the reason became as clear as if I was reading it off newsprint. The news media wanted to know about me and my delusional coworker turned kidnapper. The connection with Tom was the newsmaker—not social awareness issues—which would make audiences tune in. Even if I tried to steer the conversations to trafficking, my story and his were at the heart of it. The interviewers at my door had twisted their questions to be about him and his treatment of me. So would the national ones. My testimony would have put the paparazzi on a man hunt for Tom. The under-funded police detectives might give up, but the press wouldn't. They'd find him, and then the Feds would swoop in.

What an idiot I had been. In the effort to keep him from danger I might have shoved him further in. Maybe he didn't know the goons roughed me up so much. I had to tell him. Was he still in the store?

I scanned the parking lot and noticed a familiar white van. Mae Lin leaned against it as she filed her claws.

Tom brushed past me. Before I could speak, he sauntered over to the van. He placed his hand on Mae Lin's waist and whispered into her ear. She grinned as she zeroed her eyes on me. They turned to thin slats in her round face.

I got in my car and left. In my rearview mirror, I saw her wrap one hand around the back of Tom's neck and a long, skinny jean and boot-clad leg around his thigh. She planted her mouth firmly over his.

At least this time no syringe had been jabbed into me. Only a dagger to my heart.

My eyes stung. "I hope you will be very happy together." I

spoke in a choked whisper.

CHAPTER NINE

FOR THE NEXT week, I spent a good deal of time online reading about trafficking and illegal immigrants. It gave me something to focus on besides the image of Tom with Mae Lin, which still haunted me. I became fascinated with peeling the onion of information beyond the surface search results. Each article provided another clue, another source to Google. Somewhere, imbedded in all this information, were roads which might lead me to Monica or Marisol.

Poor Marisol. I made up a calendar and figured out her due date as best I could. I handed the flyers out in pregnancy clinics hoping, that if she would have been filtered through this area and dumped by the coyotes, she would seek them out for help.

Because she was Catholic, I doubted she would've gone to an abortion clinic, so I didn't visit any of those. How could I? My own memories prevented me.

Marisol would be too far along by now anyway. It was almost

Thanksgiving.

THE NATIONAL HUMAN Trafficking Resource Center clerk took down my information. She explained they were mostly in the business of assisting already discovered victims with health and legal services. Trafficked victims can receive free assistance in exchange for information on their abusers. If Marisol ever contacted them, they'd ask her permission to contact me.

Maria Gonzales-Taylor was assigned to be my local contact. I met her over lunch in a diner just a few blocks from campus. She carefully went over the program with me.

"We intervene by requesting the local law enforcement officials grant immunity to any girl who has been prostituted in exchange for information. By law, if they lead us to their captors, the girls get cash assistance as well as medical and social services."

"So, they agree to help you?"

Maria shook her head. "Very few actually do. You have to understand these girls came to the U.S. to make money so their families could have better lives. The coyotes say they will send the money home. These girls have revealed where their families live. That's the hold over them."

I gave her a blank look. "So?"

"They have been told their families will suffer the consequences if they do not obey."

"Aw." I sighed back the tears. Marisol's frightened face loomed in my mind. "That's why it's hard for them to break away?"

She nodded. "Exactly. Unless the vultures are caught first, they fear they'll be endangering themselves and their loved ones back home. But they're also afraid to be part of the process to catch them."

I shook my head. "What a hold those scumbags place on these

poor girls."

Maria stirred sweetener into her coffee. She took a sip, grimaced, then reached for another packet. "The coffee is strong here."

"Sleep-deprived students like it that way." I leaned toward her. "So I have to first convince Marisol and Monica their families will be safe, when I find them."

She shook her head again. "Fear keeps some from running away. But it isn't always the case. Some of these girls were abused at home. They escaped to the U.S. to get away from that."

I handed her the bowl of individual creamers. "But then they are sexually abused here as well."

Maria clinked her spoon around the ceramic mug. "Yes, but it is all they know, so it seems, well, normal. It is what men do. At least here, they are told, they will make good money letting men do that. They will receive decent living quarters, clothes, good food, and cash to send home. They are told if they get pregnant or come down with something, their 'uncle,' so to speak" — she used her fingers as quotation marks — "will take them to clinics who do not ask for papers and get them treated."

"So, the girls figure this is better than life back home." All this seemed so unbelievable, yet after what I had seen in the New Mexico desert, very believable to me. "They just want a better life. These young women have been convinced they don't have the power to achieve it on their own."

Maria took a gulp of her coffee and nodded. "Exactly. But the opposite is true. Once they get here in the U.S., they live in squalor. All the money goes to the trafficker. If they become pregnant, they are often dumped out somewhere to fend for themselves, or they are killed."

My heart jolted. Was Marisol still alive? "Why?" I squeaked.

"Once they begin to show, they are useless. Abortions cost too much money. These girls are expendable commodities, Jen, not people. Only occasionally will one of the coyotes pay for an abortion, if the girl is particularly popular with his clients. Sometimes, they let the girl stay pregnant, then once the baby is born, sell it on the black market."

"So maybe Marisol is being cared for?"

She shrugged her shoulder. "Maybe. But that kind of situation is rare."

My eyes welled. I blinked and turned away.

"Of course, most of them get hooked on drugs they are given to keep them skinny and, well, tireless. That is the other bond their pimps have on them. I wish I could be of more help."

I handed her a piece of paper. On it were sketched renditions of Monica and Marisol. "I hired a street vendor artist to draw their faces from my memory. He did a great job. I want to make these into flyers to plaster in and around the Metroplex. I thought I'd start with the DART light rail commuter stops and bus stops."

Maria shook her head. "That kind of action could make their traffickers take them elsewhere, or just get rid of them. Their clients won't want to be with girls whose faces are known. They will no longer be useful."

"They'll die?"

She looked me in the eye. "If these girls are in the Metroplex, and they very well may be, you have to be careful about how many waves you make."

I nodded and looked at my sketches. My finger rubbed across the innocent faces staring back at me. I renewed my vow to find them. But how?

"Jen?" Maria's voice softened to a tender whisper. "Don't do this alone. If you spot them or their captors, call me. We know how to take it from there."

I smiled back and clasped her hand. "I will. I promise."

She slipped me her home phone number and cell phone number. "Good."

ON SUNDAY, JAKE pulled me aside at the coffee hour after services.

"I've been praying for you."

I grinned. "I have something to tell you. I've talked with the government agencies in that pamphlet you gave me."

"And?"

"I was assigned a local contact. I told her all about Marisol and Monica. She gave me good leads."

"Be careful, Jen."

I patted his sleeve. "I will. I know who to call if I spot the girls, or the men who have them."

"I'd like to see you again." His eyes pleaded, then widened. "I mean in counseling of course. We have some unfinished business concerning your feelings about certain men in your life. You still have some issues to sort through, no?"

My back straightened. "No. I'm fine. Really. Washed that man right out of my hair, as the old song goes."

"Ahhh." Pastor Jake's expression didn't waver. "But is he out from under your skin, as another old song goes?"

I shifted my gaze to my shoes. Was I that transparent, or was he that intuitive?

I felt the weight of his warm hand on my shoulder. "Call Mrs. Edwards to set an appointment for this week."

Soon, he was off to chat with another member of the congregation.

Meeting with him was the last thing I wanted to do. Perhaps I was swallowing my feelings, but I was tired of tasting them in my mouth all the time. Was it so wrong to want to bury them deep in my gullet like the whale did to Jonah in today's church reading? I wanted to taste only the sweetness of normalcy for a while.

As I watched Jake move among his flock, I bit my lip and wished he was twenty years older and balding, instead of being so close to my own age. Why did young ministers look so handsome?

Tom's crude comments echoed in my head. I had to get a grip. Right now what I needed the most was to stay away from all men.

THE HOLIDAYS WERE a blur to me. I didn't have family and didn't feel like celebrating with anyone except Tom Cat. I went to church services, then spent the rest of the time downloading movies. I told myself Jake was too busy for counseling sessions, and even phoned Mrs. Edwards to tell him I'd make an appointment after the New Year. To pass the time until my classes began, I searched the Internet for more anti-trafficking organizations. I sent checks to several missionary groups and hosted a jewelry party in my apartment complex and at the church to raise money for one called Women at Risk, or W.A.R.

TIME MARCHED ON. Cliché as it sounds, it really seemed that way. Once my courses started, my life became regimented again. I made several friends in the same classes. None of them knew what had happened to me, which was a blessed relief. It felt good to be normal again. I did tell them I was widowed and seeking new avenues. Vivian, another widow who was twenty years my senior, tried to talk me into attending her grief group. I told her I was in private counseling.

The lies just kept rolling off my tongue. I never made an appointment to see Jake. I'd quit going to worship. I didn't feel like being asked any more questions. I wanted answers.

Instead, I contacted another resource in Washington, D.C. which was a key player in the war against illegal immigration abuse. A woman named Rebecca headed their anti-trafficking department. I emailed her, saying I was doing a research project for my degree. Yes, another lie.

In a conference call, she and one of the education coordinators for moral issues, named Steve, told me more about the plight of these victims. I learned sex was not the only angle.

Many worked in restaurants as dishwashers and in motels as maids, sixteen to eighteen hours a day. All of the money went to their traffickers. Boys, too, were trafficked, though more often they were put to work on farms picking produce. But some were used for sex as well.

"My world has been so sheltered." My voice weakened. "I had no idea."

"I felt that way at first as well." Empathy softened Rebecca's tone. "If these women try to leave, or turn these men into the authorities, they are threatened with their lives, and the lives of their loved ones back home. That is why TVPA is not very effective."

"Yes," Steve agreed. "Plus, they are often hooked on drugs to further create a bond of dependency. The coyotes give them meth so they don't gain weight and have more energy."

"And if they get pregnant?" My voice carried an ounce of hope for Marisol.

"Well," Rebecca heaved a deep sigh. "The good money makers have illegally acquired pills shoved down their throats to make them abort. Otherwise, they are tossed on the streets to fend for themselves."

I choked back the tears. I knew all too well about that pill. Again I lied. "Yes, it's what the local agent for the National Human Trafficking Resource Center told me."

I heard the woman shift in her chair. "Did she explain this life is all they know, so if these girls are tossed out, they find other drug dealers and other pimps?"

"Yes. It seems so...useless."

"You feel helpless to do anything, right?" The coordinator's voice filled with empathy. "We understand, trust us."

"How do you do this day in and day out?" I swallowed. "How heartbreaking."

"We pray together a lot." A clear, sweet faith echoed in her voice. "We also keep hope that, through public awareness, we can put enough pressure on these coyotes to make a dent."

I hesitated to ask the next question. "How do men find these girls? You know, the ones who want to, well..."

Steve spoke up. "Different communities have different symbols. These men know what they are. You're in Texas, right? Watch for cowboy boots with spurs. If you see them on a logo for a business, trafficking may be going on in the back rooms. Not just sex, but slave labor, too."

"The DFW area is a prime spot because so many Interstates connect there," Rebecca added. "The main routes of trafficking follow the Interstates because they can get their victims to their locations quicker. Besides, the traffic volume is greater so they can maintain anonymity."

It began to make sense. The pieces of the puzzle became less gray. "Because bigger cities are easier to hide in?"

"You got it. Also, remember, these girls do not trust police because in their countries government is so corrupt. If they spot law enforcement, they will scatter like flies."

I learned from talking with them that Hispanics are not the only victims. Girls from Asia, Africa, and even European countries are enticed to the U.S., then thrown into the world of trafficking. I also read a true story about how our nation's girls are trafficked by other cultures here in the U.S. For political reasons, some Arab men enjoy abusing white American girls and pay top dollar to do so. Such was the case of blond-haired, blue-eyed teenager Theresa Flores.[1] Her middle class East Coast parents never knew. The more I read, the more confused I became about how to proceed.

What could I do besides wander the streets, or patrol in my car at night, trying to get a glimpse of young Hispanic women, in the hopes one of them would talk and lead me to Marisol or Monica? That seemed not only dangerous but impractical. How could I, an Anglo, tawny-red haired, American woman with hazel-blue eyes, ever enter such a world and come out unscathed?

I couldn't. Nobody could.

I CHOSE TO write letters to congressmen and speak to women's church groups. At least locally I had a bit of something akin to fame. My name, thanks to my faked death and resurrection, still opened doors. I concentrated my talks, however, on the trafficking issue, saying my story was less important. My answer became rote. "God protected me and yet opened my eyes to greater horrors through the experience. Because I was kidnapped, I can relate to these girls even though my captor treated me well."

I was careful not to mention his name. Either one of them.

Word spread throughout the Metroplex. I even got on two talk show radio programs and was a keynote speaker at the Rotary Club's meeting. The agent with a top publishing house contacted me again, but I turned them down for now.

"I want to concentrate on my primary goal."

The literary agent's voice was metered but kind. "We'd already assigned a ghost writer. You know that."

I remained silent.

After a moment she agreed. "You know, if you actually find the girls, it would make it an even better book. Maybe even a TV movie."

I promised I'd stay in touch.

I NEVER HEARD from Tom again. Not even a stealth Snickers on the door stoop for Valentines or sneaked into my Easter basket. I shoved his memory to the back of my heart.

The weather turned warm and sultry, as springtime often does in Texas. I was getting the hang of Spanish, surprised I actually recalled as much as I did. So far I had made B's on the pop exams Señora Ybarra loved to throw at the class. The tests were a manifestation of her unyielding power over the eighteen of us, who ranged anywhere on the spectrum from businessmen to housewives, from young twenties to early sixties. As an exercise, I learned to pray in Spanish for Monica and Marisol. Somehow, I hoped it would help them get the message that someone cared. Marisol must be almost six months along, if she was still pregnant.

AFTER EASTER, I sat with two women I'd met in one of my classes, Mindy and Vivian, the older widow. We were in a busy Mexican restaurant, a popular local chain with both indoor and outdoor seating. We sipped Diet Cokes, chomped on nachos, and talked about study schedules so we could prep for our term exams.

I excused myself to go inside to the ladies' room. As I walked the corridor to the restrooms in the back, I heard a clamor in the kitchen and raised Hispanic voices. A man stormed out. As the double-doors swung, I saw a young girl being slapped to her knees. A shock gripped my heart when she turned toward the door. I knew her face. Monica.

I rushed to the door. In an instant, two strong hands pulled me back. "You lost, Señora?"

I turned to see a tall man with tattoos on his arms and neck. "Restroom?"

He jerked his head toward the back. "Over there."

I dashed inside the women-only room, locked the door, and fell to my knees. "Thank you, Lord. I've found one of them. Now, what do I do?"

I laid my head against the tile wall. Dare I involve my classmates? How much would I have to explain?

I gathered my composure before returning to my table on the patio. I desperately wanted to catch Monica's eyes, but I remembered what Maria had told me. I could endanger her life. So, I fumbled through my handbag to keep from looking toward the kitchen. After I'd meandered through the maze of tables to my seat, Mindy looked at me.

"We were wondering where you were."

Vivian touched my arm. "Are you okay? You look like you've seen a ghost."

I sighed. They wouldn't believe half of what I told them. So, I lied. Again. "I saw a huge sewer roach in the restroom. It crawled over my foot when I was on the toilet. I am so scared of them."

Vivian laughed. "For me, it is snakes, my dear."

Mindy shuddered. "Mice, rats, even hamsters freak me. Gerbils? They're way worse."

"I have a real fear of coyotes, too," I muttered. My friends gave me blank looks. I took a sip of soda, keeping a half-eye on the swinging kitchen door. After a few minutes, I pretended I'd forgotten an appointment and told Vivian and Mindy I had to leave.

I dashed to my car and grabbed my cell phone to call Maria Gonzales-Taylor. "I found her. I found Monica. She is here in Fort Worth at the Taco Shack near TCC." I gasped for breath. My heart pounded in my ears. "You know. Where I've been going to classes. Tarrant Community College."

"Whoa. Slow down." Her voice remained calm. "Are you certain?'

"Yes, absolutely. It was her. She's working in the kitchen."

Maria sighed into her receiver. "Are you there now?"

"Yes. I'm in the parking lot. In my car." Movement caught my eye. The tattooed man was taking trash to the dumpster behind the restaurant. He glanced my way. I turned my head and slouched behind the wheel.

"A man saw me look at her. He's outside, right now."

"Then leave. Now."

I turned my ignition key, backed out of my parking space, then headed for the street. With my cell phone clutched on my shoulder near my ear, I waited for a space in traffic. "Okay. Now what do we do?"

I heard her shuffle papers on her desk. "Come to my office. We'll talk."

"I'll be there in twenty minutes." I slipped my phone from my shoulder and went to click it off. A male hand reached from the back seat and grabbed it.

"No, you won't, hon."

I turned to see black locks and deep, iced-blue eyes peering at me. Familiar cologne whiffed into my senses, jump-starting my endorphins. He leaned forward and pecked the corner of my wide-open mouth.

"Hi, lady. Missed me?"

CHAPTER TEN

I WANTED TO scream and tell him to get out of my car. I also wanted to jump into the back seat and wrap him around me. Instead, I sat there with the engine running, dumbfounded. He got out, came around, and slipped into the front passenger-side seat.

"You should lock your doors."

"You'd figure out how to open them." I squirmed and tightened my grip on the steering wheel.

"I've liked your speeches. And that was a great interview on the Morning Commute with Carl show. You are becoming quite the star."

Under my breath, I counted to three. "I want you to get out." In the rearview mirror, I saw a car pulling up behind me. I motioned to the car door. "Right now."

His hand grabbed mine. "We need to talk, Jen. You can't tell them about Monica. Not yet."

I stared at him.

"Yes, I know she's here. In fact, I helped make that happen. It's better than where she would have ended up."

I whirled to face him. "You knew?" I slapped the fool out of him. I couldn't help it. My hand was across his face before my brain registered what it was doing.

"Okay," he moved his jaw back and forth. "I deserved that, I guess."

I lowered my hand, fisted it, and held it in my lap to keep it from shaking. Tears stung my eyes. Since I had met this man, I had begun to hit, lie, and hate. "I want you out of my life. And out of hers."

He inched over to me and rubbed my shoulder. "You don't mean it, hon. You love me as much as I love you. Admit it."

The man in the car behind us blared his car horn. In my rearview mirror, I saw him raise his hands in frustration.

Tom looked in the rearview mirror. "You'd better move. You're blocking the drive." I gunned the car into traffic, turned the corner, and pulled into a convenience store. I pulled the key from the ignition, and shoved it into my purse. "No," I hissed. "I hate you."

He reached for me, but I was already out of my seat. I slammed the car door in his face.

I had to get away to call Maria. Once again a restroom would work as my refuge. Then, I could call the police, too. The stalking had to end. Tom really was insane.

My finger had already curled around the store's door when he snatched it. "I said, we need to talk. Hear me out, Jen. Then decide. Please."

A black woman with three small children in tow pushed past us, one eyebrow cocked. I shoved my hair behind my ear, looked down at the sidewalk, then up to the top of the store's marquee—anywhere but into his eyes.

"Jen? Look at me."

"Don't you dare tell me to trust you, Tom. So help me..." My hand was shoulder-height again. He reared back and raised both of his in front of his chest. I swallowed my anger and headed for my car. He rushed ahead to open my door.

"You won't go away, will you?"

"Jen, this may be all wrong, but it's time you heard the whole story." He held the door open, his knuckles white. "Hear me out, then decide if we should ever see each other again."

I sucked all the air I could through my nose and exhaled. "And you will abide by my wishes?"

"Absolutely."

I edged toward the front seat. "Where are we going?"

"Just get in and drive. I'll give you directions. It'll be some place safe, with people. No back alleys or open fields."

I spied a wry smile inch toward the sparkling blue in his eyes. My heart tumbled. I sighed and dug for my keys. They weren't there.

Puzzled, I saw them swinging between his fingers as he got in the passenger side. "Didn't want to you leave without me." He fastened his seatbelt, and plopped them into my waiting hand.

"At least this time you aren't burning my car."

"Nice one, by the way. Mazda, right?"

I didn't respond. I turned the ignition and tried not to look into his face, afraid I might crater. *Remain calm, Jen. Play along Find out what he wants...just keep your head straight.*

He gave me directions as I continued my self-help mantras.

I nodded and did as I was told. We drove up Highway 360 to Grapevine, and then turned onto Main Street. It was an historic area with a nineteenth century city hall claiming majesty in the middle of the town. Quaint shops and boutiques lined the street. Traffic became bumper-to-bumper and was diverted to side street parking lots offering safekeeping for ten dollars a day. Banners stretched above the road announced the festival was called Main Street Days.

Tom pointed to a parking lot and motioned me to pull in. "Safety in numbers. Besides, we deserve to have a good time. I hear the homemade ice cream is fabulous." He reared up, took his wallet from his right hip pocket, and handed me a ten dollar bill.

"Thanks. Money's a bit tight right now." I punched my automatic window button and handed the attendant the money. He pointed to a vacant stall on the left, two rows over.

Tom winked. "I know. You're a starving student now. Don't worry, it's all on me. Whatever you want to eat, drink, or buy. Let's go."

"And then you'll tell me what this is all about?"

"Uh-huh. Promise." He got out, came around, opened my door, and extended his hand like a gentleman. Once I swiveled out, he laced his arm through my elbow.

I slung my purse onto my other shoulder. "Okay. Where to?"

"Those shops look fun." He motioned up the block and began to walk, me in tow. We entered the crowds, jostling left, then right at a snail's pace. He pulled me closer to him so our hips rubbed together as we walked. Leaning close, he spoke into my ear. "Let's just window shop for now, blend in. In a while maybe we can find a quieter side café and talk."

I nodded and pointed to a store with candles, cows, and bluebonnet-painted cups and saucers sprinkled amongst antiques. We went in. At least ten other people were browsing the shelves as an elderly lady with a red gingham blouse and denim skirt painted with sequin-lined stars grinned a Texas welcome. Tom eased us over to the candle section and picked up one for me to sniff. "I knew those coyotes who have Monica, Jen. They were part of the group we were trying to infiltrate for the government."

"Get real."

"Jen, I've never lied to you. I've just withheld some truths. Now, I want to tell you everything."

I put the candle back and spun to face him. "Why now?"

He raised his eyes, tipped a pretend hat to some ladies who had also eyed the candles and pulled me toward the jars of jams. His voice volume lowered. "Because you're getting too close to danger. You have to back off."

"So this isn't a social call?" My sarcasm was thicker than the cactus jalapeño jelly I held in my hand.

He rolled his eyes, set the jar down, and grabbed my elbow again. He pulled us back into the mob of tourists. How they could be so eager to come here on a sweltering Texas day in order to part with their money was beyond me. A bank marquee flashed 92 degrees even though it was only May. A droplet of sweat rolled down my temple to my cheek.

He nudged me in the back. "Let's go down this way. Ice cream will cool us off."

Tom bought two double-dipped vanilla ice creams in waffle cones with peach pecan syrup. He handed me one and guided me toward a bistro set for four in a side alley.

"I thought you said no alleys?"

"Ha, ha." He pulled out a chair for me.

"Jen, Homeland Security is getting more efficient at shutting down the borders. Part of that process is identifying the smugglers who are delivering these girls—and boys, by the way—to the traffickers. Originally, our job was to find out as much as we could about their network."

"Yours and Mae Lin's?" Her name was poison in my mouth.

"No. Mine...and his." His eyes rose as a shadow crossed our table. I turned to see a face I thought I'd never see again, sipping on a Coke.

"Hi, sweetheart."

My dead husband slid into the chair next to me.

CHAPTER ELEVEN

MY HEART STOPPED. The alley spun. Two hands grabbed me before my face smashed into my ice cream cone. "Take a deep breath, Jen."

"I—I...Robert?" The words stuck in my throat. Tears cascaded down my cheeks as I tossed my ice cream on the table and threw my shaky arms around him. I felt his heart beating against my ear. *He is alive.* I clung to him and sobbed.

He pulled away. "Get a grip. Not in public. You'll make a scene."

I wiped my eyes and looked at Tom for answers. His face was pained. I straightened my posture, and then looked back and forth between them. Robert's olive-colored eyes narrowed in on Tom and went cold.

Tom got up. "Right. I'll give you five minutes with her. But that's all." He screeched the metal chair out of the way and meandered across the street, hands shoved deep into his jean pockets.

I spun to my husband. "Five minutes?"

"It's all a dead man can afford, Jen."

I cupped his chin. A half-day bristle had formed. "Why?"

He pulled my hand away. "I was putting you and me in too much danger. I had to plan it this way. I couldn't tell you because it had to be believable."

Venom rose in my throat. "Your death devastated me."

His green eyes misted. "I know." It came out in a whisper. He blinked and his Adam's apple thrust. Then, he shook his head. "This was not a good idea."

My husband stood and moved away. I reached for him. "Robert!"

He grabbed me by the shoulders. "Jen. Hear me. I am dead. For your sake. I've gotten too deep to come back. I am a head coyote now. The white *Jefe*."

My words barely slid out of my mouth. "The man Marisol said raped one of them every night?"

A vicious sneer came across his face. "Part of the job, sweetheart."

So it was true. Or was this just another lie to weave into the web of deceit he'd manufactured for so long? Had he *ever* told me the truth about anything? I shook my head, not wanting to believe him.

He clenched his hands, his fingers pressed into me. "Jen. Those girls you are so desperate to find? Don't bother. I traffic hundreds of them."

I jerked away from his touch and cupped my ears. "No."

He pulled my fingers away. "Yes. I have broken our vows time and again. I sleep with them, Jen. Break them in. Show them what American men expect. It is all part of it."

I bit my lip. His words hung between us, my brain refusing to absorb them.

"Marisol is carrying my child."

"Nooooo!" I screamed and ran into the crowd.

Tears flowed from my face, as I shoved people aside. The truth I'd feared had spewed from his lips along with a vile look in his eyes—a look I'd never seen before, nor cared to see again.

I didn't know where I was going. I couldn't feel my legs. Pure instinct kept me moving block after block until my sides wrenched with pain. I wrapped my arms around my waist and slid to the ground, curling myself into a fetal position behind a dumpster.

I couldn't have his baby and Marisol could? He chose to give his seed for her to carry and not me? Bile pushed into my throat.

"God help me. I hate him. I hate him. I hate You!"

I threw up. Months of tears, hurt, fear, and anger all spewed onto the ground between my knees, right along with the ice cream. I felt Tom's hands on my back. I jerked myself out of his grasp.

"Here." A cool, damp hankie was placed in my lap. I rocked back and laid my pounding head against the searing heat of the metal dumpster wall. My shoulder muscles eased, but my chest still heaved.

"Oh, God. Comfort this woman. Give her strength." Tom grabbed the cloth and washed my face in soft, gentle strokes.

Footsteps crunched on the caliche path in the semi-paved alley. I squinted to see black boots, and sunglasses under a Stetson hat. A badge gleamed in the afternoon sun. "Ma'am? You need help?"

Tom rose to his feet. "Heat got to her, I think. I thought the peach ice cream would help, but it made it worse."

How easily he lied—just as he'd taught me to do.

The two men lifted me to my feet as my legs tried to find the ground.

"You want me to call an ambulance?"

"No. Our car is a block over. Help me get her to it, and I'll take her home."

I didn't care. Let them drag me to wherever they wanted. My life was over. Nothing mattered now.

ALL THE WAY back I leaned against the car window staring out into space as fields and fences zipped by, then turned into pylons and concrete lanes in the city. My body shook, in spite of the heat. The AC blasted my face, drying my tear ducts. My brain felt numb.

Tom pulled into a dilapidated duplex somewhere off McCart Lane in Fort Worth. "This is my home now."

I don't care. Take me back to the bomb shelter coffin and dump me. Zombie-like, I let him shuffle me inside and down the hall. He laid me on a bed, pulled my legs around, and took off my shoes. Then he placed a pillow under my head with the care of a professional nurse. I stared at the ceiling.

When he sat next to me, the mattress gave under his weight. His body heat chilled me. I inched away, rolled onto my side, and drew my legs tight to my chest.

He brushed my hair back from my eyes. "Rest, Jen. I'll be in the next room."

"Watching through a black hump in the ceiling?"

I heard his breath suck in, then release through his nose. "No, hon. Not this time." He caressed my shoulder. "Whenever you want to talk, scream, cry, or whatever, I'm here. Call for me."

The mattress thickened under me as his body left it. I heard his footsteps, then the light switch click and the door hinges squeak. I squinted and waited for another click—of the lock—but none came. I half-turned to see. In the shadow of the ceiling I saw a wedge of reflected light. He'd left the door ajar. Well, wonders never ceased. I sucked in a deep breath and felt a residual shiver before my body relaxed. I closed my eyes and let my mind drift.

I didn't need to be drugged this time. Pure exhaustion did the trick.

WHEN MY EYES opened again, the room was pitch black, except for the wedge of light, which now stretched onto the wall, brighter and more yellowed. In the distance I heard the muted hum of TV voices and laughter, then a familiar commercial jingle coming through the wall from next door. Duplex. Right. He had neighbors.

My whole body ached as if I'd been kicked and dragged by a mule. A wave of nausea pumped rancid bile into my throat. I flipped over, aiming my face at the floor just as an acidic stream burst through my lips.

Immediately Tom was there, washcloth in hand. "Maybe I should get you to the hospital."

I shook my head and spat out the last of the phlegm. I wiped my face and the back of my neck with the cloth. The coolness calmed my nerves.

He sat on the edge of the bed and rubbed my back. "Do you want me to stay?"

Unlike my time in the bomb shelter, this time I knew the answer. "Yes, please stay with me."

He collected me into his arms and rocked me as the sobs began again, then turned into wails. His voice cooed, and his hands caressed me until I was all cried out. First, he soothed my nerves. Then, his lips moved from my neck, to my cheek, to my mouth and pressed my breath to mingle with his.

My whole being floated into a warm place as his mouth pushed harder. I went limp. He lowered himself onto the bed and drew me to him. I lay there, cradled in his arms, eyes closed, as he gently swayed our bodies back and forth. The TV next door hummed with muffled laugher, jingles, and organ music.

Still, I heard him barely whisper. "I love you, Jen. Enough to wait until you are free from him."

I felt the blanket cover me. I nestled my head on his chest. Sleep again took over, this time more peaceful.

CHAPTER TWELVE

I JOLTED AWAKE as the swoosh of the curtains across the rod blasted sunlight onto my face.

"Good morning, sleepyhead," Tom sang in a high-pitched sickly sweet voice as he hovered over me.

I groaned. "Let me guess. Another of your mother's obnoxious sayings?"

"Yes. Does the trick, doesn't it?"

"No, the sunlight streaming in did." I shaded my eyes and tried to lift myself on my elbow. I half-opened one eye to see. When he turned back to face me he was grinning with a faraway look in his eyes. Oh, no. It was the same look Robert used to have after...I crunched the blanket to my neck. "What happened?"

"Nothing. You fell asleep." His tone was flat, but his eyes fogged with a touch of hurt as he lowered them to the floor. "I'd never take advantage of you like that, Jen. Honest."

I rubbed my hand over the back of my head and slid my body against the wall behind the bed. "Okay, Tom. I believe you. I trust you now. I do."

He sat on the edge and handed me a steaming mug of Earl Grey tea. The glimmer returned to his eyes. "About time, lady. Here, take slow sips."

"Why were you grinning, then?"

"If I told you I liked seeing you first thing in the morning, would you get the wrong idea?"

I shrugged and breathed in the soothing aroma. From the time I was a teenager, Earl Grey solved all my problems from cramps to heartaches. Robert had known that. He probably told Tom. A boulder of new grief crushed my chest. "Robert." It came out in a graveled whisper.

"Yes." He eased off the bed. "Drink your tea, and if you tolerate that, I'll make you toast." He stopped at the door. "Then we'll talk about him." Hand on the door knob, he added. "Oh, the bathroom is right next door."

The door clicked closed. I shut my eyes and opened them again, just to make sure it had not all been a bizarre dream. No. Same room. Same facts. My husband was alive and a horrible man. I was no longer a widow. I was not free. Tom had always known.

I sipped my tea and gazed around the sparsely furnished room. The walls were scuffed and in dire need of a paint job. The door had a huge, splintered tear in its veneer. The edges around the light switch were smudged in dark gray. The splotched tan carpet was matted with age, yet the room smelled of fresh linens. Why? Then, I spied the plug-in air freshener in the socket across the room. Tom's attempt to dispel the mustiness, no doubt.

The old bed made my back ache. The springs groaned under me when I moved. Where was I?

A chill hit me. Was this a...no. He wouldn't take me to one of those places. Not where those poor girls met their men for the night.

I jumped up and rubbed my arms, as if cooties or lice crawled on the bed. I dashed out of the room, my eyes so wide my lids stretched. Tom was at the other end of the short hall on a plaid couch in shades of tan and brown. He jolted to his feet. "What is it?"

I stopped in the hall, shaking. "Where have you brought me?" My teeth clenched back an angry scream.

He dashed to me and grasped my shoulders. "You're all right here. This is my safe house. No one knows about it. Not Mae Lin, not Robert. No one." He emphasized the last sentence in a slow, firm tone.

I looked around the dingy walls. "This isn't one of his...you know, a brothel?"

He rocked back. "Dear God in Heaven, no." Tom led me to the sofa and coaxed me on to it. Then he pouted. "Don't like my decorating style, huh?"

"Did you have to pick a place so—" I scanned the room with a sour look. "So grungy?"

"It's not that bad. It came furnished. It's cheap. Doesn't attract attention. I'm not here much, anyway."

I bobbed my head. "Typical guy answer."

"No creepy crawlies or sticky webs. Promise." He waved his hand. "See? Windows. We're above ground this time."

I curled my knees to my chest. "Uh-huh. I'm counting my blessings."

"Good. Hang tight." With a wink, he disappeared into the bedroom, but quickly returned with my cup of tea and a box of tissues. He crouched on the floor in front of me, hands flat on the sofa cushions on either side of my hips. "You ask, I'll answer."

I patted the cushion beside me and took a deep drink of the tea. It slid down and coated my stomach with blessed warmth. Tom sat next to me, an arm stretched across the sofa behind my back. One foot crossed in front and slightly bounced on his other knee. His gaze landed softly on my face. "Whenever you're ready."

"Robert knows about us?"

"Yes."

"He doesn't mind?"

Tom's hand played with a strand of my hair and then dropped. "I'm sure he does. But he chose the direction he went, Jen. He knew you couldn't follow."

I nodded. "I see."

He sniffed in a quick breath. "I doubt it." With that, he took the mug from my hand. "Let me get you a bit more."

I watched him head for the kitchen as he rubbed the tension out of the back of his neck. This was hard for him as well. My heart softened. Maybe we were both pawns.

My bladder decided to come to life. "Tom?"

He turned back toward me, brows knitted. "Yes?"

"Do you mind if I..." My eyes pointed down the hallway.

"Knock yourself out. Take a shower, too. You'll feel better." His bare footsteps slapped across the linoleum. "There are towels, shampoo, soap. Sorry, no clothes. I would have bought some, but I was afraid to leave you alone."

I gingerly stepped down the hall. As stained as the carpet was, I wasn't so sure there were no creepy crawlies.

He peeked out from the tiny galley kitchen. "You can borrow my robe, though. It's clean. Sort of. It's hanging on the peg."

I shot him a grin. "Thanks."

"Oh, Jen?"

"Yes?" I stopped and grabbed the doorjamb which opened into the once-harvest gold bathroom floor.

Tom's face widened into a smile. "No cameras. Take your time. Screw the water bill."

His eyes glittered under raised brows. He returned to the sink

to dump the lukewarm tea out of my mug.
    A hearty laugh burst from my mouth.

CHAPTER THIRTEEN

THE BATHROOM WAS clean, thank goodness. Old, chipped porcelain bore hard water stains, but it smelled freshly scrubbed. The shower spray steamed with a hint of chlorine.

This time, I washed that man right out of my body, hair, heart, and soul. Robert, that was. I let the showerhead's water spray me until I felt red and raw as my brain shuffled through each question and cleansed it from my mind. How dare he enter this underworld of prostitution? What had lured him? Was he in it before we met?

A thought flashed across my mind. The woman at the hotel Becky saw him with the night before his wreck. Had she been one? No. She was older and had come to the funeral, in the daylight. Her English was impeccable. A contact then, helping him plan his demise? Or just an evening of fun? I'd never know.

I slammed my back against the almond-colored, preformed tub enclosure and cursed my husband for all he held dear, if he held anything dear anymore. Obviously, I didn't fit in that category. Whatever love I had for him slipped down the drain with the residual suds from the drug store shampoo.

I had legal papers to prove I was a widow. I never wanted to see or hear from him ever again. In my mind, I shoveled the dirt back over his coffin and walked away. His "death" was one lie I could live with.

WE SAT ON Tom's scratchy couch, his oversized robe tucked around me in folds. Armed with dry toast and more Earl Grey, I was ready to ask. He seemed ready to finally answer.

He nodded toward the bathroom door. "Now that you've had some time, has any of this soaked in?"

I snorted a laugh. "No. It's down the drain. Over." I swished my hand back and forth erasing my husband's memory. "No more Robert."

"It's not that easy, Jen."

I blew into my tea. "I know. But my whole marriage was a lie. A sham."

Tom spoke softly. "His love for you was real. Still is."

I slammed the mug onto his wobbly side table. "Don't you lie to me, too."

He rocked back in the couch and banged his head against the wall. "I don't approve of his choices. He's deeper into this thing than I thought he'd ever get. But initially his reasons were honorable."

I jumped to my feet and wheeled around to face him, hands thrust against my hips. "Honorable? Sleeping with young girls to make them prostitutes is honorable?"

Tom's eyebrows emerged as one line amongst several on his forehead. His jaw line jerked. "He told you that?"

I grabbed my lower lip with my teeth to keep it from quivering.

Tom leaned back again and rubbed his eyes. "Idiot."

I kept my stance. "For telling me the truth?"

He looked at me, red-eyed. "For telling you anything at all. It puts you in jeopardy." He leaned forward, hands clutched between his knees. "What else did he tell you?"

My gaze shot to the ceiling as I took a deep breath, then spit the words out before they hurt again. "About Marisol."

Tom groaned. "It's true."

I slung a dagger look back at him. "You knew?"

"At the time we were at the shacks, no. Robert didn't even know then."

"Robert never wanted kids. I did. Badly." I hit the air with my fists. Then, I tucked them under my arms and grabbed my sides.

"Jen, I'm so sorry. You'd make a great mom. Maybe someday..."

I closed my eyes and inhaled through my nose. I had to keep my emotions under control if I was to get any answers. I planted my feet into his grubby carpet and took a deep gulp of courage. Then I asked what I already knew deep down in the middle of my gut. "Truth, Tom. He was there? At the shacks?"

"He showed up that night, yes. To check on you and make sure they left you, and me, alone. I knew the general vicinity of the shacks, so I led us there."

"Why?"

His eyes rolled to a water spot on the ceiling. "To tell him about Mae Lin, so she'd back off. I knew the traffickers would get a message to him." He stood, and plunked his finger at the tip of my nose. "And to ensure a way for you to get back to safety, lady."

I shifted my weight to the other foot. "Wasn't that risky? I mean, I could have seen him."

Tom spread his hands, palms up. "That's why you were isolated in the shack with the girls. So you wouldn't."

I knew it would pierce me even deeper, but I had already fallen on the sword of truth. So I asked anyway. "And did he 'train' Monica some more while I was right next door?" My fingers made the quotation marks for emphasis.

He stuck his tongue in his cheek, broke eye contact, and nodded.

An invisible force shoved the pain deeper into my chest and tore open my heart. I slunk back to the couch. "I see. Because he loved me so very much."

Tom sat as well, so close our legs rubbed against each other. I didn't move away, not this time. His closeness gave me comfort— and strength as if it transfused from his flesh into mine.

"He had to stay in the role to save you. We couldn't tell them you were his wife or they might have used you against him one day. So, I'd told them you and he once were lovers, until your husband found out. I told them Robert feared for your life because your husband had a violent temper so he'd told me to bring you—"

I threw my hands into the air. "Enough. More lies. I don't care." I scooted away to put space between us, then pretzeled my arms as I tried to think of what to say next. All my tears were spent, but my heart, ripped to pieces like a paper Valentine, bled with each painful beat.

Tom waited. I could hear his breathing in the stillness lying like a fog between us.

I turned to him and stared into those blue abysses for the truth. "Do you do this as well?"

His expression didn't flinch. "No."

I narrowed into him. "Who's Mae Lin, really?"

He remained stone-faced. "An operative I report to. Nothing more."

"And she drugged me and had you transport me to New Mexico because...?"

"It was part of the original relocation plan. I was to get you to New Mexico where Robert could make arrangements for your new life. Mae Lin was to make sure that happened. He left it up to her as to how. But she added her own little twist. She decided when she saw us together she wanted you out of the way permanently."

"Why?"

"I was falling for you. Number one mistake for any asset. She was taking us in the van to Robert in hopes he'd get jealous, maybe beat me up, and traffic you." He looked away, his eyes narrowed for a moment, then returned to mine. "He'd never do that to you, Jen."

My eyes rolled into my forehead. I shifted my weight with a humph. "Don't defend him, Tom."

Sigh. "Let me finish, okay? When I realized her motives, I knew I had to get us away from her and get to Robert first so I could talk with him. He was running point in this whole deal. She was answerable to him."

"That's why we stayed off the roads and took the shortcuts over the ranchland."

Tom nodded.

"And when she figured out we'd escaped, she thought you'd head anywhere but there."

He gave me a quick grin. "Yeah. Now do you get it?" With a quick snap of his neck he leaned back, closed his eyes, and spoke in slow, forced words. "It was risky, but I knew he'd secure your safety. When I figured out the other stuff about his involvement with Marisol and Monica…" He looked back at me, his face somber. "And the drug running, I knew I had to get you out of there fast, and under the protection of the authorities. Let them persuade you to testify against me and put you in witness protection. Robert agreed to the plan because he could slither back into the dark and no one would be the wiser. He also agreed to spring me from jail if I took the fall."

The light dawned. "So the gunshot in the hotel room was part of the plot? That's why you called 911."

He shrugged. "Consider it Plan C."

I shook my head. "Then why the cloak and dagger at Walgreens?"

He looked at the floor. "Two-fold. I wanted to convince Mae Lin you had no feelings for me so she'd quit tailing you." Then he looked into my face. "And I wanted to see if perhaps you still did. After all, you didn't testify, did you? I hoped it meant you loved me. Because..." He swallowed hard. "I couldn't get you out of my head, or my heart." His eyes swam.

I wasn't buying it. "What was the love scene between you two at the van all about, then?"

Tom heaved a deep sigh and stood up. "She was jealous of you, okay? She wanted me. So she decided to show you she'd won."

"Oh, right. I saw how you resisted her." I had had enough. I walked toward the hall.

"Where are you going?"

"To gather my clothes and get out of here. You men are liars and cheats. I want nothing more to do with any of you." Now that I was a practicing Christian again, maybe I could go into the mission field in deep Africa and dedicate my life to feeding orphans.

"Jen, Stop." He spun me around, grasped the sash of the robe I'd borrowed, and drew me to him. With hands cupped around my cheeks, he kissed me, hard and long, yet with so much tenderness. I tried to catch my breath but he pushed in stronger, moving his tongue over mine. Just as the world began to swirl, he pulled away.

"I have never, ever, kissed any woman the way I just kissed you."

I watched him stomp into the kitchen as the taste of him faded from my lips. I wobbled back, plopped on the couch, and wrapped my arms tightly around my legs. My aching spine pressed into back cushions mimicking the throbbing heart which pressed against my chest.

Maybe the reporter Veronica and Dr. Jacobs were right. I really needed outside help—like outside of this universe, Creator-type of help.

"Dear God." It was all I could muster to say. I hoped the Almighty understood the thoughts which couldn't form in my brain and would respond to them anyway.

After a few moments, Tom came back in the room. His cheeks were still flushed. He popped a can of soda and sat in the chair across from the couch. It was Naugahyde in a rusty color, cracked in the cushions and torn at the arch of the arm. He rubbed the cold can back and forth over his forehead before shooting me a glance. I looked away toward the sliding glass door. It was gray and gloomy outside.

"Where's my car?"

"At your apartment by now I imagine, tucked safely in your garage. That's what I had another asset do. Nice digs, by the way." His tone was as flat as the land around Canyon, Texas.

"I gather you've seen it?"

"Told you I was watching you."

So he'd bugged my apartment. The slight whiff of cologne I had smelled wasn't all in my head. He'd probably been the gravelly voice on the phone as well. I refused to react in astonishment. Enough was enough. Instead, I continued my original train of thought. "It's not here because...?"

"Your car?" He sighed and gave me a look as if I was a moron. "So no one finds out that you're here with me. As I said, this is my safe house. Nobody else knows where it is. I prefer to keep it that way."

Tom exited the chair with a humph and walked over to me on the couch. He loomed over me, then bent down and sat on his heels. "Are we going to talk it out or not?"

I curled my legs tighter and looked back outside. "What is there to say?"

"Volumes, or nothing. Your choice."

I looked at him. His eyes shone with emotion.

"Legally I am a widow."

"Yet, you're still married."

He was right. The reality soaked in. "It will never work, will it, Tom? I can't be in your world, or in your life. I can't live with a man out of wedlock. It's not how I was raised."

He took my hand. "I know. Robert knows as well."

I jerked my hand away. "Never mention his name again."

He raised both hands, palms out in surrender. "Okay. What do you want me to do, Jen? Just tell me. Where do we go from here?"

"Help me find Marisol."

He rocked back and stood. He motioned to the couch. "May I?"

"Please do."

He sat next to me and ran his finger along the cushion band. "I sort of know where she is. She's in a house somewhere in Grand Prairie with some others, but she doesn't have to do tricks. He's making sure she gets prenatal treatment as well. Mae Lin's found someone to take her."

I jumped. "What? Tom, why didn't you tell me?"

"And have you go off on your high horse like you did with those lectures and talk shows, even after you were warned to drop it?" He shoved his finger into my face. "You are one stubborn woman, you know that?"

[291]

I pushed his hand away. My turn to sit in the Naugahyde chair. I drummed my fingers on the puffed arm and asked the next question. "Will she keep the baby or will he make her sell it on the black market?"

Tom shrugged. "They will probably tell her to drop it off at one of those safe places. A library stoop, fire station, or the steps of a school."

My stomach became queasy. "Robert doesn't want his own child, does he? Some things never change."

Sympathy gleamed in his eyes. "Look. The only reason I can figure is she's getting treatment because he is doing this for you."

"Me?"

"He saw you connect with her. That made her different from the others."

I sat erect. "Different? Others?"

Tom glared at me. "Do you really want all the ugly facts, Jen? How many young girls he's dumped on the streets once he knocked them up because abortions are pricey and raise questions? How many he has terrorized or gotten hooked on drugs so they'd perform? Do you want to learn how long he has been doing this undercover work as a coyote?"

I shook off new tears with my response. The nice Greek Orthodox man I thought I'd married who was honest, loyal and moral was a fantasy.

Tom snorted. "I didn't think so. Besides, you told me not to mention him, right?"

I inhaled what air I could. My chest felt as if it was wrapped in a too-tight elastic bandage. I massaged my ribcage. "How did you get involved?"

He cocked his head. "With...?"

"Him. Them."

He crossed one leg over his other knee. His foot began to jiggle again. "I told you. I am under him. Even in the Navy, he was above me in rank and skill level. You don't mess with the 6th Seals."

"So, you were just following orders, per usual?"

He sat up straight and saluted. "I'm the errand boy. I do what I'm told." Then, he slouched again. "Well, most of the time."

"And you were assigned to watch out for me, the woman who stole your best friend. You must have hated me in the beginning."

Tom shrugged. "I tried to. But the more I observed you then got to know you..." He kicked his foot into the carpet. His voice volume lowered. "Now do you see why it upset me so much when he became involved with you? I knew you deserved more."

"But why was it necessary to fake my death?"

"Because you-know-who, since I'm forbidden to mention his name, got wind you were in danger."

I raised my hands in the air. "Why?"

He scratched his head. "I thought I'd explained that."

"Try again. How could I possibly be any threat?"

"By association. You were his wife. He may have confided in you."

I huffed into my bangs. "Right. Obviously that was not the case."

Tom twisted his mouth to one side. In his eyes I detected some glimpse of leftover loyalty mingled with hurt. I wasn't the only one Robert had stabbed in the gut.

"Anyway," Tom continued, "some of the coyotes suspected he was a mole. He had to go deeper to convince them he was legit. Then, the Feds got the players mixed up and began putting pressure on him. It got ugly. He was forced to pick sides."

I repositioned my legs half yoga style. It helped my backache, a residual twinge from rolling on his lumpy mattress, not to mention my whole body had been in an emotional knot for two days. "So, he faked his death and reemerged on the dark side."

"Exactly. But not right away. He laid low for a while. That meant he needed a middle man to keep watch on the agency movements, and yours." Tom pointed to his chest.

"So he chose power and money over duty, right?" Like the Invisible Man in the old black and white movies, each new tidbit of information unwrapped the ugly truth and made the man I thought I knew disappear even more.

Tom stood and came over to me. He sat on the floor beside me, his head against the sliding door, and took a deep swig of his soda. "Both sides thought the other had taken him down. They were watching you to make sure you were not in on any of it. At first, to verify his demise. Then the traffickers had to be reassured he hadn't given you instructions to go to the Feds. This is all tied to organized crime, Jen. If you knew anything which would incriminate them, they'd have to eliminate you."

"They thought I'd turn them in?"

Tom raised his soda can. "Bingo. You might. Out of revenge for your husband's death."

My brain was rattling. This was like a TV movie gone haywire. "But I didn't know anyone had killed him. Or not. Whatever."

"They didn't know that. They set up your little accidents as warnings. But you weren't paying attention."

"So you arranged for me to disappear."

He sat erect. "Yes. Now you get it?"

I slunk deeper into the chair. "No."

He groaned and rose to pace the floor.

"Was Robert planning to join me or not?"

"At first. That was the plan. Fake both your deaths. His, then a few months later, yours. You'd go into WITSEC, and start over with new lives."

"Federal Witness Security Protection?"

Tom stretched out his legs. "Right. I took the call to make it happen."

"What?"

He wobbled his head. "Agreed to the assignment. To set things in motion for him to get out and you to join him. Then he'd cry uncle, turn state's witness, and you two, both now reported dead, would vanish. No one would be looking for you."

"But in the meantime, he got the thirst for power."

"I guess, among other things."

I peered into Tom's face. "He was there in the coffin room when I was coming to. I did hear his voice, after all."

"Yeah. We came close to blowing that one."

"Why was he there and why couldn't I see him then?"

"He'd been spotted alive. To save his skin, he told the cartel he faked his own death to shake the Feds. The trafficking lords were impressed. It moved him up the ladder as an untouchable. Gave him more control. That's what he came to tell me. The plan had changed and he was headed to New Mexico." Tom's voice became more animated, his voice louder. "Do ya see now? That's why I had to detain you. When I got word I was to take you there to join him, it made my skin crawl. So Mae Lin got involved as back-up."

It all began to make sense. Yet it didn't. "What happened to him?"

Tom twisted toward me. "He turned, Jen. I don't know why. I just knew. I didn't recognize him anymore that night at the shacks. He knew you'd never join him. He'd made his choice—it wasn't power over duty, it was power over love." Tom looked down. I watched his Adam's apple bounce. "I told him I wanted to save you from knowing the ugly truth. He saw I'd fallen for you. Maybe he hoped I could give you what he no longer could. I guess that's why he agreed to let us go."

"I doubt it. Tom. He won't let me go that easily." Still, Agent Hernandez had been right all along. "So he didn't let us go because you ran drugs for them." My tone was flat. "You lied to me."

"I had to tell you something. What was I supposed to say? The truth? That your deceased husband was screwing illegals in the shack next to you and he was the one running drugs?"

"Yes."

"Would you have believed me?"

I bit my lip and looked down. For a moment neither of us spoke.

My voice cracked as if my heart wanted to prevent my mouth from asking the next question. But I had to know. "He's not undercover anymore? You're really sure?"

Tom's silence confirmed what I already knew. I ran my hands over my left ring finger. It had been bare too many months. The white was almost gone, the skin now as tan as the rest of my hand. I had lost Robert to death, and now to life.

"He's too much a part of the whole organization he has helped to build, and being Anglo, maybe he has more power. Who knows." Tom waved his hand sideways in an erasing motion. "I told him it was a game I didn't want to play any longer. I promised him three things, then I was out." He held up his forefinger. "I told him I'd see after you, since you didn't testify against me and go into WITSEC the first time."

His words pierced my heart. "How could I, Tom?"

He ignored my question. I watched his other hand grip into a fist, but his face remained stoic. He held up another finger. "I also vowed to watch over the two girls you took to heart. I got Monica the kitchen help job and Marisol out of circulation." He raised a third finger. "And, I'll make sure his kid, when it's born, finds a good home."

"Good. The child deserves a decent life." I looked away and swallowed back the sorrow.

Tom reached to clutch my fingers. "You do too, Jen."

We sat in silence. Then his words sank deeper. I peered into his eyes. "So you've been in contact a lot with Robert since...all of that."

He looked at his hand and released mine from its grip. "Yeah. He's been watching you. So have the Feds, Mae Lin, the traffickers." He wagged his head as he named them off, then he winked. "And so have I. To make sure none of them got to you. You've become my full-time job with all your publicity stunts." His eyes danced as he pointed his finger at my nose. "It wasn't easy to guard you and not be seen by the rest of the crowd keeping tabs on you. You know that?"

I bit my lip. "I'm sorry."

"I'm sorry too. About the New York thing. They moved too fast, I..." He dipped his head.

"I know. It's okay. I'm not mad about that anymore." I leaned in to catch his glance and squeezed his fingers. "Can you get out? Is it even possible?"

He shrugged. "I broke the law, Jen. I doubt it."

A thick hush draped between us again. He'd said way too much.

I knew Tom had put himself in danger to save me more than once. Now he was risking his very life to protect me. If the traffickers didn't get him for knowing more than he should, the Feds would make him the scapegoat and imprison him. Tom, or Travis, or whoever this man was in this grungy duplex with me, had no future as long as my husband was a free man...and declared dead.

A strong resolve surged through me. Tom had saved me, several times. It was my turn to save him. That was it. I'd tell them about Robert, then divorce him. That way I could bargain to get Tom and me into WITSEC. We could be together—lead a normal life.

I turned to see his lost-in-thought expression. Poor man. This was all deeply hurting him as well. I was more than the one woman he couldn't have. Truth be told, I was one burden he didn't need right now.

But I still needed him. I now knew Tom could help me ensure Marisol and Monica had a better future. I had vowed to God I'd find them and give them one, just as Tom had vowed to make sure Robert's child by Marisol had security and safety. Our purpose was one and the same.

Our intertwined vows bound us. Until we accomplished them, we'd be unable to move forward together. WITSEC would have to wait.

"So." I stood up and brushed myself off. "You say you know where Marisol and Monica are?"

He stared into my eyes. "So?"

I leaned in. "When can I see them?"

Tom buried his head in his hands. "Ah, geez, Jen."

CHAPTER FOURTEEN

"FORGET ABOUT THEM, okay?" His eyes pleaded with me.

I bolted from the chair and paced. "I can't. I'm a woman who has been wronged, just like them. Even before I knew all of this, I felt a bond." I stopped, wrapped my hands around my waist, but kept my back to him. "Now I know why. We were hurt by the same man."

I felt his footsteps, then his hands on my shoulders. "I'm still wanted, Jen. I can't run around with you as you try to save two Hispanic girls."

"I can't do it by myself."

He smirked. "At least you have the common sense now to know that. Besides, they may not want to be rescued."

I spun around. My eyes widened and my mouth dropped. "What?"

He gave me a sympathetic look. "Jen, honey. Look. This is the only life they know. This is their world. The coyotes have convinced them if they run they'll be tracked down and killed, or their families back home killed. They are not going to come with you at the drop of the hat."

"I know. I've been told that. But, I have to try."

He shook my shoulders. "You are not their Savior. God is. Turn to Him and let Him handle it."

I thrust my shoulders away and laughed. "Oh, you are one to talk. You are so pure and holy."

He chewed his lower lip. "I never said I was. But that is between Heaven and me." He raised his eyes to the ceiling.

Talking about the Almighty with him hardly felt comfortable. I switched gears. "So you won't help?"

His face sunk. "I can't. You know that, Jen."

My Irish shot to the surface. "Yeah. So much for *your* vow. I am not giving up on mine."

"To Robert?" His voice croaked.

"No, silly." I threw his answer back as I traipsed down the hall. "To Marisol and Monica. The night they disappeared in that van."

I grabbed my cell phone from my purse. It still had some battery power. Maybe God was helping after all. I pressed the button to redial Maria Gonzales-Taylor's number.

Tom had followed me. He reached to grab the phone. I twisted and backed away.

"What are you doing?" he hissed.

A female voice came on the line. "Hello?"

"Maria. It's Jen."

"Jen? What happened? You never came—"

"I know." I looked up at Tom and sat cross-legged on the bed. "I got violently ill. Food poisoning I guess. I am in bed right now."

Tom gave me a wide-eyed look and leaned against the wall. I gave him a shrug and continued. "I really am sorry."

"I'm sorry, too, Jen. We went to the Taco Shack. She was long gone."

I sat forward. "Oh, no. No. Is there any way to find her? Talk to other workers there?"

Tom gave me an I-told-you-so look.

I returned a go-to-you-know-where look. He pushed off from the wall and stood in the middle of the room, hands in pockets.

"Jen, the truth is, if we pursue this, it may put her in grave danger. Plus, as I said, we don't have the manpower..."

"I know. I understand." I took a deep breath. "Maria. Thanks. Really."

"If you happen to see her again, call. You did the right thing."

I smiled into the phone. "Thanks. Bye."

I rubbed my finger over the dial pad. "She could be anywhere, couldn't she? Even in a pit lying unconscious. Or worse."

Tom moved toward the bed. "*Now* do you get it?"

My eyes welled again as I looked up at him. His face fuzzed through my tears. "What do I do?"

He came and sat on the bed. "First, go to that church of yours. Say a prayer for them, for Robert, and for me. Then talk to the young minister. Tell him all that's happened."

I lowered my gaze to the carpet.

He raised my chin to peer into my face. "Promise you will. Tell him everything. You hear me? Everything. He'll know what to do."

I bobbed my head.

"You need to help yourself first, Jen. Find yourself, then find them."

I looked at him. "That's what he told me."

"The minister? Smart man."

"What will you do?"

He shook his head. "I'm not sure. I am sort of burned right now. No one trusts me, understandably. I really blew it when I escaped from the van with you instead of following protocol."

I grabbed his hands in mine. "Then get out, now. Like you said. We'll secure the girls then go into protection together."

He withdrew them. "Sweetie, it's not that easy. I kidnapped you. Faked your death. Broke the law. Then broke out of jail. I'll do time." He looked at the crumpled bedspread. "I don't want to do time."

"Even if you gave evidence..."

He laughed. "Against who? Blow my cover? Spy comes in from the cold?"

"Haven't you already?"

Tom shifted his weight and looked at the wall opposite us.

After a moment, his Adam's apple shifted again. His eyes shimmered as his voice quieted. "That smudge on the wall by the door? It resembles a giraffe, don't you think?"

His words crashed around me. With his change of subject, I knew our conversation was over. So was our future.

Maybe he was right. He knew more about all of this than I did. If whatever I chose to do caused him to go back behind bars...No. I couldn't have that. I must pretend I'd never had any contact with him, now or ever.

I rose, snatched my purse and clothes, and slipped into the bathroom. I let the water rinse the tears from my cheeks...but a few reached into my heart where they couldn't be washed away.

AFTER I GOT dressed, Tom shoved fifty dollars in my hand. "For a cab."

I crammed the bills in my pocket. "Thanks."

His blue eyes clouded. His hands cupped over mine. "I won't be here after today, you know."

I swallowed hard. The words "I know" barely eked from my mouth. My eyes swam in the bleak knowledge I'd never see him again.

He kissed me one last time, then peeled me from his arms.

"Goodbye, Jen." His voice cracked again as he closed the door.

I stood on the stoop as fresh tears cascaded down my cheeks. More than the chipped, wooden front door of a dilapidated duplex separated us now. My gut and my heart both felt hollow to the core.

I pressed my face into the wind to dry my eyes and walked toward a drugstore's sign on the corner of McCart and Westcreek. I pulled out my cell, phoned for a cab, then went inside.

Comfort food. That's what I needed. I regressed into my childhood and bought a pint of chocolate milk and a package of graham crackers. The combination had always made a scraped knee feel better. A shredded heart, well, that was another matter entirely.

The cab arrived soon after I'd swallowed the last of the milk. I gave him the address, told him I wasn't feeling well, and scrunched down into the back seat so he'd leave me alone and not chit-chat, as cabbies so often do. He obliged.

I half-closed my eyes and let the rumble of the tires drown out my sorrows. When the cab driver dropped me off, he told me the fare was $38.25. I handed him the whole fifty. He smiled and thanked me. I was glad to get rid of it. It smelled of Tom's cologne.

I fumbled for the key to my apartment. Tom Cat rushed to me and made several S curves around my legs. At least one man in my life was faithful and true. He made no bones about what he wanted from me—a can of food and hours of petting. I agreed to his wants as we snuggled on my sofa and watched the noise on TV.

As my vacant eyes absorbed the sitcom, my mind pleaded to God. Was He really there and could He find them? Could He find me?

FINALS WERE TWO days away and my brain would not focus. I felt as if I was in the vortex of a tornado. The facts of the past few days swirled around me, yet something barred them from touching me, hurting me. A strange calm beyond numbness acted like an antibiotic cream on my heart.

For two days, I shuffled through the motions of getting dressed, eating, going to pre-exam cram sessions, and coming home. I saw Becky as I climbed the stairs to my apartment. She waved at me and called out my name. I closed the door. Rude, I know, but I just didn't want to chat. I vowed to call her back later.

Within two hours, the phone rang. I thought it would be her. But it wasn't.

"Jen. It's Jake. I had to call and check on you. Are you okay?"

I gave him a short laugh. "Did the Powers that Be tell you to call?"

He was silent.

Suddenly I felt ashamed. My voice began to quiver. "Oh, Jake, I'm sorry. Can we talk?"

"I have some time right now. Do you want to come here, or for me to go over there?"

"Is it Kosher for you to come here?" I wrapped the end of my shirttail around my finger. "I don't think I feel up to—" My sentence ended in a stifled whimper.

"That's okay. I'll come to you."

I gave him the address and the name of the apartments.

"I know that complex. I'll be there in twenty. What's the gate code?"

I rattled off the code and told him which unit was mine. Exactly twenty minutes later there was a rap on my door.

I flung it open with the sweetest smile I could muster. Then it faded. Two blue-lined, pink shadowed, narrow dark eyes peered into me.

"Where is he?"

I leaned against the door praying Jake's steps would sound any second. "Who? My pastor? That's who I'm expecting. You want to pray with him as well?"

She shoved the door open, yanking it from my hand. She pushed me against the wall of my vestibule and pointed a long claw at my nose. "Where's Tom?"

"Oh, you mean Travis?"

She slapped me. "Don't mess with me, witch. That love sick idiot sought you out." She thrust past me and strutted down the hall in four-inch stilettos. "Still in your bed?"

I slammed my fist against the opened door. Heat pressed against my cheeks and my ears. "My Tom Cat is here." I yelled from the foyer. "And he is the only Tom that shares my bed."

She spun around, then looked to my right. Her scowl became a wicked leer.

I turned to see a black tie over a white shirt standing on my threshold, along with a hand clutching a Bible.

"Jen?"

I lowered my face in penitence. "Hi, Pastor Jake."

CHAPTER FIFTEEN

"Excuse me." Mae Lin brushed past us, but not before she shot silent Chinese curses into my eyes. She flew down my stairs in a huff. Her tight mini-shorts stretched across her backside, revealing the lower curves of her buttocks.

Jake raised an eyebrow and jerked his thumb. "Was that...?"

"Yep."

He patted the Bible with his other hand. "Looks like I came just in time." He took two steps then stopped. "May I enter?"

I folded against the door. "Oh, God, come in, yes." Then my hand flew to my mouth.

Jake leaned into my ear. "It's okay to invite Him in as well. If you didn't, I would have."

All the tension spurted from my mouth in a laugh. I motioned him into the living room. He chose the straight back chair at an angle to the couch. Pastoral protocol.

I responded with proper Southern hostess etiquette. "What can I get you? Water, a Coke?"

He crossed his leg. "Water. Thank you." A mechanical bling

sounded. "Excuse me, I must respond to this text."

"Oh. Okay. A pastor's work is never done, huh?"

He raised an eyebrow, got out his phone, and began to click away. I went into the kitchen. Through the pass-through I noticed him slip his phone back in his pocket and scan my apartment. He caught my glance and smiled. "Very nice. Cozy. You have a good eye for decorating."

"Really, or is that the 'make the member of your congregation feel comfortable 101' response?" I handed him a glass of water.

He took a sip and gave me a wry smile. "Tell me. How did an intelligent girl like you get involved in all of this?"

I rubbed my hands up and down my arms. My jaw tightened to keep the storm from pressing in, but it engulfed me. Tears rushed down my cheeks. "My husband's alive, Jake. And he's trafficking teenage girls."

Hearing the words out loud from my own lips made me shudder all over. The room twirled. My body ached as if ten elephants were sitting on me. I felt nauseous, and then weak all over. Suddenly a wail burst forth from deep in my gut. I flung myself at Jake's feet, grabbed hold of his legs, and blubbered. "Dear God, help me. Help me."

He crouched to stroke my hair and whispered a prayer.

After a while, I brushed my eyes and nose with my sleeve. His pant leg was soaked, poor man. He didn't seem to mind. He reached down, gathered me to my feet, and eased me over to the couch.

"Time for me to get you water." He raised my legs as I laid down and covered me with the afghan I kept draped over the sofa arm. I sank into my throw pillows and covered my eyes with my arm.

Jake came back and handed me a glass. I rose, took it from him, and mouthed a thank you. He pulled one of the dining room chairs over and sat facing me. "Take your time."

I sighed the last weighty shudder off my chest and took a gulp of tap water.

Jake reached into his jacket and pulled out his phone. He punched in a number with his thumb then raised it to his ear. "Mrs. Edwards? I have a member of the flock in crisis. Cancel my other appointments for the day, okay?"

I darted to a sitting position as I sloshed the water. "Oh, please. Don't do that."

He hung up. "Already done. Don't fret. It was just the financial committee. In fact..." His eyes twinkled as he took the glass from me. "I should thank you."

I grabbed a throw pillow and drew it to my heart. "I'm sorry I haven't been to see you."

He looked at me. "Where are you now, Jen?"

I knew he didn't mean my apartment. "In a silent storm whirling around me as if I am at sea. Every once in a while a wave slams into me. I don't see it coming."

The minister, too wise for his years, nodded and reached into his shirt pocket to pull out a folded piece of computer paper. "Perhaps that is why when I read this, I immediately thought of you and lifted you in prayer."

I leaned forward and reached for it. "What is it?"

He eyed the paper then me. "This is from a lady named Marilyn who writes devotionals on the web. Do you know the story of Jesus walking on the water?"

I shrugged. "Sort of."

"She writes that what is amazing to her is not the part where Jesus walked on the water toward His disciples and then calmed the storm."

I scrunched my brows together. "No?"

Jake raised his focus from the paper and looked at me. He shifted his weight. "What she found incredible was Jesus chose to be with His disciples rather than waving His hand to still the storm from the mountain where He'd been praying—which He could have done."

I shook my head, still not grasping his point.

He swallowed the rest of the water in his glass. "Jen. God has already come down to be with you in this storm. You just have to see Him, and like Peter, walk to Him."

New tears filled my eyes. "Why would He do that for me?"

Pastor Jake lowered his eyes to the gold cross around my neck. "Don't you know why?"

He left the paper beside me and excused himself to get another glass of water. I clutched the cross. A warmth spread across me. The sentimental gift from my parents suddenly became so much more than that. It was as if by touching it, peace shot into my soul.

Tom's words echoed in my mind. *You have to find yourself before you can find them.* I jolted and snapped my fingers. "I get it!"

Jake came back into the room. "Good."

I raised my back straight as a soldier's. "I have to find God and go to Him. He'll lead me to Marisol and Monica. I can be like Jesus and walk into their storm to calm them."

"Whoa, Jen." He raised his hand. "If that is His will. Don't assume it is."

I gave him a blank look. "But I feel such a strong connection."

He sat in the chair and took a long sip. Then he lowered his glass to the carpet and peered deep into my eyes. "Do you know why you feel this connection?"

I pressed my lips together and turned to stare out the slider to the tree branches. The world outside was sunny. Mine was anything but that. "Yes, I do." I returned my gaze to him. "It's as if in my search to find them, God has found me again. I understand why they will resist me. I resisted God way too long. I was too scared to change. Just like them. It's why I can reach them."

The pastor's face warmed.

I heard Tom's advice in my head. *Tell him everything.* "There is more, Jake. I feel the connection because..." I took a deep breath and spit it out. "They have been with my husband as well. He forced them to. Marisol is carrying his child."

Were ministers supposed to show surprise? Perhaps he couldn't help it. Jake widened his eyes, then clicked his tongue. "Oh, Jen. I am so very sorry. Adultery is sited as legitimate grounds for divorce in the Bible, but I can't counsel you to do that."

I laughed. "Why would I? I'm a widow, right?" A giggle burst from my gut, then turned into sobs. I grabbed a tissue and blew my nose.

"But if he's alive?"

I shook my head. "Only a few people know, and they aren't likely to go to the cops and tell. The State of Texas says I am a widow. He's dead to me, legally, and emotionally."

He wrung his hands. "But is he morally? This is not your average theological scenario."

"No? They didn't include this in your seminary counseling courses?" My tone dripped onto the carpet, but he took no offense.

Jake ran his hands over his face and sighed. "Jen, I want you to promise me something here and now."

I unwrapped the tissue from my fingers, and blew my nose again. "Okay."

He moved forward in the chair to where our knees almost touched. I could smell the remnants of the breath mint he must have popped into his mouth on the way over. It touched my heart that he'd care enough to do that. Or maybe seminary taught them to do that as well. Commandment Number 12: Never be offensive to the flock.

He stared into my pupils. "I mean it."

"Okay." I wiggled to break his stare.

"Drop this whole thing. It is too much for you. Give it to God. Let Him handle it. You'll sink in this storm, Jen, if you don't cling to Him."

I leaned back and shook my head. "How do I?"

Jake pressed the palms of his hands on to his knees. "Daily. Trust me. It's the only way you can."

THE NEXT DAY—sure I'd flunked my exams—I walked to my car feeling totally defeated. I wasn't sure who I was or where I was supposed to go. My clothes no longer fit, but I had no idea where to buy new ones, or even what size I was.

I startled easily at every sound. Every Oriental girl or muscular Hispanic man I saw tripped my heart rate into overdrive. Everywhere I turned, I saw them staring at me—in cars with loud music blaring, on street corners, in restaurants.

After Jake's visit, I'd dug my anti-anxiety pills out of the back of my bathroom drawer. There were five in the bottle. Today only one remained. And it was at home.

Jake left a text message for me to come to his office at 4:00 p.m. When I arrived, Mrs. Edwards was packing up for the day.

"Computer being nicer to you, Mrs. Edwards?"

She smiled. "Yes." She placed her black patent leather purse onto her arm. "They're waiting for you."

"They?"

I tapped on the mahogany door jamb. There, Jake stood with a large muscular Hispanic man. I felt the blood in my face rush to my toes.

Jake extended his hand and motioned me inside. "Ah, Jen. This is Agent Gonzales with the FBI. You two should meet."

I gave him an are-you-nuts look.

His mouth curved upwards. "Let him explain. He came to me asking if I'd pray with him over his job. You see, he is undercover trying to help get trafficked teens off the streets. He might be the answer to your prayers in finding Marisol and Monica."

I laid my purse on the desk and slid into one of the green leather chairs. Agent Gonzales also sat, crossing his leg over his thigh. I stared into his eyes, trying to read him.

Jake settled in behind his desk. "Lemonade, anyone? The women's group left a jug of it in the fridge." He stood up.

I reached out my hand to him. "Don't leave."

Agent Gonzales warmed his smile. "I won't bite, Mrs. Westlaw. I think I may be able to help you in your plight."

I shot my pastor a look. "This agent knows of my plight, huh?"

Jake tented his fingers and nodded.

I raised my chin. "And what do you want in return?" If he thought I'd give him information about Tom, or Robert, he was dead wrong. I wanted Robert to stay buried, and Tom to stay free.

The two men exchanged glances. Jake shifted in his chair.

I flung an icy glare toward my minister who was supposed to keep confidences. "What have you told him?"

"I read the papers, ma'am," the agent said in a flat, official tone. "I know who you are. You were so adamant about getting the media to help you locate these trafficked girls you met while kidnapped in the desert, then suddenly became silent. Then, months later, you reappear on Christian radio and begin speaking at churches about trafficking. Then, you miss a speaking engagement and disappear from view again." He leaned toward me. "I want to know why, Mrs. Westlaw. Who's been putting pressure on you?"

I still stared at Jake. Was he yet another man who'd betrayed me? Could any of them be trusted? "My pastor told me not to pursue it. That I couldn't handle it and to give it to God."

My supposed confidante rocked back in his chair. I broke eye contact and slowly turned them to Agent Gonzales. The brass clock in the bookcase ticked off the seconds of silence.

"Good day, gentlemen." I rose from the chair and reached for my purse.

Jake grabbed for my elbow across his executive desk, almost losing his footing. "Wait, Jen. Please...hear him out. He has risked as much as you coming here."

"Perhaps more." The man's voice lowered. "If he knew, I'd blow four years of investigation and endanger my life."

I turned to him. "If who knew?"

"The Anglo man who leads the cartel ring in the New Mexican desert. I believe his name is Roberto. I am also guessing you know all about him?"

My knees buckled beneath me as I slumped into the chair.

"How much do you know?" I croaked the question out. My heart thumped in my ears. Did they know about Tom? Had they captured him? Had I led them to him?

"We think Roberto is still alive, even though he faked his own death. He's an asset gone rogue. Do you know what that means?"

I nodded but kept my focus on Jake. His expression remained blank, but his eyes beckoned me to trust.

Gonzales's gaze darted to Jake's face, and then back to mine. "Mrs. Westlaw?"

My finger shivered in anger as I pointed it at my pastor. "I trusted you. You broke the confidentiality rule. How could you?"

He raised both hands. "Jen. I didn't. I only told him..."

I stomped my foot and screamed. "How dare you tell him anything!"

Agent Gonzales held out his hand. "Calm down. I'm on your side. I am your ticket to freedom, and those girls' too. Let me help. You owe Roberto nothing."

Pastor Jake pleaded with me. "Jen, trust me. I sought counsel before I called Agent Gonzales to make sure I wasn't violating your confidentiality. I had your best interest and safety at heart."

I bore a hole into them both for so long their faces began to fuzz.

"All he has told me is that you know your husband is alive and involved in the trafficking of young illegal girls. The fact you know those things alone is enough to warrant your need for protection."

Jake leaned across the desk, his hands clutched as if in prayer. "It's okay. You can tell us everything. What is said in this room remains here."

I shot him an incredulous look. "Really? What proof do I have you will this time?"

He pointed to the agent and then back to himself. "Trust us. Your government and your faith will protect you."

A nervous laugh spewed from my throat. "How can I be sure? You haven't so far."

The anxiety rose. I shuddered all over as my breath labored. Why had I left that bottle of pills at home? My legs and hands became chilled.

I heard Gonzales' voice in an echo. "Pastor Jake, get her some water."

I closed my eyes as the room spun furiously around me.

The agent shoved my head between my knees. "Breathe, Mrs. Westlaw. Breathe."

I tried to raise my head but it felt tied to floor. "Oh, dear God," I moaned, cradling my face in my hands.

Another hand patted my arm as a pair of women's shoes came into view. I lifted my eyes to see Becky's smiling, warm face. "Hi, neighbor."

I squinted to bring her more into focus. "What are you doing here?"

CHAPTER SIXTEEN

BECKY PUSHED THE hair off my face, and handed me a glass of cool water. I blinked to make sure I wasn't hallucinating. Yes, it was her. Her face was now in full view.

After a few sips, my brain cells revived. "You aren't just my neighbor. Otherwise, you wouldn't be here, right?"

Jake scooted a chair closer. "Smart girl. And I am not just your pastor. Well, I am. But more than that." He motioned to Becky then back to himself. "We're both what they call undercover assets, Jen. We've been helping the Feds. Becky's with the U.S. Marshals. She's been tracking your husband's illegal immigration activities for over a year before he died. I was brought in after your, er, resurrection, shall we say, landed you at my doorstep. I must admit it sounded a bit exciting and all. I knew I could help you. You needed someone you could—"

"Trust?" I interrupted with a sarcastic smirk.

He hung his head.

I groaned. "And I told you he was alive."

Agent Gonzales looked into my eyes. "We suspected as much.

He was getting bold. Before all of that, Becky was assigned to monitor your whereabouts and Robert's as well, which is why she moved in across the hall and made friends."

She squeezed my arm. "I didn't do too great a job of protecting you, though, did I?"

"Not your fault." I eased up more into the chair and raised my hand to my neck. "My throat. It feels so dry."

She handed me the glass of water again. "Small sips, dear. Not too much."

I was tired of people telling me that, but I obeyed. The cascading coolness revitalized my vocal chords, and more of my gray cells. "Why did you tell me you'd seen him at a hotel with another woman?"

"Because I had. And I wanted to test your reaction. To see if you had any idea who your husband was. Later, I found out she was another agent trying to trap him. Governmental agencies don't always coordinate well. They call her Mother."

So that's who "Mother" was. I widened my eyes. "He saw you. He figured you out. That's why he faked his death."

Agent Gonzales spoke up. "It's exactly what we suspect. Though at the time, we weren't sure the traffickers hadn't fingered Becky as his watchdog. We thought they had taken him down."

I repositioned my shoulders into the back of the leather chair. My head felt heavy, but my hunger for answers was stronger than my emotions. "Why didn't you get involved with the investigation into his…" I still found the words hard to say. "Into his death?"

My neighbor leaned in. "We were doing our own. He went pretty deep below the surface for a while. No one saw the ripples. We weren't sure he'd ever float up."

I pictured a bloated, stinky, dead fish and gave a short chuckle. The three of them knitted their brows in unison. Pressing the smile from my lips, I waved my hand. "Never mind, it was just an image. Forget it."

They gave each other a shrug. I turned to my minister, now agent. "And so, you got involved because ...?"

"Agent Gonzales came to me. They knew I was counseling you. They wanted me to convince you to come into WITSEC."

Now it was my turn to lower my head. "And testify against my husband and Tom."

The Federal agent responded. "Well, at the time our purpose was to find this Tom or Travis of yours. Now that we know Robert is alive, it changes the picture."

I popped the crick out of my neck and turned to Agent Gonzales. My head felt less heavy now. "What do you want from me?"

He repositioned in his chair to face me. "What I want is the information you have regarding this man Roberto and his colleagues. In return, the FBI will give you full protection and relocate you anywhere you like."

I straightened my shoulders. "And help me find Marisol and the baby when it's born." It wasn't a question.

Agent Gonzales clucked his teeth through a sigh. "That wouldn't work. She ties you to your past."

"Right. If I'm given a new life in a new city, my search would have to end."

His eyes darted to the ground then back to me. "That's correct."

I felt the blood sprint from my cheeks into my chest. My mind bounced against the walls of my skull. What should I say? Yes? Give up on my quest to save them so I could save myself? And if I refused? These were the Feds. That would mean Federal prison. I heard Tom's voice in my head. *"I don't want to do time."*

Neither did I.

I turned to face Agent Gonzales full on. "What if I refuse to testify? Will I go to jail for withholding evidence?"

He shifted in his chair. "It all depends."

Jake gave Agent Gonzales a strong-eyed look. "Jen needs rest. We can discuss all that later."

The man stood, took several steps backwards, and went to the window. He gazed into the garden, hands clasped behind his back.

Jake moved to his bookcase and pulled out a small olivewood cross, but it was strangely shaped—thick and a bit skewed as if it had melted. His mouth curved up to one side as he placed it in my hand and curled my fingers around it. It fit my clutched fist perfectly.

"I really am your pastor. Would you like to take this to the Lord?"

I looked at the picture of Jesus on the wall above his desk and nodded. Agent Gonzales stepped from the room into the outer office.

Becky squeezed my other hand. "May I stay?"

My free hand reached for hers. "Please."

Jake prayed as he spread his fingers over my forehead. Warmth oozed over my scalp. I let it soothe my soul.

When he sat down, an earnest look drenched his face. He spoke in a low voice with tented fingers to his chin. "And now, I must ask you to forgive me. I never revealed any of your heart's struggles, Jen. Yes, I have compromised your trust but the information you gave me changed everything. Lives were at stake, Jen. Yours. Young girls..."

I reached for his forearm. "I know." Then the proverbial light bulb clicked on. I sat upright. "Tom knew, too. He made me promise I'd talk with you. He said for me to tell you everything. He knew I'd tell you about Robert. Then, he parroted your words almost verbatim. He said for me to find myself, then find the girls."

"Ah." Jake looked at Becky. "He held the ace after all."

BECKY TOOK ME home to rest. After long talks over hot tea as I fluctuated between shaking and crying, she spent the night on my couch in case I needed her. The next day, she drove me to the agency's doctor's office in Dallas. Jake and Agent Gonzales met us there. After the doctor heard everything I had been through the past few days, he hospitalized me for thirty-six hours with strict bed rest and a full psychological evaluation. I insisted on a Christian counselor, if possible. I had round-the-clock guards, not because I was suicidal, but because I was in danger.

In layman's terms, I suppose I had a nervous breakdown. For me, it was a breaking apart so God could put me back together again, like Humpty Dumpty. The eggs shells I never wanted anyone to walk on had finally cracked.

A MAN CAME into my room one morning after breakfast. From his smile, suit, and clipboard I gathered he was the agency shrink. He came around the bedside table, and then extended his hand. "I'm Bob. I've been read in on much of your plight. Feel like talking? I'd like you to tell it to me in your own words."

The warmth of the sun's rays through the window fell on to my chest. Or was it the trust reflected in his eyes? I swallowed and motioned him to sit.

"I'm much better now that I have had a chance to sort through it all."

He crossed one leg over the other. "Are you? You've had a lot to absorb, Jen."

I closed my eyes and began the spiel I had rehearsed. In low, even tones I proceeded to tell him about Robert's deception, my attraction to Tom, and my fervor to save the girls and others like them.

"You saw evil up close and personal. Of course you wanted to get involved. You *are* a good person, Jen." His tone was not mocking, but soothing. Obviously he was professionally trained on how to respond, yet under his poised demeanor, there was honesty in his face. Was that part of his schooling as well?

I grinned. "I still have trust issues, you know. Like whether to trust you, a total stranger with the authority to release me or wrap me in a rubber room."

He blinked, then threw his head back in a loud laugh. "You sound very normal, Jen. Very normal indeed." He wiped his eyes on his sleeve. As he did, his face lessened in color and became more serious. "But you do know you don't have the power to be superwoman and rush in to save the day?"

I looked at the blanket on my bed and nodded.

"You see, it's best to let someone who is trained in this sort of thing pull those girls out, *if* they want out."

I rubbed my hand along the knobby white cotton. It sent off a faint whiff of institutionalized bleach. "Yeah."

Tom had been right. I searched the counselor's face. "What will happen if I back off? Do I have yours, or anyone else's guarantee they'll be found?"

"There are no guarantees in this world, Jen."

"True."

I bent my head and ran my finger over the spot where my wedding ring once lay on my left hand. "But there is something I can do, isn't there? Testify so more girls can be spared."

I'd changed my mind, or maybe finally made it up for good. Wanting to keep Robert buried only denied my own pain. Justice had to be served. Maybe my job was to help lead the Feds to Robert so they could slice off one of the trafficking octopus' arms. It'd make me a married woman again, but it was the truth anyway. Besides, Tom would never be safe as long as Robert was free. And Tom was the only one who could save the girls, and perhaps me, even if it was from a safe distance.

The psychiatrist waited as I sorted through my thoughts. He watched me without staring at me. His face seemed expressionless, non-judgmental. I swallowed and gave him a swift bob of my head. "I'm ready to give my report now. Set it up."

Bob's mouth stretched up at the edges. He covered my hand with his and squeezed. "I'll authorize your release. The agency will be in touch in a couple of days."

I RELAYED OUR conversation to Jake when he visited that afternoon. He gave me his wise, pastoral smile. "God has spoken, and at last you have heard." Still, his demeanor appeared more penitential in nature than clandestine.

"What is it?"

"Have you forgiven me?"

My face warmed. "You acted with my best interest at heart. There's nothing to forgive."

I saw his shoulders slacken.

"But tell me, when you approached me that day after church in the fellowship hour and said you wanted to see me again, was it because the Feds had contacted you?"

"That's classified." Jake winked. "I am glad, however, if even in a small way, I could be…" He paused and coughed into his fist. "Let's just say, an asset to you."

I laughed out loud.

"There's another reason I came." His face became like stone

and his eyes darted to the ground.

I scooted forward in the bed and then took in a gulp of air. "What?"

"Here." He pulled an envelope from his inside coat pocket. From my point of view, it looked official. "It's from an attorney I know. He drew this up. Legally, you have ample grounds to divorce Robert on grounds of infidelity and fraudulent vows, and may apply to do so without his consent once he's in prison." He raised a finger. "If that's what you decide to do. I'm not counseling you to do so. I only want you to know it's an option."

Relief and sorrow mingled in my eyes. I tried to steady my hand as I took the papers from him. I laid the envelope on the tray-table that swiveled over my hospital bed. My fingers hovered, not yet willing to open it.

"Take your time, Jen. Pray about it—a lot. This is not an easy decision." He squeezed my hand, and left the room.

A few minutes later, the reality sunk in. Five years of my life, five years of deception, could be dissolved as if they'd never happened. Yet, they had happened, and I had very fresh heart wounds pounding away in my chest as proof.

After a good, cleansing sob session, I packed to go home to my apartment with the legal papers, Becky, and another female agent in tow. Once home, I tucked the envelope into the stack of ever-growing "to-do's" on my desk.

LATER THAT WEEK, I basked in the apartment complex's atrium watching the finches flit around one of the birdfeeders. Becky brought Agent Gonzales for a visit.

He assumed in his normal posture, hands clasped behind his back in a military at-ease. Becky spoke first. "Their chirps are so sweet."

I turned to Becky. "The birds? Yes, they must be hungry. They aren't scrapping as much over the food. And there are more of them."

Becky nodded. "See the little ones, the fledglings flapping their wings so hard? That and food prepares them for flying."

I raised my hand over my eyes to block the sunrays. "And what are we preparing for?"

"May we be seated?" Agent Gonzales motioned to the chair across from me.

I agreed. "Official visit?"

He raised an eyebrow. His eyes, however, remained friendly. "Do you think you are ready?" He plopped his briefcase on to the wicker table next to us, then sat down.

I placed the bookmark in my novel and set it aside.

Becky laughed. "Hmm. The Spy Who Came in from the Cold. Classic."

I wiggled my eyebrows, then shut off my smile. I turned to Agent Gonzales. "I'm ready."

He winked and popped the latch on his briefcase. He set a small, silver recorder on the table. "Maybe you shouldn't read that novel. You might learn all of our secrets."

"Oh…" I grinned with my back straight. "I've learned enough of them through all of this, so don't think you're pulling anything over my eyes, mister."

Becky reached into her bag and brought out a plastic container of spinach-artichoke dip and a bag of sea salt pita chips.

"My favorites. You all must want something big from me to bribe me with pita chips." I chunked one into my mouth. Deep down, a small part of me wished I was eating them in a dark mausoleum with a black hump in the ceiling. Then I'd know Tom was safe, and watching me. Funny how perspective can change things.

"Not at all, ma'am. Only need you to relay what you are comfortable telling us."

I put on my friendly face. "I know. And, please call me Jen, Agent Gonzales."

His shoulders relaxed for the first time since we met. "Okay. I'm Luis."

Becky's eyes darted between us, then she slid back in her chair, hands folded over her bosom, legs crossed at the ankles. "Don't mind me. I'm just here as a witness."

I heard a pita chip crunch in her mouth.

Luis spelled out the deal they offered. In exchange for any information on Robert, I would be given a new identity. At first I objected, but in a few minutes, they'd convinced me it was necessary because the cartel might retaliate. After all, Roberto was the American *Jefe*. When he went down, his kingdom would tumble as well. The cartel wouldn't be happy.

At last, I had a concrete idea of my role in all of this. I knew how I could make a difference. Testify to save others from Marisol's fate, then vanish to save myself. Too bad the idea of my memoirs would have to be ditched. I kinda liked the idea of the TV movie. And the money.

"But how will you explain my disappearance this time? I've already been dead once."

Luis smiled. "Nervous breakdown works."

I rolled my eyes.

He shrugged those broad shoulders supporting a linebacker's neck. "Lost at sea? Terminally ill aunt in the south of France?"

Becky chuckled. "How about fell in love with a billionaire and scooted off to his secluded island?"

I waved a pita chip loaded with dip in her direction. "The last one, yeah. Can you make that happen?"

Luis shook his head. "We're the Feds, not God."

"Oh, well." I plopped the chip in my mouth. "Doesn't matter. I'm still married." I dashed a look at Becky. "I haven't decided to file. Will that affect my ability to testify?"

"No. But if you want to go through with the divorce, I suggest you do it now. The agency's lawyers can push it through before you fully enter WITSEC."

A piece of chip almost stuck in my throat. I gulped several ounces of water, then coughed. "Give me a day or two, okay?"

Becky looked at Luis. "Let me talk with her, woman to woman."

He clicked his briefcase closed. "Okay. Two days. That's all, though. I'll be back on Thursday."

Both of our eyes watched him round the corner before Becky put the question to me. "Why haven't you filed? You can't still love him?"

"No." I shook my head. "And I know the Bible says adultery is just cause. Jake told me."

"So?"

The truth lodged in my throat where the pita chip had. "I have to forgive Robert first. I'm still working on that. Only then will I be able to really take this to the Lord and seek His counsel."

"Okay." Becky sighed and rose to leave. "Do what you need to do. Just remember you only have forty-eight hours. See you Thursday."

I SPENT MOST of the night on my knees. I cried, I prayed. But finally, I found it in my heart to begin to forgive. Now I knew I could testify without an ounce of vengeance. But divorce him? Something inside made me hesitate.

Was it my new-found faith? I'd Googled Christian views on divorce. Jesus said in the book of Matthew that infidelity was grounds for divorce. But he also said what God had joined together no one was to separate, and if a man married a divorced woman, he'd be committing adultery. That seemed harsh, but if it was true, then Tom would never agree to marry me even if they allowed him to come with me into WITSEC.

I paced the floor. Faith issues aside, I wasn't ready to feel that last stab of pain in my heart. Could a tiny part of me still feel love? Or, was my hesitancy because the divorce would slap my own face with how naïve and stupid I'd been? I obviously had a lot more to sort through than a bunch of papers on my desk.

The next morning, I dug out the legal documents. Still, my hand hovered over the highlighted place I was to sign to begin the process. I'd been raised believing marriage vows were for life, better or worse. However, marriage was supposed to be about trust and fidelity. Mine never had either of those. Did that mean it was never real?

I called Jake and left a message.

Within ten minutes he responded. "I have three visitations to the hospitals this afternoon, sorry. You can come into the office early tomorrow morning and we can talk, but the bottom line is this, Jen." I heard his chair squeak. "It's between you and God. He's the one you need to talk with."

My throat tightened. "I have, all last night. This morning, too. I am at a place where I think I can begin to work on forgiving Robert. I'm just not sure I can end my marriage. It was real to me. I meant my vows even if he didn't."

"Is he the man you thought you were marrying, though? Was he ever that man?"

The question stabbed me in the gut. "I don't know."

"When you can answer that, you will have answered whether or not you should sign those papers. I won't push you either way." Jake stopped. The silence at the other end at first made me wonder if he'd hung up.

Then, his voice came through. "One thing I do know, Jen. God's forgiveness is vast. So is His ability to change people. Robert knew of Him once. That seed is still buried somewhere in his hardened heart. Maybe his love for you is there as well."

ON THURSDAY, LUIS set the documents before me. "Your written testimony is all that is required. You won't have to appear in court and face him."

I felt fifteen tons lift from my chest. "Thank you."

Luis handed me a pen to sign the agreement to testify. I scrawled my name, Mrs. Jennifer Wade Westlaw. The words blared back at me, a stark reality of the other papers still on my desk.

"Have you thought about the other issue?"

"I've thought of little else." My voice cracked. "It's all so much at once."

He patted my hand. "It's okay. None of this can be easy. Let's talk about your relocation first. Becky will be going with you to settle you in. She'll be your elderly auntie."

"You will?"

She placed her arm over my shoulder. "Sure. And you'll like where you're going. And the career we've lined up for you."

"Where am I to go?"

Becky scooted forward. "We've set you up in Bonita Springs, Florida at a public library as an assistant to the librarian. It's located across from the middle school. You can also teach English as a second language there. We can get your teaching license in order since you already have the credentials and degree. Would you like to return to teaching?"

My eyes swam with joy. "Yes," I whispered. "It's not math, but... yes."

Luis slid the papers in front of me. "All you need to do is sign and we'll begin the process. You will still be a widow. Your husband did die in an auto accident, just in San Antonio, Texas where you were married. But you were born and raised in Abilene and went to school there. They'll drill you on all that."

My heart sank. "I had hoped the lying was over."

Becky took my hand. "I think God will understand."

I wasn't so sure. "I'll live a normal life? I can go out, go to church, go to the beach..." I opened my hands. "Without any Feds watching my every move?"

"Absolutely. You will have an agent assigned to you if you ever need help. You will also have access to confidential counseling through the U.S. Marshals to help you adjust."

I slouched backwards into the chair, my hand on my chin.

She patted my knee, the way my mother used to when I'd had a bad day at school. "Jen, it's their job. They are there for you, 24/7, if and when you need them. No pressure. And initially, I'll be around as well."

I inhaled her words. "Okay. Just for information on Robert?"

They shot each other a glance, then Becky shrugged. "Yes, he is who we're after."

I squared my shoulders. "I want more. I want immunity for Tom, uh, Travis Walters."

Luis leaned in. "You realize you can never, ever, see him again."

I nodded rapidly. "I understand." But a whisper in my heart refused to believe it. He'd find a way. That day at his duplex was not the final act. I hung every ounce of hope on the idea.

Becky looked at Luis. "Can she know?"

Luis shook his head.

"Know what?" A cold splash of worry spread across my breast. "Tell me. Is he okay?"

My female companion reached over and flicked off the recorder. "She has the right to know, Luis."

He slunk back. "Okay. I guess. Off the record."

Becky looked to me. "Tom turned himself in three days ago. He's already told the Bureau everything he knows. Your testimony will only confirm what he's said."

I grabbed at the proverbial straw and held tight. "So he is cleared of all charges? He's free? Or does he have to go into WITSEC as well?" Perhaps we could be together after all.

Becky opened her mouth.

Luis cleared his throat. "No more. She is not authorized to be read in on that." Then he turned to me. "Your friend will be fine, Jen. He is still of value to us. Let's leave it at that, okay?"

I peered deeply into his male eyes, and finally found truth. If Tom continued with the agency, he'd embark on a path I couldn't follow. But he would be fine. Above all else that was what mattered. I nodded and signed the Memorandum of Understanding, acknowledging I could have no ties to my past and no contact with anyone from it either.

Had the Feds solved my moral dilemma? As I saw it, there was no need to file for the divorce after all. With a few strokes of ink, Mrs. Jennifer Wade Westlaw would no longer exist.

I CALLED JAKE with the news. "Robert was sentenced to thirty years without parole. He'll be sixty-two when he gets out."

Jake's voice was flat. "Have you decided what to do?"

"I seriously doubt if I can wait that long to see if time, and perhaps any tiny bit of conscience, has changed him." A nervous giggle spewed from my lips. "Besides, I can't have any contact with him starting tomorrow."

"You're going into WITSEC, then."

I nodded into the receiver. "I have to. That won't stop me from praying for a miracle though, for Robert's sake more than mine. One thing I'd learned—no one is out of reach from God's mercy if he asks for it. If God can forgive Robert, I must continue to try to as well."

His chair squeaked. I pictured him leaning back, a wise grin on his face. "Good, Jen. Good."

"Jake. As I prayed, the affirmation I could not file to dissolve my marriage grew. My vow was to God as well as to Robert, even if I didn't realize it at the time. That means only Robert's death can free me." I swallowed back the sorrow. "But then, the only man I want to be with is banned from any contact with me, so what does it matter? I've decided to leave it all in God's hands—or I'll try to do so."

He sighed. "Daily. It's the only way."

"So you've said. How can I ever thank you?" The "goodbye" caught in my throat.

"It's been my pleasure." Jake's deep breath came through the phone. "I will be praying fervently for you, Jen. And for Tom, and even for Robert. Go with God, my friend. He'll give you strength."

CHAPTER SEVENTEEN

TWO MONTHS LATER, hurricane season hit Florida. Major storms were predicted. I had a small, two bedroom bungalow about three blocks from the library and a mile from the beach. Tom Cat loved to watch the birds flitter in the front yard's oak tree beyond the living room window. According to my elderly neighbor across the street, he spent hours perched there each day until I came home.

I found a church within a few miles from my house and joined a small Bible study group. The pastor was happily married, middle aged and balding. No temptations there.

However, I'd caught the eye of one of the deacons. A widower, Brad, in his late thirties had lost his high school sweetheart-turned-wife of eighteen years to ovarian cancer two years ago. His son was a freshman in high school and his daughter a junior. Brad was a social worker who liked cats and refused to wear any cologne. Besides, his eyes were brown. I'd had enough of green or blue ones to last me a lifetime, and then some. He seemed honest, unpretentious, and he made me laugh. Still, I let him know my heart was not free. We could only be friends.

I let him believe it was due to the fact I was a new widow, the legitimate lie WITSEC had created for me. In a way, it was true, I guess. I was mourning two-fold—the death of the man I thought I knew so well, and the loss of the man I'd never get the chance to know better.

MRS. BURNETT, THE head librarian, was down with the flu, so I agreed to open. The air this Saturday morning held a noticeable stillness. No usual rustle of leaves in the trees from a sea breeze. The clouds were overcast and a dark, bluish gray. An eerie calm lay over the world.

"This," I told Tom Cat as I stroked his fur, "is what they call the hush before the storm." A tropical storm was predicted later that day moving in from the Gulf of Mexico. I kissed his fur, told him goodbye, and closed the front door. When I looked back, he was already in the window.

I tucked my raincoat tighter around me and quickened my pace. My heels clanked on the concrete sidewalk and echoed against the rows of houses, each similar to mine. A few blocks later, I took the back steps into the library. After I'd disarmed the alarm, I wound my way through the bookshelves to the main check-in and check-out area. I punched the remote button under the return desk drawer to unlock the main door. The digital clock read 9:01.

No rush of bodies waiting to use the library followed. It was, after all, the weekend. People would filter in as the morning lengthened, unless the storm hit.

My English as a Second Language class wasn't to begin until 10:00 a.m. I fixed a cup of Earl Grey, and was logging in the overnight drop returns when eight-year-old Joshua Holder dashed in.

"Mrs. Williams. Come quick."

I rushed to the front door.

At the bottom of the stoop, swaddled in a pink blanket, lay a round-cheeked, Hispanic baby with ebony hair and tanned skin. She couldn't have been more than a month or so old. I bolted down the steps and knelt to pick up the infant. "How did you get here, wee one?"

"This was taped to her." Joshua handed me a small card. "Read it."

My business card. But how? Who? On the back, a distinctly scrawled note. *She's yours if you want her.*

My fingers became icy. A baby. My heart's desire. But…mine?

With a coo, the infant turned her face toward me. I gasped. Gray-green eyes, not the normal Hispanic brown, focused on my face. A shudder zipped through me. I knew those eyes. This was Robert and Marisol's baby. How could this be? No one was to know where I lived.

As if a shade had been pulled down, everything around us darkened. A gust of wind swirled dead leaves off the stoop in a lopsided waltz. Thunder rumbled.

"Let's take her inside. It's about to rain." Joshua darted up the steps and opened the library door. "Ms. Williams?"

"Right." As I gathered the baby into my arms, I scanned the block for anyone watching. Across the street, a well-built man in tan Dockers and a black T-shirt raised his hand in a wave. The approaching weather whipped dark locks about his face—a face I longed to caress. I could almost smell the aroma of his citrus-musk cologne drift across the street and melt into me.

"Who's that?" Joshua scrunched his nose.

"Just a man saying hello, I guess."

I waved back as a hopeful vision of Tom dashing across the street to take me into his arms yanked my heartstrings. Instead, he dipped an imaginary Stetson in my direction and back-stepped further from me.

The momentary giddiness faded as reality set in. This cooing baby in my arms meant Tom had kept his vow to Robert. But so had I—and Tom knew it.

We were both still bound—Tom by the law to have no contact with me. I by morality to my husband. Neither of us could live a lie. If the Almighty destined us for each other, we'd have to leave the how and when in His hands.

Our eyes locked on to each other. In his, I saw a love deeper than I thought I could ever know. I also saw trust that somehow God would find a way for us to share that love. I nodded back with a smile as my heart pounded—*I'll wait. I'll wait.*

Tom's lips curved into a grin, and then with that famous wink, he turned to walk away.

Despite the brewing storm overhead, a hush fell over my soul.

POSTSCRIPT

When I began this novel, I had no idea this was where it would lead. But God knew. As my fingers flew over the keyboard, He instilled in my heart to write about human trafficking, but to encase it in a story about love, betrayal, and restoration. What my main character, Jen Westlaw, went through is mirrored in the experiences of the two teenage illegals, Monica and Marisol. All three women had been lied to and mistreated by the same man. The girls were physically raped. But Jen was emotionally raped of her belief in who she thought her husband was. Her trust in him had been ripped from her heart, just as the girls' innocence had been ripped from them. Jen's efforts to seek and rescue Marisol and Monica reflect God's efforts to seek and heal her through Pastor Jake and Tom.

I would like to extend my deepest thanks to Jaime Welch and Toby Scrivener of the United States Catholic Council of Bishops (USCCB) for their eye-opening guidance concerning the plague of human trafficking and the plight of the trafficked victims. This group has been the lead lobbyers in anti-trafficking legislation for two decades. Also, thanks to Marilyn Ehle who writes for Truth Media's *Christian Women Today* daily devotional blog along with me, and who authored the devotional Jake shared with Jen. Finally, thanks to my AWSA sister Peggy Sue Wells, and Teresa Flores, co-authors of *The Slave Across the Street**, which tells the story from the victim's point of view. I also thank critique partners Gail Morris and Sandy Wright, Joy Brooks of Prayer4Freedom, my editor, Delia, Prism Book Group president, Joan Alley, and fellow author and speaker Angela Breidenbach, who gave so many great suggestions, and to my real life sister Anne and my niece Melissa who are my dearest encouragers.

Here are the bare facts about human trafficking.

It is a growing issue worldwide and a vast majority of victims are illegal immigrants, according to statistics. They come from many countries, not just Mexico. Girls from Eastern Europe, Russia and Asia are trafficked. (*So are teenagers born in the U.S.) In 2005, the U.S. Department of State estimated between 14,500 and 17,500 immigrant boys and girls who had been duped into human trafficking had already entered our borders. Sex is not always the purpose. Sometimes the victims are used as slave labor in restaurant kitchens and dry cleaners, for crop harvesting, and for transporting drugs. In third world countries, child soldiering is also commonplace.

Human trafficking is often tied to drugs and/or organized crime. A majority of the victims are lured with the promise of legitimate work in the U.S., and a better way of life. They are most likely taking the risk in order to escape extreme poverty and abuse in their home country. This makes them easy targets for such schemes because they are already broken and vulnerable. Many are prostituted to "pay for their passage," thus initiating the pattern.

Human trafficking is believed by many to be responsible for the increased percentages of disease infestation in the United States over the last fifteen years including malaria, HIV/AIDS, drug-resistant tuberculosis and polio.

FOX News reported on the increase in trafficking in North Carolina in 2011. They interviewed Delbert Richburg, ICE North Carolina Assistant Special Agent in Charge. He stated, "The average citizen has no idea of the magnitude of the problem that exists here, in our backyard, and which has been growing with time. So we need people to help and report cases... The traffickers seek out teenagers in remote towns in Latin America with the promise of getting jobs in restaurants or caring for children. On arriving here, they keep them captive and isolated. The traffickers usually take the migrants' identification and travel documents and threaten to harm them or their families if they try to escape."[2]

Legislation to assist human trafficking victims and bring more traffickers to justice was passed by Congress in 2000 under the Trafficking Victims and Protection Act (TVPA). Opponents see the act as convoluted because, while it provides victims financial help and medical care in exchange for identifying the traffickers, it does nothing to deal with why the victims agreed to break the law. In a 2006 report, a California social worker named Johansen, said, "'Crisis'-centered interventions emphasizing the criminal justice system needs while neglecting vulnerable victims are not likely to have an impact on human trafficking. The best interests of individuals, human rights, or public protection are not served under existing programs. There is a need to look at larger issues including economic inequities, gender and racial discrimination, if there is to be any real reduction in human trafficking."[3]

Governmental assistance and legislation only bandages the gaping wound of supply and demand. Through social awareness and education, public intolerance can significantly reduce this problem.

Above all, fervent prayer for these victims, the people who desire their services, and their captors is needed. It is the best remedy we can offer to a broken world.

For more information about how you can help, contact one or more of the organizations and fundraising opportunities listed in the reference section at the end of this book, or do a computer search for anti-trafficking organizations. The referenced lists are not inclusive. More and more people are getting onboard to support and rescue victims both in the United States and worldwide.

If you identify a person you feel is a trafficking victim in the United States, call the National Human Trafficking Resources Center (NHTRC) at 1-888-373-7888. In Canada, contact Public Safety Canada at 1-800-830-3118.

Thanks,
Julie B. Cosgrove

REFERENCES

Organizations

1. Coalition of Religious Congregations to Stop Trafficking of Persons (NY-CRC-STOP)

http://lifewaynetwork.org/coalitions/nycrc-stop/human-trafficking-of-young-women/

2. Girls Education and Mentoring Services (GEMS), http://www.gems-girls.org/ 212-926-8089

3. Prayer For Freedom www.prayerforfreedom.com 817-229-8947 Based in the Dallas-Fort Worth Metroplex, this organization also has an informative website and weekly blog from missionaries about human trafficking and sex slavery all over the world, and how prayer in beginning to make impacts.

4. Coalition of Catholic Organizations Against Human Trafficking, jkuh@usccb.org mrstvics@usccb.org, 202-541-3220, one of the premier organizations with lobbying power in Washington, D.C.

5. Bridging Refugee Youth and Children's Services (BRYCS) http://www.brycs.org/ 1-888-572-6500

6. Shared Hope International sharedhope.org 866-HER-LIFE (866-437-5433). Based in Vancouver, Washington. Access to state-by state

resources as well as statistics and glean reliable information on how you can become involved at one of many levels. Also has a Facebook page.

Fundraisers

1. WAR- Women at Risk International, www.warinternational.org 616-355-0796. Sell or buy jewelry, scarves, handbags from trafficked victims to help them off the streets. Ninety-three percent of monies raised goes to the safe houses in Asia and Africa. You can host a party at no cost to you.

2. Thistle Farms- Love Heals, http://www.thistlefarms.org 615-953-6440. Body care products handmade by survivors of prostitution and trafficking. Located in Nashville, TN., they also have retail outlets spreading across the U.S.A. Tours and café open Monday-Friday. "Every product bears witness that love is the most powerful force for change in the world."

3. Polaris Project, www.polarisproject.org 888-373-7888. Sell products and host house parties, book a speaker, or watch informative films. Website has free handouts that inform about human trafficking. Based in Washington, D.C., it also has a state-by-state map that lists non-profit organizations.

ENDNOTES

[1] Flores, Theresa, with Peggy Sue Wells (2010) *The Slave Across the Street*. Ampleon Publishing. ISBN 978-0-982386-8-2

[2] Read more:

http://latino.foxnews.com/latino/news/2011/01/21/human-

trafficking-immigrant-women-girls-rise north-

carolina/#ixzz1aEA5US26

[3] P. S. Johansen / Californian Journal of Health Promotion 2006,

Volume 4, Issue 3, 34-41, "Human Trafficking, Illegal Immigrants

and HIV/AIDS: Personal Rights, Public Protection"

http://www.csuchico.edu/cjhp/4/3/034-041-johansen.pdf

ABOUT THE AUTHOR

Julie B. Cosgrove is a freelance writer, professional speaker and published author. She is a member of Advanced Writers & Speakers Association, American Christian Fiction Writers, Christian Authors Network, North Texas Christian Writers, The Christians Writers Group Two, and Christian Writers Fellowship International.

She represents Women at Risk International, a Christian missionary group who sponsor safe houses for women and children snatched from human trafficking and slavery in thirteen countries and is actively involved in Prayer For Freedom, a nonprofit anti-trafficking ministry.

As a speaker, Julie has achieved the highest level of communication award, the Advance Communication Gold, in Toastmasters International. She has led quiet days, workshops and retreats as well as spoken to many women's and church groups throughout Texas, Louisiana and Florida, and in Indianapolis.

Julie writes regularly for several Christian websites and publications. In the past three years alone, her articles have been featured in *Devozine* and *Alive Now Magazines* published by the Upper Room, *Chicken Soup for the Soul: Find Your Happiness, Faith-filled Family Magazine, Good News Daily, The Secret Place, Light from the Word,* and *The Journey.*

She has also published five nonfiction works: *P.R.A.Y.I.N.G.: Bringing Power and Purpose to Your Prayers* (2009), *Song Notes: Devotionals from the Book of Psalms* (2010), *What Can She Tell Us?*

(2011), *Between the Window and the Door* (2012), and *Squeeze More God-time Into Your Day* (2013).

Julie has authored three contemporary faith-based novels. *Focused,* set in the Texas Hill Country, which follows a woman's journey to find God in her empty nest, was released in 2012. She is working on the other two novels in that trilogy, *Grounded* and *Rooted*. The sequel to *Hush in the Storm, Legitimate Lies*, launches through Prism Book Group in early 2015.

Contact her at www.juliebcosgrove.com or through her blog, http://WhereDidYouFindGod Today.com

Thank you for your Prism Book Group purchase! Visit our website to enjoy free reads, great deals, and entertaining, wholesome fiction!

http://www.prismbookgroup.com

Made in the USA
Middletown, DE
07 May 2021